MERLIN

BOOK 10

SHADOWS ON THE STARS

D0097535

T. A. BARRON

PUFFIN BOOKS
An Imprint of Penguin Group (USA) Inc.

PUFFIN BOOKS
Published by the Penguin Group
Penguin Young Readers Group, 345 Hudson Street, New York, New York 10014, U.S.A.
Penguin Group (Canada), 90 Eglinton Avenue East, Suite 700, Toronto, Ontario, Canada M4P 2Y3
(a division of Pearson Penguin Canada Inc.)
Penguin Books Ltd, 80 Strand, London WC2R 0RL, England
Penguin Ireland, 25 St Stephen's Green, Dublin 2, Ireland (a division of Penguin Books Ltd)
Penguin Group (Australia), 250 Camberwell Road, Camberwell, Victoria 3124, Australia
(a division of Pearson Australia Group Pty Ltd)
Penguin Books India Pvt Ltd, 11 Community Centre, Panchsheel Park, New Delhi - 110 017, India
Penguin Group (NZ), 67 Apollo Drive, Rosedale, Auckland 0632, New Zealand
(a division of Pearson New Zealand Ltd.)
Penguin Books (South Africa) (Pty) Ltd, 24 Sturdee Avenue,
Rosebank, Johannesburg 2196, South Africa

Registered Offices: Penguin Books Ltd, 80 Strand, London WC2R 0RL, England

First published in the United States of America as *The Great Tree of Avalon: Shadows on the Stars* by
Philomel Books, a division of Penguin Young Readers Group, 2005
Published as *Shadows on the Stars* by Puffin Books, a division of Penguin Young Readers Group, 2011

1 3 5 7 9 10 8 6 4 2

Patricia Lee Gauch, Editor

Text copyright © Thomas A. Barron, 2005
Illustrations copyright © David Elliot, 2005
Maps copyright © Thomas A. Barron, 2004, 2005
All rights reserved

THE LIBRARY OF CONGRESS HAS CATALOGED THE PHILOMEL BOOKS EDITION AS FOLLOWS:
Barron, T. A.
Shadows on the stars / T. A. Barron.
p. cm. – (The great tree of Avalon ; bk. 2)
Summary: As the warlord Rhita Gawr tries to gather enough power to destroy Avalon,
Tamwyn—the heir to the powers of his grandfather, Merlin—and his friends
embark on separate quests to try to save their world.
ISBN: 0-399-23764-X (hc)
[1. Magic—Fiction. 2. Avalon (Legendary place)—Fiction. 3. Wizards—Fiction. 4. Fantasy.]
I. Title
PZ7.B27567 Sha 2005 [Fic]—dc22 2005047590

Puffin Books ISBN 978-0-14-241928-1

Design by Semadar Megged
Text set in ITC Galliard

Printed in the United States of America

Praise for T. A. Barron's Merlin saga:

"An extraordinary journey of mind, body, and spirit—both for Merlin and for ourselves."   —Madeleine L'Engle

"Rich with magic."   —*The New York Times Book Review*

"In this brilliant epic, T. A. Barron has created a major addition to that body of literature, ancient and modern, dealing with the towering figure of Merlin. Barron combines the wellsprings of mythical imagination with his own deepest artistic powers. Through the ordeals, terrors, and struggles of Merlin-to-be, we follow an intense and profoundly spiritual adventure."
                                                          —Lloyd Alexander

"This is a brilliant epic tale with memorable and glowing characters—a real gift."   —Isabel Allende,
          author of *House of the Spirits* and *Daughter of Fortune*

"All the elements of a classic here."
          —Robert Redford, actor, director, and conservationist

"Barron has created not only a magical land populated by remarkable beings but also a completely magical tale . . . that will enchant readers."
          —*Booklist* (boxed review), on *The Lost Years of Merlin*

"Set on the legendary island of Fincayra, this novel about the childhood of the wizard Merlin is imaginative and convincing."
          —*The Horn Book*, on *The Lost Years of Merlin*

"The quest for one's true identity, of puzzles and tests of intelligence, and moral courage are all here. . . . The climactic ending offers a twist to seeking one's identity and heritage. A good bet for those who enjoy fantasy, mythical quests, and of course, Merlin, the greatest wizard of them all."
          —*VOYA*, on *The Lost Years of Merlin*

What are those stars?

Tamwyn peered at this star—and suddenly blinked in astonishment. The Heart of Pegasus seemed to be beating! He opened his eyes just a sliver more, as wide as he could stand, to look more closely. And yes, that star was indeed pulsing like the heart of a great steed.

A lizard scurried, just then, across his foot. Tamwyn flinched in surprise. In doing so, he lost sight of the pulsing star. He started to look for it again, but found himself gazing instead at a different constellation.

A darkened constellation.

The black hole that had once been the Wizard's Staff.

He stared hard at the spot where those seven stars had once burned so bright, hoping to find some clue about what had really happened to them. And what all this had to do with Rhita Gawr.

Something strange caught his attention. Peering closely, he could detect vague circles of light up there. Yes . . . seven of them. And the circles sat in precisely the same places as the lost stars!

Though his whole body shook with excitement, Tamwyn fought to keep himself steady. The stars, or some parts of them, were still there. And if they were still there . . . they could, perhaps, be lit again.

He swallowed. Could only Merlin himself do such a thing?

READ THE WHOLE MERLIN SAGA!

To Mother Earth,
beleaguered yet bountiful

With special thanks, once again, to
Denali Barron and Patricia Lee Gauch,
brave companions to Tamwyn, Elli, Scree . . . and myself.

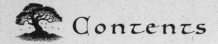 # Contents

Part I

Part II

Part III

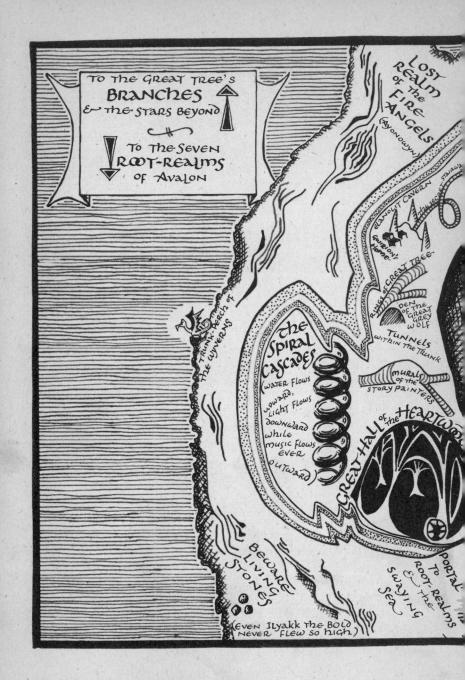

Seeking the Stars

IN TRUTH, I WONDER JUST WHY I HAVE CHOSEN now to embark on this long and dangerous voyage to the stars. Surely not because my strength is at its peak; surely not because the timing is auspicious. Perhaps I am not seeking the stars after all, but merely fleeing my own past. The stars are bright and far away, but my wounds are dark and ever near.

—*Fragment from a letter, dated Year of Avalon 987, left by the explorer Krystallus Eopia, son of the deer woman Hallia and the wizard Merlin*

Sway, Broad Boughs

Sway, broad boughs of Avalon,
Shielding from the storm—
Bend so far, yet never break:
Ev'ry day newborn,
Mystery's true form.

Rise, tall trunk of Middle Realm,
Stretching ever high—
Reach for misty, branching trails:
Stairway to the sky,
Stars are flaming nigh.

Sink, great roots of Seven Realms,
Plunging under sleep—
Hold the farthest, lowest lands:
Celebrate or weep,
Wonders ever deep.

—Ancient ballad of Avalon, believed to
have been composed by High Priestess Rhiannon

Prologue: The Greatest Power

DEEP UNDERGROUND, IN A CAVERN OF DARK shadows, something even darker hovered in the air. Slowly it spun—a venomous snake of smoke. As it twirled, the air around it crackled with black sparks. And wherever its tail brushed against the cavern floor, stones burst apart like trees shattered by lightning, leaving only heaps of smoldering ash.

The dark spiral floated menacingly toward a small, radiant crystal on a stone pedestal. The crystal's light, frail but still defiant, glowed white with ribbons of blue and green. As the shadowy being approached, it swelled a bit brighter.

"Now observe," hissed the smoky serpent. "I will demonstrate how to destroy this crystal of élano, just as we will soon destroy our enemies." The serpent laughed, its voice bubbling like molten rock. "But first, my pet, we will turn its power to our own purposes."

His back pressed against the cavern wall, Kulwych shifted nervously. The cloaked sorcerer chewed his once perfectly clipped fingernails, then ran his hand across the scarred hollow of his empty eye socket. "M-m-mmmyesss, my lord Rhita Gawr."

"I have but one small regret," hissed the spiral as it hardened, coalescing into darkness that was almost solid. "By now, no doubt, you have already dispatched the one who calls himself *the true heir of Merlin*. And I would have rather enjoyed making him my crystal's first victim."

Kulwych bit harder on his fingers. "Er, well, in that case, my lord . . . you'll be pleased to learn that—"

"He *isn't* dead?" spat the spiral. Instantly, it shot at the sorcerer's face, stopping only a hair's breadth away from his throat. "Have you failed me, my little magician, my plaything?"

Shivering, his head against the wall, Kulwych made a frightened gurgle.

The dark being swayed back and forth, sizzling like a tongue of lava. "You have seen my wrath before, haven't you?"

Kulwych's one eye darted to the headless corpse of the gobsken on the cavern floor. He tried to speak, but could only gurgle again.

For an endless moment, the smoky serpent hovered, crackling in the air by the sorcerer's throat. Then, with a whiplike snap, it pulled away, floating back toward the crystal. Kulwych gasped and crumpled to the stone floor.

"You are fortunate, even if you are a simpleton."

Kulwych's lone eye narrowed at the insult, but as he stood again he said only, "Mmmyesss, my lord."

"Fortunate indeed," continued the spiraling coil. "You see, my pet, I still require your services, at least until I am strong enough to take solid form. One day soon, however, I shall assume my true shape—and my true role as conqueror."

"Conqueror," repeated Kulwych, bobbing his hideously scarred head.

"Yes!" cried the smoky spiral that was Rhita Gawr, with such force that black sparks exploded in the air, sizzling and steaming on the wet stone walls. "And not just of this puny little world, this hollow hull of a tree. Once I control Avalon, the very bridge between mortal and immortal, I will soon control everything else, as well! From the Otherworld of the Spirits to mortal Earth—all the worlds will be mine."

In a quieter, almost pleasant tone, the dark being added, "And perhaps yours, too, my Kulwych. If, that is, I choose to keep you at my side."

Slowly, Kulwych straightened himself and brushed some dust off his cloak. His jaw quivered as he said, "Always your faithful servant, my lord."

"Just be certain it is *always*," hissed the shadow of Rhita Gawr, sounding more dangerous again. "Or I will do to you what I am about to do to this obstinate little crystal."

Before Kulwych could even respond, the dark coil snarled viciously, then stretched all the way around the crystal's pedestal. Circling slowly in the air, it bound itself end to end, like a noose, and began to tighten around its prey. At the same time, it grew flatter, widening so that it looked less like a rope and more like a shroud—dark enough that it couldn't be described as merely black. Rather, this shroud seemed like the essence of emptiness, so dark that nothing resembling light could ever penetrate its depths, give it shape, or touch its bottomless void.

The crystal pulsed bravely, as relentlessly as a beating heart, even while the shroud closed over it. Tighter and tighter the darkness drew, enveloping the glowing object, squeezing ever closer. Although light still pulsed beneath the shadow, and a few white rays broke through to illuminate the cavern walls, the crystal grew dimmer by the second. The whole cavern darkened.

Standing by the wall, Kulwych watched in fascination. Delightedly, he rubbed his smooth hands together. Here was power, true power, at work! And yet . . . in the back of his mind, he remained uncertain. No one—not even Rhita Gawr—had ever before corrupted a pure crystal of élano. Was it truly possible? Or would the crystal's stubborn magic prevail? After all, its magic ran deeper than anyone had been able to comprehend, flowing from the very resin of the Great Tree. Why, even Merlin, that sorry excuse for a wizard, had understood that his powers were nothing compared to élano.

The dark shroud continued to shrink, until at last it covered the crystal completely. No large openings were left, not on the top or bottom or any sides, for light to escape. And yet, even now, a faint glow still seeped through some cracks. The crystal continued to resist.

Kulwych leaned closer, his lone eye twitching anxiously. *Trolls' teeth and ogres' tongues,* he cursed to himself, *what is happening?*

Tighter the shroud squeezed, like a smothering blanket. But under its folds, the crystal glowed ever so slightly. The vaguest shimmer of light still radiated from beneath the layers of darkness.

Suddenly the shroud crackled with black fire. Heavy, rancid smoke rose from the pedestal. The darkness itself started to pulse, as if it were a fist squeezing the last spark of life out of its enemy.

The cavern's air thickened, growing steadily more foul. Kulwych choked back a cough. He felt more and more nauseated, until it was all he could do not to retch. He leaned against the rock wall for support, as the sickening air burned his lungs. Near his feet, a stray mouse lost its way, groped wildly for some way to escape, then twitched one last time before it died.

Seconds passed, stretching into minutes. At long last, the

shroud of darkness released its hold. It pulled gradually away from the crystal, forming itself again into a spiraling coil that hung in the air, slowly spinning. And on the pedestal, the crystal still glowed—but with a light far different than before.

Dark, smoky red it shone. Veins ran through it as if it were a diseased, bloodshot eye. And with every strangled pulse of its core came a repulsive odor like rotting flesh.

Kulwych took a cautious step nearer. "It is . . . done?"

"Oh yes, my pet magician, it is done." The voice of the spiral sounded drained, much weaker than before. "You did not doubt my powers, did you?"

"No, no," said Kulwych quickly. "I would never doubt you, just as I would never disobey you."

"So then," hissed the dark being, "you would obey my command to lay your hand upon this crystal?"

The sorcerer cringed in horror. He glanced at the dark red object, the color of dried blood. "T-t-touch th-that?" he stammered.

"Yes, Kulwych. Touch it. I command you."

Shivering uncontrollably, the sorcerer lifted up his arm. The sleeve of his cloak ruffled like a sail in a stiff wind. Then, gritting his teeth, he reached his hand toward the dark crystal. Closer he came, and closer. Meanwhile, the smoky spiral twirled in the air, sizzling softly.

As his hand approached the crystal, Kulwych cast a final, pleading look toward his master. But the shadow of Rhita Gawr said nothing. Perspiration glistened on Kulwych's fingers as he lowered them toward this thing that looked less like a crystal than a pulsing clot of blood.

Just as his fingertips were about to touch it, the edge of his sleeve brushed against the crystal. Instantly the cloth burst into dark red flames. The sorcerer screeched in fright and drew back his arm, even as the flames went out. Only then did he notice that the flames hadn't really burned his sleeve—but had, instead, made the cloth disappear.

Kulwych shook his arm in surprise. Where the bottom of his sleeve had been, there were no fragments, no charred threads, not even any wisps of smoke. The entire section of cloth had simply vanished.

He looked over at the smoky serpent that had commanded him. "My lord . . . do you still wish—"

"No," snarled the dark being. "You needn't touch it now. You have shown me your loyalty, such as it is."

Kulwych gulped. Then, turning back to his sleeve, he mumbled to himself, "Ironwool threads, shouldn't have burned." Facing the serpent once more, he asked, "Tell me please, my lord, just what is this crystal's power?"

A low, sizzling laugh echoed in the walls of the cavern. "Behold, the utter opposite of élano! *Vengélano*, I hereby name it: the greatest power in all of Avalon."

Kulwych just stared at him, confused.

The spiral twirled, hissing with a mixture of impatience and triumph. "Do you not understand, my foolish minion? Élano holds the power to create—which is why that scoundrel Merlin used it to end my Blight centuries ago. Or to heal—which is why a filthy little spring in Malóch can work such strange wonders. Why, even the very dirt of that realm is so rich in élano that it can bring forth new life."

"But my sleeve just . . . disappeared."

"Have you no brains at all? That is the power I have unleashed!

Where élano creates, vengélano destroys. Anything it touches, no matter how well made, will be instantly unmade."

Anxiously, the sorcerer squeezed his fingers—fingers that had nearly touched the corrupted crystal.

"Whatever flesh vengélano meets," crackled the voice, "will simply slice open, or vanish. Blood vessels will bleed without end. Healthy trees will wither, sturdy weapons will crumble, and freshwater streams will turn to poison."

Kulwych's lone eye widened in amazement. "So with this new power, we will seize control—" A sharp sizzling halted him midsentence. "Er, I mean, *you* will, my lord. Avalon will be yours at last."

The dark shape swirled around the bloodred crystal, circling it slowly, admiring it as a painter would admire the work of a lifetime, savoring its subtlest detail. "That is true, my pet. But first, before embarking on grander plans, I shall take care of one minor detail."

"Which is, my lord?"

"I shall destroy, once and for all, the true heir of Merlin."

The spiral continued to circle. "He is just seventeen years old by my count, barely a newborn to me. But his meager powers should soon start to emerge. And although the day of my triumph grows near, we have much to do before then. This young wizard could become a nuisance, a distraction. Besides, eliminating him will be easy enough, as well as entertaining. Fool that he is, I suspect that he fears his new powers almost as much as he fears me! And so, my Kulwych, I shall relieve him of his worries—along with his life."

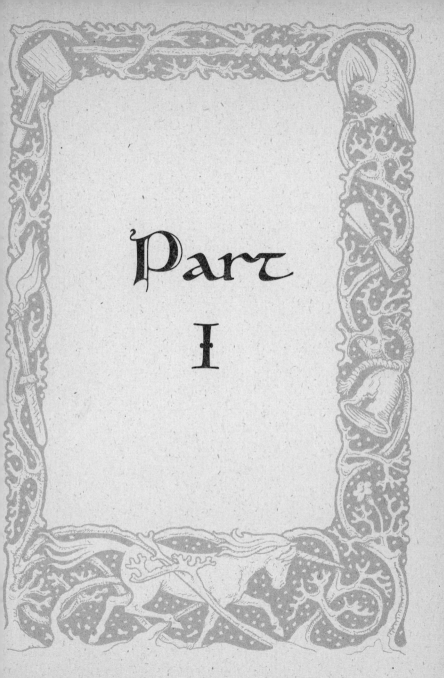

Part

I

1 · A Vast Hand of Darkness

WIND, COLDER THAN AN OGRE'S BREATH, blasted over the mountaintop. Sharp bits of ice, hurled by the gust, slapped at the broad, flat stone on the summit—and at the two people huddled there.

"So c-c-cold," said Elli with a shiver. She slid closer to Tamwyn on the sitting stone, so that their shoulders barely touched. Her hair, frosted by the icy gusts, gleamed white under the nighttime stars, making her curls look like wintry waves.

He blew a cloudy breath, then winced as a chunk of ice bit into the back of his neck. "I know it's cold. But it'll be t-tolerable again, once this cursed wind settles down."

Elli's teeth chattered. "Can't you just make the wind let up? With your new powers?"

He winced again, this time for another reason. His gaze strayed to the gnarled staff he'd set beside the stone—a staff that had been entrusted to him, though he really wasn't sure why. He thought about Elli's words, and frowned. *New powers? If only she knew the truth.*

Was it time, perhaps, to tell her what was really happening inside him? What it felt like to have these strange, often violent powers surging through his body—appearing when he least expected them, didn't want them, and couldn't even begin to control them?

Before he could speak, the wind suddenly died. Ice and snow ceased flying; the mountaintop fell silent. All around, the ghostly heads of nearby peaks glistened in the starlight, though none of those summits rose higher than Elli and Tamwyn. For they were sitting atop Hallia's Peak, the highest point in all seven root-realms of Avalon, so high that it was the only place where the Great Tree's trunk could actually be seen.

Tamwyn studied the vista. There were the other peaks of Olanabram, and beyond, the starlit ridges rising steeply upward that he knew were the bottommost reaches of Avalon's trunk. As a wilderness guide, he'd always been struck by the stark contrasts of mountains—starting with their howling storms that could melt instantly into profound stillness, a quiet so deep you could almost feel its weight upon the air. He also loved how, by day, the ridges shone with light, sliced by the shadows of clouds. And how, on nights like this, they rippled like a glowing sea beneath the stars.

Turning back to their sitting stone, he gazed at the frosted rocks that surrounded them, looking like thousands of miniature snowcapped peaks. Only the sitting stone itself had no trace of snow. Tamwyn slid his feet, bare as always, over its smooth surface, feeling the strange warmth of this stone that no wind could ever chill.

For this was Merlin's Stargazing Stone, touched long ago by the magic of the great wizard himself. And its eternal warmth, strong enough that ice and snow never stayed on its surface, was but the least of its wonders. Even now, it gleamed mysteriously—as well as darkly, for it was nearly as black as the gaping hole in the starry sky above their heads.

The hole where, less than a month before, the seven stars of the Wizard's Staff constellation had abruptly disappeared.

The hole that had brought Elli and Tamwyn to this remote summit. And to the Stone itself.

For this was not only the best spot in Avalon to view the stars—or a gap between the stars. More important, it was the one spot where anyone from any realm could come and ask for a vision. Such was the lasting gift of Merlin.

And so they had trekked all the way here, joined by their closest companions, who were now exploring the summit to pick a suitable place to camp (or, like the shrunken giant Shim, already sleeping soundly by a nearby hot spring). Elli and Tamwyn's goal was simple: to call for a vision that would reveal the truth of what had happened to the vanished stars. Elli had insisted that Tamwyn, with his emerging powers, should be the one to ask for it. And while he'd at first resisted, he had finally agreed.

"So are you ever going to do it?" Elli turned from the starry sky and nudged Tamwyn impatiently. "Or are you just going to sit here like a mindless lump of snow?"

He shook his long black hair, irked at her tone. Even though he guessed that her impatience was really masking her worries about the hole—and what it meant for Avalon—she had about as much patience as a hungry raccoon.

"Well?" she demanded. "What are you waiting for?"

"You know, Elli, you are the single most impatient, stubborn, thick-headed, exasperating . . ."

She cut him off with a fetching grin. "We're so much alike, aren't we?"

Despite himself, he almost grinned back. For he knew she was right. And, to his surprise, he wasn't angry anymore. Right now, instead of berating her, he mainly wanted to hug her. Just how did she do that—changing his feelings as fast as a mountain storm? On top of that, she could somehow see right into him, as if he were a clear alpine pool—even when he himself felt hopelessly murky.

He blew a long sigh. Although he had no idea where their relationship might go, it had definitely come a long way from the pair of black eyes she'd given him when they first met.

He reached over and lightly touched the simple yellow band she was wearing around her wrist, a sturdy bracelet of astral flower stems that he'd woven for her last week. But when their eyes met, he could see that she had other things on her mind. Worrisome things.

"Tamwyn," she whispered, "I'm scared. What if you ask for a vision—and nothing happens?"

He ran a hand through his locks. "I'm more scared of what *could* happen."

Lifting his face, he gazed up at the stars—masses and masses of them, more than he could possibly count. There, flanking the black hole of the Wizard's Staff, were other constellations he knew well: Golden Bough, that lovely ring of light; Pegasus, soaring high over starry fields; and Twisted Tree, which tonight seemed as large as the Great Tree of Avalon itself.

Though dawn was drawing near, the stars still blazed with the sharp clarity of night. Often, as a guide, he had set his course by them. So often, in fact, that they had long since become his companions, as much as Elli, Scree, and the others. Yet in all his years of camping, they'd never looked so bright as they did right now, in the clear, cold air of Hallia's Peak.

Stars, he said to himself. *What are you, really?* Dimming at the end of every day after the golden flash of starset, and swelling bright again every morning at dawn, they were Avalon's ultimate mystery. And, for Tamwyn, its ultimate beauty.

He clenched his fists. For he knew that the stars had also called to his father, the famed explorer Krystallus Eopia. So much that they had lured him to make the expedition that would be his greatest—and his last. Somewhere up there, climbing the trunk and branches of the Great Tree on the way to the stars, Krystallus had perished.

Or had he? Over the past few weeks, that question had clung like a burr to Tamwyn's thoughts. After all, no one knew for certain what had really happened to that expedition . . . or to Krystallus himself.

Struck by a new idea, Tamwyn caught his breath. After calling for a vision about the vanished stars, why not call for one about his father?

The very thought made his heart pound as fast as a wood elf's drum. For more than he'd been willing to admit, Tamwyn longed to find his father. To know him, as he never had, as a son. Even for just a moment. And to learn what his father had discovered about the stars. And maybe also, since Krystallus had seen up close the wizardry of Merlin, to learn what was needed to control these growing magical powers—powers that had caused Tamwyn to freeze a ripe melon in his hands, confuse some flying moon geese with a simple whistle, and knock over an old elm tree with a single breath, when he hadn't intended any such things to happen.

All right, he told himself. *I'll do it. Right after—*

Elli squeezed his forearm, still impatient. This time she didn't speak, but merely raised an eyebrow.

Tamwyn nodded. Drawing a deep breath, he gazed up at the black hole that seemed like a gash in the night sky. He focused his thoughts on just one question: *What does the hole mean—for Avalon, and for us?* And then, thinking of the young woman by his side, he added: *And are we safe?*

At last, remembering the words that the old sprite Nuic had taught him, he started to chant:

> *Great starscape on high, deliver me thy*
> *Vision of truth, as in Merlin's youth;*
> *Use all heaven's light to answer tonight*
> *This question my own, by Stargazing Stone.*

As his words melted into the air, a slight gust of wind blew over the mountaintop. Elli shifted a bit closer on the Stone, peering up at the stars. Anxiously, she muttered, "Nuic said it might take a minute or two before anything magical happens."

Tamwyn didn't answer. He was watching the sky and listening to the buffeting breeze with the keen attention of a wilderness guide. Suddenly he heard a voice—no, two. He stiffened, listening intently, as did Elli beside him.

Then, as one, they breathed a disappointed sigh. They faced each other, knowing that those voices hadn't come from any magic.

"It's only Scree," grumbled Tamwyn. "And Brionna. Somewhere over there, behind those boulders."

"Sounds like they're having another argument," added Elli.

"Or they never finished their last one." He shook his head. "That brother of mine, stubborn as a headless troll! Why can't he just realize that he doesn't really like Brionna? All they ever do is argue."

Elli looked surprised, then gave her frosted curls a shake. "You really think that? He argues with her *because* he likes her. A lot, in fact."

"Really? Are you sure? Well, Brionna certainly doesn't feel the same way about him."

"Oh, yes she does. Just the same." Elli peered at him thoughtfully. "Your brother's not the only man around here who's clueless when it comes to women."

Tamwyn returned her gaze, then gave a reluctant nod. "You might have a point there. He's about as awkward with her as I am with . . ."

He stopped, realizing what he was about to say. Sheepishly, he averted his eyes.

Elli laughed, a sound as lilting as a lark's morning song. "You know," she said gently, "Scree, being an eagleman, may look a lot older than you. But he's still just a boy when it comes to women. A lot like you."

Slowly, he turned back to her. "And is that, um, all right with you? My being awkward around a woman?"

Her eyes sparkled. "That depends," she answered, "on what woman you're thinking about."

Feeling suddenly warmer than even the magic of the Stone could explain, Tamwyn shifted uncomfortably. He decided to try to turn the conversation back to Scree. "You're right about my brother, that's for sure. Remember that big mistake he sometimes mentions, without ever telling us what it was? Something that happened years ago when he was living alone, guarding the staff. Well, I'd bet my beard that it had something to do with a woman."

Elli grinned mischievously. "You don't have a beard, Tamwyn." Then, with her fingertips, she brushed the stubble on his chin. "But it won't be long now."

As she touched him, he felt an unexpected prickling. His heartbeat quickened; he leaned a little bit closer. He could almost imagine bringing his face to hers, and . . .

He suddenly pulled back as a bitter blast of wind raked across the summit. Chunks of ice stung their cheeks, necks, hands—anything exposed. The cold pierced Tamwyn's old tunic and Elli's tattered robe, and drove down deep into their bones.

"Owww," she cried, hunching her shoulders and putting her hands on the sides of her head. "That hurts my ears!" She shivered as another frosty gust whipped them.

"Here, let me help." Though shivering himself, he reached up and pushed her hands aside, replacing them with his own. Very gently, he cupped his palms over her ears, trying to hold back the wind.

As the last gust subsided, taking the edge off the cold, Tamwyn also felt his inner warmth grow again. Here she was, her face so close, looking at him gratefully. He studied her hazel green eyes, her lips that seemed so soft . . . and slowly drew her nearer. A new, dizzying feeling surged through him.

Without warning, an image flashed through his mind. An image from just a few days before, when he had held something utterly different in his hands. It was nothing remarkable, just a simple melon—but he'd held it in exactly this way, his hands cupped against its sides. The melon had been the gift of a friend, the farmer Abelawn, whose fields Tamwyn had often helped to harvest: the very last one from his vegetable garden. Tamwyn had hefted the fruit, thinking playfully how good a snowball it would make if only it were frozen. Then, all of a sudden, the melon turned to ice! In the blink of an eye, it froze between his hands—turning completely white before it shattered, exploding into a thousand icy shards.

Could the same thing happen now to Elli? Was this feeling rising inside him really just another violent, misdirected burst of power?

"No!" he shouted, roughly shoving her head away. Elli shrieked and tumbled backward off the Stone. But he could only stare down at his hands, aghast at what he'd almost done.

Elli slowly picked herself up, brushed the snow off her shoulders, and sat again at the far edge of the Stone. She glared at Tamwyn, rubbing her sore neck. Anger showed in her eyes, but there was also a hint of tears.

Just as she opened her mouth to speak, the night sky abruptly flashed with light. So much light that the whole sky seemed to be swallowed by flames. Then, just as swiftly, the light vanished, and was replaced by another night sky—one with only seven stars, grouped in an unmistakable constellation.

"The Wizard's Staff," whispered Tamwyn, blinking in astonishment.

Elli stopped rubbing her neck and just gaped at the sight.

As they watched, awestruck, the seven bright stars of the Wizard's Staff flickered, as if some bitter winds on high had made them shiver. Then, one by one, they faded, pulsed with a final gleam of light, and disappeared—just as they had actually done less than a month before. But now, in this vision, when the last star went dark, nothing else remained in the sky.

All at once, something moved. Both Tamwyn and Elli sensed somehow that what they were about to see had not yet happened—but would very soon. As they watched, strange shapes, even darker than the sky itself, began to flow outward from the vanished constellation. The young viewers squinted, trying to see just what those shapes could be. But it was impossible to tell. They looked misty, undefined, and yet undoubtedly evil, like plumes of noxious gas. Combined, they resembled a vast hand of darkness, stretching deadly fingers toward Avalon.

Another flash! The evil shapes abruptly disappeared. Yet Tamwyn and Elli couldn't stop seeing them in their minds, just as they couldn't stop wondering what they really were.

Suddenly the sky filled with a procession of scenes, drawn darkly upon the night. Unlike the vision of the shadowy shapes, which belonged to the future, these scenes seemed more present—as if they had recently happened, or were happening right now. Each one came from somewhere in the Seven Realms. And each one spelled some new disaster.

Elli gasped as she watched a towering stone pillar topple and smash to the ground. Surely that couldn't be one of the pillars of the Great Temple in the Drumadian compound? Then the scene shifted to an angry mob of people, shouting and hurling stones. Next came a band of eaglefolk, flying out of the smoking cliffs of Fireroot—and straight into battle. But they weren't fighting their traditional enemies, the flamelons, or even humans: Rather, they were battling *other* eaglefolk.

From behind the nearby boulders, Tamwyn and Elli heard a

shout of disbelief. Evidently Scree, too, could see the vision. And didn't like at all what it showed.

Next came a series of scenes that moved by so rapidly they blurred together. There was a gobsken warrior forging a broadsword; a water dragon's tail rising out of the waves; and an ancient hand grasping desperately for something, clutching at the air, before it finally fell still.

And then those images melted into another scene, one that made Tamwyn stiffen. For staring down at him from the darkened sky was the brutally scarred face of White Hands, the wicked sorcerer who had enslaved hundreds of creatures and killed more, all in his quest to gain a powerful crystal of pure élano. Tamwyn, helped by his companions as well as his staff, had done his best to stop White Hands. Yet there was a satisfied gleam in the sorcerer's only eye that made Tamwyn feel sure that he was still alive. And that he possessed the crystal.

Suddenly the scarred visage moved—and spoke. The sound of the sorcerer's hoarse voice bubbled out of the air. "So what lies ahead, my lord?"

My lord? wondered Tamwyn. *Who could he mean?*

Something shifted behind the image of White Hands. It was hard to make out, barely more than a thin trail of smoke. Or a gaseous sort of serpent. Then the smoky form itself spoke, in a voice that crackled across the sky like a bolt of black lightning. And in that moment Tamwyn knew exactly who this was. For though he'd never heard the voice before, somewhere deep within himself he recognized it instantly.

Rhita Gawr. Wicked warlord of the Otherworld, where he'd been banished long ago by the great spirit Dagda and the wizard Merlin.

Rhita Gawr—here in Avalon.

"My ultimate triumph," crackled the voice, "is but a few weeks away! First will fall Avalon, this miserable world in between. And then more worlds will follow."

White Hands, rubbing his palms, nodded vigorously. "And the sign, my lord? What will be the sign?"

The snakelike form coiled slowly. "When the great horse dies, the storm will come." A harsh, hissing laughter filled the air. "Ah yes, my pet, it will come."

The sky flashed again, so bright that it took Tamwyn and Elli several seconds before they could see anything. When at last they gazed skyward, they saw no more visions. Only stars. And one dark, gaping hole where a certain constellation had once shone.

Tamwyn recalled the vision of those strange, shadowy shapes emerging from the void of the missing stars. Shapes that would, he felt sure, soon appear in reality. What were they? What did they mean? And what in the name of Avalon had Rhita Gawr meant about his triumph just a few weeks away—and by those words *when the great horse dies?*

He grimaced. This vision had raised more questions than it had answered!

He turned to Elli, and saw the same questions on her face. As well as all the anger and hurt that he himself had caused. His heart seemed to wither in his chest.

"Listen," he started. "I can explain."

She shook her head, jostling her curls in every direction. "Don't explain. Just go."

"But Elli—"

Her eyes seemed to sizzle. "Just *go.*"

He stooped to retrieve his staff as well as his pack, wanting to say more but certain now that it would take some time before he could even hope to speak with her. All the things he'd like to tell her would simply have to wait. Just as his plan to ask for a vision about his missing father would have to wait. How long, he couldn't even guess.

He turned and trudged off through the snow, troubled by the demons he'd seen on high—and, even more, by the demons he'd seen in himself.

2 · Magical Wood

THE MAN, TALL AND RUGGED, STOOD ALONE on a mountain ridge. Wind blew his long gray locks across his face, barely lit by the flickering light of his torch. Dark shreds of mist swirled about him, wrapping him in shadow.

But Tamwyn recognized him instantly. "Father!" he cried, though he wasn't sure whether the man was on the same mountain as himself, or somewhere far distant. "Father, I'm here!"

The man suddenly started. His coal black eyes, bright in the torchlight, opened wide. And in that instant Tamwyn knew beyond doubt that this was indeed his father.

Slowly, the man turned toward the voice. His weathered, hawk-like face seemed exactly right for Krystallus Eopia—voyager to Avalon's farthest reaches, born of the wizard Merlin and the deer woman Hallia. Right now he looked both surprised and puzzled, as if he couldn't tell whether the voice he'd heard was very near or very far away. But he seemed to sense, somehow, that it came from his son—his only child, whom he'd never had the chance to know. His face creased in the very first hint of a smile.

"It's me," cried Tamwyn, his throat suddenly tight. "It's me, your—"

Just then Krystallus faltered. He clutched his chest, as though he'd been pierced by an arrow, and fell to his knees on the rocky ridge. The half-smile vanished, replaced by an agonizing look of pain. And something more, as well: a look of having found something precious, at last, before losing it for all time.

"Father!" screamed Tamwyn, trying to stretch out his arms. But his arms couldn't reach far enough. He could only watch helplessly as his father crumpled. The torch, still blazing despite the fierce wind, dropped to the ground beside him—then went out.

• • •

"Don't die!" shouted Tamwyn, sitting up. "Don't—"

Someone shook him by the shoulders, while a pair of pink eyes stared down at his face. "There now, Tamwyn me laddy. Wakes up! Even with me oldsy ears, I'd have heard you ten leagues away."

Tamwyn wiped his brow, wet with perspiration, then blinked his eyes. They felt strangely swollen. "I'm fine, Shim, just fine."

"Must dine? You is waking up hungrily?"

The young man grimaced. And then, to make sure that Shim heard him clearly, he shouted, "Just fine!"

Shim frowned, adding several more wrinkles to a face that was more than a thousand years old. "No, no, you isn't. I is maybily just a smallsy and midgetly giant, but I knows a bad dream when I hears one."

Tamwyn simply shook his head, making his hair swish against his shoulders.

The pink eyes narrowed. "Nobody who dreams so shoutingly is just fine! I is surely of that, as surely as I am of me own little sniffer." For emphasis, he patted the tip of his large, potato-shaped nose.

Because it was so difficult to talk with his hard-of-hearing companion, Tamwyn just waved him away. He looked around, trying to remember exactly where he was. But his dream was still so vivid, so real, he felt disoriented. His father—and that torch—had seemed almost near enough to touch.

He gazed above his head at an overhanging slab of rock, coated so thickly with mosses and dwarf ferns that almost none of the rock itself could be seen. More moss lay beneath him, thicker than a black bear's fur. Steam, rising from the hot spring that bubbled near his feet, made the air moist and warm—much warmer, he felt sure, than out there beyond the overhang, on that snow-covered summit.

Hallia's Peak! All at once, he remembered where he was. And everything that had happened to him before he trudged over here to the hot spring, where he'd fallen asleep. He remembered the Stargazing Stone. The terrifying vision of dark shapes in the sky, White Hands, and Rhita Gawr. And, on top of that, what he'd done to Elli.

Now she hates me, he thought angrily. What an ogre's lair he'd made of everything! At least none of their companions on the summit—especially Henni, that crazy hoolah who just loved to ridicule him—had seen what he'd done.

But his problems with Elli, painful as they were, didn't compare to the problems facing Avalon. Across his mind flashed the images of that vision—images of such peril and terror that he couldn't even fully comprehend them, let alone hope to prevent them from coming true.

Why had such a vision, concerning the very survival of Avalon, come to him of all people? He was still, at heart, just a bumbling wilderness guide—as far away from being the true heir of Merlin as Shim was from being a true giant.

Sure, he'd shown some flashes of magical power in the past few weeks, but most of that had been unintended—as well as destructive. What little good he'd done had been the work of the staff, not himself. And no matter how hard he'd tried to direct his growing powers with his thoughts, he'd always failed. The only power he could rely on was his ability to understand the languages of non-human creatures. But that wasn't true magic; it was really just another kind of listening.

He sliced a hand through the rising steam, as if he were cutting to the unavoidable truth: The vision *had* come to him. Avalon *was* in grave danger.

But what could he possibly do about it?

Pondering that question, he pulled his dagger from the sheath on his belt. Slowly, he twirled it in the dim light from the stars beyond the overhang, light that constantly wavered in the misty air. The dagger's blade and hilt were so old and battered that rust covered everything, even the random scratch marks. With a nod, he recalled the day, years before, when he'd plowed it up in a field. The old farmer he'd been helping had given it to him, calling it "a gift from the land." And for Tamwyn it soon became his favorite tool, useful for everything from slicing fruit to carving wood.

Carving wood . . .

Suddenly an idea burst into his mind. Whether or not he could find a way to save Avalon—maybe he could, at least, find a way to save his relationship with Elli. If only he could just explain to her what had really happened there on the Stone, she'd understand about his fears. And also, perhaps, about his feelings.

Reaching for his pack, he pulled out a triangular slab of wood. He turned it over, watching its dark brown grains, streaked with orange, gleam in the misty light. As always, he was amazed at the lightness of this wood, called *harmóna* by the elves. It seemed more the stuff of clouds than of trees.

And lightness wasn't its only special quality. Tamwyn gently tapped its side and listened to the reverberating echoes that rumbled within, like a clinking chorus of wooden chimes. They took more than a minute to fade away. For harmóna was the fabled wood, found only in the westernmost forests of Woodroot, that elves had used for centuries to carve magical musical instruments: flutes so soft and gentle that their voices could calm a rushing river; drums so soulful that they could make the heart of any listener beat as fast as a hummingbird's wings; lutes that could play a lilting, sensuous song after only the slightest pluck.

Tamwyn had earned this slab of harmóna, in the days following Tressimir's funeral, by working as a woodcarver in Brionna's home village, while Elli went to visit her old friend High Priestess Coerria. He had stayed there for five days, carving furniture and waterwheel gears during the mornings, exploring deer trails and faerie glens in the afternoons, and joining elven songfests in the evenings. He'd been offered other forms of pay for his work, including a length of elven rope far more sturdy than the twine he wore around his waist, but he'd said no. For he'd needed this wood.

He stroked its edge, visualizing the contours of the harp that he was going to carve for Elli. It would play wondrously, as only this magical wood could do. And it would replace Elli's first harp, made by her beloved father—which Tamwyn had managed to crush within seconds of first meeting her. She had, it seemed, almost forgiven him for that, until he'd ruined things all over again last night. Now this new, magical harp was his best—maybe his only—hope.

He looked at the slab of wood. *Yes, by the bark of the Great Tree.* This new harp would be both an apology for the past . . . and maybe, as well, an invitation for the future.

He swallowed. What future could they have, though, if Avalon was conquered by Rhita Gawr? If the warlord from the spirit realm won what he'd called his *ultimate triumph?*

Even through the rising mist, the lines of Tamwyn's jaw and brow looked suddenly hard-edged. *I must do something. What, I don't know. But I still have to try.* He nodded at the slab, as if he were speaking to it. *By morning, I need to have a plan. Or at least the beginning of one.*

Yet morning was just an hour or two away.

Chewing his lip thoughtfully, he took up his dagger again. Then, with considerable care, he made his first slice in the wood. It cut as easily as the froth on a mug of Stoneroot ale, seeming to sense the movement of his blade even before he did. He began to work on what would eventually become the instrument's soundbox, not yet daring to carve on its delicately curved neck. The slab trembled ever so slightly in his fingers. All of a sudden, he realized that it was *asking* him something—a question that lay between wood and hand.

A harp, he answered in the same silent language that helped him speak with creatures of any kind. *Become a harp. One that is light to hold and lovely to play. One that will give endless joy to Elli.*

The wood made an airy, sighing sound. The dark brown grains seemed to realign, shaping themselves magically in Tamwyn's hand. And he knew beyond doubt that this would be the most beautiful thing he had ever carved.

Just right for her, he told himself. Then he blew a sigh, scattering the steam from the hot spring. For he knew that if the harp turned out well, it would be less because of his own skill than because of the wood. Once again, he needed a magical object to do something right. Not his own magic, his own power.

His gaze shifted to the ancient staff that lay on the moss beside him. Wisps of steam curled around its shaft, partly covering the green runes that stood for Merlin's Seven Songs, giving the staff an eerie, mysterious look. As if it belonged more to the Otherworld than this one. And perhaps it did. For this was Merlin's own staff, the legendary Ohnyalei, whose name meant *spirit of grace* in the Fincayran Old Tongue.

Tamwyn frowned. How he longed to truly deserve that staff! To be a real wizard—someone who had fully mastered his powers, who could wield magic just as confidently as he could now wield a whittler's knife. Someone who could rise to the crisis that his world would soon confront—in just a few more weeks, as Rhita Gawr had boasted.

Trolls' tongues! he cursed to himself. *Quit dreaming, will you? You're the last person who could possibly help.*

Perhaps, he thought grimly, he really had no choice but to accept his fate as the child of the Dark Prophecy . . . whose destiny was to bring about the very end of Avalon. No matter what the Lady of the Lake had told him about choosing his own fate, more and more the Prophecy seemed inescapable.

A frosty gust of wind tore across the mountaintop, hurling

snow and ice over the rocks outside the overhang. Even under the shelter, some snow blew into the hot spring, making the water hiss angrily. Steam scattered, Shim's white hair stood on end, and all the tiny ferns on the overhang shivered in unison.

Out of habit, Tamwyn looked around for some wood to build a fire. But there was nothing that he could kindle with his iron stones. *A real wizard could start a fire without any wood,* he grumbled silently. And the only magical flame he'd ever made was just an image—an *illusion*, as Nuic liked to call it. Not the real thing.

Angrily, he slammed his fist down on the bed of moss. For he knew, in his heart, that what really stood between him and wizardry—between him and some sure way to save his world— was not the lack of ability. No, what held him back most of all was something very human. Something that had shown itself at the worst possible moment out there at the Stargazing Stone.

Fear.

Fear that his powers could never be controlled, or directed in the ways he wanted. And, even worse, that they could arise without warning, entirely unbidden, and harm the people he loved most. People such as Elli.

Yet . . . unless he somehow found a way to master those powers, how could he ever help Avalon in its time of need? Or avoid fulfilling the Dark Prophecy? And, closer to home, how could he ever be with Elli? Or hope to find his father?

Suddenly something shot under the overhang, speeding like an arrow. It glowed, leaving behind a trail of green light as it zipped through the steam. It struck Tamwyn hard in the chest. Like his father in the dream, he hunched over, wincing in pain.

3 · Starlight and Torchlight

TAMWYN GROANED, RUBBING THE SORE SPOT on his chest. The glowing green missile that had struck him bounced off, swerved in the steamy air above the hot spring, and shot at him again. He managed to duck just in time, but it still clipped the top of his ear.

"Batty Lad!" he shouted. "Why do you have to—" He ducked again as the green-eyed creature zipped by his other ear. "Have to nearly chop off my head like that?"

"Ooee ooee, manny man," squeaked the little beast as it did an erratic loop, skidding through the mosses that grew beneath the overhanging rock. "Me feeling very bouncy, after hunting lotsa bugs."

With that, he scrunched his batlike face into something resembling a smile, and plunged straight into Tamwyn's tunic pocket. When Tamwyn opened it to peer inside, all he could see was a tiny ball wrapped inside a wrinkled wing. Right away, the ball started snoring contentedly.

Tamwyn shook his head at this mystifying little creature. What was Batty Lad, anyway? It seemed that the Lady of the Lake had known more about him than she'd been willing to say. Then again, there were *many* things the Lady seemed to know that she hadn't wanted to reveal.

Even so, Tamwyn longed to speak with her again. About last night's vision—and about the wild, dangerous plan that was now forming in his mind.

A sudden change in the light caught his attention. As he crawled over to the edge of the mossy shelter and looked outside, the stars swelled brighter. Dawn already! The snow-ribbed slope of Hallia's Peak turned silver, then white, in the strengthening glow from above. As always, with the brighter light of day, the sky's constellations became harder to see. Within seconds, he couldn't even see individual stars—just blue sky, utterly clear.

So different from his own thoughts. He scowled, stuffing the magical slab of wood back into his pack. Morning had arrived—and although he was now fairly sure what he had to do, he had no idea at all how to do it. Or how to explain it to Elli. For while she probably hated him now—and would keep right on hating him until he told her about her harp—she surely wouldn't want him to die. And with this new plan of his, death was more than likely.

Turning back to the summit, he watched her sitting up on the Stargazing Stone. She stretched out her legs on the snowless surface, like a waking mountain lion, then raised both arms high above her head. All of a sudden, as if she felt Tamwyn's gaze, she stopped stretching and turned around. The look she gave him was colder than last night's icy wind.

Beside the Stone, a small round figure sat up in the snow. It was Nuic, Elli's ever faithful (and ever sassy) maryth. His little body swirled with streaks of dark red, which told Tamwyn that the pinnacle sprite had also seen the vision last night. Erasing any doubt, Nuic put his tiny hands against his sides and said dryly, "Hmmmpff. Nothing like seeing the world being destroyed by an immortal monster to ensure a good night's sleep."

"I saw it, too," declared someone's deep voice from across the slope. It was Scree in his human form, bare-chested despite the chill mountain air, walking toward them. "But I don't believe a bit of it."

"Really?" demanded Elli. "Why do you say that?"

"I just don't, that's all." He glanced over his shoulder at the slender elf maiden who was striding gracefully across the snow behind him. "Visions like that are as unreliable as elvish folktales."

Over by the mossy overhang, Tamwyn winced. He could tell that, as graceful as Scree could be in flight, he had landed with a crash when it came to Brionna. Just as Tamwyn himself had done with Elli.

Indeed, Brionna's green eyes flashed angrily. But she kept her voice calm as she turned to Elli. "What he's really saying is that he didn't *like* what he saw. Especially those eaglefolk battling each other, which offended his precious sense of honor."

Scree's brows lifted over his large, yellow-rimmed eyes. "At least when we have to fight, we use our own talons and wings—not some clumsy old weaponry that breaks if you step on it."

Brionna's hand, which had been fingering her braid, moved to touch her longbow. "The elves have a curse for creatures as war-like as you."

"And we're not going to hear it now," declared Elli, cutting her off. "We have more important things to discuss."

"Wait now, watching them argue is fun!"

Everyone turned to Henni, who had called out from his perch

atop a tall, angular rock. He wasn't exactly on top, however. The hoolah's toes were stuck into a jagged crack so that he could hang upside down. His grinning face dangled just above several knife-like quartz crystals.

"Eehee, hoohoo, heeheehahaha," he laughed raucously, waving a hand at the others. "You people are almost as entertaining as clumsy old Tamwyn!"

He laughed again, clearly enjoying himself. The only question was whether his good mood came mainly from watching Scree and Brionna, or from the simple delight of risking a broken neck.

But Elli was not about to be deterred. She looked grimly at Nuic. "What did that vision really mean? Those dark shapes, whatever they were, pouring out of the spot where the stars had been. And those images of gobsken and water dragons."

"Along with eaglefolk," muttered Scree unhappily, shaking his shoulders as if ruffling his wings.

"And then," continued Elli, "there were those words spoken by—"

"Rhita Gawr," finished Nuic, his color darkening to deepest black. "*When the great horse dies.* We need to know what that means. But even more, we need a plan."

"Which I have." Tamwyn stepped out from under the overhang.

Elli started in surprise, but like Nuic, she just stared at Tamwyn, saying nothing.

Scree's eagle eyes widened. "Do I sense a quest coming on, little brother?"

"Yes. But I'm *not* your little brother. We're the same age, and you know it. Just because you look ten years older—"

"And act ten years wiser," added Scree with a smirk. Ignoring Tamwyn's glare, he asked, "So tell us, then. What is this plan of yours?"

Tamwyn stepped toward them on the snow. He moved slowly but deliberately, his bare feet crunching on the hardened crust. Just short of the Stargazing Stone, he stopped and drew a deep breath.

"Well," he began, trying not to look at Elli, "I think there's just one thing to do."

"Which is?" probed Nuic, his liquid purple eyes locked on Tamwyn.

"Go up there. All the way to the stars—before those dark shapes, whatever they are, really start to appear."

"And just what," demanded the sprite, "would you do if you ever actually reached the stars?"

"Relight them. Restore them somehow. That could be the only way to stop Rhita Gawr."

"But," objected Elli, "that's crazy! No one can do that."

"Lighting stars is no simple matter," stressed Nuic.

Still unwilling to look directly at Elli, Tamwyn spoke instead to the sprite. "Look, when those same seven stars went dark, way back at the end of the Age of Storms, Merlin said it was essential to relight them. And he found some way to do it, didn't he?"

"Sure, but he was—"

"A wizard," said Tamwyn bitterly. "And I'm not, as all of you know. I'm just a stupid fool, with a wizard's staff."

His throat, suddenly dry, grew hoarse. "But maybe I could still find a way. Still figure it out." He glanced, ever so briefly, at Elli. "Before it's too late."

Elli, blinking the mist from her eyes, watched him in silence.

Brionna, as observant as ever, caught the softer look on her face, but also said nothing.

Shim, who had ambled over, shook his white mop of hair. He had, for once, heard well enough to understand, and frowned up at Tamwyn. "You is full of madness, lad. Certainly, definitely, absolutely."

"Maybe so, but I'm convinced it's the only way to save Avalon."

"I think," declared Nuic, "you also have another reason for going. Tell me now, hmmmpff, am I right?"

Tamwyn swallowed. "Yes, old one, you're right. I also want to try to find my father."

"Your father?" repeated Scree. "Krystallus? But he's long dead."

"No one knows that for sure."

Scree scratched his hooked nose. "That's true, I suppose. And if he's even half as stubborn as you, Tam, he just might have survived."

Tamwyn grinned. "Everything I know about stubbornness I learned from you, brother." Turning back to Nuic, he explained, "Maybe I can find him, somewhere between here and the stars."

"Hmmmpff. Or at least his torch."

Tamwyn caught his breath, remembering his frightful dream. "Torch?"

The pinnacle sprite shifted on the snow. "His precious torch, said to have been a gift from Merlin himself. He carried it everywhere, on all his expeditions." His black color rippled with a bit of red. "I heard him say once that the torch would never go out—until the moment he died."

Tamwyn stiffened. His mind flashed with the final moment of his dream, when his father's body crumpled. And the torch went out.

At last, Elli spoke again. "Listen to me, Tamwyn. You *are* a stupid fool. But that's still no reason to throw your life away, questing for things that are impossible. The stars, your father—can't you just see how crazy that is? They're both out of reach."

He didn't answer.

"Maybe there's something we can do right here," she continued. "In the Seven Realms. Maybe Rhita Gawr is already down here! He could be hiding in some cave, along with his minion White Hands."

At the mention of the sorcerer's name, Brionna tensed. He had stolen her beloved grandfather, her only family—and left her with a scar across her back, as well as deeper scars inside. Awkwardly, Scree reached out and touched her shoulder. But she just brushed his hand away.

"Elli," whispered Tamwyn, "I *know* this is crazy. And I'm scared, too—of more things than you know. But honestly, I have to try! To see what I can do. And also to see what I'm really meant to be."

For a long moment, she studied him. "Just what," she whispered back, "are you scared of? Besides the stars, and what might be up there?"

He cleared his throat. "I'm afraid of, well, what's . . ." He moved closer to her, working his tongue. "What's happening inside me."

She peered at him, a fathomless look on her face. "I understand," she said gently. "The same thing has been happening inside me."

He frowned. "No, no, it isn't. It can't! You don't know what I mean, what I'm feeling."

Suddenly her eyes seemed to burst into flames. "Oh, I don't? I can't? Is that what you think, you rock-brained excuse for a man?"

Angrily, she slid off the Stone and stood facing him. "Well, I'll tell you something, Tamwyn. If I ever *did* have feelings like that for you, I'd be—well, even stupider than you!"

"Wait, no," he sputtered, trying to explain. "You don't understand."

"I understand just fine," she snapped. "Just fine!"

She turned and strode off, kicking up snow with every step.

Before Tamwyn could do anything, Nuic tugged on his leggings. "Did I ever tell you, my boy, about your remarkable way with women? It's a quality you inherited from your grandfather Merlin."

Tamwyn merely growled at him and started after Elli. Then, abruptly, he halted. He stood as still as the snow-frosted rocks all around, his expression one of utter surprise.

Someone else was approaching—someone he recognized instantly from the songs of bards. But Tamwyn had never expected to see this creature. Not in all his years of trekking. For the bards, with good reason, called her *the most elusive beauty in all the lands.*

4 · Bonds of Two Brothers

TAMWYN'S JAW WENT SLACK. THOUGH HIS bare feet sank deeper into the cold snow, he didn't care. This was the sight of a lifetime—a creature more of legend than reality.

He glanced over at Elli, who had also stopped in her tracks. By the Stargazing Stone, Scree, Brionna, Nuic, and Shim all stood in silence. Even the irrepressible Henni stopped swinging from his upside-down perch and simply gaped at the creature.

It was the Sapphire Unicorn. She was, as all of them knew, unique. While there were a few other unicorns with patches of blue in their horns or manes, only this one shone deep blue all over, as if her whole body were a glowing gemstone. Long ago, at the very moment that Merlin's mother, Elen, arrived in Avalon, the first creature she had seen was the Sapphire Unicorn—and since then, this exquisite being had come to symbolize all that was rare and wondrous in the world. For through all the ages of Avalon, there had been one—and only one—of her kind. The sight of her was just as unusual, and full of portent, as an appearance by the Lady of the Lake: Sometimes centuries would pass between sightings. And then, without warning, some voyager in a remote region would catch a glimpse of her spiraling blue horn.

She loped up the steep slope to the summit with the ease of a gentle wind, her head held high, her hooves kicking up puffs of sparkling snow. Her horn glowed lustrous blue, as did her fetlocks, her mane, and her flowing tail. Powerful thigh muscles flexed as she bounded over the drifts.

It was her eyes, though, that most arrested Tamwyn. Deep as an endless slice of sky they were, and just as blue. There was something old about them, as old as the Great Tree itself. They seemed to shine with the sorrows and hopes of all living creatures. And yet they gleamed with newness, too—as vibrant as the first rays of light from a newborn star.

Struck by the unicorn's beauty, Tamwyn could barely breathe as he watched her climb toward them, her hooves clicking quietly across the snow-frosted rocks. He had known, from the songs of bards, about her elusiveness as well as her beauty. But he found himself, even so, amazed by her loveliness.

She's like grace come alive, he mused. *Too beautiful, almost, for a mortal creature.*

Mid-stride, the Sapphire Unicorn turned her head and fixed one of her eyes on Tamwyn. Instantly, he realized that she had heard his thought. And then, in a full, whinnying voice, she spoke directly into his mind:

Perhaps that is so, young man. But I come on an errand fraught with misery and grief.

Tamwyn tensed, twisting his feet in the snow. *And what is this errand, graceful one?*

Soon you shall know. For it was the Lady of the Lake herself who sent me.

"The Lady," he said aloud, surprised. Could this be somehow connected to last night's vision? And to his decision to go to the stars?

At that instant the unicorn leaped over a mound of loose rocks and loped straight toward Elli, who smiled broadly as the shimmering creature trotted right up to her. As a gentle breeze rippled the unicorn's mane, she studied the young woman carefully. Then, tilting her head, she offered a small shred of cloth that she'd been holding at the edge of her mouth.

Elli took it—and abruptly went pale. She looked anxiously over her shoulder at Nuic and Tamwyn. "A piece of Coerria's gown! The one worn only by the High Priestess. She must be in trouble!"

Unbidden, Tamwyn caught the thoughts of the unicorn. *More trouble, young woman, than you can imagine.*

"I'll go to her," declared Elli. She squeezed the silky shred in her hand. "Right away."

The Sapphire Unicorn's ears twitched anxiously. She shook her head, scattering the hair of her mane.

Again, Tamwyn caught her thoughts. He shouted to Elli, "She wants you to go first to the Lady of the Lake!"

"But why?" demanded Elli. "Coerria is the one in danger, not the Lady. And I must—"

At that instant, a strange green shoot, capped with a dark red bud, popped right out of the snow beside the unicorn. It shivered a bit, swelled in size, and lifted to its full height. Meanwhile, the bud swiftly opened into a magnificent flower.

Everyone, including the unicorn, stared at it. *A flower in winter?* thought Tamwyn, astonished.

Even if it hadn't appeared in the midst of a snow field, atop a remote mountain peak, this flower would have seemed miraculous.

Though only seconds old, it stood nearly as high as Elli's knee, with a single bell-shaped blossom and no leaves. A deep red color glowed on its largest petals, while the rest were darker, the color of dried blood. It gave off a scent like lilac blossoms, which seemed impossibly sweet on this frozen mountainside.

The unicorn's ears lay back, and she swished her flowing tail. Gracefully she bent her head to look more closely at the flower. Her great blue eyes sparkled with curiosity.

Tamwyn, though, felt a sudden sense of foreboding. He raised his hand, and was about to shout, when someone else called out first.

"Wait," yelled Scree. He sprinted through the snow toward the unicorn, his muscular legs pumping. "This feels wrong. I've lived on mountains all my life, and never seen a flower like that!"

The unicorn simply ignored him. Bending her head to the flower, she sniffed at it with wide nostrils, drinking in the sweet smell.

"Wait!" shouted Scree and Tamwyn in unison.

Gently, she touched one of the bloodred petals with the tip of her spiraling horn. All at once, the flower exploded with a thunderous roar that echoed across the summit and the surrounding ridges. As if it had been made of glass, the flower shot out dozens of jagged shards—which struck the unicorn with devastating force.

She shrieked in agony, a heartrending whinny. Staggering, she fell on her side, kicking wildly in the snow. Her horn, which had been hit directly by several shards, lost its lustrous glow, sizzled, and then broke apart, crumbling into flecks of ash that blew across the slope. A shard had also lodged in her eye, tearing a wide gash in the crystalline blue. Meanwhile, all over her magnificent body—her long neck, her sturdy haunches, her elegant nose—

gaping wounds appeared. Fountains of silver-blue blood spurted from them, staining the snow all around, as the creature writhed in pain, whinnying helplessly.

It was over in seconds. Elli, who had been standing behind the unicorn and so hadn't been hit, screamed in horror. Before she could even think to pull out her gourd that was filled with healing waters from the Secret Spring of Halaad, the great being shivered and fell still.

The Sapphire Unicorn, whom bards had long celebrated as *the most elusive beauty in all the lands*, was no more.

Elli fell to her knees in the snow beside the gruesome corpse. "Why?" she cried, hurling her question across the mountainside.

Tamwyn charged forward, his mind reeling. Who had done this? Why would anyone destroy such a wondrous creature, the only one of her kind? To keep her from completing her mission for the Lady? Or some other reason?

Suddenly, he knew. *Rhita Gawr did this. I'm certain.* And then he realized something else: This terrible trap might not have been meant for the unicorn! That deadly flower could have been set to explode when the first person with any magical power touched it.

He caught his breath. That flower could have been meant for *him*.

"Aaaagh," came a moan from near the corpse. It was Scree!

Tamwyn, Elli, and Brionna ran over. Scree was crouching in the snow, squeezing his thigh, his rugged face contorted in pain. Blood dribbled from a tiny gash above his knee, soaking his leggings. "One of those shards . . . hit me. And it's working its way in deeper, I can feel it."

Bending his other leg with the dexterity of an eagleman, he scratched at the wound with his sharply pointed toenails, trying desperately to remove the shard. But the blood flowed freely, more than his scratching alone should have caused.

"Wait," commanded Elli. "This will help."

She pulled out her water gourd and poured several drops onto the wound. As the magical liquid seeped in, Brionna stepped to her side. The two women traded a grim glance, each of them recalling the day when that same water had healed the elf maiden's gashes—and saved her life.

"Something's wrong," said Tamwyn anxiously. "The potion's not working!" He knelt and pressed his hand against his brother's wound.

Blood flowed more and more, seeping through Tamwyn's fingers. It poured over Scree's thigh, painting the snow dark red. The young eagleman slumped back on the snow.

"Too much blood," he said weakly. "Just a little thing . . . shouldn't bleed like this."

"And shouldn't *keep* bleeding," added Elli, confused. "Not after the water."

Shim pushed his way through the snow, his face a mass of worried wrinkles. In his arms he carried Nuic, whose color had shifted to somber gray. The pinnacle sprite gazed down at Scree, then said, "This is evil, such as I haven't seen since the War of Storms."

"Have you got any herbs that could help?" asked Elli.

Nuic frowned. "No herbs can help with this. Nor any magic I know."

"What are we going to do?" cried Brionna, her hands twisting the end of her long braid. "He'll bleed to death."

Elli turned to Tamwyn. "Your powers! Use them."

He didn't answer. For he was already wrestling with the same idea—and with his own fears. If he tried to call on his new powers, and lost control, he could destroy Scree. But if he did nothing—

He ground his teeth, thinking hard. All the other times he'd tried to direct those powers, to guide them with his thoughts, he'd failed. And he'd never dared to turn his powers on someone he knew and loved, someone he couldn't even hope to think clearly about.

Think clearly about . . .

"Aaaagh," Scree moaned painfully. He writhed on the snow, much as the unicorn had done just moments before. Elli touched his brow, her face contorted with fright.

Think clearly . . .

All at once, a new idea struck Tamwyn. Maybe thinking clearly wasn't the point. Nor *any* kind of thinking! That could be just the wrong way to direct his magic. Maybe it had to be guided by something deeper than thought. Something not from his head, but from his heart.

"Tamwyn!" shouted Elli. "He's going to die."

"No," he declared.

Placing both his hands on Scree's thigh, he did more than just press against the wound. He closed his eyes, searching within himself for his powers, and for whatever feelings could guide them. But the only feeling he sensed now was fear. He could kill Scree with just the slightest mistake! And he didn't even know what powers he was looking for. All he knew was that now, for the very first time, he desperately wanted to find them.

Come, my powers, he commanded. *Grow strong! This time I really need you.*

But he felt nothing. Just the surging of Scree's blood, running thick and warm through his fingers.

He dug deeper into himself. *Powers, whatever you are, help me!* Now his strongest feeling was another kind of fear—for the life of his brother. And with it came an edge of panic, rising swiftly.

But he could tell that this still wasn't enough. He searched his feelings, hurrying through emotions like a man dashing blindly through a forest at night. Loyalty. Guilt. Sympathy. Sorrow.

Nothing happened.

Then, from somewhere far away it seemed, he heard another long, wrenching moan.

Tamwyn's eyes closed tighter, holding back his tears. He just couldn't do it! Scree—his only brother, his only family—was dying. And it was Tamwyn's fault. He could save him, even now, if only he knew how!

His hands gripped the bloody flesh more tightly. Memories flooded through him, visions of their rough-and-tumble adventures together as children, their quarrels, celebrations, discoveries, and losses. Their years of painful separation. Their surprising reunion, less than a month ago. Their special way of speaking that went beyond any words, any language known by others.

Don't die, my brother. Please listen to me! Don't die.

As the first tear flowed down Tamwyn's face, the first tingling of magic started to flow out through his fingers. Down, down, down—deep into Scree's skin, veins, muscles, and bones. Reaching for life. For love. For the bonds of two brothers. He tried to knit the flesh back together, to stem the bleeding. But even as he succeeded, he always found fresh wounds that seemed just beyond his grasp.

Don't die, Scree. Don't.

All at once, Tamwyn sensed that he had found something sharp. Something lethal. Something that didn't belong. The shard!

It was swimming away from him, out of his reach. Straight for Scree's heart!

He lunged for it, but missed. Again he tried—and this time caught hold. He wrapped his magical fingers around it. Held it firmly. And started to pull it back—out of Scree's body, into the open air. For an endless moment he carried it, holding tight.

Shaking, Tamwyn opened his eyes. There, in his hand, lay the bloodred shard.

What are you, evil thing? And who sent you?

He heard no answer. Instead, within his trembling fingers, the shard cracked, split into pieces, then dissolved into smoke. The dark red plume rose into the air and curled, snakelike, before wafting away on the wind. All that remained was the slightest scent of lilac blossoms, impossibly sweet.

Tamwyn's gaze shifted to his brother, who had also opened his eyes. For several seconds they looked at each other in silence. Then Scree said in a hoarse whisper, "What took you so long?"

The corner of Tamwyn's mouth lifted slightly. "Oh, you know me. Always a slow learner." Bending closer, he added, "Just don't ask me to do it again, all right?"

With effort, Scree wiped a drop of sweat from his hooked nose. "Don't worry."

Tamwyn straightened up, giving his brother's muscular shoulder a squeeze. Along with feeling relieved, he felt amazed: He had, at least this once, used his powers—and used them well. Then he caught sight of Nuic, whose color had changed to a rich, burnished gold. The sprite merely growled, "Not bad for a beginner."

Knowing he couldn't receive a higher compliment from Nuic, Tamwyn gave him a nod.

"You is still full of madness," said Shim with a bob of his head. "But you is also most handily clever."

"Sometimes," replied Tamwyn.

"Almost never," countered Henni, who had scurried over to watch all the excitement. He grinned at the person he so enjoyed tormenting. "Just wait, give him a minute, and clumsy man here will do something stupid! Eehee, eehee, hoohoohoohoo."

"Probably true," grumbled Elli. But her face showed more than a hint of gratitude. So did Brionna's, although the elf was looking not at Tamwyn but at Scree.

Weakly, the eagleman tried to sit up. But he quickly collapsed and fell back on the bloodied snow. "Guess I'm . . . going nowhere," he panted.

"Yes, you are," declared Tamwyn. "You won't last long up here on the mountaintop after losing so much blood. I'm going to take you down the west slope, to that clan of eaglefolk who live there. They'll take care of you until you're back on your feet. Or wings."

Reluctantly, his brother nodded. But even that seemed a strain.

Tamwyn waved to Henni. "Come here, you worthless hoolah. How about doing something useful for a change? Help me hoist this big stump onto my back."

Grinning at the insult, Henni obliged, shoving Scree onto his crouching brother's back. Tamwyn stood shakily under the weight. Despite the snow, which now came up to his knees, he took a few plodding steps.

Scree tapped him weakly on the shoulder. "Sure you can manage, little brother?"

"No," grunted Tamwyn. "But at least my feet are all covered with calluses. Gives me some padding, you know. Anyway, big as you are, you're no heavier than that dead troll we dragged out of his cave years ago."

Hearing a weak chuckle from his passenger, he added, "You look like him, too."

Scree then proved that even in his condition, he could manage to kick Tamwyn in the ribs.

"Ow! No more of that, or I'll dump you in that snowdrift over there."

But Scree didn't respond. He had passed out, his head slumped against the back of Tamwyn's neck.

Tamwyn turned to Shim. "Grab my staff, would you? And also my pack? They're back at the hot spring." Seeing that the old fellow didn't understand, he shouted, "What you called *the hotsy pool!*"

Shim's pink eyes narrowed. "Snotsy fool? That's no way to calls a friend."

Tamwyn shook his head in frustration. But before he could say another word, quick-footed Brionna had already sprinted to the overhanging rock that sheltered the spring, and was emerging with his belongings. A few seconds later, she slid the staff into the hip sheath that he had woven out of willow bark. Then she hefted the pack, clearly curious what sort of lightweight object it held.

"Just hang it around my neck," he said, not giving her any chance to ask about it. He glanced uncertainly at Elli. Was this the moment to tell her what the pack held?

Elli strode over, her face more troubled than ever. She peered at him. "After you've taken him to the eaglefolk, will you still . . ."

"Try to go to the stars?" He drew a deep breath. "Yes. To light them again, if I can. And also, maybe, to find my father."

"Find your death, more likely." She shook her curls, thick as a faery's bed of flowers. "Why don't you come with me, Tamwyn? Together we can help Coerria, then find some way to stop Rhita Gawr, right here in the Seven Realms. Doesn't that make more sense than throwing your life away on some wild idea?"

He said nothing.

Elli turned to Brionna. "*You'll* come with me, won't you?"

The elf maiden nodded. "For as long as you'll have me." Then, her face grim, she tapped her longbow. "And if there is any chance of finding whoever did this to the unicorn—and Scree—so much the better."

"What about you, Nuic?" asked Elli.

"Hmmmpff. Need you ask? I'll stay with you." He glanced up at the white-haired fellow holding him. "As will Shim."

The little giant, seeming to hear his name, nodded.

"And you, Henni?"

The hoolah cocked his head playfully. "Me? Hoohoo, I'm staying with clumsy man here! Life's much more entertaining that way."

Tamwyn groaned, and not from the weight of Scree on his back.

Elli turned back to him. "Well then, what's your decision?" Her hazel eyes studied his rugged features. Softly, she said, "I can help you face those fears, Tamwyn."

He swallowed, glanced at Scree's bloodstains on the snow, and sputtered, "Those fears—they, well, it's . . . um, different now." Then, gathering himself, he added, "And besides, Elli, they're not what you think. I mean, they're not about you."

"Is that so?" she snarled. "No, I suppose not! They're about *you*. As always! You're just plain selfish, Tamwyn. Selfish! Why don't you ever think of anyone besides yourself?"

He bit his lower lip. No doubt about it, he had to tell her about the harp—right now. Then she'd change her mind about him! He started to speak, but she cut him off.

"Go to the stars, then. See if I care!" She glanced over at the mutilated corpse of the Sapphire Unicorn, and her frown deepened. "Me, I'm going straight to Coerria."

"Not the Lady?"

"No."

"But the unicorn said—"

"Don't tell me what to do."

"I'm just—"

"You're just impossible!" She punched him in the shoulder, so hard he stumbled and nearly dropped Scree.

Regaining his balance, he snapped, "And you're a stubborn fool."

"Better than a dead fool." She glowered at him. "Oh, I wish I'd never met you!"

With that, she spun around and strode off through the snow, kicking angrily at the drifts. Tamwyn watched her go, feeling angry himself, as well as frustrated and hurt. The weight on his back now seemed far less than another weight he carried inside.

Slowly, he turned and trudged off in a different direction.

5 · Friendship

DAMN THAT MAN." ELLI THREW A PUNCH AT the air to emphasize her point. But her stride never slowed as she neared the crest of the snow-dappled hillside.

Brionna, who was walking a few paces ahead, stopped. With her sharp eyes, she scanned the serrated ridges of the high peaks in the distance, including the windblown summit of Hallia's Peak, now three days' trek away. A long, curving plume of snow was blowing off the summit, and its shape, like a great white eagle's feather arching over the horizon, reminded her of Scree. She gazed at the blowing snow, a touch of worry on her brow.

Hearing Elli come up behind, she turned—just in time to hear another angry outburst. "Who," she asked, "are you cursing now?"

Elli scowled. "Not Rhita Gawr, this time—although I wager he's to blame somehow for what happened to the Sapphire Unicorn. And maybe also for whatever danger is threatening Coerria."

She blew a long breath. "No, this time I was just cursing Tamwyn."

"Still?" asked Brionna gently. "After three days?"

Elli gave a grudging nod. "He makes me so mad! I don't know how, but he does."

Brionna's deep green eyes twinkled. "The wood elves have a saying, you know:

> *"Find the tree who spurns the vine,*
> *Trying not to intertwine,*
> *Fighting often, wrestling more,*
> *Twisting hard till both are sore:*
> *There you find eternal strife—*
> *Leading to a mate for life."*

Elli grimaced, her face taking on the same greenish hue as the pinnacle sprite who sat on her shoulder. "Mate? Him? Are you *crazy*?" Her eyes narrowed. "If that's what fighting means, then it's you and Scree who are just perfect for each other."

"Wha— me? And that big, that oafish, that—"

"Yes," agreed Elli with a grin.

"But I . . . never ever, well no! It's not even poss-possible," stammered Brionna, turning pink at the tips of her pointed ears.

Old Shim, who had ambled up, tugged on Elli's Drumadian robe. Cocking his head of floppy white hair at the elf maiden, he said, "She talks confudoozedly, don't she? But I still likes her."

As Elli nodded, Brionna sputtered some more. Finally, the elf regained her composure. Changing the subject back to Tamwyn, she said, "Listen. Don't let him get you so upset! He can't help being stupid. He's just a human."

Elli arched an eyebrow, thoughtfully tapping the water gourd at her side. "I'm a human, too."

"Yes, yes. But at least you're a female one."

Then, as if she'd felt a chill wind from the high peaks, Brionna shuddered. "Oaf that Scree is, I do hope he's all right. That leg . . ."

"Should heal just fine," finished Elli. "He's an eagleman in his prime."

"But he lost so much blood," continued Brionna. "He passed out just as we were leaving them, did you see? Slumped on Tamwyn's back, as limp as a broken willow branch."

"You know, if I didn't know any better, I'd say you were really worried about him."

Brionna's cheeks reddened, but she said nothing.

"Anyway," Elli went on, "they should have reached that clan of eaglefolk by day's end. And surely there's a healer there. By now Scree is probably strutting around like a young fledgling." She paused. "Unless Tamwyn got lost on the way there. With him, that's always a possibility."

"A big possibility," added Nuic grumpily from his seat on her shoulder. "Which is why I wouldn't worry about him going to the stars if I were you. He'll probably lose his way and wind up in Shadowroot instead."

Elli stiffened. "Not Shadowroot, let's hope. Nobody deserves to go there, not even him."

Beside her, Brionna's expression darkened. "I did go there once," she whispered. "With Granda. And I almost died."

She straightened her back, pinching the long scar that she'd received from a slave master's whip. It still hurt—especially when she thought about Granda. For she couldn't help blaming herself, at least in part, for his death.

Elli squeezed her friend's forearm. "Why are we talking about

Shadowroot? Even those two troll-headed brothers have enough sense to stay away from there."

The elf maiden sighed. She kicked at a patch of snow on the hilltop; the icy crust broke off, revealing some frozen tufts of grass. "They certainly are troll-headed! But, to be fair, they were right about that evil flower. Both of them sensed it, remember? They tried to stop the unicorn, but she was just too stubborn to listen."

Elli chewed on her lip. "Some creatures are like that. Even females."

"*Especially* females," corrected Nuic. He sidled closer to Elli's ear. "And most especially ones that are priestesses."

The last word seemed to freeze her blood. Her hand squeezed the torn strip of the High Priestess' gown that was tied to her belt. Woven of ancient spider's silk, it felt as smooth as an owlet's wing. "I just hope that Coerria will be at the compound when we get there. And that we're still in time to help."

"She'll be there, all right," declared Nuic. "If I know her, that's the place she'd most want to be in a time of danger."

"Right," Elli agreed, even as she started walking again, her feet crunching rapidly over the snow. Brionna, right at her side, gave an encouraging wave to Shim, to hurry him along. Then Elli, whose thoughts hadn't left the compound, spoke again.

"Do you think," she asked Nuic, "that the toppled pillar in our vision was from there? That could mean—"

"Trouble," answered the sprite. "Serious trouble."

"We're now less than a day's walk away." Brionna took hold of her long, honey-colored braid and tossed it over her shoulder. "But Elli, I have a question."

Elli turned to the elf maiden striding so gracefully beside her. "Sure. What is it?"

"It's about High Priestess Coerria. What is she like? What makes her so special that you'd drop everything and walk all this way, just on the chance you could help her?"

Thoughtfully, Elli pursed her lips. "Where do I start?" she said, stepping over the frosted bank of a rivulet. "She's . . . well, she's—"

"Hmmmpff," commented Nuic. "So articulate."

"Just give me a moment," snapped Elli. "It's hard to describe." She kept walking briskly, thinking hard, but the right words just wouldn't come.

Suddenly she stopped. Bending low, she reached down to a mound of snow that rested among the roots of a gnarled old elm. There on the mound lay a small branch, thinner than a finger, which had fallen from the tree. Elli lifted the branch, shook the snow off its tattered leaves, and said simply, "Watch."

Grasping the branch with both hands, she snapped it in two. Deep in its center, well beneath its hard brown surface, there was a slender ring of green. Looking just as vibrant as a newly sprouted leaf, the inner ring could have belonged to a sturdy young sapling.

"That's Coerria," she said softly. "Weathered on the outside, but still green within."

Brionna ran her finger along the wood and smiled. "I understand."

Then, quick as a shifting wind, her expression changed. Peering at Elli, she said, "Something still worries me, though. The Sapphire Unicorn didn't want you to go straight to Coerria. She wanted you to see the Lady first."

"But there might not be time! Coerria needs me—that's all I need to know." Elli gave the sprite on her shoulder an uncertain glance. "The Lady will understand, won't she?"

Nuic's color darkened to grayish purple. "No," he answered flatly. "She won't. After several centuries of being her faithful maryth—and several weeks of being yours—I can assure you that she's just as stubborn as you are."

The young priestess swallowed. "Well then, I'll just have to hope she can understand that I'm doing this out of friendship."

The sprite's little mouth turned down in a scowl. "We'd better get going again."

6 · Never to Fly

GRASPING THE STRIP OF COERRIA'S GOWN, Elli started to stride, with Nuic holding tight to her shoulder. Her pace was even faster than before, since she wanted to reach the Drumadian compound—and Coerria— before nightfall. Brionna adjusted her longbow and followed, treading lightly over the patches of snow and dry grass. Behind them, running to keep up, came Shim.

Out of the hills they strode, and into the sprawling farms of central Stoneroot. Although the climate here was generally warmer than in the hills, drifts of snow lay in every furrow and in the shade of every fruit tree. The companions passed through fields where people had long planted barley for ale-making, as well as unfenced pasturelands where horses and sheep chose to winter.

More and more they heard the sound of bells: chiming from rooftops, barn doors, and weather vanes; clinking from the legs of ducks and geese who flew overhead; and clanging from the necks of goats and the hips of women, men, and children who lived in the flatrock homes that filled every village. For this region was truly the land of bells, where bells made from stone or metal or wood sounded constantly.

Elli, stepping through a field where melting snow had turned everything to mud, stopped to shake a clump from her leather sandal. In the distance, she could hear the bell of a trotting colt; the sound reminded her of the small quartz bell that hung from Tamwyn's hip, always clinking as he moved. Her jaw tightened.

As she started off again, her thoughts shifted to another bell, one she had grown to love in her short time at the Drumadian compound. The Buckle Bell—made from the belt buckle of a giant, melted down by the breath of a fire dragon, and crafted by dwarf metalworkers and faery artisans—dated back to Elen the Founder. For nearly a thousand years, as long as the Society of the Whole had existed, it had symbolized the Society's highest ideal of harmony among all creatures. If that ideal was the heart of life in the compound—or perhaps, Elli wondered, of life in Avalon—no single object better signified it than the Buckle Bell.

And what a sound it made! She smiled to herself, remembering the first time she'd heard it toll. She had arrived only that morning, and decided to skip formal prayers—something she would come to do often. Hiding by a thick bush of ripe blackberries, she was eating a juicy handful when suddenly, right behind her, the great bell sounded—so loud that Elli had fallen over backward, scattering blackberries everywhere.

Onward they marched, through Stoneroot's living quilt of pastures, cornfields, and wild meadows. With every step, it seemed, their shared sense of urgency increased. As did their speed, so that Shim often had to run to keep up.

Suddenly, as Elli topped the brim of a hill, she stopped—so abruptly that Nuic barely managed to cling to her shoulder.

Brionna halted as well, and like Elli, stood as still as a sapling on a windless night. Until, that is, Shim charged into them both from behind.

"Well, I neverly!" he growled, rubbing the tip of his bulbous nose. "You shouldn't stop like that, Elli. Nor you neither, Rowanna."

The elf maiden growled, "Brionna. For the hundredth time, Brionna."

"What dids you say, Rowanna?" he asked, cupping his ear.

But she didn't respond. For, like Elli and Nuic, she was staring at the outer wall of the Drumadian compound. Or what should have been the outer wall. For a gargantuan hole had been torn in it, scattering slabs of flatrock and broken timbers in every direction. The wall now resembled a row of broken teeth, with a great gap in its center. From behind it, where the Society's buildings, temples, gardens, and jeweled caverns had long rested, plumes of smoke curled skyward.

"Great Dagda," muttered Nuic, changing to scarlet. "What could have happened?"

In answer, Elli and Brionna broke into a run. Shim followed, hobbling a bit from age but just as anxious to reach the compound. They ran past the scattered debris, through the broken wall—and then stopped once again.

There, lying on its side in the dirt, was the Buckle Bell. Its huge, flaring mouth had been crumpled by heavy blows. Several jagged cracks ran up its sides. One great chunk of metal had broken off completely and now lay on the ground. The intricate designwork on its rim had, in many places, been scraped away. And its ancient clapper, said to have been the gift of Elen herself, was nowhere to be seen.

Elli shook herself out of her shock and disbelief. "Coerria!" she shouted, dashing past the ruined bell and deeper into the compound.

Everywhere she turned, she saw devastation. It assaulted her gaze, as well as her heart. What buildings hadn't been burned to the ground had been torn apart, their windows smashed and their decorated doorways shattered. The Garden of Birds, which held nests of all sizes that belonged to birds from every realm, had been ripped to pieces, as if struck by a hurricane. Elli's stomach twisted to see the ancient nest of the halomyth seagull, which took three-and-a-half centuries to build, torn to shreds. And she nearly cried when she spied the crushed remains of a fledgling larkon bird, named for the spiral-shaped fruit that its kind loved to eat, whose mangled body lay in the dirt. The tiny bird, no bigger than Elli's thumb, would never taste again its favorite fruit, nor sing with celebration at the dawn, nor spread its wings to fly.

What caused all this? she asked herself, as she and her companions ran past the smoldering remains of the apprentices' dormitory—the very spot where she herself had lived not long before.

They ran down long corridors of oak, beech, and rowan, whose massive trunks and arching boughs had been viciously slashed. Rude symbols had been carved on them, as well as on the gleaming pathways of stones that marked the compound's inner Rings, stones whose white glaze of élano was now streaked with excrement. When they passed the Drumadians' famed moss garden, which had covered a whole hillside and held more than five thousand varieties of moss, Nuic suddenly turned jet black. For the hillside now bore very little besides smoking heaps of charcoal and the marks of heavy boots.

Even the towering pillars of the Great Temple, carried here

from Lost Fincayra in the earliest days of Avalon, hadn't escaped damage. Some—just as they had seen in the vision atop Hallia's Peak—had been toppled. Others had been used as targets for hurled mud and rotten fruit. On one stone pillar, someone had scrawled the words *Down with Harmony—Up with Humanity.*

All at once, Elli realized that something else was wrong— something less obvious, but just as frightening, than all the devastation around her. It wasn't something that she could see, but rather, something that she could *not* see.

"Nuic," she panted, as they sped through the smashed remains of the oaken gateway that had marked the entrance to the residence of the High Priestess. "Where is everyone? No priestesses, no priests, no maryths. The whole compound is empty!"

"Lifeless as a tomb," intoned the sprite on her shoulder.

Up the steps to Coerria's cottage Elli leaped, followed by Brionna and Shim. Wood from across the Seven Realms had been donated to build this residence: ancient oak from the alpine groves of Stoneroot; sturdy ironwood from Fireroot; liquid boughs of branwenna, found only in the Rainbow Seas of Waterroot, which were so fluid they could be poured into place; always-green cypress from the jungles of Africqua in upper Malóch; harmóna from Woodroot, so rich with musical magic that even the slightest breeze would cause it to hum melodiously; some nearly invisible bark from the eonia-lalo, Airroot's tree of the clouds; and ravenvine from Shadowroot, which would produce heat but no flames when burned. There was even, above the main door, a silvery strip of wood from Elna Lebram, the most famous tree in El Urien, among whose roots elves had long buried the bodies of their wisest scholars and bards.

All these kinds of wood, and more, lay broken, splintered, and strewn about the floor of the cottage. Just after the group entered, what remained of the ornate oaken door—carved by Thule Ultima, greatest of the faery artisans—crashed to the floor. And then, for Elli, came the worst sight of all.

Coerria lay motionless, eyes closed, on a cot in the main hallway. Her body, and the shimmering gown of spider's silk that she wore, were covered by a brown woolen shawl peppered with wood chips. The High Priestess' long white hair, twisted and tangled, fell over the cot's edge and onto the debris on the floor. A tiny bee with purple wings buzzed around her head, trying frantically to untangle the strands: Uzzzula, the old woman's devoted companion. Like every maryth, Uzzzula had taken an oath of loyalty to a priestess or priest—an oath that had clearly, in this case, been severely tested.

Beside the cot knelt a lanky figure whose torn Drumadian robe bore smears of blood. Both he and the silver-winged falcon perched on his shoulder turned their somber faces to Elli as she approached.

"Lleu," she gasped, breathing hard from the run across the compound. "Is she . . ."

"Not dead. Not yet." His eyes, no less sharp than the falcon's, studied Elli. "And if you have brought the elixir from the Lady of the Lake, she may yet survive."

Elli froze. "The elixir?"

Lleu nodded impatiently. "Come now, give it to me." He cocked his head to the side. "You do have it, don't you?"

Though Elli tried to speak, her mouth wouldn't move.

"She has no elixir," grumbled Nuic. "And no sense, either."

"But the Lady!" blustered the priest, his brow deeply furrowed. "She came to me in a dream—four nights ago, right after all this happened. Told me you'd come with Coerria's cure."

"She hadn't counted on certain things," answered Nuic gravely.

"Such as my stubbornness," declared Elli. "I'm such a fool!"

"No more than I," replied Lleu. "You see . . ." He started to stand, then clutched his ribs with a groan and slid back to the floor.

"You're hurt," said Elli as she rushed to his side. Seeing a swollen gash through a hole in his robe, she unstrapped her water gourd. "Here. This should help."

She hesitated, recalling how useless her healing water had been for Scree. But that wound had been caused by some sort of dark magic, while this looked more like the stab of a dagger. In any case, she just had to try. And maybe at least do something right! She poured a trickle onto the gash, waited, then poured some more.

Slowly, Lleu's expression changed from pain to surprise, and finally, to wonder. He clutched his ribs, tearing open the robe.

"It's gone," he whispered hoarsely. "The knife wound—so deep. How did you do that?"

Elli shook her head and tapped the gourd. "Not me. Water from Halaad's Secret Spring." Suddenly her eyes brightened. "Lleu. Could this help Coerria?"

His frown returned. "No, child, I'm afraid not. What afflicts her is a wound not of the flesh, but of the spirit."

"Tell us who did this."

"A mob, Elli. They just burst into the compound and flowed over us like an evil wave, destroying everything they touched. Everything! And when Coerria saw what they were doing—to her Order, her buildings, her gardens, her life's work—she simply collapsed, overwhelmed by the horror of it all. She must have lost all her hope, all her will to live."

Uzzzula, upon hearing these words, flew past Lleu's ear, buzzing angrily. Then the little hive spirit went right back to work on the High Priestess' hair.

Lleu smiled ruefully. "Some of us will never lose hope."

"That's right," declared Elli. She moved closer to Coerria and knelt by the cot. Gently, she stroked the woman's wrinkled cheek, recalling the radiant blue of those eyes now hidden by closed lids. "Really, Lleu. It's her life we're talking about! We can't give up."

Shim ambled closer. The old fellow bobbed his head, having caught her meaning if not her words. "Certainly, definitely, absolutely."

"I agree," added Brionna. She stepped forward, gracefully avoiding a hole in the floor. "But first, if we're to know what to do, we must know more of what happened."

The falcon on Lleu's shoulder piped a sharp note. At that, the lanky priest cleared his throat. "There isn't much to tell. They suddenly attacked, a whole raging mob of men and women. Farmers, smiths, traders, vagabonds—all whipped into a frenzy of hatred. They stormed the compound, broke down walls, smashed the bell, destroyed the gardens, and so much else. By the bones of Basilgarrad, if Coerria hadn't commanded everyone to flee, they would have murdered us all!"

Elli eyed him gratefully. "Someone didn't flee, though."

Lleu just snorted. "A lot of good it did. Within seconds of bursting in here, they'd made her collapse. Then they stabbed me, tore the place apart, and left us both for dead."

"The mob," asked Nuic, "was strictly humans? No other kinds of creatures?"

The priest nodded grimly. "And so very angry! I can't explain why. Even though, for months now, we've been hearing reports of growing violence out in the realms, everyone had hoped that our troubles would end after the dam at Crystillia was destroyed."

At the mention of that place, Brionna's whole body tensed.

"But alas," the priest went on, "they didn't end. Far from it!" He gazed around grimly. "If only I'd been paying more attention, I might have seen this coming. Why, in just the past few weeks, I've heard some shocking stories of humans attacking other creatures: wolves who were out hunting for their food, elves who happened to be living in desirable trees, or dwarves who were resisting fences being built across their lands. And of course, we also have that movement of Belamir's—Humanity First, he calls it. Well-intentioned as it may be, it seems to be fueling those fires, by claiming that humans know better, and maybe *are* better, than anybody else."

Lleu turned and looked at the still, frail body of Coerria. So feeble were her breaths that her shawl and gown didn't seem to move at all. Then, to no one in particular, he asked, "Who was behind this attack?"

"Belamir," said Nuic darkly.

"No, no, that's not possible. I'm sure, at least, of that. For all his flaws, he's basically just a gardener who's gotten carried away with his notions of humanity's special role in this world. Calls us Nature's *benevolent guardians*, I believe."

Nuic erupted in a spasm of coughing.

"I know, my friend, that's a sure path to arrogance. But I doubt that Belamir is even aware of how his theories can be twisted and abused by greedier people. At heart, he's really a good man. A teacher. And also a friend of Coerria's."

Elli shook her head of curls. "No, he's not. He said some things about her that weren't friendly at all, right to me and Llynia."

Lleu's eyebrows arched higher. "Llynia? What ever happened to her?"

Elli shrugged. "Don't know. But my good sprite here thinks we'll see her again."

"Hmmmpff," growled Nuic. "Just as we'll see plagues and hurricanes again."

"Enough," said Elli as she rose to her feet. "It's time to go."

"Where?" asked Brionna with a shake of her braid.

"To the Lady." Her eyes gleamed with determination as she turned, kicking some wood chips across the floor. Then she bent and whispered to the motionless form on the cot, "And I'll come back with your cure, I promise."

Ever so lightly, she touched the old woman's brow. In a whisper, she spoke, as if Coerria could really hear. "There's a song that my father taught me a long time ago:

> *"Avalon lives! The last place to keep*
> *All the songs of Creation alive.*
> *Sing every note—sing high and deep:*
> *Voices uplifted shall thrive;*
> *Singers themselves shall survive."*

She drew a long, slow breath. "Please survive, Coerria. Please."

Lleu stood up. He brushed some wood chips off his shoulder, then gazed warmly at Elli. "You know," he said, touching her arm, "that look on your face just now reminded me of someone."

Puzzled, she blinked up at him.

"Your father."

She blushed. "Really?"

He nodded. "He was my best friend, you know. Saved my skin many a time during our days as young priests." Then, his voice soft, he added, "Maybe that's why I'm going to come with you."

She started. "But what about Coerria?"

"There's nothing more I can do for her now. Uzzzula here has been pouring fresh water on her tongue, and mopping her brow with eucalyptus leaves, several times a day. Beyond that, whatever might help her only the Lady can provide."

"Then," declared Elli as she clenched her fists, "let's go get it."

7 · Arc-kaya

WHEN SCREE AWOKE, HIS MEMORY WAS AS hazy as his vision. Where the frill-feathers was he? And how did he get here?

He blinked his large, yellow-rimmed eyes, but everything still looked blurry. Then, drawing a fitful breath, he caught some familiar smells. Eagles' feathers. Broken shells. Droppings. Timbers scraped raw by talons.

He knew those smells, from the nests of other eaglefolk. And from his own childhood, those days when he'd felt the touch of his true mother—days that had ended all too quickly. For she'd been felled by the arrows of some murderous men. Since then, practically all his life, he hadn't lived in nests like the rest of his kind, but in caves of fire-scorched rock, out of reach from anyone or anything.

Except his longings. In the years that he had lived all alone, trying to protect Merlin's staff, he'd often yearned for some clear idea of his purpose in life. And even more, he'd yearned for some companionship—especially from his brother Tamwyn and from the eaglemother he'd known so briefly. She often visited him in his dreams, soaring overhead with her wide, powerful wings, or calling to him with her rich, screeching voice, part human and part eagle.

A face appeared before him now, fuzzy at the edges but distinctly that of an eaglewoman. Like Scree, she was in human form, and she peered down at him, her fierce yellow eyes showing a hint of softness. Long gray hair, as fluffy as a fledgling's feathers, fell over her shoulders.

"M-mother?" he croaked in disbelief.

She smiled, wrinkles curving like talons around her eyes. "No, no, I am not your mother." She frowned and added in a whisper, "Though I was once someone else's." She cleared her throat. "My name is Arc-kaya."

Gently she placed the palm of her hand on his forehead. "Good. The fever's a bit less."

"Fever?"

"You were badly wounded when you came here to the village Iye Kalakya—carried by a human and a hoolah, of all creatures. They said you'd lost a lot of blood, in addition to ripping most of the muscles in your thigh. And you've been delirious with fever ever since you arrived."

She moved away and started to unwrap the layers of bandages on his leg. "Your name is Scree, isn't it?"

Suddenly everything came back, in an avalanche of images. The night on Hallia's Peak, and that vision in the starless sky. The unicorn. The evil flower. And the bloodred shard, turning to smoke in Tam's hand.

Scree's eyesight cleared. He was in a nest, huge and deep in the manner of all eaglefolk. Feathers of every size, some as long as his own arms, lay everywhere on the logs and branches that intertwined around him, as well as the table, chairs, and chests made of sinew-lashed wood. But instead of the usual gnawed bones and bits of shell common to eaglefolk's nests, this place looked exceptionally clean. And against one wall stood three large cabinets, their shelves packed full of vials, bowls, strainers, splints, bandages of all sizes, and numerous tools for mixing and measuring potions.

A healer, he thought. *So that's who she is.*

"Arc-kaya," he demanded, "just how long have I been here?"

She continued to unravel the bandages. "Well, let's see now. It's been three days."

"Three days!"

He started to sit up—but his head exploded with pain, as if a boulder had been dropped right on his skull. With a groan, he fell back on the feather-cushioned logs beneath him, his bare chest heaving from exertion.

"Shackle my shells," he panted, his head still pounding. "Hurts just to move."

"Patience, Scree," said Arc-kaya, clacking her teeth, beaklike. "You'll be weaker than a hatchling for several more days, if not weeks."

"Weeks?" His eyes flashed like golden orbs. "But I must—" He tried again to sit up, but fell back right away. "Must go . . ."

"Now, now. You'll not be going anywhere soon."

"But Tamwyn! He needs me."

"That dark-haired human who brought you? He's gone now. Left yesterday, after he was sure you'd recover."

"Left? That stump-headed fool! He's gone without me."

She began carefully peeling off the bottom layer of bandaging.

"He did seem in a great hurry—like most humans. Though why anyone in his right mind would want to go anywhere with a crazy hoolah tagging along, I don't know."

Her hands paused. "He did say something odd, though. About *finding the route before it's too late.* Just where is he going?"

"The stars," groaned Scree. "He's trying to find some way to reach them."

"The stars! That's pure folly."

"And pure Tam. He left before I revived enough to talk, since he knew I'd do everything I could to—"

"Stop him," finished Arc-kaya. "That's sensible."

"No, to *join* him."

She turned and peered at him with her large eyes. "Maybe you *are* still delirious."

Scree didn't answer. What was the point? He turned his cheek against the pair of silver feathers that made his pillow. His fool brother!

Outside the arching walls of the nest, he could hear the sounds of village life: eaglefolk laughing, arguing, or screeching as they landed; young fledglings scampering after one another; someone ruffling feathered wings, preparing to fly. Those sounds seemed so normal here, so ordinary. And yet they were so far away from his own solitary experience.

Arc-kaya, having gone back to work on his leg, removed the last strip of bandage. She whistled with concern. "Such a savage wound you have here! What gave this to you? A barbed spear?"

"No. A flower."

Her eyes narrowed. "Either you're toying with me, Scree, or you're wounded even more badly than I thought."

He turned his head so their gazes met. "That's the truth, Arc-kaya. You don't have to believe me, but it is. There are new kinds of evil out there in the world, more than you can imagine."

She pursed her lips thoughtfully. "You know, for some reason I do believe you. Maybe it's because you remind me of someone."

"Who?"

"Someone I lost."

Though her words made him curious, he didn't press her any further.

Arc-kaya, meanwhile, reached for a stone vial, opened it, and poured some gray, oily ointment onto his thigh. Scree winced, less from the stinging sensation than from the pungent smell.

"Smells awful, doesn't it?" she asked, beginning to rub the ointment gently into his muscles.

"Like troll turds."

"Crushed bark from the rancidnut tree, actually. The best thing for healing torn tissue." She heaved a sigh. "You are right, I'm afraid, about new kinds of evil. I've even heard there's now a renegade clan of eaglefolk, from some distant realm, that's taken to attacking other clans, murdering their people and stealing whatever is valuable."

Scree's whole body tensed. The vision! So it was true! "But why? That's never happened before in the history of our people."

"I know, I know." She sighed, reaching for some more ointment. "That's always been the province of humans and gobsken, attacking their own kind."

"But why would they do it?" Scree demanded.

"Well," she replied grimly, "some say they are ruled by a leader whose greed knows no bounds. And some say they've been hired to steal as much as they can by a wicked sorcerer."

"Sorcerer?" Scree lifted his hand, which felt as heavy as stone, and squeezed her arm. "Does he wear a hooded cloak? And have pale white hands?"

She stopped massaging his leg and squinted at him. "So you know of him? Kulwych is the name I've heard."

His hand fell back to the nest. "I know him, yes. And his lackey swordsman." He ground his teeth. "What else have you heard?"

"Not much," she said, resuming her work. "Just what comes to me as the village healer, and it's hard to tell what to believe. Why, I've even heard that Kulwych is using the treasures stolen by the eaglefolk to pay for all the weapons he needs for an army of conquest."

Scree grimaced. An army—one that would serve not just White Hands, but Rhita Gawr! He needed to tell Tam about this. But how could he? His brother was already on his way, and soon would be somewhere deep inside the trunk of the Great Tree, a region probably many times as large as all seven root-realms combined. And that wasn't all: Once Tam found his way into the trunk, he'd be searching for an unknown route—if indeed such a route existed—that could take him all the way up to the branches, and then to the stars. Why, before long he'd be harder to find than a white feather in a cloud!

In frustration, he groaned. For even if he knew where to find Tam, what could he do? He was too weak even to stand up, let alone change himself into winged form and take flight.

"Here, Scree, taste some of this." Arc-kaya held a feather quill, dripping with something that looked like mashed strawberries, over his mouth. "It will help you relax."

Somewhat warily, he licked the tip of the quill. It tasted sweet, like clover honey, so he licked some more. Just seconds after he'd swallowed, a heavy mist seemed to flow into his mind, dimming his thoughts. Soon he fell into a dreamless sleep.

After he awoke, many hours later, Arc-kaya propped up his head and fed him a thin, tangy broth, one spoonful at a time. For the next several days, she almost never left his side, departing the nest only briefly to visit the communal cooking area, or to find some implement or ingredient that she needed.

Scree watched, with growing admiration, how generously she gave of herself. When she wasn't changing his bandages, applying new poultices, or massaging his leg muscles, she was busy making potions, creams, or splints for the variety of other eaglefolk who came to her nest. Whatever the time of day or night, she welcomed villagers young and old, whether their problem was allergy to weasel fur, swollen talons, infected gashes, or bad dreams. She treated everyone with care and patience, even when Scree himself was tempted to give them a good scolding for waking him and Arc-kaya up from a sound sleep. And if someone wasn't able to pay, she'd merely wave her hand and say, "Just bring me a feather or two when you can."

In time, he grew strong enough to hobble over to her table and help her prepare medications. He sliced herbs, roots, and bark fibers with her flint knives; crushed seeds with her mortar and pestle; and (his favorite task) cracked basketloads of nuts with her quartz hammer. He learned how to make bone marrow paste, lemon balm oil, and tincture of carrot and aniseed for calming children's coughs. All the while, he talked with Arc-kaya about village life and the history of her clan—but never about the loved one she'd lost.

Finally, on the ninth day, he was strong enough to climb out of the nest with her. Together they visited the communal hearth, where he saw eaglefolk cooking rich venison broth, baking feather-light barley cakes, and steeping reeds to make baskets and rugs. At the village market, Arc-kaya inspected numerous dried herbs and flowers, but only bought a bundle of rosehips. On the way home, they paused to watch a group of children playing catch-the-hare, which looked like so much fun that Scree would have joined in if he'd had the stamina.

More days passed. As his strength increased, Scree ventured out for walks on his own around the village. He found eaglefolk practicing their talon-fighting skills, a rough sport that often sent men and women to Arc-kaya's care. He discovered craftspeople who could feather-paint vivid pictures on polished eggshells, carve jewelry from purple amethyst and red rubies, and make all sorts of tools from sun-dried bones and crystals from the mountainside. Yet he enjoyed more than anything the warm welcome that Arc-kaya always gave him when he returned to the nest.

In fact, he enjoyed it enough that he felt almost glad that, for now at least, he couldn't go anywhere else. Tam, as well as Brionna, were often in his thoughts—along with the vision they'd seen on Hallia's Peak. So he made plans for what he would do after his strength came back: Since finding Tam would be impossible, he'd try to locate Elli or Brionna and tell them what he'd learned about White Hands. But for now he was here. In a village, and a nest, that felt nearly like home.

One morning, when Scree came back panting and covered with dust after a game of catch-the-hare, Arc-kaya nodded knowingly. "Well? How did you do?"

"Terribly! Some of those two-year-olds, only half my size, had me spinning in circles. Especially one golden-eyed boy whose name, I think, was Hawkeen." He flashed her a smile. "But I had a great time."

She grinned, though not quite happily. "That's just what Ayell would have said."

Scree lifted an eyebrow. "Was he . . . ?"

"My son. He lived with me until he was five, nearly a full-grown adult who could build his own nest, his own life. And then one day . . . he died."

Gently, he asked, "How?"

She blinked and shook her fluffy gray hair. "By the arrow of a human."

He winced. *Just like my mother.*

"We were flying together, over the northern ridge of Hallia's Peak. Looking for cliff hares, we said aloud—but our real reason, we both knew, was just to fly together." She sighed, remembering. "Ayell loved nothing more than soaring freely, his wings open to their widest."

"And then?"

"Men. With bows and arrows. One of them aimed at me—why, I don't know. Who can explain the vile acts of men? But Ayell saw him shoot. He veered instantly, and threw himself right into the arrow's path."

Angrily, she raked the air with her fingers, as if she had assumed her winged form and was scratching out someone's eyes with her talons. "Gave his own life for mine! Aye, if only he'd never done that, he could be soaring in the sky today."

Her shoulders drooped. "That is what I wish, with all my eagle's heart."

Scree nodded, then said, "He died with courage."

She stared at him blankly. "But he died."

Abruptly, she straightened herself, marched over to the table, and started dicing some tubers. "What a foolish old bag of feathers I am," she mumbled in embarrassment. "Burdening you with such prattle."

"Arc-kaya," he chided. "That wasn't prattle."

Slowly, she lifted her face, her yellow eyes now rimmed in red. "What was it, then?"

"A memory, a cry of pain. For your son, who was your family. Nothing is more precious to have—or more painful to lose."

She pondered him, and a little of the bitterness faded from her eyes. "Something tells me you've had your own share of losses."

He swallowed. "That's true." Joining her at the table, he added, "But you know, in these days here with you, I've found a few things, too."

She gazed at him gratefully. "In just another week, Scree, you'll be strong enough to change form and fly. To leave, if you like." And then hesitantly, she added, "Or maybe . . . to stay."

His heart quickened at the thought, and he looked around the nest, at the piles of splints and bandages, the feathers scattered everywhere, the vials and bowls and colorful potions. Then he slowly shook his head. "I can't, Arc-kaya. There are people I must find, and help if I can. Far from here."

Biting her lip, she nodded. "I understand, aye. Our clan's oldest blessing, you know, is *Soar high, run free.*"

"I like that. It's simple, strong, eagleworthy."

The corners of her mouth turned up slightly, as a breeze tousled her long gray hair. "I'm glad you came here," she whispered. "Even just for a while."

"So am I."

Thhwaaack.

A thick-shafted arrow struck her back, plunging deep between her shoulder blades. Her mouth opened wide, as if to scream. But no sound came. She teetered, glanced at Scree, and toppled onto the floor of the nest.

"No!" shouted Scree as he knelt beside her, drawing her face to his chest. At the same time, he looked up to see who had done this terrible thing—just in time to see another arrow plunging straight at him.

He rolled to the side, just barely in time. The arrow grazed his shoulder and buried deep into one leg of the table. Straining to the limit of his strength, he dragged Arc-kaya over to a sheltered spot between two of her potions cabinets. But not before he caught a glimpse of who had shot at them.

It was an eagleman! He was young, but fully grown, and from the look of him already a seasoned warrior. His face haughty and sneering, the attacker grinned smugly as he swooped overhead, heavy bow clutched in one talon, before disappearing beyond the rim of the nest. Several more eaglemen, all bearing weapons, followed close behind.

"Cowards!" shouted Scree wrathfully. "Buzzards! Why don't you fight with your talons, like real eaglemen?"

His cry, though, was lost in the sudden cacophony that rose on all sides. Just beyond the walls of Arc-kaya's nest, he heard the shrieks and wails of many eaglefolk. The village, moments ago full of the sounds of ordinary life—laughter, debate, and tools at work—echoed now with howls of rage and agony.

Looking at the woman slumped against him, whose fluffy gray hair was now streaked with blood, Scree turned onto his knees. He grabbed the arrow and tried to pull it free. Arc-kaya moaned painfully, arching her back. But he wasn't strong enough! The arrow just wouldn't budge.

Leaning her gently against the cabinet, he started to get up. *At least I can fight them*, he told himself. *Even if I can't change into eagle form, maybe I can—*

Arc-kaya stirred, opening her eyes. Though she clearly had trouble focusing, she recognized Scree and grabbed his forearm. "No," she said hoarsely. "Don't go. They'll just kill you, too."

He shook loose. Eyes brimming, he said, "I must go! Must fight them! To help somehow."

Feebly, she brushed a finger against his jaw. "Help by living. Aye, Scree. Just stay alive . . . my son."

She gasped, then whispered her final words, so softly that Scree could hardly hear. "Soar high . . . run free."

8 · Beyond Any Tears

BY THE TIME SCREE LEFT ARC-KAYA'S NEST and stumbled out into the village, the massacre was already over. Bodies of eaglefolk—children and elders, artists and vendors, women and men—lay everywhere, most of them struck by deadly arrows before they had even a chance to transform into their eagle forms. The few who had sprouted wings and tried to defend their village had been brutally mauled, their bodies slashed and their talons severed.

The communal cooking area, where many villagers had died, was a shambles. Scree found equipment and market stalls overturned, food scattered, and hearth coals smelling of burning flesh. Smoke, thick and dark, rose somberly into the sky, blocking out the summit of Hallia's Peak. What few survivors remained were either wandering about in shock or weeping over the bodies of loved ones.

While most of the goods from the village market had been left behind, the attackers had taken all the jewelry, tools, and crystals—anything valuable. It seemed clear that the purpose of this brutal attack had been thievery. Scree felt sure that this had been done by the renegade clan that was in league with White Hands and Rhita Gawr.

And he felt sure of something else, as well. When he had glimpsed the haughty young warrior who murdered Arc-kaya, he had noticed his red leg bands and black-tipped wings: unmistakable markings of the Bram Kaie clan. He knew them from his travels across Fireroot. And he also knew their leader.

All too well. For he had been lured into trusting her, and that misplaced trust had very nearly cost him Merlin's staff, which he had promised to guard, as well as his own life. He had never told anyone else about that terrible mistake, not even Tam, for some secrets were just too painful to share.

Yet he could never forget it.

For the rest of that heart-wrenching day, he set himself to the task of finding and helping the survivors. There weren't many, fewer than a dozen out of the sixty or seventy eaglefolk who had lived in these nests. He found three women and two men, all wounded, along with one old fellow in winged form, who was so dazed he could only stumble around blindly, his wings singed and dragging. Five children had also survived—including Hawkeen, the golden-eyed eagleboy who had, that very morning, so enjoyed their game of catch-the-hare.

Using Arc-kaya's supplies, and what little knowledge of healing he had learned from watching her, Scree tried his best to clean and bandage the wounds of as many people as he could. But the severest wounds, as he knew well, lay behind their eyes.

On the following day, the survivors began the most difficult task of all. Burying the dead, in the traditional fashion of eaglefolk, required building an earthen mound covered by stones. And in this case, with so many bodies, the mound would have to be an enormous one.

Though it tapped his strength to the limit, Scree joined the other villagers in hauling dirt and stones to a wide field near the now-silent nests. Throughout the day, the survivors did their best to help each other, although very few words were spoken. Even when they paused to sip from bowls of water or chew strips of smoked boar, they ate in silence, staring in grief at the rising mound. Like the others, Scree felt that he was burying more than just a village.

Nothing he carried that day felt as heavy as the limp form of Arc-kaya. She was the very last person to be buried. As he'd already done too many times, he placed her body on the mound, arms spread wide in the way of all eaglefolk. Gently, he covered her as best he could with a layer of feathers and dry grass.

Before pouring the first basketload of dirt over her body, he knelt beside her. Using one of her flint knives, he cut off a single lock of her gray hair. As soft as a fledgling's tail feather it felt, and he studied it for a long moment before tying it around his ankle.

At last, when the final stone had been laid, Scree stood grimly facing the mound. He stretched his arms, stiff and bruised from the long day's work, and rubbed the sore muscles of his thigh— muscles that she had worked so hard to heal. He lowered his head, and in a voice heard only by the wind, he whispered, "Soar high, Arc-kaya. Run free."

Then, just behind him, voices suddenly lifted in song. He turned around to see the adult eaglefolk, arrayed in a line that bent like a wing, starting to sing the sacred chants of their clan. Surprised, Scree found himself caught by their music, and lifted by it, as if he were a feather on a breeze.

As the chanting continued, Scree realized that he'd never heard such beautiful sounds from the mouths of his people. Simple though this music was, and tinged with sorrow, it swept him up and bore him aloft, twisting on currents of feeling that had flowed through eaglefolk for generations.

In time, the children joined in, hesitantly at first, their voices broken with sobs. But soon they were singing clearly, their small voices blending with the others as smoothly as separate feathers merge into a single wing. And they added more than voices, Scree knew. They added a touch of hope. For the fact that there were still children left meant that this village, and this people, would live on.

He turned away from the body of Arc-kaya and looked at the faces of the children. They were, as he expected, full of grief and loss, for among those buried had been their mothers, fathers, sisters, and brothers. And yet, despite their youth, they also showed hints of the eaglefolk's legendary ferocity, courage, and will to survive. Especially in the face of Hawkeen, Scree saw those qualities. And something else, too. For in that sad but sturdy youth, whose somber eyes glinted with gold, Scree saw a reflection of himself years ago. Such anguish and resolve, all bound together, seemed terribly familiar.

What he hadn't expected was what Hawkeen did next. The lad lifted his chin toward the sky and started to sing on his own, his voice blending the plaintive call of a child with the screeching cry of an eagle:

High overhead
In islands of clouds
Sailed the good ship I knew best.
Her feathers so soft,
Her wings wide aloft,
She carried me safely to rest
Settled in our downy nest.

O Mother, my ship,
My vessel on high,
You have flown beyond sight, beyond fears.
I miss you beyond any tears.

Sleekness and strength,
So graceful in flight,
Eagle wings riding the sea—
You taught me to fly,
To sail in the sky,
And grandest of all how to be
Master of all that I see.

O Mother, my ship,
My vessel on high,
You have flown beyond sight, beyond fears.
I miss you beyond any tears.

Mere moments ago
You promised to take
Me flying above haze or cloud.
Two sailors we'd be

Afloat on the sea—
But our journey was never allowed:
The haze has become your death shroud.

O Mother, my ship,
My vessel on high,
You have flown beyond sight, beyond fears.
I miss you beyond any tears.

Silent you sail
Where I cannot go,
Behind veils of gathering mist.
Though hard have I tried
To stay by your side,
I must fly alone and exist
Far from the ship I have missed.

O Mother, my ship,
My vessel on high,
You have flown beyond sight, beyond fears.
I miss you beyond any tears.

As the boy's voice trailed off, he started to walk back to the empty nests of the village. But as he turned, his gaze met Scree's. For an infinite moment they looked at each other, one's eyes flecked with gold, the other's rimmed in yellow. Then, as if they had said everything they needed to say, they gave a simultaneous nod. The boy stepped solemnly toward the village, while Scree turned back to the burial mound.

While the other survivors continued to chant, Scree's

thoughts turned to Arc-kaya. To her kindness, her generosity, and her love.

Then, in his mind's eye, he saw the sneering face of the young warrior who had murdered her. It was a face eager for battle. Hungry for blood. And also . . . something else, a strange quality that Scree couldn't quite identify.

"I'll find you, brutal warrior," he growled under his breath. "You'll pay for what you've done! By the Thousand Groves, you will."

For his plans had changed. Knowing that he had no hope of finding his brother Tam, who was probably now deep inside the vast expanse of the Great Tree's trunk, and also knowing that he could spend weeks searching for Brionna and Elli, who could be anywhere in the Seven Realms, he had hit upon a new course of action. It was highly risky, and bold to the point of moronic. But if it worked, it just might give him the chance to upset the wicked plans of White Hands—as well as his master, Rhita Gawr. And if he succeeded, he would be helping, in his own small way, to save Avalon from the gathering storm that would strike very soon.

He would return to Fireroot—and find the Bram Kaie clan. Whatever it might take, he would track them down and kill their leader, who had made the gruesome pact with White Hands. And, if he could, he would kill someone else as well: the young assassin who had stolen Arc-kaya's life.

His eyes glinting like sharpened blades, Scree nodded gravely. Dangerous as this idea was, he knew it was the right thing to do. Even though he couldn't actually join Tam on his quest, they would at least be working toward the same goals. So while they'd be separated by enormous distances, they would still, in this way, be together. Doing their parts for Avalon.

He swallowed hard, realizing that this plan appealed to him for other reasons, as well. For one, whether he succeeded or not, he would seem like less of a buffoon. To himself—and maybe also to Brionna. And for another, he could win a small measure of revenge for Arc-kaya.

For a moment he seemed as hard as the stones that he had carried to the mound. He'd find that brutal warrior, all right. Find him and kill him. And he'd do it the old-fashioned way, with no weapons but wings and talons.

He glanced down at his anklet of Arc-kaya's hair. In the late afternoon light, it glowed like a radiant ring of silver. He thought of the truly loving welcome that she'd given him—so very different from the welcome he'd received that day, six years ago, from Quenaykha, the leader of the Bram Kaie clan.

When he first met her, among the flaming cliffs of Fireroot's Volcano Lands, it was entirely by accident. They had both been flying low, hunting the same pack of wild boars, when they nearly flew into each other because of a crag that blocked their vision. Right away, he'd found her beautiful—with streaming auburn hair, a shapely form, bright yellow eyes, and a sense of enormous power that guided her every movement. But while Scree was himself a powerful figure, brawny and skilled at hunting beyond his years, down inside he was still just a boy.

For all his life, he had lived on these cliffs, cut off from other eaglefolk. Because of his promise to Merlin, he had stayed hidden away, especially after murderous ghoulacas had killed his adopted mother and separated him from his brother Tam. So without any family or friends, he lived all alone, sleeping in remote caverns, avoiding contact with others.

Then he met her. Even in those days, as the newly chosen

leader of her clan, she preferred to be called simply Queen. Naive as he was, Scree didn't understand what this said about her—nor what her true motivations might have been for luring him back to her village.

He'd been easy prey for her. He understood that now. She had seemed so strong, attractive, and completely self-assured. And also so drawn to him, which had felt as intoxicating as the richest mead. Scree, meanwhile, was lonely, confused, and desperately craving affection. While she had given him that—leading him to a hidden grove of ironwood trees and wrapping him in feathery softness beyond anything he'd ever dreamed—she hadn't done it out of love.

No, she had done it out of greed. For she had seen Merlin's staff, sensed its power, and wanted to own it. When they returned to her village, she had kissed him warmly and promised that he'd be safe, even as she was stealthily signaling to her guards. Bathing in her affection, he hadn't suspected a thing—until, all of a sudden, he was viciously attacked.

Only thanks to his superior strength and speed, and his experience battling ghoulacas, did he escape with the staff. Not to mention his life. And from that day to this, he'd cursed his gnome-headed foolishness. For he had made, he knew, the worst mistake of his life, almost losing everything he valued in a single mindless moment.

Scree straightened his back and turned away from the mound. Raising his gaze to the ridges above the village, he scanned the windblown summit of Hallia's Peak. And then, peering beyond, he traced the dark brown ridges that rose in the distance.

Those ridges lifted steadily starward, climbing higher and higher until they vanished in ever-swirling mist. Scree knew that none of his own people, not even the legendary flyers Hac Yarrow and Ilyakk, had ever flown as high as the places that his brother was now seeking. They hadn't even attempted to fly up to the branches of the Great Tree, considering such a journey beyond the natural reach of their kind. And yet that was just what Tam was trying to do—to voyage not just to the branches, but onward to the stars.

Tam, wherever you are right now, I hope you're still in one piece. And behaving more sensibly than I am.

Raking the air with his hand, he strode off to stay his last night among the nests of this village. Tomorrow at dawn he would leave, hoping that his strength would fully return during his trip to Fireroot. For although he had less distance to travel than Tam, he knew that he had no less danger to face. And he also knew that, like his brother, he simply had to try his best to survive.

9 · To Live Forever

REACHING UP, TAMWYN GRABBED HOLD OF A lip of rough brown rock above his head. He pulled, hoisting himself higher, straining his sore arms to gain the upper ledge. Sweat from his brow dribbled into his eyes, stinging.

Just a bit higher, he thought with fierce determination. *Almost there now.*

Suddenly the lip of rock broke off, spraying pebbles into the air and sending him tumbling backward. He slid and bounced down the cliffside, finally rolling to a stop. For a moment he lay on his back, dust swirling about him, listening to the echoing ring from the quartz bell on his hip—and the softer, deeper note from the slab of wood inside his pack.

"Trolls' tongues!" he cursed, forcing himself to sit up despite his dizziness.

He stared up at the cliff looming above him. So steep, so lifeless. For two days now, all he had seen—other than the smirking face of that hoolah now and then—was rock. Rough brown rock.

It was everywhere, rising higher and higher, climbing straight up to the sky just like . . .

He shook his head, sending up a cloud of dirt and dust. *Just like the trunk of a tree.* Which was, of course, what he was climbing. For this was no ordinary tree. This one, it seemed, went on and on forever. And these endless brown ridges were, in fact, its bark—the crusty surface of the trunk's lower reaches.

Blinking the dust from his eyes, he peered into the thickening clouds of mist that swirled above him. The cliffs beyond the ledge rose upward until, at last, they vanished in the vapors. How far he'd come he couldn't guess, but he did feel sure that in the time since he'd left Scree he'd only managed to climb a tiny fraction of the trunk.

Why, he hadn't even glimpsed the Swaying Sea, which was supposed to be somewhere up here. Nor his true goal, which was not the Sea—or the strange appendage, neither root nor branch, that held it. No, what he wanted to find was the portal that was somewhere near the Sea: the highest portal in the lower realms, which could take him deep into the Tree itself. For he knew that his hopes lay not in climbing up the Great Tree from the outside, as he was doing now—which could take forever—but in finding a passage somewhere *inside*.

The same inside passage that, as Tamwyn had learned from bards, his father had hoped would carry him to the very top with the speed of portals. After all, Krystallus had ridden portals to every one of the seven root-realms, even Shadowroot, and survived. Despite its dangers, portalseeking offered the fastest way to move around great distances.

And even the vast distances between the root-realms were

small compared to the utter enormity of the upper reaches of Avalon. Why, Krystallus himself believed that the trunk alone dwarfed all Seven Realms put together. And then, if you considered how huge the branches, and all the lands they contained, could be . . .

Tamwyn shook his head, overwhelmed by the mere thought of such magnitude. *And here I am, trying to travel all the way to the top, and to the stars beyond! And to do it in just a few short weeks, before Rhita Gawr can crush us all.*

But he knew he shouldn't think about that now. Better to focus on his next steps. First, he'd find that portal near the Swaying Sea, and enter the trunk from there. Then he'd go to the legendary Great Hall of the Heartwood, deep inside the Tree, which his father had discovered on one of his earlier expeditions—and which Krystallus believed held the key to traveling higher, into the upper trunk and branches. And ultimately, to the stars.

Tamwyn brushed some chips of rock off his eyebrow, then took from his pack the flask he'd made from a supple leaf of leathereed. Unplugging the flask, he took some water—his final sip, just a few piddling drops. Licking the last trace of moisture on his lips, he knew that he would find no more to drink until he reached the Swaying Sea. If he ever got there. And where he'd find his next meal, he could only guess.

What matters more, he told himself, *is finding that portal.*

Closing the flask, he replaced it in the pack. His hand brushed against the slab of harmóna wood and it vibrated again, a low, quivering note. He hadn't touched it since parting from Elli. And given how upset he felt, even now, he didn't want to hold the wood in his hands, let alone carve on it again.

He adjusted the pack strap on his shoulder, and straightened his staff and dagger in their sheaths. Then, once again, he started to climb. Hand over hand he pulled himself higher on the rough-hewn rock, moving upward bit by bit. Another handhold broke, scraping his thumb, but this time he caught himself before falling. It took him twenty minutes of hard work to regain the spot below the ledge where he'd tumbled backward.

He paused, breathing hard as he reached up to the ledge to grasp a new hold. *This is tough*, he told himself. *Toughest thing I've ever done.* A wry grin creased his dirt-smudged face. *Except for trying to talk with Elli.*

His hand found a knob. It was not very big, and almost out of reach, but he managed to clamp his fingers around it. With a grunt, he tried to pull himself up onto the overhanging ledge. Quaking from the effort, he drew his body higher. His bare feet left the rocks below the ledge, so that all his weight hung on the knob. This was just the place he'd been last time, when—

Craaack. The knob broke off!

Tamwyn roared in anguish as he started to fall. His fingers scraped against the rock, trying desperately to hold on somehow. But he kept sliding backward. He couldn't stop himself now.

Suddenly a strong hand appeared above him and grabbed his wrist. It clasped tight around Tamwyn's sweaty skin.

"Henni!" he shouted, relieved even as he flailed, hanging over the ledge. He kicked his legs wildly. "Pull me up, you fool."

"Hoohoo, eehee, ahahahaha," chuckled the hoolah, clearly savoring his new position of power. His silver eyes widened, filling his circular eyebrows. "Well, well, clumsy man. Just look at you now."

"Pull . . . me . . . up," grunted Tamwyn, trying to wriggle up over the edge.

Henni tilted his head and, with his free hand, scratched his temple below the red headband he always wore. "Er, could you tell me why?"

"Why?" blustered Tamwyn, flailing desperately. "Because I'll kill you if you don't!"

"Kill me? Hoohoo, eeheeheehee. Sounds like fun."

"It won't be, I promise!"

Henni's face turned somber. "No fun?" He heaved a sigh. "Oh well, then. What's the point if it's no fun?"

With that, he let go. Tamwyn cried out and plummeted backward, smashing into the rocks below, then rolling and bouncing until he finally came to a stop. He groaned and straightened his left leg, twisted beneath him. Weakly, he raised his head. Even through the spinning collage of brown cliffs, he could make out the face of the hoolah above him, grinning happily.

"You, you . . . little heap of dung!" He waved his clenched fist. "Just wait until I catch you. I'll beat you, chop you, and feed you to a fire dragon! Then I'll rip you out and do it all over again. And that's just the beginning!"

"Eeheeheehahaha," laughed Henni. "You were wrong again, clumsy man. This really *is* fun."

Tamwyn's eyes blazed. Then, hearing a tiny whimper from his tunic pocket, he pulled it open and peered inside. "Batty? You all right?"

"Noee no, manny man. Me's having a very bumpsy-umpsy dream."

"That," growled Tamwyn, "was no dream. That was the hoolah."

Within his pocket, a bright green glow expanded. Then out poked a scrawny, mouselike face with cupped ears, looking very angry indeed. "Batty Lad will teachy him a lesson, oh yessa yessa ya ya ya."

Tamwyn worked his stiff neck and nodded. "Be my guest."

With a flash of green from his eyes, Batty Lad lifted his crumpled wings and took off. He whizzed around the cliff for a moment before catching sight of Henni up on the ledge. The little fellow screeched wrathfully, then zoomed after him. Henni's face looked suddenly worried before he disappeared up the slope.

A moment later, there was a very loud (and for Tamwyn, very satisfying) yelp of pain from the rocks above the ledge. The young man grinned in admiration. Whatever Batty Lad lacked in size, he surely made up for in zeal, at least when he was angry.

Slowly, he got up again, straightened his pack and sheaths, and started to climb back up to the overhanging ledge. The trudge seemed longer than ever, and the cliff steeper, but eventually he reached the spot. This time, however, he tried to work his way around the side of the ledge, cramming his feet into vertical notches in the rock. Bit by bit, he ascended, dragging himself up the sheer face.

Finally, with one last tug, he hauled himself past the barrier. A jutting edge scratched against his cheek, drawing blood, but he didn't care. He'd made it! He pulled off his pack strap and collapsed against a smooth, gray boulder, panting heavily.

Looking to either side, he saw no sign of Henni anywhere. This only improved his mood. In addition, he'd arrived at a flatter area where the trunk seemed to bulge outward. Could it be that his days of hard climbing were almost over?

He swung his head around and looked at the terrain above him—and his brief moment of joy vanished. The cliffs swooped higher again, reaching endlessly upward, until at last they were swallowed by mist. There was nothing ahead of him but rock, rock, and more rock. No sign of the Sea, or the portal.

Then, to the west, a patch of mist opened. And he saw it—hardly more than a flash of blue, deeper than the color of sky, against a rim of brown shoreline. But that was all he needed.

Tamwyn blinked just to be sure. It was really there! So the Swaying Sea wasn't out of reach after all. All he had to do was climb a bit more, until he approached it. Then somewhere up there, if the bards were right, he'd find the portal that would take him to the Great Hall.

But where, exactly? The ballads he'd heard were all vague, just calling it *the portal near the Swaying Sea*, or *the portal on the cliffs*. Even now that he was in the region, it could take him hours—or days—to find it. Or was it too much to hope that he might have some good luck for a change?

He sank back against the boulder, rubbing his tired shoulders on its smooth surface. For an instant the oddity of that intrigued him. Why should there be a boulder like this up here, so different from the rising ridges all around? Looking higher on the cliffs again, he glimpsed a few more such boulders above him—all smooth, round, and dingy gray. Strange that he hadn't seen anything like that down below.

Ah, well. Just another one of those unanswered questions. His brow furrowed. *These days I've been finding lots of those. And most of them have to do with myself.* He glanced down at his pack, holding the wood that could have become a magical harp. *Or with her.*

His gaze moved to the splash of bright blue to the west. The appendage whose broad cup held the Swaying Sea was an unanswered question of its own. Was it Avalon's highest root, an eighth realm, as some supposed? Those who had visited it, including many of the representatives of Avalon's diverse peoples who had signed the treaty that ended the War of Storms, described a place much like Waterroot, though smaller.

Or was it really more like Avalon's lowest branch? That was the view of many at the school that Tamwyn's father had founded, the Eopia College of Mapmakers. But who could really say, since no one—save possibly Krystallus or one of the explorers who had gone with him on that final, ill-fated expedition—had ever seen a true branch of the Great Tree?

Feeling drowsy from all his exertion, Tamwyn gave up speculating. He concluded that someday, if he survived this quest—and if Avalon survived Rhita Gawr—he would just have to explore the Swaying Sea himself. He leaned his head back against the boulder and closed his eyes. He hadn't planned to nap, not really. Just to rest a bit, to gather his strength before the final push to the portal.

Mist from the heights drifted lower, surrounding him in thick, gauzy vapors. Closer and closer the mist swirled, until he could feel its chill on the back of his neck. Then he heard a shout—from someone nearby. Someone in trouble. It was a voice he had never heard before. Yet even so, he recognized it instantly.

"Father!" cried Tamwyn, leaping up from the boulder. Stumbling through the thickening mist, he ran toward the voice. Suddenly he saw his father, or what was left of him. The man's head, in a swirl of long gray hair, was vanishing into the rocks. No more of him remained—just his face, fast disappearing. Beside him on the ground lay his torch, its flame sputtering weakly.

Tamwyn blinked in astonishment. His father was being swallowed, eaten alive! By the Great Tree itself.

Krystallus tried to speak, but this time his voice sounded

inhuman, like scraping rocks. His eyes, as black as Tamwyn's, opened wide in terror. Tamwyn lurched toward him, arms outstretched—

But he couldn't move. The rock beneath him was pulling at him, tugging him downward. He, too, was being sucked down into the rocky ridge! The scraping sound grew louder, swelling all around him.

He cried out, but all he heard was the grinding scrape of stone against stone. Louder it grew, and louder. Now his legs were inside the stone, up to his knees, his thighs, his waist. Then his chest. His hands, his wrists, and soon, despite his struggles, his shoulders. His neck.

Glancing over at his father's face, he caught one final glimpse of the great explorer's eyes. They shone bright, burning through the mist like black fire coals, full of feeling that would never be expressed. Never be shared. Then the ridge swallowed Krystallus completely.

And his torch went out.

"No!" shouted Tamwyn above the grinding noise. Teeth of rock gnawed at the back of his neck, tugging the hair at the base of his skull. "Don't—"

All at once, he woke up. It had all been a dream!

Panting with relief, as cold sweat dribbled down his brow, he surveyed the stark brown ridge around him. It looked the same as before. No mist, no father, no torch.

And yet the back of his neck still hurt, more every second. Too much for a dream. And what was that grinding, gnawing sound so near?

He tried to lean forward—but couldn't budge his head. It was stuck fast to the boulder behind him.

Not a boulder, he realized with a sudden jolt of terror. *A living stone!* He'd heard of them in his travels, and in the ancient tales of Lost Fincayra, though he'd never actually encountered one.

Until now.

Panic seized him, gripping his heart as fiercely as the stone's open jaws gripped the hair of his neck. He pulled harder, trying to tear himself away. But he couldn't break free. Slowly, inexorably, the lips of stone were swallowing his head.

My powers! I'll use them, just as I did for Scree. He shut his eyes, trying his best to concentrate, despite the scraping sound so close to his ears, a sound that had grown to a roar. Now he could feel the living stone's mouth, so close it was starting to tear at his very flesh.

Help me! he cried to those mysterious forces inside himself, remembering that the only way to guide them was through his deepest feelings. But what feelings did that mean? In the case of Scree, it had been the bonds of two brothers, but right now all he felt was his own swelling panic.

No time. His powers, still elusive, weren't coming to his aid. He would die, here and now, ground to bits by the jaws of this creature. Unless . . .

He drew his dagger from its sheath. Reaching behind his head, he sliced downward, cutting off locks of hair—and a chunk of skin as well. He jerked forward, tearing some more hair.

Free! He rolled away, stopping an arm's length below the boulder, near the ledge he had worked so hard to climb. Blood trickled down his neck, and the back of his head stung sharply. But he had escaped.

He stared at the living stone. Its smooth gray surface had

cracked apart, revealing a jagged seam that opened into darkness. Black hair, spattered with blood, clung to the edges. The entire stone vibrated, still scraping its jaws.

All at once, Tamwyn realized that he could understand its words. *Come back to me*, it rumbled angrily. *You are my food, the first I've tasted in centuries.*

No, he answered. *I don't want to die!*

So like a mortal man, said the living stone, its jaws grating. Ever so slowly it started rolling toward Tamwyn, pushing him toward the lip of the ledge. But Tamwyn, for some reason, didn't want to move—just to listen.

You churn with motion, you flame with desire, like all your kind. And yet you know less than a tiny mote of dust. Joining me is not to die, but to live forever! That is true, young man, for I have lived to see the birth of new stars and the death of old worlds. I am the blood of volcanoes, the landing place of lightning, the sediment of eternal seas.

Despite the stone's growing nearness, Tamwyn couldn't resist the sound of its words. He was caught by a strange, dark magic that gripped him, holding fast.

Join me, mortal man, and live forever. The words grew steadily louder. *Join me and be as strong as stone. Join me now.*

At that instant, Tamwyn felt something brush against his hand still holding the dagger. It was the stone! He shook himself, breaking out of his trance.

He spun sideways, rolling on the very lip of the ledge. With a bound, he leaped past the assailant and landed just beyond it. There he stood, shaking the cobwebs from his mind. That had been close—too close.

"Good-bye, living stone. You'll just have to go on eating dust."

He turned to go, when the creature released a roar of rage that echoed across the cliffs. And then the living stone did what Tamwyn had least expected. It started rolling up the slope, straight at him—much faster than before, crushing pebbles under its weight.

Tamwyn ran. All around him, more gray boulders sprang to life. They came crashing down from the heights, bouncing across the ground, pursuing him from all sides. He sprinted along the flat part of the ridge, dodging them and hurtling out of reach. The whole area roared with rocks being smashed and split apart, as if the cliffs themselves were exploding in wrath.

Suddenly, just ahead, he saw a flash of green flames. The portal! He pounded toward it, preparing to leap inside—when he heard another sound, the shrieking wail of someone about to die.

Henni. Tamwyn swerved to miss an oncoming boulder, then halted. He spotted the hoolah, writhing on the ground, his foot caught in the crushing jaws of a living stone. Batty Lad was there as well, buzzing around frantically, but to no avail. In a few more seconds, Henni would be swallowed.

Damn that hoolah!

Back across the ridge Tamwyn charged, right into the oncoming boulders. He veered, sidestepped, and leaped over the attackers, finally skidding to a stop at Henni's side. The hoolah released another howl of pain.

Without thinking, Tamwyn raised his dagger and stabbed at the stone. The blade just snapped off, falling into the dirt. He grimaced, cursing himself. How could he have been so stupid?

Just then the living stone opened his mouth to bellow in rage.

Just for an instant, and barely a crack—but that was enough for Henni to wriggle free. He clutched his sore foot with his oversized hands and glanced up at Tamwyn.

His expression serious for a change, Henni rasped, "You saved me, clumsy man."

Tamwyn scowled, thrusting the remains of his broken dagger into his pack. "Everybody makes a mistake now and then."

"Oohoo, eeheeheehee," laughed the hoolah, having already forgotten his pain. "Let's do that again."

"Let's not." Tamwyn grabbed him by the arm and yanked him upright, even as the living stone started after them. At the same time, three more boulders rolled toward the spot.

They leaped away just as all the enormous stones crashed into each other. Jagged shards flew everywhere. Batty Lad squealed in fright at the explosion and dived into Tamwyn's tunic pocket. Meanwhile, Tamwyn did his best to guide the limping Henni toward the tower of green flames.

They ran, spun, twisted, and ran some more, dodging their rolling pursuers on every side. Henni chuckled constantly, despite his injury, enjoying what seemed to him a great game of tag. But his companion knew that losing this game would mean losing their lives.

Just as they neared the portal, an especially large boulder came hurtling down at them. It slammed through the air, roaring like a wrathful dragon. Tamwyn poised himself to jump, grabbed Henni by the neck, and shouted, "To the Great Hall of the Heartwood!"

The boulder flew past, whizzing right through the spot where Tamwyn's head had been only an instant before. Yet there was no impact, no cry of pain. For no one at all remained.

10 · The Great Hall of the Heartwood

A GREAT FIST OF GREEN FLAMES SQUEEZED Tamwyn tight.

There was a loud crackle, an explosion of light— and then, in the span of a single heartbeat, his skin, bones, and organs condensed down to nothingness. All he could feel, all he could sense, was green fire, searing his very soul.

And yet, at the same time, that fire welcomed him, warmed him, and held him. For he had joined with the Great Tree as wholly, as seamlessly, as a shred of mist joins with a cloud.

Into the tree he spun, riding rivers of flame through canyons of glowing brown. Deeper, deeper, and deeper still—into the very heart of the Tree, the living world that bound all creatures mortal and immortal. As small as a torch beside a star was he, when compared to Avalon itself, yet having entered its inner rivers of élano, he belonged to the Tree no less than its powerful roots.

Rich, resinous smells surrounded him. Entered into him. Became him. As he traveled steadily deeper, the Tree was all he knew, all he felt, all he was.

Suddenly the pulsing river of green veered sharply. He spun

upward, spiraling, toward a mass of bright flames. They crackled, restoring his body instantaneously as he shot through.

He landed face-first on hard ground. And he knew from the sharp squeak in his pocket that Batty Lad had arrived, as well. Then Henni thudded beside him, rolling across the dirt.

Tamwyn sat up, checked to be sure his staff and pack had both survived the journey, and looked around. They were inside a cavern. But this was unlike any cavern he'd ever seen before. He gazed upward, astonished, at the Great Hall of the Heartwood.

Supported by enormous, rootlike buttresses, the ceiling arched high above his head—so high that this place seemed like a grand temple within the Tree. Countless veins twisted and twined across the ceiling's surface, creating a pattern as intricate as a faery queen's filigree. Like the floor where he sat, the spaces between the webbing were filled with some sort of hardpacked dirt, or maybe matted bark, that shone reddish brown.

As he often did in caverns, Tamwyn released a loud whoop, wanting to hear the echo. But this cavern was so vast, with so many niches in its webbed walls, that his voice simply disappeared, swallowed by the space around him.

"Oohoo, eehee, look at this."

Tamwyn trained his gaze on Henni, who had climbed partway up one of the root buttresses, and was now hanging upside down. Apparently the hoolah's narrow escape from the living stone was now nothing more than a memory, if that. Even the bruises on one of his feet didn't seem to concern him. For he hung there, his sacklike tunic falling over his face, tittering with glee and swinging playfully.

"You should try this, clumsy man. Everything looks better upside down."

"No thanks. Unlike you, I value my head."

Henni stopped swinging—looking, for once, sincerely puzzled. "Er . . . why?"

The corners of Tamwyn's mouth turned up slightly. "Nothing you'd understand, my friend."

"Oh well, eeheeheehee. Then it can't be anything important." He went back to swinging. "Besides, if I ever fell, I'd just land on you."

"Hmmm, I guess it's time for me to move." Tamwyn stood, adjusted his staff, and walked over to the portal through which they'd just arrived. But he stopped a pace away, for he could see now that this was no ordinary portal.

Many times taller and broader than any others that he'd seen, this tower of green fire filled a good portion of one wall of the cavern, and the entire space between two vertical buttresses. Layers of undulating flames shimmered up and down its surface, making it ripple like a radiant curtain. It wavered, sparked, and crackled, pulsing with the pure energy of élano. Its top narrowed to a peak, giving it the look of an enormous archway.

For some time Tamwyn pondered the Great Hall's portal, puzzled by its vast size. Suddenly he punched the palm of his hand, recalling some of the lore that he'd heard. While all of Avalon's portals could take travelers to a few other root-realms, and sometimes to random destinations as well, no single portal could reach every other portal—except for this one. It was said that this one alone could carry a traveler to all Seven Realms, as well as to the Swaying Sea. Or at least to six of the realms, for the only portal in Shadowroot, at the Lost City of Light, had been destroyed long ago by the dark elves.

Looking up at the wall of green flames, Tamwyn pushed some

black hair off his brow. His thoughts turned to the explorer who had discovered this place, the first person to travel through its portal: his father. As the bards often sang, Krystallus first came here sometime in the Year of Avalon 700s, at the height of his career as the greatest mapper of the Seven Realms. He had vowed someday to return—and surely did, on his final expedition: his journey to the stars.

The same journey that Tamwyn himself now hoped to make—before time ran out for Avalon.

Tamwyn's throat, already dry, seemed coated with sand. *So it's possible that my father stood right here, not so long ago. With his famous torch in hand.*

Something made him need to swallow, despite the dryness. *I wonder if he ever thought about his wife, Halona, after everyone gave her up for dead. And about . . . his son.*

Just then he noticed a new sound, apart from the ongoing crackle of the portal and Henni's inane chuckling above him. It was very soft—just a whisper, a bubble, a gentle gurgle. He caught his breath. A spring!

Scanning the circular hall with a woodsman's eye, Tamwyn quickly spotted the source of the sound. It was, indeed, a spring, at the far side of the hall. It flowed beside a patch of emerald green moss at the base of the largest root buttress. He strode over and knelt beside it.

Cupping his hands, he filled them with the clear liquid, and drank. Many times before he'd tasted fresh water from a spring, but never like this. The water, not so cold as snowmelt but still cool enough to make his tongue tingle, poured over his dry mouth and throat like a sweet mist, awakening his taste buds even as it revived them. More nectar than water, its sweetness thrilled his lips, strengthened his limbs, and lifted his spirits. It seemed more like a meal, or a week's worth of meals, than just a drink. What water! What life!

Tamwyn sighed pleasurably, then took another drink. At that moment, a furry little head with oversized ears poked out of his pocket. Unfurling the wing that he'd wrapped around his face, Batty Lad sniffed the air with his tiny black nose.

"Me smelly some wetwater?" he chattered. "Oo, manny man. Me lovey-do wetwater."

"Come on out then," offered Tamwyn, wiping the dribbles off his chin. "Have some."

The batlike creature hopped onto the pocket's edge, flapped his wrinkled wings, and drifted down to the spring. He plunged his tiny face right into the flow, gurgling with delight. Eagerly he swallowed, then came up for a breath of air, only to plunge right back in for more.

Henni, seeing that something new was happening, climbed down from his perch. Limping slightly, he scurried over to join the others. As soon as he realized there was fresh water, he, too, bent over the spring. He pursed his lips, slurping loudly as he drank. Soon his circular eyebrows glistened with water droplets.

After he'd drunk all he could hold, Tamwyn filled his water flask, sure that no matter how many times he refilled it, the flask would always contain a hint of this water's wonderful sweetness. Then, having returned the flask to his pack, he lay down on his back to rest. He set his head on the small patch of moss that grew by the spring, careful not to scrape the sore spot behind his head. This moss, he guessed, would be softer than any pillow he'd ever known.

But it wasn't. Something jabbed into him, a sharp corner of

some kind. He frowned, sitting up again. What sort of moss was this, anyway?

Peering closely, he saw nothing unusual. Curious, he patted the thick pad of greenery with his hand. It seemed as soft as he'd imagined, luxuriant and deep. Then—he felt an edge.

He sucked in his breath. Something was buried under the moss! It could be just a rectangular stone, or perhaps a slab of wood. Or it could be . . . well, he'd just have to find out.

Swiftly, he dug his fingers into the soil beneath the moss. He felt something smooth, and a perfectly straight edge. He lifted, tearing it eagerly out of the green tendrils. For he was sure now that this was no stone, or slab of wood.

This was a box.

He pulled it free, brushed off the clumps of moist dirt, and held it before his face. In the flickering green light of the hall, it glowed eerily—a small box of smooth, tan-colored wood. There were no markings to be seen on its surface. But when he shook it gently, something rustled inside.

By now both Henni and Batty Lad had stopped drinking to watch. Tamwyn didn't speak to them, though, focused as he was on his discovery. Could it, perhaps, have been left here by Krystallus or one of his band of explorers?

With trembling fingers, he lifted the lid. Inside was a gold-edged piece of parchment, tied into a scroll with a lock of gray hair. Even if he hadn't seen that hair in his dream, Tamwyn would have known it by its touch, its sheen, which spoke a single word in his mind.

Father.

He carefully untied the lock of hair and squeezed it for a moment in his hand. Then he set it next to his pack, which held the rest of his possessions: the broken blade and handle of his dagger, the water flask, and the harp that he'd barely begun to carve.

At last, he unfurled the scroll and began to read its message. Written in blue ink, in bold yet flowing script, the words seemed to leap straight into his mind. He could almost hear his father's rumbling voice and thoughtful cadence.

> *Dagda's Day,*
> *the 27th since midsummer*
> *Year of Avalon 987*

Ah, for those long ago days! When I first set foot in this Great Hall of the Heartwood, more than two hundred years ago, I bore no cares beyond the adventure I had chosen, no worries beyond the perils at hand.

Now I return, feeling very different indeed. My stated purpose is even grander than before—to find a route upward into the trunk and limbs of the Great Tree. But to my closest friends I have confided that my true goal is to seek the very stars on high, to solve at last the great mystery of their nature. This is a quest that has called to me since childhood. Yet now that it has begun, and I stand again in this hall, I bear a burden far heavier than the magical torch from my father. It is a burden I carry within: the faces of my wife and child, Halona and Tamwyn. For I have lost them. And yet, even now, in this faraway place, I see their faces as clearly as on our final, starswept morning together.

In truth, I wonder just why I have chosen now to embark on this long and dangerous voyage to the stars. Surely not because my strength is at its peak; surely not because the timing is auspicious. Perhaps I am not seeking the stars after all, but merely fleeing my own past. The stars are bright and far away, but my wounds are dark and ever near.

My route, what little of it is known to me, is simple. I shall find, somehow, the way to Merlin's Knothole, a place he described to me once long ago. If I cannot get there by portals, I shall seek out another way, perhaps even a way that is portalfast. I am eager to reach the Knothole! For Merlin told me that, from there, one could view something that no one from the Seven Realms, besides himself, had ever seen: the very branches of the Great Tree, leading to the stars.

He also said, with one of his secret smiles, that the view from the Knothole was almost as dizzying as the journey. What he might have meant by that, I know not. But I intend to find out.

And he did, as well, say one thing more. When I asked him how, if I ever reached the Knothole, I could ascend further—all the way to the stars—he did not answer me directly. Rather, in that maddening way of his, he simply recited a riddle:

> *To climb ever starward,*
> *To vault through the sky,*
> *Discover one secret:*
> *The Great Horse on High.*

Again, I know not what he meant. But as before, I intend to find out.

Tamwyn stopped reading. Furrowing his brow, he repeated the riddle's final phrase: *Great Horse on High.* Could that possibly be related to Rhita Gawr's mysterious words *when the great horse dies?* And if so, how? He hadn't even the vaguest clue what this horse could be. Or how it could die.

Puzzled, he turned back to the scroll:

Old and weighed down as I am, I suspect that this voyage will be my last. Or next to last, for the Otherworld itself now beckons. Because of that suspicion, I have chosen to leave this missive for any person who is bold enough to journey here and find it. And who, I hope, will carry on my quest if I do not succeed—for it is only right that a mortal man or woman should, at last, touch the stars.

Who, I wonder, might that person be?

And so I depart on my final expedition in Avalon. Just where it will take me, I cannot guess. Yet when, at last, it comes to an end, I shall meet that end with whatever grace I can muster.

For my life has been a long and wondrous walk, with experiences far too many to remember. And one far too bitter to forget.

Krystallus Eopia

Tamwyn closed his eyes, crumpling the page. And in his mind, once again, he heard his father's words: *The stars are bright and far away, but my wounds are dark and ever near.*

"I will follow you," he whispered. "Wherever you've gone, I will follow you."

11 · Deth Macoll

DEEP IN THE DARKNESS OF SHADOWROOT, not far from the underground cavern where Rhita Gawr and Kulwych gloated over their newly corrupted crystal, an elderly woman approached. She came very slowly, hardly more than a shiver in the shadows. But she came.

Hunched over so far that her face nearly touched her knees, she couldn't have walked at all without the help of her cane, an old piece of cherry wood as gnarled and beaten by time as the hand that grasped it. Covered by her ragged brown cloak, she looked like some sort of humpbacked beetle that had wandered the underground caverns for ages.

Hesitantly, she made her way through the maze of dark corridors and stone stairwells, dimly lit by flickering torches of oiled rags. It helped to tap her cane against the walls and floor, since the echo often alerted her to turns and pits ahead. And fortunately, her hearing was still quite good. Even now she could hear, above the machinery clanging and squealing in the distance, the wheezy breathing of the gobsken warrior who stood guard around the next corner.

Making no effort to hide, she hobbled around the corner. She surprised the burly gobsken, who started and drew his huge broadsword, grabbing its hilt with his three-fingered hand. Jabbing the point at her head, he thundered, "Who in Harshna's name are you?"

"Just a tired old traveler," rasped the crone. She lifted her head to look at him, revealing a fringe of white hair under the cloak's hood. "I must be lost."

"That you are, ol' hag."

The gobsken stared down at her. The greenish gray skin of his brow furrowed. He seemed to be wondering which was more amazing: that he'd met any intruder at all down here, or that the intruder was an addled old woman.

With a snarling laugh, he sheathed the sword. "Get out o' here, hag. I'd kill you meself, but then I'd have to carry your body down to them furnaces for burning. Harrarr, harrarr, wid all the weapons ol' scarface is having 'em make down there, they always need more fuel! Though your shriveled ol' body wouldn't amount to much."

She bobbed her white head and hobbled a step closer. "How very kind of you, good sir. I am deeply in your debt."

"Begone, hag! Before I change me mind." He raised his powerful hand to hit her.

Quick as a striking snake, she lifted her cane and clicked a button on its handle that extended a dagger blade from its tip. Before the astonished warrior could even gasp, she used her lower height to aim upward and thrust her blade into the gap under his breastplate. He fell to his knees, green blood spurting from his riven heart. She pulled out the weapon as he collapsed dead on the stone floor.

"Be fuel yourself," she snarled, in a voice that sounded more strong and assured than before. Quickly, she retracted the blade and cocked her head, listening.

"Ahhh," she murmured in satisfaction. For behind the heavy door where the gobsken had been standing guard, she could hear the voices of those she had been seeking. The voices of Kulwych and Rhita Gawr.

• • •

On the other side of the door, the smoky shape of Rhita Gawr floated in the air, slowly circling the bloodred crystal. The cavern echoed with his hissing laughter. For he felt immensely pleased with his work.

"Now, Kulwych my pet, you see my power. A marvelous thing to behold, is it not?"

"Mmmyesss, mmmyesss, my lord." The face of the sorcerer, so terribly burned and scarred, bobbled nervously as he spoke. "You have created this crystal of vengélano, just as you promised."

"I have done more than that, my duckling. Much more! Though I would not expect you to perceive it, limited as you are with your own feeble powers."

Kulwych winced at the insult. But he remained motionless by the cavern wall, saying nothing. Only the narrowing of his one eye gave a hint of his burning resentment.

The smoky form continued to spin around the crystal that rested on its pedestal. As the dark serpent moved through the air, black sparks exploded in its wake.

Leaning against the wet stone wall, Kulwych watched carefully. Although he couldn't be sure, Rhita Gawr's shape seemed to be more solid already, just two weeks after he'd appeared so suddenly. Now he looked more like a black coil of rope than a spiral of smoke. The sorcerer gulped, for he knew that this could mean just one thing: The spirit lord was swiftly gaining power, and would soon take his true form—whatever that might be—at which time he would launch the attack that would utterly demolish his enemies in Avalon. The only question was whether, at that stage, he would still have any more need for Kulwych.

The dark being hissed in satisfaction. "You see, my magician, I have also done something else." His voice sharpened, like a dagger slicing the air. "Something you tried to do, but failed."

Kulwych stiffened. "You have destroyed the heir?"

"Indeed I have! He received a little messenger, you see—a token of this crystal's new power, sent to the spot where I sensed his presence." There was a crackle of laughter. "I disguised it as a flower, so beautiful he couldn't resist, and set it to explode the very instant it was touched by someone with deep magic."

"B-but my lord," asked Kulwych anxiously, "how can you be sure that the person it killed was the true heir of Merlin?"

The dark spiral snapped in the air like a whip. "Are you so foolish as that? My senses are keener than you know, Kulwych! I felt him there, atop some mountain peak in Olanabram. I felt the flower explode. And now I feel him nowhere—not in any of the root-realms of Avalon."

Kulwych's hideously scarred face gave a ghoulish smile, as the lipless gash that was his mouth curled upward, melting into the jagged scar that ran from the stub of his ear down to his chin.

"And now," continued the floating form of Rhita Gawr, "there is one more person I would like to destroy, before initiating my ultimate plan. She will not be felled so easily as the heir, for I cannot sense her whereabouts as easily as I could someone who carried the rancid blood of Merlin in his veins. But Kulwych, I want her dead. And soon."

The sorcerer, eager to prove his worth, rubbed his pale white hands together. "I have just what you need, my lord. An assassin of the highest order."

"Not that stupid ox of a man you have been using to whip the gobsken into making weapons?"

"Harlech? No, my lord, not him. This work you describe requires a thousand times more delicacy." Kulwych nodded eagerly. "In fact, anticipating your needs as ever, my lord, I have already called for this person to join us. Mmmyesss."

The spiraling form crackled, sending up a shower of black sparks. "Good. Then that must be the dangerous presence I sense even now, behind the door."

"What?" asked Kulwych, caught off guard. "So soon?"

Slowly, the heavy door swung open. A frail, hunched woman shuffled into the cavern, leaning heavily on her cane. She glanced at the sorcerer from the side of her hood, then turned to the serpentine shape hovering beside the corrupted crystal.

"Yes," she said in a thin, wavering voice. "So soon."

"Show me who you are," commanded Rhita Gawr.

All at once, the old crone stood up straight, doubling her height. She threw back the hood of her cloak, whipped off the wig of white hair, and ran a hand over the bald spot that shone red in the light of the crystal. A sallow face peered at them with flinty gray eyes. Then, with a flourish, the man—for it was indeed a man—bowed in greeting.

"Deth Macoll," he announced. "At your service."

The snakelike form floated away from the crystal and approached this new arrival, inspecting him closely. As Rhita Gawr encircled him in a smoky noose, moving just a hand's width away from his chest, Deth Macoll merely stood there, relaxed, showing no sign of nervousness. His gray eyes followed the circling form as if he himself were the hunter instead of the prey.

"Very good," declared Rhita Gawr at last, his voice bubbling like hot lava. "You are a master of disguise, I see. But not a changeling."

The man did not answer.

"That's right, my lord," said Kulwych proudly. "He is human, the superior race."

"Bah," spat the spirit lord. "Superior to what? Cockroaches, perhaps?" His dark tail crackled in the air. "But perhaps I have spoken too harshly, Kulwych. After all, both you and your friend here are human."

Deth Macoll squinted at the sorcerer, and spoke again. "He is not my friend," he said casually. "Merely someone who provides me with interesting work from time to time."

Kulwych bristled. "You mean someone who pays your exorbitant fees."

The other man's voice dropped to a growl. "My real pay, as you should know by now, comes not in coin." His chin angled toward the sorcerer. "I choose my work for other reasons. My own reasons."

"Maggots of Merlin! You ungrateful—"

"Silence," snapped Rhita Gawr, still circling. "You have proven my point, Kulwych. Humanity may have some superior gifts, I suppose, but also superior flaws. And it is the flaws that make them so very useful to me. For their very natures are arrogant, greedy, and superstitious."

Neither man said anything more. Their eyes, however, glinted like sword blades.

"And now," declared Rhita Gawr, "are you ready to hear my command?"

"To hear your request," corrected Deth Macoll. "Tell me your target, and then I will decide."

Sparks of darkness flew into the air, and the spinning form hissed, "For your sake, let us hope you decide correctly. Your target is a woman of considerable power."

"Who?" asked the assassin, shrugging his shoulders lazily.

Kulwych stepped forward. His wretched face was so contorted by anger that he would probably have grabbed Deth Macoll by his cloak and shaken him, but for the dark form that sizzled between them. "Are you really that stupid? Who else but the Lady of the Lake?"

"No, my plaything," corrected Rhita Gawr. "It is not the Lady."

As Kulwych froze, openmouthed, the other man smirked ever so slightly.

"The Lady is old," continued Rhita Gawr, "too old to trouble me now. And besides, just as I have planned, she will very soon give away the greatest source of her remaining power."

Taken aback, Kulwych shrank away. "Then if not her, who?"

"A young woman, a priestess in the Society of the Whole. Her name I know not, but I have felt her as a growing threat. By herself, she has no power worthy of any concern. But she will carry with her that gift from the Lady that I mentioned—an object so powerful that it could conceivably disrupt my plans."

Deth Macoll, suddenly intrigued, raised an eyebrow. "And what is this object?"

Rhita Gawr stopped circling and just hung in the air, a rope of darkness suspended by nothing. "A crystal of pure élano, the last one in Avalon. Until I can break its magic and bend it to my will, as I have this one here, it remains a threat."

Deth Macoll nodded. "I see. All right then, I will kill her for you." He grinned savagely. "I have just the right disguise to get close to her."

"And after you kill her," added the sizzling form by his chest, "you will bring back the crystal. To this very cavern. Though I myself may not be here to greet you, Kulwych will be. And he will tell me if you try any treachery."

The man bowed his head. "But of course. It will be a plea-sure."

Part

II

12 · A Faery's Flight

TIME FOR A BATH," GRUMBLED NUIC FROM his perch on Elli's shoulder. His skin color, an over-heated shade of burgundy, could barely be seen under all the mud and dust.

"And a drink," Elli answered, stepping through a grove of tree-sized ferns whose fronds had been decorated with wreaths of pink berries. She looked admiringly at the wreaths, knowing that they were probably the work of starflower faeries, those yellow-winged creatures whose artistic urges had long enlivened Woodroot.

Hearing the splatter of water nearby, she turned toward a rivulet. It flashed silver in the morning starlight, a luminous ribbon that flowed through the lush forest. Sprigs of brightmint grew along its banks, bejeweled with drops of dew that rimmed every edge of every leaf. This rivulet looked, sounded, and smelled of one thing above all else: freshness.

As Elli knelt by its edge, Nuic leaped into the water with a splash. Within seconds, his color had changed to a sparkling ice blue.

She bent lower and drank. Instantly, the chill liquid moistened her tongue, while the sharp scent of mint tickled her nose. For some inexplicable reason, she thought of Tamwyn just then, feeling a hint of sadness at the way they'd parted. *Where is he now?* she wondered. There was no way she could know that, at that very moment, he, too, was sipping some fresh water, high above in the Great Hall of the Heartwood.

She frowned, wiping some drops off her chin. *Probably he's lost.* Her frown deepened. *In more ways than one.*

She heaved a sigh. *So why should I care where he's gone?* In the time since she'd left the ruins of the Drumadian compound, retracing her route back north into the high peaks and then trekking into Woodroot, the realm of the Lady of the Lake, she'd thought about little else besides the Lady, Coerria—and Tamwyn. She'd even felt the touch of his strong hands as she climbed down the rope ladder that he had so carefully spliced and hung in the tunnel of the Rugged Path. His work had saved them plenty of trouble (as well as scrapes and bruises).

As silently as a leaf falling onto a bed of moss, Brionna knelt beside her. With a quick glance at Elli, she took a drink of her own, then said, "Still thinking about him, aren't you?"

"Yes. But I don't know why. He's not—well, just not . . ."

"What?"

Elli's curls bounced as she shook her head. "I don't know. Just *not.*"

Brionna studied her for a moment. "Well, I'm grateful for one thing, at least—that he's a dependable woodsman. That rope ladder he made was a fine piece of work. Elvish, almost."

Elli's hazel eyes narrowed. "What are you telling me?"

The elf maiden paused to watch a family of foxes, their bushy rust-colored tails held high, prance along the opposite bank. Then she bent low, holding her long braid to her chest so it didn't plop into the water, and took another drink. When she came up, she replied, "Look, I know he's impossible. That just goes along with being a man. But there really is something about you two. Do you feel it?"

"Sure," answered Elli. "Like a punch in the gut."

Thoughtfully, Brionna scratched one of her pointed ears. "No, I mean something more like this."

She dipped a finger into the rivulet. Out it came, with a single droplet on its tip. She shook it gently, so that half the droplet fell into the open palm of her other hand, then shook off the other half as well. The two small droplets stayed there in her palm, quivering, until something new started to happen. Even without any apparent movement of her hand, the two glistening specks seemed inclined to move, wobbling down the creases in her skin until, at last, they rejoined. It was as if they'd been drawn together from the start.

Elli said nothing for some time, though her fingers touched her bracelet woven from the stems of astral flowers. Finally, she asked, "And what about you and Scree? Are you also like drops of water?"

Now it was Brionna's turn to scowl. "More like drops of wax from two different candles. Sometimes, near a flame, we might melt together. But our natural state is separate. And—like the resinwax candles crafted by my people—hard, very hard."

"Lard?" repeated Shim, plopping his round little body down on the moist bank of the rill. "You don'tly have much of that, Rowanna me lass."

The elf maiden opened her mouth to speak, then, deciding it was hopeless, closed up again.

Shim suddenly reached over and pinched her muscular arm.

She jumped back and swatted him, but his pink eyes gleamed with mischief. "Sees there, lassie? Not even a smidgely bit of fat upon you! Lotsly different from old Shim here." He gave his bulging bottom a pat. "Nobodies would everly think we're related, you and me. Certainly, definitely, absolutely."

He bellowed in laughter, then broke into a rhyme:

> *You be fitty,*
> *While I be lardly,*
> *You're so pretty,*
> *And I'm so . . . hardly!*

> *You're fair and tall*
> *(And a pigsy grump);*
> *But I'm short and small*
> *With a bigsy rump.*

> *Men fight and steal*
> *For your every whim.*
> *Just never reveal*
> *I'm your uncle Shim!*

He gave her a broad wink. "And you is my most favoritest niece."

Brionna tried her best not to laugh, hoping not to encourage him. After all, anyone else who had dared to pinch her would have instantly found himself facing a longbow loaded with a barbed arrow—and no more than three seconds to apologize. Even so, as hard as she tried, she just couldn't hold back a grin.

For her part, Elli didn't try at all. She burst out laughing, as did the gangly priest, Lleu, who had just joined them at the rivulet. Even the silver-winged falcon on his shoulder joined in with a coarse screech.

Shim gave Brionna a gap-toothed grin. "You knows I'm just being teaserly, don't you? Surely as your name is Rowanna."

She nodded—then suddenly reached over and pinched *his* arm.

The little giant yelped, then chuckled at the rudeness of elves—and nieces. Finally, he turned to Elli. "So where is your friend, the Ladily of the Lake? Is we close now?"

Elli's face turned suddenly somber. "I hope she still is my friend."

From his bathing place, his tiny feet propped against a stone that kept him from floating downstream, Nuic snorted. "Hmmmpff. She'll probably boil you in oil, stretch you thinner than a spider's thread, and pound you into dust." His color brightened just a bit. "But she'll still be your friend."

Lleu waved his long arm at the endless greenery that surrounded them. Right there within his reach were trailing vines studded with petals of blue and gold, dense shrubs that looked like miniature maple trees and smelled vaguely like cinnamon, thick pads of moss on the water-soaked stones, mint and dill and lavender growing on the banks, as well as the towering ferns draped with pink berries.

He touched Elli's forearm. "I wouldn't worry, really. Anyone who chooses to live in such a lovely place must be both wise and forgiving."

"Hmmmpff," growled Nuic. "And irascible, too. Believe me, having seen her over enough centuries, I know."

Elli twirled one of the hanging vines around her finger. "If she's angry, that's just what I deserve. I just hope we can find her soon."

"That won't be easy," warned the sprite, rolling over to splash himself with water. "Her lair is hidden by layers of magic. Even if it's somewhere near here, it could take us many days to find it."

"We don't *have* many days!" objected Elli. "Coerria needs help. And the vision—"

"I know, Elliryanna." Nuic's color darkened. "I, too, saw the vision." His voice lowered to a whisper. "And heard Rhita Gawr."

Peering into the forest, Brionna said quietly, "Granda used to tell me that the pathway to the Lady is made of mist. And, if I'm not mistaken, there's a creature just over there that could guide us."

"You mean that wren in the nest over there?" asked Elli doubtfully.

"No."

"The worm by those roots?" guessed Lleu.

"No."

She pointed, but none of the others—except perhaps Catha the hawk—could see any other creatures amidst all the greenery. Elli shook her head in exasperation and asked, "What is it?"

"Come and I'll show you," Brionna replied. As gracefully as a dragonfly lifting off a lily pad, she rose and stepped soundlessly along the bank.

The others followed, doing their best to be quiet. This wasn't at all easy for Shim, whose feet seemed to crunch on every twig and scrap of bark. Quietest of all was Nuic, who simply let go of his stone and drifted slowly downstream.

A moment later, Brionna stopped. Gently, she pulled back a curtain of leaves from a willow bough. There, napping in a knothole of the willow, was a tiny person with delicate, light blue wings. Female, she wore a matching blue robe, stockings, and sash, all made from cloth so thin it was almost transparent. A pair of miniscule silver bells adorned her curved antennae. She could have fit inside the bowl of an elm leaf, and seemed lighter than a milkweed seed.

A mist faery, Elli said to herself in wonder. She had seen them many times, flocking in the early morning hours, but never so close. Usually a blur of silvery blue motion, mist faeries were both skittish and almost never at rest—two qualities that made this sight one of Avalon's rarest.

A breeze stirred the tall ferns, as well as the willow, and Brionna turned to Elli. "How to wake her—that's easy," she whispered. "How to speak with her, though, will be hard."

Before she realized what she was saying, Elli replied, "If only Tamwyn—"

She caught herself, but Brionna finished her sentence. "Were here, I know. He could speak the faery's language."

Elli just chewed her lip.

"I'll just have to try my best," the elf maiden continued. "Before she flies off."

With that, Brionna bent lower, until her face nearly touched the knothole. Very gently, she blew on the sleeping faery, making the delicate wings flutter. At once, the faery's blue eyes popped open. With a shriek of fear, she leaped into the air and zipped off in a misty blue streak.

Brionna started to speak, but by then it was too late. Before she'd even said a word, the faery had disappeared into the forest.

Behind her, Lleu sighed. "Looks like we'll just have to find the Lady the old-fashioned way."

"By getting lost, you mean." Nuic climbed up the bank of the rivulet and shook himself dry. As Elli stooped to return him to her shoulder, he added gruffly, "She never did like visitors."

Just then a terrible roar shook the forest. Wrathful it sounded, echoing among the trees. The companions froze, trading nervous glances. The roar came again, much closer this time. A flock of crested doves took off, whistling in panic as their wings slapped the air. Branches cracked and snapped in the distance. Then came the sound of an entire tree—or several trees—uprooted and thrown down with a sickening smash.

Elli's eyes met Brionna's. "A dragon!"

"But," said the elf, shaking her head, "we've seen no dragons in Woodroot for ages."

"You're about to see one now," declared Lleu. "In just a few seconds, if you don't get moving."

The whole group broke into a run, while the falcon on Lleu's shoulder took wing. Elli leaped across the waterway, carrying Nuic in her arms so he wouldn't tumble off her shoulder. All the others followed, crashing through the underbrush, dodging vines and tree trunks, hurtling past scurrying hares, hedgehogs, and squirrels. All around, more animals sought shelter: a speckled green snake slithered into a hole by a tree root; a pair of hedgehogs burrowed into a bed of pine needles; a doe and her spotted fawn flashed past, bounding over a fallen branch.

Behind them, the dragon's shattering steps only grew louder. So did its roar, loud enough on its own to shake great oaks and hemlocks down to their roots. Now they could hear the heavy, snarling breaths of the beast.

"It's right behind us!" cried Elli.

She glanced over her shoulder to see a tall spruce smash to

the forest floor, taking several smaller trees with it in an explosion of branches. In the space the fallen trees left against the sky, she watched in horror as an immense neck rose upward. Armored with shiny orange scales, each one broader than a boulder, the neck flashed like fire as it lifted. Impossibly long, it stretched on and on, until at last came the colossal head. Trailing towers of smoke from its flared nostrils, the dragon's face was covered with green and purple scales that were blackened by charcoal. Its enormous ears swiveled wildly, as did its eyes, deep pools of orange flames that glowed with unending anger.

Then the dragon's mouth opened. Within its long black lips, flecked with saliva, Elli saw hundreds of murderously sharp teeth—rows upon rows of them, each tooth as tall as a full-grown man or woman. Between them hung the remains of rotting carcasses and strips of blood-streaked fur, licked now and then by the mighty black tongue.

Again the dragon roared, louder than thunder. Like the others, Elli ran with all her strength, tearing through branches and leaves and spider's webs, heedless of where she was going.

All that mattered was escaping the dragon. And those teeth! Her heart pounded inside her chest, her lungs burned. She leaped through a thick wall of greenery and then—

Fell. Down into a deep pit she tumbled, spinning head over heel, kicking up clouds of dirt and dead leaves. All the companions except the falcon plunged into the pit as well. They spilled down the side, rolled to the bottom, and landed in a tangle of limbs.

Though her neck and back ached badly, Elli shook the dead leaves off her face and sat up with a groan. She blinked, trying to focus. What she saw made her want to scream: the gargantuan head of the dragon drawing close to the edge of the pit. Its shadow, dark as doom, fell over the group. Elli drew a sharp breath, just as one of those fiery eyes fixed on her.

She sat there, utterly frozen in heart and mind, as the colossal jaws opened.

13 · Time to End All Secrets

THE DRAGON'S HUGE HEAD BENT TOWARD the pit, as the long black tongue flicked hungrily. Rows of teeth, smeared with dried blood and rotting flesh, gleamed just above the trapped companions.

Then from the dragon's mouth belched a thick cloud of smoke. Like lava of the air, it poured down into the pit, slowly covering the group, suffocating them in vile, sulfurous fumes. Elli, like the others, coughed and gagged. She covered her mouth, waving her arms frantically to clear the air.

But that didn't help. Dark smoke stung her nostrils, her throat, her watering eyes. She couldn't breathe at all without spasms of coughing. The poisonous smoke was everywhere.

And then, all of a sudden, it wasn't.

In half a heartbeat, the dark cloud brightened. As if suddenly shot through with light, it turned shimmering silver. Its noxious fumes vanished, replaced by moistness that seemed as soft as a cloud, and fresh as a woodland stream.

Mist, Elli realized. *It's turned to mist.*

The vapors swirled about them, sparkling, then slowly pulled apart. Luminous shreds lifted, twirled, and spun, throwing spiraling rainbows into the air. At last, the radiant mist had thinned so much that it seemed to be made more of light than water. Elli and the others in the pit could only blink in the wash of brightness.

Then Elli realized that the pit, too, was gone. The steep sides had disappeared, leaving them in the middle of a misty plain that stretched on and on in every direction, farther than she could see. Elli turned around, scanning this vast meadow of mist that rolled away endlessly. Nothing but curling waves of whiteness rose above the horizon.

Except for one thing.

Out of the farthest edges of mist, a dark shape appeared. Elli tensed, still fearful of the dragon. But this was no dragon.

The Lady! She's come to us.

Yes, answered the woman's airy voice that spoke inside Elli's head. *With you, though, I am as angry as any dragon.*

Elli winced as the shape drew closer, striding toward them through the vapors. And yet she couldn't help but appreciate how lovely the Lady looked—just as lovely as she remembered, despite the grim expression. Her vibrant, gray-blue eyes, and the silvery hair that tumbled down in curls as abundant as Elli's, shone with the magic of the enchantress. Her textured green gown, as light as mist itself, glittered as she moved. So did her shawl, resting like a cloud upon her shoulders.

And Elli knew what lay beneath that shawl. Wings! Luminous wings, glowing like feathered starlight. For the Lady's true identity was the legendary Rhiannon—great leader of the early Drumadians, daughter of Elen the Founder, and sister of Merlin. This secret she had willingly entrusted to Elli, Nuic, and Tamwyn. No one else. And how had Elli repaid that trust?

"Forgive me," she whispered hoarsely. "I didn't mean to . . ."

Oh, but you did, came the stern voice in her mind. *You heard my plea, through the valiant Sapphire Unicorn. Then you ignored it, by your own choice. Elliryanna Lailoken, you have put Coerria, as well as the rest of us, in danger. Great danger.*

Elli bowed her head. "I am sorry, Rh—er, I mean, Lady. So sorry."

The Lady approached, tongues of mist licking the hem of her green gown, until at last she stood before them. Elli bowed, more stiffly than Brionna, whose honey-toned braid swept through the cloud at her feet. Lleu bowed as well, very low, and as he rose, the hawk Catha floated down and landed on his shoulder. Even Shim did his best to be polite, although his bow looked more like a clumsy curtsy.

Then, to everyone's surprise, the Lady herself bent low. Not in greeting, though, for she was actually bending to gaze into the eyes of Shim. "My old friend," she said wistfully. "You are just as small as you were when we first met. And, I suspect, just as big in other ways."

Perhaps because of her magic, the little fellow seemed to have no trouble at all understanding. Even so, he looked confused. "Didly you know me, Lady, all that long ago?"

She didn't answer, though. She merely turned to Brionna and said gently, "Welcome, daughter of the wood elves. What is your name?"

"Brionna, good Lady." She lowered her head gracefully. "I am honored by this meeting."

"As am I." The Lady observed her thoughtfully. "All the more since I perceive you come from the family of my dear friend, Tressimir."

At the mention of her grandfather, Brionna stiffened.

With a sympathetic nod, the Lady whispered, "I miss him, as well."

The elf maiden said nothing.

Facing Lleu, the enchantress said, "You and I have already met, haven't we? In your dream?"

"Yes, Lady. Though as lovely as you were then, you are still lovelier now."

"Quiet, Lleu," snapped Nuic. "You'll just give her a big head."

Amused, the Lady of the Lake bent to pick up the sprite. And as she lifted him in her arms, he sparkled as much as the surrounding mist.

"Hmmmpff," he said, trying unsuccessfully to sound gruff. "Terrible trick, that dragon. But I knew it was you all the time."

Elli started. "You mean—"

"That's right," the Lady replied, waving her hand through a rising shred of mist. "It was all just an illusion. The roar, the rampage, and of course those terrible teeth. But no creatures were harmed, not even a twig."

"Just my backside," muttered Lleu, rubbing his spine.

"I hope you enjoyed yourself," grumbled Nuic. "Scared me yellow, you did."

The Lady's eyes twinkled. "I thought you said you knew it was me the whole time."

Nuic turned a deep shade of crimson. "Er, well, ah . . ." he sputtered. "I did, really. But I just forgot how formidable your sense of humor can be."

She studied him, her eyes now melancholy. "My dear Nuic. If you must know, that had nothing to do with humor. I did it partly to let loose of my anger."

"At me," said Elli ruefully.

"At you, my dear." She peered at the young priestess. "Now, though, I forgive you. After all, your rash behavior reminds me of no one more than myself."

Elli's lips quivered, but she said nothing.

Nuic swatted the Lady's sleeve with his little hand. "You said partly. So there was another reason?"

The enchantress nodded. "I also did it to frighten off the person I sensed was following you."

Everyone tensed. Brionna's hand went to her longbow. But the Lady shook her silvery head. "He or she is gone. For now, at least. And it might have been someone innocent . . . though I doubt it. Even after your success in foiling Kulwych's plans at the White Geyser of Crystillia, there is evil now in Avalon, such as I have not felt in many years."

She blew a long, steady breath of air into a shred of mist floating by her face. Right away, the mist transformed into a gleaming circle. Within it, another circle formed, and another, and another, until the rings grew so small they could no longer be seen. Elli gazed at this infinity of circles, wondering how many mysteries—and how many worlds—they might hold.

Watching Elli, the Lady almost smiled. Then, all at once, her face hardened. "I cannot be sure, but I sense a new shadow in our midst, a shadow that lengthens every day. Already it is long enough to blot out the stars of the Wizard's Staff—and also the brighter sides of human beings, so they act like mindless trolls."

Lleu's brow furrowed deeply. Catha, on his shoulder, piped a shrill whistle.

"I've felt it, too," Nuic said, his color going gray. "It is a shadow we have felt before, you and I. Long ago."

The Lady of the Lake lifted him a bit higher, so their faces nearly touched. "Yes, my old friend. The shadow of Rhita Gawr."

At the mention of that name, a chill wind blew over the mist, stirring the white waves, scattering them as a squall would the sea. The wind, or the name itself, made Elli shiver. Even the Lady drew her shawl a bit higher on her shoulders, covering the amulet of leaves she wore around her neck.

"We saw him," began Elli, but she had to stop to clear her throat. "In a vision."

"I know," said the Lady. "For the vision came to me, as well."

"Still, I've been hoping that it wasn't really true. That he wasn't really here."

Mist curled about the Lady's slender wrists. Gravely, she declared, "He is here, child. As surely as the Sapphire Unicorn is not."

The enchantress drew a deep, slow breath. "There is still a chance to stop him, and to save our world—though it is slimmer than a spider's thread."

"What is it?" asked Elli. "What must we do?"

"Many things, I fear. But two most of all. First, we must somehow relight the stars of the Wizard's Staff. And soon! Since your friend Tamwyn is not here, I assume that he has already embarked on that quest."

Elli nodded stiffly.

"I only wish I had spoken to him first," the Lady said ruefully. "There was much I could have told him about the Tree, the stars, and also his foe. But now he must discover all that on his own."

Elli asked, "So you don't even know if he's still . . ."

"Alive? Yes, I believe he is. And beyond that, just knowing him, I also feel hopeful. And so can you."

Gratefully, Elli peered at her. "And what is the second thing we must do? Bring the elixir to Coerria?"

"No, my dear. The fate of Avalon is not bound to the fate of Coerria. The second quest is something else."

Elli ran a hand through her curly brown hair. "Then I'll have to bring her the elixir first. Before starting the quest."

"No." The Lady shifted Nuic so she could hold him in one arm, then placed her free hand on Elli's shoulder. "You do not have time for both. That might have been possible, if you had come here first, but now that chance is lost to us."

Elli bit her lip. "Then I must go to Coerria. Whatever it means for Avalon, I just can't abandon her."

"You love her that much?"

"That much."

The Lady regarded her with a mixture of admiration and affection. "I expected you would feel that way. Which is why I have decided, if you take the larger quest, to go to Coerria myself."

"But," objected Elli, "you never leave the forest, except in visions."

"I will now," she declared. "Whether to help my world or my old friend, I must. For I love them both dearly. And I would take the quest for Avalon, if I could. But now, I fear, I am too old and worn down to succeed in the larger quest. So I shall leave these woods, and my lair in New Arbassa, to go to the High Priestess."

Lleu and Brionna both started to speak, but the Lady raised her hand to silence them. "I know, dear ones, that you would go in my place. But you are much more needed by Elli's side. If, that is, she takes the quest."

Elli straightened her back. "I'll take it, if you'll promise to save Coerria."

"I promise to try. In this time, that is all anyone can do." She pursed her lips. "If only my brother were still here! He'd be as old and frail as I am now, but at least he'd have some ideas."

"Stupid ones, most likely," said Nuic.

The Lady smiled at him. "Most likely. Even so, I do miss him, gone from Avalon all these years."

She turned back to Elli, her expression again grim. "Your quest, my child, involves the crystal of pure élano that Kulwych made from the magical waters of Crystillia."

Brionna started, feeling the sting of the whip across her back. And the greater sting of the memory of her days as the sorcerer's slave.

"So he still has the crystal?" pressed Elli.

"Yes. But that is not all." The Elder drew a ragged breath. "With the help of the wicked spirit lord, no doubt, he has changed it somehow—corrupted its power. I can feel it. The crystal has gone from a source of great good to a thing of great evil."

"Exactly what sort of evil?" asked Elli.

"That isn't clear to me. But I suspect that it could be just as destructive as pure élano is creative. Instead of spawning new life, it could destroy whatever it touches."

Elli gasped. "Like that flower! The one that killed the unicorn, and almost Scree, as well."

The eyes of the Lady filled with mist of their own. "The Sapphire Unicorn, the only one of her kind. What a loss! To Avalon . . . and to her unborn filly."

"Filly?" repeated Elli. "She was going to have a child?"

"A magical child. There is never more than one Sapphire Unicorn in Avalon, with this exception: Near the end of that unicorn's days, she always gives birth. And I knew my friend well enough to know that her time was approaching." She pinched her lips. "I just didn't think that her death would happen so soon."

"Nor did she," said Elli bitterly. "That evil flower. I'm sure it must have come from the crystal." She tapped the side of her water gourd. "Even these healing waters couldn't stop it."

Nuic's color darkened still further. "Where is this corrupted crystal now?"

"I don't know. I cannot see it, no matter how hard I try. Yet I feel it, most definitely. Somewhere in the Seven Realms." She squeezed Elli's shoulder. "You must find it, wherever it is. And then destroy it."

"But how?"

"With this." The Lady set Nuic down in the meadow of mist, then reached under her shawl to remove her amulet of oak, ash, and hawthorn. As she peeled back some leaves, there was a sudden flash, dazzlingly bright.

Shim, who was leaning close to the Lady, fell back in surprise, scattering mist in all directions as he landed.

"Élano!" exclaimed Lleu. "So you, too, made a crystal."

"No," replied the Lady. "Someone else made this, long ago."

"Wait," said Brionna. She gazed in wonder, remembering the tales she'd learned from her grandfather. "I'll wager this is the crystal that saved Woodroot from a terrible blight centuries ago. Why, that crystal was made by Merlin himself."

Lleu's eyes widened. "Of course! And on that journey, he was joined by just two people. One was his beloved sister, Rhia."

Only Elli caught the glint that appeared in the Lady's eye.

"And the other," the priest went on, "was my great-grandfather, Lleu of the One Ear." At this, Catha strutted proudly across his shoulder.

The Lady nodded at them. "Right you are, my dears. This is that very crystal. Merlin later gave it to me." She touched the radiant crystal, scattering its rays—white, blue, and green—across the rolling clouds at their feet. Tufts of mist caught the light, shimmering like vaporous prisms.

"Now, though, I give it to you." She pulled the amulet's cord over her head, drawing it through her silver curls, before placing it around Elli's neck. With the tip of her finger, she touched the crystal one last time, feeling its facets, then covered it again with the leaves.

Elli herself patted the leaves, and the crystal beneath them. Was she really wearing it? Did she deserve that power, that responsibility? Then her gaze met the Lady's, and for a long moment they shared something even more precious than the amulet.

Yet still some doubts remained. She tapped the amulet and asked, "How can this crystal ever destroy the other one? I thought élano can only heal things, or create new ones."

Sadly, the Lady shook her head. "I don't really know, my dear. It's only a guess. Yet I feel sure that the crystal you are wearing is the only power in all of Avalon that could possibly defeat the corrupted one. They are opposites, after all, so perhaps you can find the way. Before it's too late."

She studied the amulet a moment longer, as if she could still see what lay hidden under the leaves. "I shall miss that crystal—its beauty, as well as its power. More than I can say. But if it can somehow save Avalon from this threat, then it will have achieved its highest purpose. Nothing it has ever done, in all the years I have worn it around my neck, is nearly as important."

Suddenly Elli blanched. "The crystal . . . it has given you strength, hasn't it? And power?"

The Lady didn't respond.

"And more," pressed Elli, following her intuition. "It's given you *life*. Without it, you will—"

"Die," finished the enchantress. "You are right, my dear. But my life has been long already, perhaps too long. And always remember this: The crystal itself came from Avalon, which sustains us all. When at last it is my time to die, my body and blood will return to its soil, my breath to its breath, my life to its life. So who can say that I have gone anywhere but home?"

She almost smiled, as shreds of mist rose up and touched her face, caressing her cheeks. "When I join with Avalon, you see, I shall join the world I have loved. And all the people I have loved, as well. Such as my mother, Elen."

Everyone but Elli and Nuic gasped in surprise.

"It is time," declared the Lady, "to end all secrets. Know me now for who I truly am."

In one swift motion, she tore off her shawl and tossed it into the rolling mist. Up from her back rose wings—as luminous as the loveliest star. They glistened in the moist air, spreading with grace and beauty.

"Rhia," said Brionna, thoroughly amazed. "With your wings from Lost Fincayra."

"It's you," said Lleu, blinking in disbelief. Catha, on his shoulder, whistled in admiration.

Shim slapped the side of his head. "I didly suspect it was you! But neverly, everly could I believe it."

"Hmmmpff," grumbled Nuic. "You always were a show-off."

For the first time since they'd all met, the Lady of the Lake—Rhia—burst out laughing. The bright, bell-like sound flowed across the field of mist, making the vapors rise and dance in merriment. Silvery tufts cavorted in the air, leaping and twirling. And as she laughed, her wings opened wide, flashing with light of their own.

At last, she reached into the pocket of her gown, which was made entirely of woven vines. "I have one more gift," she announced. "For you, Nuic, my faithful maryth."

Even the crusty old sprite could find no words. His color shifted to deep purple, much like his eyes.

From her pocket Rhia drew a jeweled pendant with a deep green stone in its center. A rich, mysterious light shone within the stone, which was wrapped with a tracery of gold and attached to a simple leather cord. Rhia doubled the cord to make it smaller, then bent down and placed it on Nuic. Since he was so small and round, with no discernable neck, it slid down to his middle and hung there like a belt.

With his tiny hands, Nuic touched the gleaming stone, feeling its contours. Then, without a trace of mockery in his voice, he looked at her and said, "You will always be my Lady." And he bowed, so low that the mist completely covered him for a moment.

When he stood again, he looked at Rhia and asked, "Are you sure?"

"Yes, my friend. The Galator is now yours."

As one, the others gasped—including Shim, who had recognized not just the word, but the stone itself.

The Galator! Here it was, the magical green stone that Elen of the Sapphire Eyes had given to Merlin long ago—something he'd fought hard to protect, since it was even more valuable than the Treasures of Lost Fincayra. Elli stooped down to look more closely, and saw lines of red, violet, and blue flowing like blood vessels under the surface of the stone. That was when she remembered the phrase that Merlin had, in legend, used to describe it: *a living eye.*

She stood up, her gaze still fixed on the stone. *But what, I wonder, can it see?*

As if in answer, Rhia mused aloud, "It has the power to look across time and space—to see someone you love. So in the centuries after Merlin gave it to me, I used it often to watch him, even after he'd left our world for mortal Earth."

"And so I will use it," Nuic declared, "to watch you." He added gruffly, "To see what new trouble you've gotten yourself into."

Rhia grinned at him. "No doubt. Too bad for you that you can only use it to see me, not talk to me. You'd be giving me an earful a day, if you could!"

"Twice a day," he retorted. "And who knows? Maybe I'll find a way to make this stone talk after all."

"If you can, my dear pinnacle sprite, you have more skill than I. Or more passion in your heart. For in all the years that I've used it, I've only been able to watch those I care for in silence. Something that you will find difficult, indeed."

"Hmmmpff. Indeed."

Elli's hand brushed against her amulet of leaves. Reminded of the new weight she bore, around her neck and elsewhere, her doubts resurfaced. "But Lady, how are we supposed to find the other crystal?" she demanded. "We don't have any idea where to start."

Rhia took her hand and said, "No, but I do."

"Where?"

"At the home of an acquaintance of mine. Not a friend, I must warn you—but not an enemy, either. He lives far from here, across the Rainbow Seas in lower Brynchilla. You see, he has a special ability with crystals of all kinds. He can sense where they are, even if they are thousands of leagues away. And he can also feel their particular powers."

Nuic's color darkened to purplish gray. "You don't mean—"

"Yes. I speak of Hargol, highlord of the water dragons."

"Dragons!" exclaimed Elli.

"Er, my lady Rhiannon," protested Lleu, clasping his hands together. "Haven't we seen enough of dragons already?"

Catha ruffled her silver wings approvingly.

"And *that* was just an illusory dragon," added Brionna. "Not a real one."

Rhia looked at them, each in turn, with a probing expression. "You decide. First, though, you should know this: Hargol is a dragon, so by his very nature he is easily angered and highly dangerous. And, like all dragons, he craves treasure—crystals and jewelry most of all. But in Hargol's case, his ability to tell where crystals are hidden, and to read their powers, makes him even more hungry to possess them. For him, they are a kind of food that he cannot live without."

Elli swallowed, wondering why they would even consider seeking out such a terrible beast.

"But there is more. Hargol is also deeply learned, a master of many languages. He is uncommonly reasonable for a dragon—as you might expect from a direct descendant of Bendegeit, the brave highlord who rallied the water dragons for peace at the worst point in the War of Storms. Bendegeit nearly succeeded, by the way, but was murdered in a revolt. So despite Hargol's incessant hunger, you will find he can be honest, thoughtful, and at times, even admirable."

She leaned closer to Elli. "And one more thing. He is by far your best chance to find Kulwych's crystal. And given what we learned from your vision, you have less than three weeks left to do that."

"Not much time," said Elli grimly. She glanced around at the others. Every one of them, even Shim, seemed to understand the risk they'd be taking. And every one of them looked willing to take it.

She nodded. "How do we get there, though? The Rainbow Seas are a long way from here. Is there a portal near the water dragons' lair?"

"No," answered Rhia, running her hands down her gown of woven vines. "But there is something better. While my former strength still lingers, I think I have just enough power left to send you there by Leaping."

"Really?" asked Elli, having heard about the power of Leaping only through the stories her father had told when she was a child. "You can do that?"

Nuic sniffed. "In her dreams, perhaps."

Eyes narrowed, Rhia scrutinized him. "So you're saying that only Merlin could do it?"

"No," he said teasingly. "I'm just saying that maybe you're not the enchantress you once were."

He gave Elli a wink. "Somebody's got to keep her honest, you know."

"Your specialty," the young woman replied. "I know from experience."

"Just watch, you old skeptic," declared Rhia. Concentrating her thoughts, she began to draw some lines in the air. Swiftly, they turned into mist. Soon a glowing white shape hung before her face—the shape of a star within a circle, the ancient symbol for the power of Leaping.

Then she started to chant:

> From the all-embracing seas
> To the stars of dawning,
> By the ever-swirling mist
> And my deepest longing:
>
> Find the trails of hidden truth,
> Lead me down those walkways,
> Take me over landscapes vast—
> Seeking ever, Leaping always.

Instantly, tendrils of mist rose higher, reaching from the companions' feet into the air above their heads. The tendrils swiftly intertwined, weaving vaporous threads into glistening patterns of mountains and valleys, shorelines and skies. Soon the weave grew so rich and complex that nothing could be seen but the mist itself.

Yet despite the thick clouds all around, Elli could sense Rhia's presence in her mind. *Good luck to you, my dear! May you find your way to the crystal—before it's too late.*

"And may you find yours," Elli replied, "to Coerria."

I will try, my dear. I will try.

Suddenly, the mist exploded in a burst of silver light.

14 · Sailing the Rainbow Seas

WATER EVERYWHERE!

That was Elli's first thought when the silver-shot clouds evaporated. She and the others were standing on some sort of ground (except for Shim, who was sitting in a murky puddle). But this was certainly the wettest ground she'd ever known. In fact, it seemed to be made more of water than soil.

For water was, indeed, everywhere. It dripped from the soggy branches of moss-draped trees, coursed down the streams that crisscrossed the ground, and floated in the misty air and the lumbering gray clouds overhead. It shone in the dewdrops that rimmed every twig and blade of grass. It seeped through the muddy soil underfoot. And it rested in countless pools—some as small as a clamshell, some as broad as a dragon's back.

"Suchly mud," groaned Shim. He tried to stand up in the puddle, lost his balance, and fell back again with a splash. "Too slipperly! And stinkerly also."

He scrunched his potato of a nose, now splattered with mud. "Totally, certainly, disgustingly."

Lleu sloshed over, the bottom of his priest's robe dragging

through the water. "Here you go, my friend." He reached down and tugged Shim, who came to his feet with a loud *slurp*.

But Shim, whose woolen vest was soaked and sagging more than usual, just frowned at him. "This neverly would happen if I hadn't gotten so smallsy again." He blinked his eyes, now more red than pink. "It just isn't fairly! Once I was big and high, as high as—"

"The highliest tree," finished Brionna, stepping lightly through the puddle to put her arm around the little fellow's shoulders. Unlike the fabric worn by the others, her green elven robe, made from sturdy bark cloth, repelled water. So while it glistened with liquid beads, it looked drier than anything else around—and significantly drier than Shim.

He blinked up at her, clearly touched. "You is a friend to me, Rowanna. A fine, courtly friend."

She made a wry grin. "Ah, but you're my uncle Shim, remember? So I'm really a fine, courtly niece."

Scowling, he pulled away. "A blind, wartly beast?" He shook his head, making his white hair slap his ears. "You is just too crazily! Even for an elf."

"Look there," urged Elli, suddenly pointing a dripping finger at the horizon.

"Why?" demanded Nuic, who had plopped himself into a rushing rivulet near her feet. Lazily rolling in the water, he had turned a tranquil shade of green, much like the pendant tied around his middle. "Anything worth seeing is right here."

"But," disagreed Elli as she stared into the distance, "what's out there is so, so . . ."

"Glorious," suggested Lleu, now gazing the same direction. Catha piped an admiring whistle from his shoulder.

The others looked where Elli was pointing—except for Nuic, who continued bathing happily. At once, they stood as still as the mossy trees around them, struck by the sight.

For as wet as this place was, it wasn't nearly as wet as what surrounded it. This was an island, they now realized: one of many sprinkled across a wide, churning sea that seemed to stretch forever on all sides. Waves rolled across the reaches, line after line of them, an endless army of whitecaps, ultimately to slap against the island's soggy shore. The breeze smelled of seawater, rich with brine and kelp, and something more, as well: a wisp of immense, uncharted depths.

But it wasn't just the size of this ocean that arrested the companions. It was the *color*. For underneath the surface, glowing currents flowed and swirled, mixing and blending waters into every conceivable hue. And so each individual wave shimmered with iridescent red, green, orange, purple, yellow, and violet, as well as the underlying blue. Like liquid prisms, the waves trembled with radiant colors, making the entire sea a vast, rippling rainbow.

And so it was that Elli knew beyond doubt that they had arrived, as Rhia had promised, at the Rainbow Seas. Somewhere in this part of Waterroot, the highlord of the water dragons kept his lair. But where? And would they find it soon enough?

Just offshore, a pod of purple-toned dolphins leaped out of the waves. Their sleek bodies glistened with lavender; their dorsal fins shone with gold. As they jumped from the colorful currents, they hung in the air for an extended moment of delight—part bodies, part water, part unjaded joy.

Behind the dolphins, past the farthest visible island, a huge, spiraling cloud rose into the sky. It started from a single point on the horizon, then lifted higher and higher, growing wider as it climbed. Though very far away, it seemed enormous to Elli—a billowing funnel of vapors that lifted into the cloud banks above, and perhaps higher still. Maybe, she wondered, it rose all the way to the magical mist that swirled around the roots and trunk of the Great Tree.

She caught her breath. That spiral didn't just rise into the mist. It *was* the mist.

"The Wellspring," she breathed in wonder. "Right there!"

"Dear Dagda," exclaimed Lleu, "you're right! I've heard so many bards' songs about it, but never thought I'd actually see it: *The Wellspring of Mist, wonder and whist.*"

Catha cooed softly, eyeing the cloud.

"All the mist that surrounds our world," the priest said in awe, "begins in that place. Or so the explorer Krystallus believed. He wrote about it after sailing across the Rainbow Seas to the Sea of Spray."

"So did Serella, first queen of the elves," added Brionna. Thoughtfully, she ran her finger down the full length of her honey-colored braid, flicking off the water at the end. "She also believed that the mist rising from the Wellspring never ends, never dies— that it just keeps on flowing out from that spot and returns as rain to the surrounding seas, only to rise once again into the sky."

"Which could mean," Elli mused, "we're looking at the same mist that hugged the shores of Lost Fincayra, ages ago. And that flowed out of the Otherworld, long before that. So the misty air we're now breathing—" She inhaled slowly. "Could have been breathed by Merlin himself."

"Or Serella," said the elf maiden at her side.

"Or Dagda," added Lleu. He glanced at the falcon strutting

on his shoulder and nodded. "Or even Merlin's own hawk-friend, Trouble."

"Hmmmpff," bubbled the voice of Nuic from the stream. "Let's not forget Hargol, now. He breathes, too—though fortunately for us, not fire."

"Once I heard an old bard say," Lleu recalled, "that when water dragons get very angry, they breathe *ice*. Blasts of ice. I don't know whether or not it's true."

"Let's not find out," suggested Elli. Then she asked the question on everyone's mind: "Where do we find Hargol?"

"Not far from here, I think." Brionna looked westward, away from the Wellspring. Concentrating on a dark patch that she could, with her extraordinary sight, make out on the horizon, she tapped her longbow, knocking off the row of drops that had gathered on its string. "Whenever I came here with Granda, to visit the sea elves at Caer Serella, he taught me about Brynchilla's geography. Since this, like El Urien, is a realm of my people, he believed I should know it well enough so I could find my way around even . . ."

She swallowed, but her voice had turned raspy. "Without him."

Elli gave her a gentle smile, encouraging her to continue.

"And so I recognize, to the west, the Willow Lands." She glanced Elli's way. "Something tells me you will like that place." Turning back to the horizon, she declared, "Just beyond that is the lair of the water dragons. Which is a spot," she added bleakly, "that Granda always warned me to avoid."

"But since we must go," asked Lleu, waving at the colorful waters, "how are we supposed to get there? Swim?"

Brionna cocked her head to the left. "If we go to that side of the island, I'll wager, we'll find a boat or two. The elves, for centuries, have left boats on the southern shore of every island in the realm. It's a tradition that comes in handy around here."

Elli gave Lleu a mischievous wink. "And if there's no boat, you can swim over to the next island and get us one."

"Certainly, my lady," the priest answered teasingly. "Right after you!" He gave her a deep bow, despite the squawking of the bird trying to stay on his shoulder. "Anyone who wears the crystal of élano has all my allegiance."

She fingered the amulet of leaves that hung from her neck. "So if Hargol steals it from me, you'll be loyal to him?"

Lleu nodded. "Maybe, but only as long as it takes to steal it back."

"Good."

"Hmmmpff," said Nuic, shaking himself as he climbed out of the stream and onto the turf. "Easier said than done."

Elli scooped him up, and the group followed Brionna through the grove of moss-covered trees, their feet squelching loudly in the wet mud. They soon arrived at the other side of the small island, where they found a crescent harbor rimmed with golden brown sand. There, above the tide line, they found a single boat, turned on its side with its mast against the sand so that the hull wouldn't fill with rainwater. Outfitted with a furled sail as well as oars, in the fashion of the water elves, it looked small but quite seaworthy.

"Ah," said Brionna with gratitude. "They've left us something else, as well."

She nodded toward a thick patch of shrubs growing farther up the shore. Berries of many kinds hung there, glistening with spray: blue rivertang, dwarf harkenfruit, purple raspberries, and more. The group needed no urging to tramp right over to the shrubs and start pulling fruit off the branches.

Like hungry bears, they stuffed their mouths with berries that exploded with flavors sweet and zesty, tangy and tart. Everyone, for the moment, forgot about the perils ahead and concentrated on the demanding task of eating as many berries as possible. Even Nuic joined right in—and turned the color of white moonberries, his personal favorite.

"Hmmmpff," he said gruffly while swallowing another handful. "No one but me has any manners." He then released a loud belch.

Elli shot him a smirking glance. But before she could say anything, he frowned at her and scolded, "Oh, Elli. That was *disgusting.*" Then he went right back to eating.

The berry feast continued, with juices dribbling down every chin and colors staining every hand. Finally, Shim patted his swollen belly and gave Elli a lopsided grin. "Wellsy now, methinks I needs a nap."

He promptly fell onto his back on the sand. Wriggling a bit to make himself comfortable, he said sleepily, "Really, truly, honestly."

Seconds later, he was snoring, his large nose blowing like a bugle with every breath.

Lleu cocked his head at the little giant. "Not a bad idea, really." He turned to Elli. "We have time, don't we?"

"Sure. Just try not to snore as loud as Shim."

"Impossible," grumbled Nuic, who had also settled down on the sand for a nap.

Lleu grinned, wiped his chin with the back of his hand, and gave a nod to Catha. The hawk fluttered over to a twisted piece of driftwood, her bright eyes scanning the shoreline for anything more tasty than berries to eat. A gray-backed beetle on the driftwood nudged one of her talons. With a snap of her beak, it was her appetizer.

The priest lay back, shifting to stretch out his legs. Before long he, too, was snoring.

Brionna worked her long fingers, sticky with berry juice. She glanced at Elli. "Are you sleepy, too?"

"Not really." She watched the prone forms of the others for a moment, then turned back to the elf. Eyes shining, she asked, "Do you have the same idea I do?"

Brionna smiled. "Of course. How can we come all the way to Waterroot and not take a swim?"

Together, they peeled off their clothes, all except the amulet that Elli kept around her neck. Pausing just long enough for Brionna to untie her braid, they waded into the water. Cool waves lapped against their legs, making their skin feel taut. Their toes slid on the algae that coated the stones in the shallows, making their first steps awkward, but soon they fell forward with a pair of gentle splashes. Brionna's long hair floated behind her like strands of seasilk, while Elli's curls glistened upon the water.

Elli's first sensation was the coolness, which slapped her neck, her belly, her arms. She felt the chill water swirl under her armpits, flow behind her knees, and slide between her shoulder blades. Then, gradually, it faded away, as she became one with the water, floating with her chin on the surface. Small underwater currents ran across her ribs, tickling.

She noticed something new. *Apples,* she said to herself in surprise. *This sea smells like apples! Crisp and tangy, like the ones Papa used to bring home every autumn.*

She drew a long breath, savoring the fruity smell that hung

there, mixing with the scents of brine and salt and kelp. Then she turned onto her back, relaxing into the water. It lifted her body, bouncing her gently, rhythmically, with the waves. She felt as buoyant as a scrap of spongewood on the sea.

In time she turned over again, the water sliding off her bare shoulders, just as a black-winged cormorant skidded to a landing, splashing her face with droplets. The bird ruffled its feathers, curled its long neck, and floated contentedly by. *The sea holds us both*, Elli thought. *And who knows what else?* She imagined a mackerel, sleek and strong, swimming beneath them even now. Under that, perhaps, a sea turtle slid past, stirring its graceful flippers. And under that, a tiny crab scuttled through the waving wands of kelp.

And such colors! Now, close up, she could see the astounding richness of the greens and blues, scarlets and violets, that wove through these waters. Like rivers of rainbows, layers upon layers of color flashed and trembled. Nothing she'd ever seen, save her crystal itself, held so much color—and didn't just hold it, but shared it, painting everything within reach.

Something more was in this sea, as well. Light. It belonged to every drop of every wave, as much as the water itself. Tiny specks of phosphorescence sparkled throughout, ringing Elli's body like thousands of shimmering stars.

Of course, she said to herself, remembering the gleaming water that flowed from the White Geyser of Crystillia. That water had been, for a time, trapped behind the dam built by Kulwych's slaves. But now it ran free again, just as it had for all the ages of Avalon—passing through Prism Gorge, splitting into the spectrum, and flowing southward through the Seven Rivers of Color all the way to the Rainbow Seas.

In time, Elli and Brionna swam back to shore. They stood on the sand for a moment, letting the soft wind dry their skin, as the elf maiden combed her wet hair with her fingers and retied her braid. Then, with grateful smiles at the sea, they quickly dressed and woke the others. It was time to set sail.

It took all of them to lift the little boat onto its hull, since so much sand had settled around its sides. With a combined shove, and a string of curses from Nuic, they pushed off. Each of them found a spot to sit: Brionna in the stern, Elli in the bow, and the others on the sides—except for old Shim, who decided to stand. Then, as soon as the craft started to rock upon the waves, he lost his balance and fell on his bulbous nose.

Minutes later, Brionna had put up the grayish green sail. Woven from sturdy fronds of elbrankelp, it had probably outlasted many a storm at sea. It fluttered in the briny breeze, bearing the ancient symbol of the water elves in its center: a rainbow-colored wave on a background of blue. All this was encircled in forest green, a reminder to all of their origins, the days when Serella brought the first elves here from Woodroot and established a settlement at Caer Serella.

With Brionna's steady hand at the tiller, the boat started to slide over the colorful waves. Elli, leaning against the bow, felt again the freedom of floating in the water. A few drops from her wet hair rolled down her brow and then her nose. One fell onto her outstretched tongue. It tasted of sea salt . . . and a hint of apples.

Wind gusted suddenly, jolting the sail and tilting the boat drastically. Shim screeched and Nuic roared as they both slipped and rolled together in a heap. Quickly, Brionna twisted the tiller, and told Lleu to yank on the elbrankelp rope, dumping some air from the sail. With a splash, the craft settled back to a safer angle. It coursed along, skimming the surface, leaving behind a glittering wake.

As Elli watched, they sped past dozens of islands. Most were as small and flat as the one where they'd landed, but some stretched for great distances. One heavily forested island rose high out of the waves, finally disappearing into the clouds. At one point she caught a glimpse of a thin, vertical shape rising in the distance. Almost as soon as she'd seen it, though, it vanished behind a swell, leaving her to wonder whether it was the mast of an elven ship—or the neck of a water dragon.

Abruptly, her attention turned to the waters close to the boat. Bubbles—thousands upon thousands of them—were popping incessantly on the surface. The water seemed to be boiling madly, more froth than waves. But when she tested it with her hand, it felt quite chilly. All around the bubbles, an oily film had formed, streaking the water with still more colors.

"What's going on?" she asked Brionna. "Is there some kind of giant fish down there?"

The elf maiden smiled. "Fish, yes. But not a giant one. These are bubblefish! They swim here, in the upper reaches of the Rainbow Seas, by the billions. And they have the shortest life span of any creature in Avalon—no longer than a single heartbeat."

She dipped one hand into the water, scooping up a bubblefish just as it popped. All that remained in her hand was the oily film, swirling with translucent shades of orange, red, and green. Examining the remains, she nodded.

"Here's the real surprise, though—something Granda taught me. Despite how brief their lives are, bubblefish are intensely happy. So happy that sailors who mix their breakfast with the oil of a few bubblefish are blessed with buoyant moods all day long." She gave a sidelong look at Nuic, who was still grumbling at Shim. "For someone like your maryth, though, it would take a few *hundred*."

Elli's laugh sounded like a lark of the sea. "I'd like to taste some," she announced. "It must be wonderful."

"Wait," warned Brionna, her face now serious. "Sailors who spend too much time in these waters become giddy—or crazed with greed—and lose control of the helm. That's why there are so many shipwrecks in this region, and why the elves call these *the isles of joyful death*."

Lleu nodded. "I remember when we sent a delegation of priestesses and priests to Waterroot—oh, ten or twelve years ago. Their boat was blown off course by a storm, straight into the cauldron of bubblefish. Only one of them survived, old Abcahn. He said the others were so intoxicated by the oil, and so greedy for more, they leaped overboard to devour as much as they could. And then drowned."

"How did he ever resist?" asked Brionna.

"He didn't. Abcahn told me he was just as crazed as the rest. The only reason he survived was that, before he could jump in, he slipped and clonked his head on the side of the boat. When he woke up, the boat had drifted into safer waters, and he was all alone on board. So he had a lump on his skull, but he also had his life."

Lleu licked the salty spray from his lips, then glanced over at Elli. "At the memorial service, our friend Coerria tried to make sense of this whole tragedy by using it to remind us of our own weaknesses. Quite useful, since I'm afraid humanity is very skilled at ignoring them! She quoted that famous passage by Pwyll the Younger:

> *"Beware all ye mortals,*
> *This warning to heed:*
> *When faith turns to arrogance, or*
> *Joy turns to greed—*

> *"Belief becomes shackles,*
> *Not wings of the freed.*
> *Then hard be thy heart,*
> *Corrupt be thy creed."*

"Be glad we're just crossing the outer edge of this region," muttered Brionna. She wiped her hand, still shimmering with color, on her robe. Then she pointed past the bow. "Over there, look."

Indeed, they saw the clear border of the frothing waters. In a few seconds, they had passed beyond them. There were several sighs on the boat—of relief, but also, perhaps, of longing.

They sailed on in silence, skimming past island after island. Abruptly, the silence ended when lightning seared the sky and a great boom of thunder echoed overhead. This was followed by several sharp gusts of wind that tossed the little craft to and fro, and then a hazy drizzle that grew swiftly into a downpour. Before long, sheets and sheets of rain poured down on the sea and on the sailboat. More lightning and thunder exploded as rain pummeled the companions.

Huddled together in their drenched robes, they lost any feeling of contentment at sea. Brionna grimaced as she gripped the tiller. It wasn't just the cold rain that troubled her, but the difficulty of keeping on course. She could barely see past the sailboat's bow, let alone keep track of the Willow Lands. And there was a real risk they'd run aground.

Brionna finally released the tiller and, with help from Elli and Lleu, took down the sail. Instead of furling it, though, they unhooked it from the mast and spread it like a roof of cloth above their heads. Now, at least, they were somewhat drier, if just as cold. Crouching close together, the companions shivered constantly as the small boat pitched on the swells, tossed by water from below and pounded by water from above.

15 · The Willow Lands

THE RAIN CONTINUED, UNABATED, HOUR after hour. Starset came and went unnoticed. Under the dark blanket of the sail, the companions lost all track of time. All they knew was the ceaseless sway of waves and the endless howl of wind, along with the relentless drumbeat of rain.

And they also knew cold—a swelling, creeping cold that chilled their deepest veins. Fingers ached painfully; toes went numb. Shim's nose turned nearly as blue as Nuic's skin.

"Me b-b-bones is fr-freezing," moaned the little giant.

"Mine, too," grumbled Lleu. "I'm worried we'll all turn to ice."

More worried that they were losing precious time, Elli cursed, "Vilrat's venom! Are we just going to drift around on this sea forever?"

"Until the rain stops, at least," answered Brionna with a shiver. "If I can't see, I can't steer."

All through the night they drifted on the stormy sea. Not until the hour before dawn did the elf maiden finally notice some slackening in the rain. She squeezed Elli's wrist, and they both listened for several moments as the world beyond the boat gradually quieted.

Slowly, with numb hands, they pulled away part of the sail. Through the opening came a rush of crisp, moist air, rich with the salty smell of the sea—but very little rain. Seconds later, the rain stopped completely. A few isolated stars even shimmered through the gaps in the clouds. By the time they had hoisted the sail once more, dawn's light had brightened both sky and sea, throwing a net of golden light across the waves.

And there, just to the west, sat the deep green band of the Willow Lands. To everyone's relief, the storm had blown them toward their goal rather than away from it. Skillfully, Brionna turned the boat just enough to billow the sail, and tacked westward. Apart from Shim's inane comments that nobody understood, and Nuic's incessant grumbling that reassured Elli he was alive and well, the companions remained quiet. For their attention had turned to the strange place they were fast approaching.

Lleu joined Elli, kneeling at the bow. At last, he said, "It's a whole lot more *willow* than *lands*, isn't it? Those trees seem to sprout right up from the water."

"Mmm," she agreed. "And look at their lowest branches. They sprout from the trunk but then they go down, not up. Why are those branches all bending down to the sea?"

"Because," answered Brionna from the stern, "they're not branches at all. They're roots. Aerial roots." She paused, adjusting the tiller slightly. "That's what makes these willows so remarkable. Unlike their cousins in El Urien, they *do* grow right from the water, in shallows such as these."

"But how will we get past them?" asked Elli. "There's no place to walk."

The elf grinned knowingly. "We won't need to walk."

Elli turned uncertainly back to the trees. Before long, though, her doubts receded in a rising sense of awe. This was more than a forest they were nearing. This was a whole new world.

The swelling light of dawn traced the graceful lines of the willows' roots, trunks, and branches, making the rain-washed wood gleam and glitter. As the companions drew near, they heard the first whispers of wind in the long, flowing tresses of the leaves that hung from every limb, swishing the surface of the water, swaying gently. Burly roots rose upward, higher than the top of the boat's mast, and curved to join the trunks, forming great archways above the lapping waves.

Through those archways, Brionna steered them. There was just enough wind to make the boat glide slowly and serenely ahead. And Elli soon realized that much more than willows grew here. She saw golden-boughed mangroves, rising out of the shallows; pink and purple aquaferns, looping around the willows' tresses like bright ribbons tied in someone's hair; Lorilanda's moss, impossibly rich and velvety, draping down from the boughs; and some translucent branwenna trees, swelling with liquid heartwood that cannot burn. She even saw a pair of yellow-finned fish leap straight out of the water and bite off some berries before plunging back into the water with a double splash.

Yet most beautiful of all, she thought, were the willows. Sailing through the flowing tresses, she felt as if she'd left her cramped, cold body behind. Instead, she was floating, free as a bubblefish, within a wondrous waterfall. Leaves rustled softly as they rippled and swayed, immersing her in a cascade of silvery green. Could there be ballads, she wondered, in the whispers of willows?

The thought of other words, other languages, made her glance at her bracelet of astral flowers. Brightly it glowed in the growing light. And for the first time, she felt a genuine pang of regret about Tamwyn.

I hope he's all right . . . Then, just as abruptly, her old anger returned. *And I also hope he's tripped on his own feet and fallen down a deep crevasse.*

A trail of willow leaves brushed against her cheek, and her thoughts returned to the present. She gazed up into the starlit boughs. *I could stay here forever,* she mused. *Right here, in this world of willows.*

Onward through the arching roots they sailed, gliding over the water. The golden light warmed the colors all around—as well as the companions' hands and feet. As the morning light swelled, Elli remembered her favorite Drumadian prayer, written by Rhia herself:

> *Listen to Creation's morning,*
> *Waking all around you.*
> *Feel the spark of dawn within,*
> *Breaking day has found you.*

She caught Brionna's eye. "You were right about this place." Stroking the amulet, she sighed. "I only wish we had more time to explore it."

"Just wait. There's something more to see, before we get to the dragons' lair."

"What?"

The elf maiden tossed her braid over her shoulder and said no more.

Elli dropped her hand over the side and let her finger slide through the phosphorescent water. Then she felt something nudge her thigh. It was Nuic, a decidedly chilly shade of blue.

"Thought I might see how this works," he said, pointing at the radiant jewel on his chest. "Rhia's had plenty of time to get herself into trouble by now."

As Elli watched with interest, he closed his liquid purple eyes, concentrating hard. Nothing happened for a minute or two—then a sudden flash of green exploded in the Galator. Light and color swirled within, as if it were a glowing drop of the Rainbow Seas.

Nuic reopened his eyes, just as an image started to form in the center of the jewel. Like Elli, he watched the colors coalesce until they showed an elderly woman walking briskly through deep woods. When she stepped into a shaft of light that had pierced the canopy of leaves, her silver curls glowed with the new day's light.

"Rhia," said Elli softly. She chewed her lower lip. "How I love her."

"That's the only reason you can see her, you silly wretch." Nuic's voice sounded as gruff as ever, but his colors told a different story. As he viewed the old woman, streaks of warm reds and yellows vibrated in his skin.

Shifting his gaze to Elli, he asked, "Want to check on that fool Tamwyn, while we're at it?"

Surprised, she caught her breath. "Why would I want to do that?"

"Hmmmpff, I don't know. Boredom, maybe."

Just then Brionna yanked the tiller hard, bringing the boat around so sharply she threw everyone against the side. Bodies jostled and Nuic howled as Shim rolled on top of him. But as they regained their balance (and in Nuic's case, composure), nobody berated her. They simply stood in awe. For now they could tell just why she had swerved—not to avoid something, but to *see* something.

"Stars," said Elli, her voice full of wonder. "Stars upon the sea."

There, before them, the willows opened into a great circle. Within the ringing boughs, and the shimmering curtain of green, was a pool of perfectly still water that reflected the stars above. And more: Somehow this water held the stars' light, captured it, and intensified it.

Slowly their boat drifted into the center of the pool, sending out gentle ripples that rolled across the reflected stars. As the ripples passed, they caught the light, becoming luminous rings that expanded ever outward, finally disappearing into the encircling willows.

Elli glanced up at the morning sky, then back at the waters surrounding them. "The sky's so bright now, it's hard to see any stars at all. But this pool is like a crystal clear night."

"With stars so near you could almost touch them," added Lleu. "And even brighter than usual."

"It's like Merlin's Stargazing Stone," said Brionna, viewing the stars all around the boat. "But different, too. At the Stone you see everything in the sky, even the tiniest points of light. Here, you see just the brightest stars, but as if you were closer somehow."

"Hmmmpff," grumbled the pinnacle sprite. "Which is why the water elves call this place the Pool of Stars. A most unoriginal name, if you ask me."

"No one asked you, Nuic." Brionna flashed him a smile almost as radiant as the stars themselves. "Right, Elli?"

But Elli didn't hear her. Struck by the mention of the Stargazing Stone, she'd been thinking of her blissful moment there with

Tamwyn. And his journey, his quest to find the stars. To get, as Brionna had said, *closer somehow.*

She turned to Nuic. "Maybe I would like to . . ."

He understood without another word. "Just touch the Galator and think about him. That should do it."

She stretched out her hand and placed a fingertip on top of the green jewel. Closing her eyes, she thought about Tamwyn: his determination, veering into stubbornness; his gentle nature, capable of surprising wisdom now and then; and his clumsiness, more endearing than he knew. And also his fears—about his feelings for her, she was sure.

You madden me, Tamwyn. Drive me crazy some of the time. Much of the time! But you do intrigue me. I'm still not sure why.

She opened her eyes. Like Nuic, she gazed into the glowing green jewel. Bright colors swirled, then started to coalesce. She thought, for an instant, she could make out Tamwyn—reading something, a letter perhaps. But the image suddenly turned smoky, blurry, impossible to recognize. The jewel flashed once more, deep in its center, then returned to its normal color.

Elli twirled one of her curls, staring at the pendant. "That's all?"

"Hmmmpff. Your feelings, I suspect, aren't exactly clear on this subject."

She frowned, saying no more.

They reached the far side of the Pool of Stars. Silently, the boat glided through the swaying tresses. Elli, like the others in the boat, took one last look at the bright lights in the water, wishing she could touch them. Then the pool, and the stars, vanished behind the greenery.

Onward they sailed through the willows, under aerial roots draped with moss and boughs arching high. In time, the growth began to thin, and the powerful trunks grew farther apart. Then, with a gust of wind that ruffled the elbrankelp sail, they emerged from the Willow Lands into the open sea.

Before them stretched the northernmost reaches of the Rainbow Seas, fading into the distant mist. To the east, a line of sheer cliffs rose out of the waves: Aquator Narrows, the land bridge connecting both halves of Waterroot. Beyond that, Brionna pointed out, there was a touch of color on the horizon, darker and deeper than the waves themselves. That, as she explained, was the very edge of the Flowering Isles, where colorful water plants bloomed all year round. The Isles stretched along the coast for quite some distance, almost to the bluffs where the Eopia College of Mapmakers had sat for centuries.

"Look!" cried Lleu, pointing his long arm at a shape on the western horizon. "Another boat like ours."

"Not like ours," Brionna corrected. She swung the tiller, coming about to tack westward. With a *whoosh*, the little sail swung over their heads, making Shim's thin white hairs blow sideways. "That's an elven ship, built by the famous shipwrights of Caer Serella."

"But it does look like ours," objected Elli. "Right down to the emblem on the sail. See it there? That boat must be no more than half a league away."

"Try fifty leagues," declared Brionna. She shook her head in admiration, making her spray-covered hair sparkle. "That's one of their tall ships. It only seems to be that close because of its size. Why, it's at least twenty times taller than ours. It has a hull lined with giant paua shells, each as big as a full-grown oak tree. And that sail must be as big as . . ."

"My appetite," growled Nuic. He leaned against Elli, who

lifted him in one arm. "What I'd give for some fresh herbs and berries right now! If these waters weren't so deep, I'd dive in and—"

"Get eaten by a water dragon," cautioned Brionna. "Nobody swims here, unless they're dolphin-fast. Though we're lucky these dragons don't fly, they can move amazingly fast through the water."

She stroked her braid thoughtfully, her brow furrowed. "It is strange, come to think of it, that we haven't seen any signs of them. Not even their guard patrols."

"They leave boats alone, don't they?" asked Lleu. He kneeled at the bow, scanning the waves.

"Sure," the elf maiden replied, "ever since their truce with Serella long ago. Except, of course, for the War of Storms, when even Bendegeit couldn't contain their greed. But even in times of peace, they're usually all over these waters, patrolling their hunting grounds."

She pointed south of the tall ship, at a dark, rounded ridge that lifted out of the water like the shell of an enormous sea turtle. "I'm certain their lair isn't far from here, just around that bit of coastline. Which makes it even more strange we haven't seen any of them."

Elli touched the amulet of leaves, and the precious crystal within. "They know we're here," she declared. "They're just making it easy for us."

"Right," grumbled Nuic, his colors darkening. "Too easy."

16 · Edge of Terror

OR SCREE, THE PAST THREE DAYS OF TREKKING through the Volcano Lands of Fireroot seemed more like three years. Three very long years.

Since leaving the portal in the Burnt Hills, the same place where he and Tamwyn had lost their mother years ago, he'd trekked incessantly, pausing only now and then to nap, drink, or eat a scrawny cliff hare. He'd passed through charred vales reeking of sulfurous smoke, scaled sheer cliffs where flame vents erupted without warning, and dodged fire plants whose ghoulish hands reached out to scorch his legs. Since he couldn't just fly to his destination—a lone eagleman soaring above the peaks would be too easily spotted—he had no choice but to walk.

And to think. All of Scree's thoughts boiled down to one goal, which burned the terrain of his mind no less than lava had often burned the slopes and crevasses of the Volcano Lands: *Stop the Bram Kaie clan.* He knew what this meant. He'd have to kill its leader, as well as that brutal young warrior, before he himself was killed. But if he somehow succeeded, he'd be helping Tamwyn—and Avalon—while avenging Arc-kaya's death.

He paused, sweat glistening on his bare shoulders. Though his stamina had steadily improved, he still felt weaker than usual. His hand went to his thigh, kneading the muscles that still ached from that evil shard. Even after so many days, the strength of that leg hadn't fully returned. Would it ever?

He turned his eagle-sharp eyes on the jagged crater on the ridge ahead, whose jutting stones reminded him of the Crater of the Crooked Teeth where he'd spent so much of his youth. In hiding. Only once had he left the safety of that place for long—and that was enough to come just a feather's width away from losing both the staff of Merlin and his own life.

Thanks to *her*.

"I can still see you, my Queen," he said in his rough, raspy whisper. "Just as I've seen you in my memory hundreds of times."

His powerful fists clenched, making muscles flex all the way up his arm. Rows of feathery hairs, which covered his skin from his wrists up to his shoulders, stiffened like bristles. "But you didn't really want me, did you? You *never* wanted me. All you wanted was the staff."

The large, yellow-rimmed eyes narrowed. "It's me you're going to get in the end, though, Queen. I'll be a present for you." He saw, in his memory, the face of Arc-kaya, as she lay dying in his arms, and he added: "And for that murdering warrior of yours."

Suddenly a flame vent blasted out of the rust-colored rocks by his feet. He leaped to the side, just in time to avoid being scorched by crackling yellow flames. But even as a plume of black, sulfurous smoke belched out of the vent, he caught sight of a small furry body darting between two rocks.

Rolling over with an eagleman's agility, he shot out one leg so fast that his toes grasped the animal's tail. Scree lay there, back against the rocks, and bent his leg to see just what he'd caught. His stomach rumbled hungrily; it had been more than a day since his last cliff hare.

There, dangling before him was a strange combination of a furry marmot, a scaly snake, and a long-tailed mouse. It writhed madly, squeaking with rage. It had a black tail as long as its slender body, grayish brown fur, and six feet covered with tiny orange scales that flashed like fire.

"You're an ugly little something, aren't you?" Scree peered into its angry eyes as the animal squirmed before him. "Can't say I've seen your kind before. Or eaten anything like you."

The creature bent itself double, trying to snap at Scree's foot with its toothy snout. But it couldn't quite reach high enough. All its snapping was useless.

Scree shook his foot. "I'll bet you'd taste pretty good, roasted over that flame vent with a pinch of char-lichen to spice you up." He licked his dry lower lip. "Pretty good indeed."

He frowned. "But I won't find out today, I guess. For all I know, you could be the last of your kind."

Abruptly, he rolled over and released his grip. The surprised creature hesitated for an instant, then scurried to dive into a crack underneath a rock.

Scree bounced back to his feet. With a squeeze to his weak thigh, he started off again. He trekked up the ridge, following the trail of a now-dry sulfur spring. Puffs of yellow dust rose into the air with every step.

He veered to the side to avoid a bubbling pit of ash, whose frothy gray fluid gurgled and belched. Then, topping the ridge, he slid down a thin chute of obsidian, as smooth as black glass. Landing on his feet at the bottom, he gazed up at the next ridge ahead. Dark with fire-blackened rocks, it loomed as large as a fire dragon's back, but with an added edge of terror.

For behind that ridge, Scree knew, were the people of the Bram Kaie clan. He'd be greatly outnumbered, that was certain. He needed to surprise them. And even then, he'd have but one chance to succeed.

All of a sudden he heard a distant screech that echoed over the volcanic peaks. He ducked into the shadow of a charred boulder just as a cadre of four warriors, all with black-tipped wings and red leg bands, sailed out of an ashen cloud. They cried triumphantly and then plunged toward the blackened ridge. But not before Scree glimpsed what they were carrying—an object so large that it took two of them to carry it in their talons.

It was a corpse, smeared with blood from the tips of its battered wings to the stubs of its severed legs. The corpse of an eagle-woman.

A plume of fetid smoke blew past, searing Scree's eyes. He waved it away, trying to get a better look. By the time the air cleared, though, the warriors had vanished behind the ridge. But he'd already seen enough.

Angrily, his hand raked the air. And then, every muscle tensed, he started to climb. He kept to the shadows, moving with utmost stealth. For he was going to the place where Quenaykha ruled, the place where he'd fight what would most likely be the last battle of his life.

17 · Memories of Avalon

BEFORE HE'D READ THE SCROLL FROM HIS father, Tamwyn could taste only the wondrously sweet water from the spring that bubbled forth in the Great Hall. Now, though, he tasted something else—something much more bitter.

He smoothed the crumpled paper and rolled it up again. Then, retrieving the lock of his father's hair, he tied it around the scroll and shoved them deep inside his pack. As he did so, his finger brushed against the slab of harmóna. Even so gentle a touch made the magical wood hum in response, as if he'd plucked the strings of an arboreal harp. Its grains sang for several seconds, and the sound was so resonant that the tiny quartz bell on his hip vibrated, echoing the note.

Tamwyn merely scowled, closing the flap of his pack. The harp's yearning note made him think of Elli, and the confusion of feelings she stirred inside him. And the bell made him think of Scree—the years he'd searched for him in the wilds of Stoneroot, the thrill of finding each other at last, and now the sting of being separated again.

He ran a hand through his black hair. *Looks like I can't keep anyone near me for long. Not Elli, not Scree, not my mother.* He studied the small wooden box that had held the buried scroll. *And not my father.*

He reached over to Batty Lad, who was sitting in the emerald green moss by the spring. With one finger, he scratched the creature's head, still dripping wet from being plunged into the sweet water. Right away, the cupped ears swiveled, while the green eyes glowed brightly. In a whisper, Tamwyn asked, "What about you, my little friend? How long will you stick around with the child of the Dark Prophecy?"

Batty Lad stiffened. "Whatsa this crazy babble-wabble?" He peered doubtfully up at Tamwyn, cocking his mouselike face to one side. "Sometimes you actsa very odd! Absolooteyootly."

Despite himself, Tamwyn grinned. "Good thing I've got you to keep me sane."

"And me," piped up Henni, sitting up from blowing bubbles into the pool under the spring. Water droplets glistened on his circular eyebrows. "You've got me to keep you crazy."

Tamwyn nodded, swishing his hair across his shoulders. "So far you're doing great at that."

Henni clapped his big hands together. "Good! So where do you want to go next?"

The young man's brow furrowed. "To a place called Merlin's Knothole. And, from there, to the stars. If that's even possible!" He rubbed his chin, reflecting on his chances. "Truth is, I don't even know if it can be done at all. Can a mere man—"

"A *clumsy* man," corrected Henni.

"Hush," snapped Tamwyn. "What I'm wondering is whether *any* man—or any mortal creature—can climb all the way to the stars."

"Probably not," said the hoolah cheerily. "Do you know anything else?"

"Nothing useful. Just that we might meet some sort of horse on the way." He thought back to the words on Krystallus' scroll. "And that the journey to the Knothole will be somehow *dizzying*."

"Eehee, oohoohoohoo, that could be a fun ride."

"Or it could be a death trap."

The hoolah scratched one of his circular eyebrows. "Haven't I told you before, oohoo eehee? Death traps are the spice of life."

Tamwyn, who wasn't so sure, started to scan their surroundings. Just how was he supposed to find this Knothole, anyway? He studied the wall of green flames that rose so high above them, filling the gap between two root buttresses. It crackled and churned with the fires of élano—the only portal in the Great Hall of the Heartwood. Could that be the way?

No, he knew better. All the lore he'd heard from bards said that this portal led to the root-realms, as well as back to the Swaying Sea, but no higher on the Tree. And besides, hadn't Krystallus written, *I shall seek out another way?*

There was still a chance, of course, that this portal could carry him upward, in some way that had eluded his father. But jumping into any portal was risky business. Even if Tamwyn had his mind completely focused on his destination, the portal could take him instead to someplace far distant. Or back to the living stones he'd just barely escaped.

He turned from the crackling curtain of flames to survey the vast cavern. All around them, great roots rose up from the dirt floor, arching high overhead, twisting and branching until they spread across the ceiling. Veins crossed and recrossed, creating an intricate web of shadowy niches far above their heads. But Tamwyn saw no sign of any exit up there.

And yet . . . his father must have found *some* way to leave the Great Hall, since no one from his expedition ever returned to the Seven Realms. Just where did they go, though? If they went any higher inside the Tree, they must have found a passageway.

His woodsman's gaze roamed around the room. Suddenly, on the rim of the ceiling, he caught sight of an especially dark spot that he hadn't noticed before. Set in the notch between two tributary veins, it could have been just another shadow, or a shallow pit. Or something more. He stood, pulled his staff from its sheath, and walked to where he could get a better view. Leaning on the staff, he stared upward.

Some kind of tunnel? he wondered. *But even if it is, how can I possibly get up there? Flipping fire dragons, if only I could fly!*

At that instant, one of the symbols carved into the wood of his staff caught his eye. It seemed to be glowing, though dimly. Was it just the reflected flames of the portal? No, he felt certain. The staff itself was alight.

Startled, Tamwyn sucked in his breath. He recognized that symbol: It was the star within a circle, symbol of the power of Leaping. Whether the legendary staff, Ohnyalei, had been touched by some of his own untamed magic, or whether it had responded to the power of Leaping being invoked by someone far away, Tamwyn had no idea. All he could do was look, amazed, at the glowing symbol.

Then, to his even greater amazement, his bare feet started lifting off the floor!

Higher and higher he rose, flailing arms and legs to keep his balance. He floated steadily upward, while both Henni and Batty Lad stared at him in astonishment. Soon he was more than his own height off the ground. He held tight to the staff, even when the magic that was lifting him tilted him way over to one side so that he was floating nearly horizontal in the air. No matter how hard he kicked, he couldn't turn himself upright again.

"Eehee, eehee, that looks like fun," crowed Henni. He rubbed his hands gleefully and rushed over to stand under Tamwyn. Then, jumping as high as he could, he tried to grab hold of his foot.

"Stop that, you bung-brained idiot!" shouted Tamwyn, flailing desperately.

"Take me with you," pleaded Henni. "I want a ride, too."

Tamwyn fought—unsuccessfully—to keep himself from rolling over in the air. "This isn't a ride, you fool! This is some kind of magic I can't control. It could vanish just as fast as it—"

All at once, the light disappeared from the staff. Tamwyn spun around and then plunged down—right on top of Henni. The staff clattered on the chamber floor, the hoolah shrieked, and Tamwyn howled. And over by the bubbling spring, little Batty Lad shook his furry head.

"Silwilly creatures," he muttered, straightening his crumpled wings. "Theya should know theya can't really fly, yessa yessa ya ya ya."

It took several seconds (and several kicks and punches) for Tamwyn and Henni to untangle themselves. At last, both of them lay back on the floor, panting heavily. Tamwyn's vision finally steadied, and he looked again at the dark spot on the ceiling.

"I've got to get up there," he muttered. "If only—" He caught himself, having learned anew the dangers of making wishes. Especially with whatever powers were burgeoning inside himself, powers he still couldn't control. For a while after he'd used them to save Scree's life, he'd felt better about having them. Now, though, he wasn't so sure. It was almost as if he held a whole new person down inside, different in every way from his former self, struggling to burst free.

But was that something he really wanted?

Tamwyn shook his head, rubbing it into the reddish brown dirt. Turning to the thin fellow sprawled beside him, he asked, "You're still crazier than a catnip faery, you know that?"

"Sure. And you're still stupider than a headless troll."

"All right then, we understand each other. Now tell me, Henni." He pointed up at the ceiling. "Do you think you could climb to that dark place up there?"

The hoolah's brow crinkled. "Looks pretty difficult. Impossible, maybe. Foolish even to try." He grinned broadly. "Just my kind of thing."

"Good," declared Tamwyn. "Here's the plan, if you can remember it."

He sat up and tugged at the length of twine that he always wore around his waist, equipment he'd found helpful more than once as a wilderness guide. As he unwrapped the twine and securely tied one end around his waist and the other around Henni's, he explained that this might save someone's life in case of a fall. Though Henni protested, saying that falling was part of the fun, he eventually relented. A moment later, they were roped together. With Tamwyn's staff back in its sheath, and a disturbingly gleeful grin on Henni's face, they began to climb up the nearest buttress. As they moved higher, Batty Lad circled them, chattering anxiously all the time.

For Tamwyn, scaling the tangled, twining veins wasn't the most difficult part. It was keeping Henni, who was climbing behind him, from making a sport of letting go of the buttress and swinging freely from the twine. It only happened once, when they were halfway up to the ceiling—and it took all Tamwyn's strength to hang on by his fingers and toes while the hoolah whooped and giggled below him. Only thanks to Batty Lad, who dived at the giddy creature's head, buzzing him angrily, did Henni finally swing himself back to the buttress.

Another harrowing moment came when they crossed a place where the wood was as smooth as newly sculpted clay—and Henni thought it would be entertaining to yank on the twine as hard as he could. But the most terrifying moment of all for Tamwyn came when Batty Lad's wing clipped his nose, making him sneeze so hard he almost fell. Somehow he managed to hold on, though only just barely. Yet at long last, they made it to the notch on the ceiling that held the dark spot.

"By the Thousand Groves!" Tamwyn hooted in delight.

For it was, in fact, a tunnel, heading diagonally upward into the Tree. But it really wasn't much of a tunnel—more like a hole in the ceiling where a crack in the Tree's trunk had broken through, or a trickle of water had opened a gap over time.

But that was enough for Tamwyn. He squeezed himself into the hole, showering his face with loose dirt. Then, overcoming a moment's hesitation, he wriggled higher so that Henni could follow. Last of all, Batty Lad zipped in to join them.

Inside, everything was dark. And damp, as well. All around, they heard the sound of running water coursing inside the walls, dripping from above, percolating in hidden cracks. Tamwyn paused to let his eyes adjust, then spied a thin sliver of light far above. He started crawling higher, bracing his arms and legs so that he didn't slide down backward. At one bend in the tunnel his head bashed into a knob of dangling roots, where a large clump of dirt exploded in his face. The bruise on his head was much easier to bear than Henni's raucous cackles behind him. But he held his temper in check and kept on climbing.

The light, green and flickering like the fire of portals, grew stronger. The tunnel bent again, and Tamwyn had to push his way past a mesh of fingerlike roots. Suddenly he saw the source of the light—a narrow hole up ahead. Finally he reached it and climbed through, showering himself and the others with dirt. He fell onto a hard surface.

Another tunnel! But this one was much larger—and horizontal, almost like a road running through the heart of the Great Tree. Its rounded walls were ribbed with parallel grooves, and it was high enough that he could stand without hitting his head.

Tamwyn stood, shook the dirt out of his hair, and peered at the tunnel walls. For they pulsed with a light of their own, as radiant as if they were made of condensed élano. They reminded him of the crystal in the amulet of leaves worn by the Lady of the Lake, with its radiant tones of green amidst gleaming white. Like these walls, and like the flaming portals, that magical light spoke of power. Of life. And, most of all, of the Drumadians' seventh Element, the one named Mystery.

Tamwyn debated for a moment which way to go, since left and right looked very much the same. Finally he chose left, for no better reason than the fact that his left arm had always been his strongest. They started down the tunnel, road, or whatever it was, with Tamwyn walking before Henni and Batty Lad flitting behind. Although he hadn't the slightest clue where this passage might lead, that concerned Tamwyn less than the fact that it was completely level. At some point, he'd need to find a way to climb higher—much, much higher, to Merlin's Knothole and beyond.

But how? Tamwyn could hardly imagine the difficulties of climbing so far upward. For now, the best he could do was to follow this passage straight through the trunk.

It wasn't long before he noticed something else. Something strange.

The tunnel's walls and floor kept changing in color, shape, and texture. At irregular intervals—sometimes, just a few paces apart; sometimes, half a league—the tunnel would go from bright green to reddish yellow to translucent lavender and back again to green. Meanwhile, its surface changed from grooved to knobby to so jagged that Tamwyn had to step carefully despite his thickly callused feet.

All the varied surfaces seemed like wood, with embedded grains of fiber. But they looked and felt like drastically different *kinds* of wood. There were even wooden crystals sprouting from the ever-changing walls: red cones of fragrant cedar, black cubes of gleaming ebony, brown spirals of mahogany, white crowns of ash, and green spheres of juniper. The only thing about the tunnel that remained constant was its underlying radiance, the pulse of élano within.

What's going on here? puzzled Tamwyn as he trekked. Shouldn't the trunk of the Great Tree be pretty much the same throughout, like the trunks of the trees he'd seen toppled by storms and avalanches? What could have caused all these stripes of different colors and kinds?

On and on the tunnel ran, without any sign that it might ever end. Or climb upward. After they had traveled for what seemed like several hours, having crossed through hundreds of changes in the tunnel walls, they paused to drink from Tamwyn's flask. The sweet water from the Great Hall refreshed them, to be sure, filling them with the strength of a hearty meal.

But over time, as more hours passed, their bodies wearied again. This tunnel seemed endless! Tamwyn pulled the staff out of its sheath so he could lean on it now and then. Henni drooped, his oversized hands nearly brushing the floor as he walked. And Batty Lad finally gave up flying, choosing instead to ride in Tamwyn's pocket.

The strange stripes continued, some studded with wooden crystals, some undulating with swirls of grain, and others as smooth as blown glass. Occasionally they passed smaller side tunnels, though all of them angled downward and consequently didn't seem worth exploring. Finally, they entered a section of the tunnel that struck Tamwyn as the most unusual yet. It was black, but not the shining black of ebony. This stripe was dull and sooty, like charcoal. And it smelled of ancient fires.

Tamwyn halted. *This wood has been burned. I'm sure of it.*

He stepped over to the wall. Rubbing his fingertip along the surface, he studied the smudge it left on his skin. No different than the soot from his cooking fires, it seemed.

And yet something about this burned part of the tunnel made him uneasy. It felt dangerous somehow. Threatening. Almost . . . malevolent.

Why?

He bent closer, examining the wall. Unlike the other stripes of wood he'd passed through, the grains here seemed almost fluid, flowing under the surface like tiny rivulets. Dark red, they glistened like muddy streams. *If only my dagger hadn't broken back there, I'd use it to chip some of this away.*

Instead, he used his fingernail. Digging into the charred wood, he ripped out a sliver. Seeing some blood on his fingertip, he shook his head at his clumsiness. How could he have cut himself on such a smooth spot?

Suddenly he stiffened. His finger wasn't cut. The blood on his skin hadn't come from himself. It had come from the wall!

For within this dark, smoky wood ran not grains but vessels. Vessels of blood. As Tamwyn stared, aghast, a slow red ooze dribbled down from the place he'd opened.

All at once, he realized the truth. What they'd been passing through weren't just strange stripes of wood. No, they were the intricate markings that could be found inside any tree, markings that told the story of its struggles, experiences, gains, and losses.

They were *rings.*

Tree rings—but of the grandest, tallest tree of all. The tree that contains within itself all the different kinds of wood that ever existed. The Great Tree of Avalon.

Each ring was unique, telling a tale of something remarkable that had happened in a particular year. So in traveling along this tunnel, Tamwyn had passed through the Great Tree's memories of many seasons—of cedars flourishing, cherries blossoming, and maple roots breaking ground as hard as rock. He had walked by the first oak to survive the long winter at the base of the high peaks. The tallest grove of mahogany trees to sprout in the jungles of Africqua. The most fragrant spring to grace Woodroot's history, when the Forest Fairlyn was born.

And now, he realized grimly, *I have entered the War of Storms.*

A year, stretching into an age, when forests burned in every realm, the very air smelled of death, and the rivers ran with blood.

Onward he walked, his feet shuffling across the charred wood, his staff tapping against the floor. Henni, who looked unnaturally glum, stayed as close as a shadow. For his part, Batty Lad dared only once to poke his furry head out of the tunic pocket—and then, with a whimper, dove back inside.

How long it took to pass through this section of the tunnel, Tamwyn couldn't guess. But when, at last, the blackened walls gave way to gray, then to rippling lines of yellow and tan, then to the green of newly sprouted ferns, his heart leaped. Though he couldn't forget the feel of that ancient blood, nor the sooty smell of smoke, he knew that in the memory of Avalon, a time of renewal—the Age of Ripening—had begun.

Though he couldn't be sure, the tunnel now seemed to veer gradually to the right. Not all at once, but over time, even with the occasional brief swing to the left. Or was he just imagining that? It was hard to tell.

Worse yet, he was starting to feel utterly disoriented. *Just where, in the whole vast space of the trunk, am I?* he wondered. Walking here was completely different from his many treks across the surface of the root-realms. In those places, even if he were lost, he could find landmarks to help him chart his course. There was always a ridge line, a mountain peak, or a lone tree in the distance. And of course, at night, he could orient himself by the stars.

Here, though, deep inside the Tree, there were no such landmarks. Where he really was, he could only guess. All he could tell was that he wasn't, at the moment, going up or down. But even that wasn't wholly certain: Maybe the tunnel had actually been sloping, but so very subtly that he just couldn't tell.

If only I had some sort of compass, he mused, continuing to stride along. Not a traditional compass, but one that could work inside the Great Tree. That could place him, wherever he happened to be. That could tell him his position vertically, as well as horizontally!

Now, *that* would be something useful. But of course, it was nothing more than an idea. And a bizarre one, at that.

In any case, right now he could only wonder where, inside the Tree's trunk, he really was. And whether, years ago, his father might have traveled down this same tunnel—seeking the same destination.

Just then his keen hearing picked up something in the distance, a vague whispering sound. It ebbed and surged, whooshing like gusts of wind. Yet it seemed somehow more than wind, deeper and sturdier.

They came to a smooth section of wall, flecked with gleaming silver. Tamwyn was reminded suddenly of the stars. He wondered whether this ring marked the moment, centuries before, when Merlin rekindled the stars of the Wizard's Staff after they had gone dark for the first time. And he also wondered whether, without Merlin around to help, he or anyone else could ever hope to light them again.

Meanwhile, the whispering sound grew louder. Now it seemed more like a rushing river, seething and coursing on its way to the sea. Tamwyn, followed by Henni, started to walk faster to find the source of the sound.

All at once, they stopped.

"Oohoo," said Henni. "A painting."

"More like a thousand paintings," corrected Tamwyn. "And all so beautiful."

Indeed, the entire tunnel, including ceiling and floor, had been decorated in bright colors and extraordinary detail. It was one vast mural, stretching hundreds of paces! Painted on the silvery surface were intricate scenes of every season in every realm, along with many scenes that Tamwyn couldn't even begin to identify. There were trees that grew upside down, mountains that seemed to float upon the air, clouds that carried purple-hued cities, rivers that ran with something like honey, and even the spectacle of a strange yellow star rising over the horizon. And so much more—places beyond description, worlds beyond count.

There was even a scene that consisted mainly of darkness. A great city loomed in the background, where a few frail lights still burned, although night deepened all around. Dark figures crouched in the shadows, clearly afraid. Could that have been, Tamwyn wondered, Shadowroot? Maybe the Lost City of Light that he'd heard described by bards?

Most of the painted scenes overflowed with creatures. Some of them Tamwyn knew well, such as mist and moss faeries, gobsken, dwarves, elves, eaglefolk, humans, and light fliers. Even the Sapphire Unicorn had been painted, bending her graceful neck to drink from a starlit pool.

And there were some beings that he'd never seen before—including one especially striking creature who resembled a winged man or woman, completely surrounded by orange flames. There were several of them, sprinkled throughout the mural. Always, they were pictured in dramatic, even heroic, circumstances: rescuing other creatures, making beautiful buildings, or soaring high over the world below.

In one starkly painted scene, the left half of the sky was intensely bright, while the right half was deeply shadowed. A group of the flaming people were pictured flying toward the left—from night into day. Or perhaps . . . out of the darkness and into the light.

For some time, Tamwyn peered at this painting. Could these people, he wondered, be flying to the stars? And if that was so, did it mean that some mortal creatures had actually made the journey successfully? Or was this painting not about what they had done, but about what they, like Tamwyn, longed to do?

Looking closely at the scene, he examined the people—their wings, their orange flames. Just who were they?

Ayanowyn. From nowhere he could explain, the word simply popped into his mind. And then, just as mysteriously, he understood its meaning. *Fire angels.*

He knocked his skull with the heel of his hand. *Fire angels? Don't be absurd!* First, nobody here was speaking, so how could he hear any words? And second, no creature, however bizarre, could live long consumed by such flames. Even the salamanders that he and Scree used to chase in Fireroot, who loved to bathe in flame vents, had to cool off regularly or they would roast.

His eye glimpsed a new painted figure, one that made him catch his breath. For he'd seen this figure before, many times, in his dreams. It was a man, tall and rugged, with a wild mane of gray hair that blew behind his shoulders. And in his hand, he held a flaming torch.

Krystallus! So whoever painted this mural had heard of him. Or maybe even had known him.

He turned a slow circle, tapping the top of his staff pensively as he studied the rows of paintings. In a flash, he understood. This mural was really a story, just like the rings of the Great Tree. The story of Avalon! But instead of telling the story of the world from the Tree's perspective, this mural told it from the painter's perspective.

Who *was* the painter? How long ago did she or he live? As part of what people? Where in the vastness of Avalon did they live? Had they made this tunnel, as well as the mural?

He shook his head. There were no answers to those questions. At least none that he could find.

Just then he spotted a new scene, painted on the ceiling. At first he thought it was just a tall, vertical column, colored rich brown with occasional streaks of green. But when he saw, at the very top, what looked like the beginnings of branches, along with some stars gleaming through mist, he knew what it really was. The trunk of the Tree!

Catching his breath, he spied something else about the painting. On one side of the trunk, near the top, there was a bump that bulged outward like a burl. In its center sat a deep, bowl-shaped valley that faced the branches above. Perfectly round, the valley reminded him of the craters he'd seen in Fireroot, except for its vivid green color. Suddenly he recalled his father's description of Merlin's Knothole: *From there, one could view the very branches of the Great Tree, leading to the stars.*

He nodded in wonder. *Merlin's Knothole.*

Then he noticed something odd. A thin, silver ribbon dropped down from the Knothole, plunging toward the lower reaches of the trunk. Painted with light, nearly transparent strokes, it was hard to tell whether it actually represented something deep inside the trunk, far beneath the bark. Whatever it was, it sloped steeply, like a near-vertical stairway.

Could that be a stairway to the Knothole? And if so, how do I find it?

His brow furrowed. More questions!

Once again, he became aware of that peculiar sound, coming from farther down the tunnel. Now it whispered, now it whooshed, now it pounded like a distant drum. *By the wizard's beard, what is that?*

He turned toward the sound, determined that at least one of his questions should be answered.

18 • Spirals

THE SOUND GREW STEADILY LOUDER, rumbling like endless thunder in the distance. As Tamwyn and his friends passed the end of the brightly painted mural, they entered a section where the tunnel's walls and ceiling were draped with moss, as rich and luxuriant as any in the misty forests of El Urien.

Indeed, the air itself became heavy with mist. Beads of water formed on the bridge of Tamwyn's nose, trickled down his staff, and shook from his ankles with every step.

Meanwhile, the sound swelled and swelled, echoing in the tunnel. Henni tugged on Tamwyn's sleeve and said something, while Batty Lad mouthed a comment from the lip of the pocket, but it was impossible to hear. Just then the tunnel swung to the left and opened onto a mossy ledge—and the most astonishing view that any of them had ever witnessed.

A waterfall, gargantuan in size and awesome in power, stretched far above them, as well as far below them. It roared like a million angry ogres, slamming into the walls of an enormous cavern that showed no top and no bottom. Spiraling plumes of spray soared into the air, showering the ledge where they stood, as the waterfall crashed relentlessly upward.

Upward?

Tamwyn leaned against his dripping staff, alternately looking higher and lower. Still unwilling to believe his own eyes, he stepped cautiously closer to the slippery edge, stowed the staff in its sheath, and crawled out as far as he dared. To look down—at the source of all this water.

Yes, the source. For the cascade was truly rising toward him, up this cavernous well in the trunk of the Great Tree. And not only that. It didn't rise straight upward, in the way chutes of water plunged down. It rose, instead, in a spiral—one that spun gracefully and continuously, like a watery dancer who has twirled since the beginning of time.

Then Tamwyn noticed something more. While water lifted starward, light fell rootward. Also moving in a spiral, the curling column of light wove in and out of the cascade. Each spiral wrapped around the other, as each Element touched its counterpart, making water droplets shine like stars and shafts of light flow like radiant rills.

Henni, who had also crawled out to the edge, turned an astonished face toward his companion. Tamwyn had never seen those silver eyes so full of out-and-out wonder. And he was sure his own eyes looked much the same. It struck him that, for all his antics, maybe this hoolah had actually changed during their journeys together. Sure, Henni was still as playful and unreliable as ever, but there was at least a little rationality in him now. And, no matter how he tried to disguise it, a hint of respect . . . for his surroundings, if not for his life.

Tamwyn turned back to the twin spirals of water and light, one climbing and the other descending. Both moved with endless grace, rising and falling forever. He watched, spellbound, until suddenly he sat back in surprise.

He shook his wet locks, trying his best to listen. Could it be? At last, he concluded it really was there.

Music. Out of the swirling swells of the cascade, beneath the thunderous pounding of so much water, rose a vibrant, lilting music. It whistled, flutelike, as water swam through the air, even as it crashed like massive drums, swelled like distant horns, and pealed like newly wrought bells.

All around him, and within as well, this music whirled. He realized that it, too, moved in a spiral, no less than the cascades of water and light. Higher notes circled upward, while lower notes wound downward, all connected to the same rhythmic sounds, the same endless dance.

"Henni," he said dreamily, listening to the swelling music. "Can you hear it?"

Perhaps because he, too, was moved by the spiraling notes, Henni wrapped his long arm around Tamwyn's shoulders.

Or perhaps not.

For without any warning whatsoever, the hoolah jumped straight off the ledge and into the water—taking Tamwyn and Batty Lad with him.

"Heeheeyahahahaaaaaaa!" cried Henni, before the churning cascade swallowed his words. Just as it swallowed all of them.

Suddenly Tamwyn heard no more music—only the smash and crash of water everywhere. His whole body was battered, pounded, and torn apart. His mouth, ears, and eyes all filled with water.

His lungs did, as well, making him retch and cough violently. He gagged, trying to draw some air, but breathed only more water instead.

Curtains of liquid struck him, less like rain than like hammers that pummeled him mercilessly. Over and over he rolled, hit in the face and chest and back. Water slammed him, twirled him, tumbled him. Part of his tunic ripped away, gone in a flash.

All the while, water carried him higher and higher, bearing him swiftly up leagues of vertical distance. Like a tiny seed caught by a powerful updraft, he rose within the trunk of the Great Tree.

Air! I need air!

His mind darkened as everything spun. But even with his dimming awareness, he knew that he'd been carried into upper Avalon—and that, after he died, his body would ride even higher. But what good was that now? For he'd never reach the stars, or find his father, or see Elli again. His last thought was simply surprise that he had, in this moment, thought of her.

Only vaguely did he feel himself thrown from the cascade, hurtling through air rather than water. His body thudded onto something hard, rolled, then collided into a wall. He lay there, utterly still.

19 · Hargol's Lair

AS SOON AS ELLI AND HER COMPANIONS, RIDing their small elven boat, neared the rounded ridge of coastline—it happened.

With a shower of iridescent droplets from the Rainbow Seas, four enormous heads suddenly lifted out of the water. There was no warning, no chance for Brionna to change course. All at once, with a *whooshhh* of spray, the heads shot straight out of the waves, riding immensely long necks. There was one on each side of the boat, plus the bow and stern. Now, four pairs of narrow, glittering eyes peered down at the companions.

"Dragons!" exclaimed Elli, staring up at the scaly necks and jaws that towered over them.

"To guide us to their lair," said Lleu caustically. He glanced at the falcon on his shoulder and shook the spray off his cowl. "So we don't somehow get lost."

"How kind of them," added Nuic, his color darkening from purple to murky gray.

Shim, who had fallen against the side of the boat in surprise, craned his neck to stare upward. "They is sureburbably big! As big as I oncely was, long ago."

For that they were: Each head, as large as a good-sized house, carried rows upon rows of blue-tinted teeth. Like the long, undulating necks, the heads were covered with scales that shone with the bright glacial blue common to all water dragons. Below their huge nostrils and inside their triangular ears, the scales were streaked with green algae.

Realizing that only a portion of their immense bodies rose above the waves, Elli peered over the side of the boat. There, moving through the colorful water, she could see the shadowy shapes of the dragons' enormous chests, broad backs, and powerful tails. In great, slow sweeps, the tails swept back and forth, rippling like muscular currents.

Since the dragons on each side were using their outstretched legs to guide the boat, Brionna let go of the till. "They don't even trust us to steer," she grumbled. As if in answer, the elbrankelp sail started fluttering noisily in the wind.

Swiftly, the dragons rounded the bend of coastline, their sleek necks leaning in unison, and guided the boat toward a sheer black cliff pocked with caves. And toward one cave in particular, which opened like a giant mouth trying to swallow the sea. All around its rim, thousands of deep blue shells had been carefully set, arranged in swirling, wavelike patterns. Even in the hazy light of Waterroot, where vapors swirled constantly, the shells glittered as bright as sapphires.

Into the gaping mouth of this cave they glided, propelled by their dragon escort. Elli and Brionna exchanged fearful glances. But as they entered, their expressions changed to surprise, for though they had expected it to be dark inside, the tunnel was actually bathed in light. Dozens of torches, radiating pearly light, lined the walls. But these were no ordinary torches: They were bubbles of seaglass filled with phosphorescent particles strained from the ocean itself.

Like melted stars the torches shone, illuminating the rock walls of the tunnel. Then, all of a sudden, a vast cavern opened around the voyagers. The cavern's walls shimmered with colors, violet and blue and emerald green, as if every speck of its surface had been inlaid with jewels.

"Paua shells," said Brionna, her voice filled with awe. "Everywhere you look! They cover this place as completely as bark covers a tree."

The companions in the boat gaped at their radiant surroundings. Even Catha the falcon whistled in outright awe. Rising straight out of the great round pool of water that formed the cavern's floor, the shell-coated walls arched high overhead. Where they converged at the top, a great seam of silver shells ran the length of the ceiling. And all around, intricate lines of red, orange, and gold sea stars formed a complex mosaic of dragons sailing stormy seas, making wide nets of kelp, or plunging down into the darkened depths. In a far corner, where fresh water flowed down a seam into the pool, dozens of silver and pink salmon leaped and splashed. The whole cavern glowed with color; it was as much a part of the Rainbow Seas as the water itself.

Elli drew a deep breath. The cavern smelled of sea salt, kelp, barnacles, and water birds—for hundreds of cormorants, gulls, windsong loons, flying crabs, egrets, kingfishers, and others had clustered on the ledges surrounding the pool and the many side tunnels that ran deeper into the rock. The air, she realized, still carried a hint of fresh apples. And another aroma, different from sea or shell, that wafted through everything else.

The aroma of dragons. It was a smell as potent as rotten fish, as ancient as algae-covered cliffs, and as briny as the sea itself. Several more dragons swam around the rim of the pool, patrolling the tunnel entrances. One tunnel in particular caught Elli's attention, for it glowed with an eerie green light. As the dragons swam, they made low, throaty sounds that were part hum and part gurgle—a deep, vibrating chant that carried the feeling of immense bodies swimming in a wondrous sea.

The boat stopped. Just as abruptly as they had appeared, the four dragons in the escort dropped back down into the pool, their heads disappearing in a simultaneous splash. And before anyone on the boat could say a word, another head rose up right in front of them—a head larger than those four put together.

Rivers of water coursed down the massive dragon's head as it lifted slowly out of the pool. But instead of rising any higher, the head stayed on the surface, resting on the water like a gleaming fortress. A titanic crown, carved of golden coral and ringed with diamonds, shards of jade, and emeralds, sat upon the dragon's brow. Hundreds of jewel-studded barnacles dotted his glacial blue scales. Countless teeth, as tall as full-grown spruce trees, glinted between his enormous black lips. And from his gargantuan ears, each the size of a great elven sail, hung earrings made from thousands of black pearls strung together with braids of kelp. With every movement of the head, the earrings clinked noisily.

All the while, the dragon's eyes studied them—Elli in particular. Huge and oval-shaped, the eyes glittered with great intelligence. Indeed, like living portals, they burned with a fiery green light of their own.

"Welllllcome to my lllllairrrrr."

The deep, resonant voice boomed as loud as last night's thunder. And from every wall of the cavern came an echo, making the words rumble and roll like endless waves. For this was the voice, the companions all knew, of Hargol, highlord of the water dragons.

"We arrrrre honorrrrred to grrrrreet two such distinguished visitorrrrrs."

Though terrified by the dragon's enormity, Elli also felt puzzled. "We are honored as well, highlord," she declared, standing as tall as she could in the middle of the boat. "But there are more than just two of us."

"Do not corrrrrect me!" boomed the dragon, his great nostrils flaring. "Neverrrrr corrrrrect me! Have you neverrrrr hearrrrrd the olllllld adage of my peoplllllle? *Henjalllllla makk sevrrrrranash.* Orrrrr, in the Common Tongue, *Rrrrroyalllllty knows alllllll worrrrrth knowing.* And besides, as the gnomes say, *He who arrrrrgues with a drrrrragon neverrrrr arrrrrgues again.*"

He gnashed his teeth, knocking loose the half-chewed head of a giant squid. "Therrrrre arrrrre two distinguished guests, and then therrrrre arrrrre the rrrrrest of you, who bearrrrr them."

Suddenly Elli understood. He meant the two precious crystals! The crystal of élano she wore around her neck, and the Galator strapped to Nuic's middle, were truly his prized visitors. And just how much he prized them, they would soon find out.

"You crrrrreaturrrrres carrrrry not onlllllly jewelllllls, you carrrrry rrrrrarrrrre beauty, grrrrreat mysterrrrry, and unfathomablllllle powerrrrr." He licked his black lips, as if tasting a delectable treat. "I have not seen such marrrrrvelllllous crrrrrys-tallllls in many lllllong yearrrrrs."

Lleu stood up, with Catha on his shoulder, rocking the craft as he moved to the center to stand beside Elli. He had to step over Shim, for the little fellow was cowering in the bow, trembling at the sight of this beast that had risen up before them. "We have come here," Lleu announced, "from very far away." He spread his long arms, beckoning to the gargantuan face. "Great highlord, we need to ask you for—"

"I allllllrrrrready know why you arrrrre herrrrre!" Hargol's immense earrings clattered noisily as he shook his head, while a sandhill crane that had landed on the tip of one ear flew off with a squawk. "You seek to lllllearrrrrn the lllllocation of the new crrrrrystalllll of powerrrrr. Forrrrr I have sensed both this crrrrrystalllll . . . and yourrrrr strrrrrong desirrrrre to find it."

Elli started to explain that they didn't want to possess the new crystal, but rather to destroy it. But she caught herself. How could she be sure of the dragon's reaction? Savoring rare crystals as much as he did, would he consider that a terrible crime?

She cleared her throat. "You are right, highlord, about what we seek. Our friend, the Lady of the Lake, told us you could help."

A distant light gleamed in the enormous green eyes. "The Llllllady?" Hargol seemed to regard them with a touch of new respect, or possibly caution. "She is indeed corrrrrect that I can helllllp you. *Illllli upsulllll ethimilllll*, as the mist maidens of Airrrrroot say: *A drrrrragon's knowlllllledge is widerrrrr than the sky*. But such matterrrrrs rrrrrequire time, you rrrrrealllllize."

"Just what we don't have," whispered Nuic grumpily. He

wriggled in Elli's arms, then raised his voice. "Just how long do you intend to make us wait?"

The green eyes narrowed slightly at the sprite. "As lllllong as I pllllease. A drrrrragon's age if I lllllike!"

He rumbled angrily—and sprayed a jet of blue ice from one nostril. The ice hit the water with a loud splash, then instantly congealed into a chunk as big as the companions' boat. An unfortunate sea otter, who had been swimming near the spot, suddenly squealed in panic, for his foreleg had been frozen into the ice. The otter fought vigorously to break free, rolling and twisting, until the ice finally cracked. Then, with another squeal, he dove beneath the surface and swam away.

On their craft, Elli and the others traded anxious glances. At the same time, the dragons patrolling the perimeter immediately ceased their chanting. Turning toward their highlord, they watched him with utmost attention. At last, Hargol flicked one of his ears dismissively. The guards resumed their movements through the water, as well as their chants.

"You ask a grrrrreat dealllll of me," he declared in a slightly softer voice. "Morrrre, I bellllllieve, than you know. Forrrrr to find the crrrrrystalllll you seek, I must strrrrretch my senses to the lllllimit. And I must allllllso . . ."

His voice trailed off, echoing around the cavern. He blinked his eyes, with regal slowness, before continuing. "I must allllllso rrrrresist the temptation."

Elli swallowed. She didn't need to ask what temptation he meant.

"So whillllle I considerrrrr yourrrrr rrrrrequest, you shalllll stay herrrrre. Allllll of you."

"But we don't have much ti—" began Elli, before the highlord cut her off.

"*Arrrrrgowzbrrrrragg!* And whilllle you wait, you shalllll feast."

Even Shim's deaf ears seemed to catch the meaning of that final word. The little giant suddenly stopped trembling and looked around expectantly.

"But highlord," began Elli again. "We—"

"Guarrrrds!" commanded Hargol, in a voice so thunderous that several sea stars broke off the walls and splashed down into the pool. "Brrrrring them to the dining halllll."

20 · Caviar Cakes

DESPITE ELLI'S PROTESTS, THE BEJEWELED head of Hargol plunged beneath the surface of the pool. The waves from his sudden descent nearly swamped the companions' boat. They might have flipped—or at least lost Shim overboard—except that a team of dragon guards arrived immediately. The four blue-scaled dragons, showing both speed and precision, steadied the craft with their outstretched legs. And then, with a simultaneous sweep of their powerful tails, they started guiding it over to a side tunnel.

"Don't worrily, good lass," said Shim, smacking his lips as he wriggled in the boat. "They're justly taking us to eat."

"Must say," added Lleu, "that does sound rather good! I'm hungry enough to eat one of those sea stars."

The falcon on his shoulder chirped approvingly.

"Feels like we're being taken to prison," Elli snapped. "Not a dining hall."

"Or a dining hall where *we're* the next meal," grumbled the sprite in her arms.

Still fuming at the highlord, Elli nodded. She sat back down in the center of the boat, arms folded across her chest. Just as they were about to enter the side tunnel, she realized that it was adjacent to the tunnel where the eerie green light flickered. As they passed the greenish entrance, she peered inside. But she saw nothing other than strange shadows trembling upon its walls.

Down the side tunnel they glided. Abruptly, it opened into a new cavern. This one was much smaller and lower-ceilinged than the central cavern where they'd met the highlord. It was also decorated far more simply, with alternating rows of oyster and clam shells set into its walls, and no graceful designs of sea stars. But it did have one advantage over the central cavern.

Food.

All around the rim, on rock ledges that jutted out from the walls just above water level, sat heavy tables of carved coral. Not just a few—more than a dozen of them ringed the cavern. And every table was piled high with the ocean's bounty.

Huge pots of steaming fish sat beside enormous bowls of salmon and dill puddings, raw fish fillets, scallop and savorykelp salads, and shrimps the size of Lleu's open hand. There were giant clamshells full of purple water chestnuts, krill-stuffed mushrooms, fresh coral onions, sugar eels, and—of course—melted butter made from rich seal's milk. Mountainous piles of cracked crabs, orange and blue and green, covered two whole tables, together with a wide array of undersea spices. Tureens as tall as Brionna and as wide as Shim held piping hot abalone soup, oyster stew, and crab bisque. Broiled lobster, steamed tuna, crab casserole, poached snapper, and mackerel steaks rounded out the menu. And everything went well with the cheesekelp biscuits that were piled high in baskets on every table.

The travelers pounced on the feast, their troubles momentarily forgotten. Lleu went first for the giant shrimps, rolling them in sea salt, while Elli started by drinking a paua shell bowl of oyster stew. Catha, squawking eagerly, tore open clamshells with her talons. Brionna and Nuic stayed with the savorykelp and other vegetarian options—while Shim made no effort at all to restrict his diet. Very quickly, the little giant discovered that dumping a bowl of seal butter on anything improved its taste.

Sticky-fingered and smelling like fish, they washed down the meal with coral mugs of seamead and waterberry ale. But as full as they were—"stuffed like those mushrooms," as Lleu put it—they managed to find room for dessert. Caviar cakes, still steaming because they were flown straight from the dragons' kitchens by white-winged albatrosses, were devoured right away. As were the orangecaper cream pies, sealime tarts, brineberry cobblers, and chocolate-of-the-abyss truffles.

At last, stomachs bulging, they were led to a hollow at the upper end of the tunnel. A pair of seaglass torches lit the area with pearly luminescence. Without a word of conversation, the tired voyagers stretched themselves out on mats of thickly layered spongefern. And promptly fell asleep.

When Elli awoke, however, she had just one thought on her mind: They were captives, plain and simple. And over the next five days, the water dragons gave her no reason at all to change her thinking. All the companions were ever allowed to do was eat, eat some more, sleep, and swim occasionally in the sparkling water of the hollow.

Elli's frequent requests to see the highlord were simply ignored. Watched by shifts of dragon guards who swam over to check on them at regular intervals, she and her friends could only worry about their fate . . . as well as Avalon's. For with each passing day in captivity, their chances of succeeding in their quest grew smaller—and would, at some point soon, vanish completely.

On the fifth night, Elli was suddenly awakened by a sharp kick from Nuic's foot against her ribs. When she sat up to look at the sprite, his skin had turned deepest black, the same color as the strange, dark shadows they'd seen in the vision atop Hallia's Peak. There was no need to ask him what he'd been dreaming about. Then she noticed that the old fellow was shaking, trembling uncontrollably. Quickly, she drew him to her chest and held him, until at last the shaking stopped.

The next morning, Elli sat on the tunnel ledge with her feet in the water. "How long is Hargol going to keep us?" she demanded impatiently. "Even if he does finally decide to help us, that could be a dragon's age from now. And we're losing precious time."

Brionna, seated beside her, swished her feet, making trails of phosphorescent sparkles. "Or he could just decide to crush us in his jaws, steal our crystals, and be done with it."

"A lovely thought," commented Nuic, who was floating on his back nearby. "Now that he's fattened us up, we'll taste like seafood casserole."

"Even if he doesn't eat us," Brionna continued, "he could simply keep us here forever—enjoying the company of his *two distinguished visitors*, as he called them."

Lleu, who was sitting against the cavern's rock wall, knees to his chest and falcon on his shoulder, looked up. "I don't know about the rest of you, but I've come to a decision."

"What?" asked Elli.

"We've got to break out of here. Escape somehow."

She bit her lip, then nodded. "I think you're probably right. But how? And if we try that, we'd just better succeed. Hargol would be furious! He'd just swallow us like so many shrimp. Or at least chain us to some wall so we'd never try again."

"All the more reason for us to escape now, while we still can." Lleu slammed his fist into his palm. "The only question is how."

"I agree," said Elli. "We must find a way."

"That we must," said Nuic, now floating in the water by her feet. "And I think Rhia would also agree, if she were here. But it's much easier said than done."

"That's true," said Lleu, shaking his head glumly. "We really could end up stuck here forever. By the crooked teeth of Babd Catha! Why did I ever come along on this quest, if this is as far as we ever get? I should have just stayed with Coerria."

Nuic's color changed a bit, as some veins of compassionate pink worked into his murky blue. "You saw her just yesterday in the Galator, don't you remember? She is still alive, if only barely. Even if you were there, you couldn't do anything to help her."

"But at least my being there would signify something. Here, I just feel like one of those empty butter bowls that Shim discards left and right."

Elli looked over her shoulder at the hollow where Shim was napping, snoring like a rumbling dragon. "How does he do it, anyway? I mean, how can he eat like a giant but still look like a dwarf?"

"Have you seen his rump?" asked Nuic. He blew a spray of seawater into the air, as if he were a whale. "Before long he'll be as wide as this tunnel, unable to budge. He'll be trapped."

"We're *all* trapped," declared Elli. "And it's worse than just having no way to escape! Even if we could find some way out of here, we'd still have absolutely no idea where Kulwych and his evil crystal are hiding."

"But at least we'd be free." Lleu straightened his back against the rock wall, causing Catha to flap her wings to keep her balance. "We could go to the last place you saw Kulwych and track him from there, searching everywhere in the Seven Realms, in every tree and burrow, until we found the crystal. Why, I'd climb up the branches of the Great Tree, all the way to the stars, if that's what it took!"

His words made Elli stiffen. She'd been missing Tamwyn—nothing more than a mild twinge, but nothing less, either—for almost a week now. And last night, after helping Nuic feel better, she had fallen asleep wondering what had happened to him. She turned to Nuic, and asked, "Could I try again?"

The sprite understood immediately. He paddled over to the ledge where she was sitting. As he approached, she lifted a dripping foot out of the water. Then, with one of her big toes, she touched the Galator, and closed her eyes. She thought about Tamwyn—his quirky ways, comforting clumsiness, and sturdy ideals. And about how he made her feel: sometimes spitting mad, and sometimes more alive than she'd ever felt before.

Just as she opened her eyes, the green jewel flashed. Light and color swirled, then coalesced into an image. Tamwyn! He was lying on his back, badly wounded, in a darkened room. Bloody bandages covered much of his body. Someone was kneeling over him, touching his forehead—someone with wings! Or were they just shadows? It was impossible to tell.

Elli peered into the radiant crystal. How severe were his wounds? How had he gotten them? And who was that winged person? A he or a she? Elli didn't like the feeling that another woman would be so close to him—and liked even less that she would care about such a thing.

Abruptly, the image blurred. Green and violet hues swirled around, as if the Galator held a maelstrom inside itself. There was another flash, and the jewel's normal color returned.

"Ho ho ho, quite a show!"

She whirled around, splashing Nuic with her foot, to see who had spoken. To her astonishment—and everyone else's—there was a bent, balding man standing right behind her on the ledge. No one had seen him approach, nor heard his leather sandals or cherry wood cane on the wet rock. Not even Catha, it seemed. Had they all been so focused on the Galator, or was this fellow more stealthy than a ghost?

His sallow face creased in a rather silly smile. Then he bowed in greeting, twirling on his cane as he did so, like some sort of children's toy. When he stood still again, he announced: "Seth be my name, jests be my fame. A pleasure to serve you, and hope not to unnerve you."

Brionna, whose hand had moved to the handle of her long-bow, eyed him skeptically. "How did you get in here? And who exactly are you?"

Before he could speak, Lleu cut in sternly. "And stop that infernal rhyming! Pretend to be sane for a moment, and just tell us who you are in the Common Tongue."

Quite pleasantly, the man nodded. He was hunching, so as his head moved up and down, his whole body bounced like a spring. Tiny silver bells that had been sewn onto the arms and shoulders of his maroon jerkin and his baggy brown leggings jingled. The whole effect was rather comical.

He cleared his throat, which took an unusually long time. "Ahemmm, as I was saying, good people, my name is Seth. I am a jester, a trickster, a beggar, or a madman, depending on the mood of my audience. And I have no particular plans this day, but to entertain you if you like."

"We don't want to be entertained," said Lleu. "We want to be freed."

Elli traded glances with Brionna. "You didn't tell us how you got in here."

He shrugged, tinkling some bells. "Came here to entertain, I did. I'd heard the dragon king, whatever he's called, fancies jesters, jugglers, and the like. And pays in jewels, or at least pretty shells. But once I arrived, the brute didn't even want to see me! He just told one of his guards to bring me down this tunnel—which he did, the scaly scalawag, by the seat of my pants, dropping me off at the food tables over there."

He danced a little jig before continuing. "So what else was I to do? I just filled my head with a bit of crabmeat and capers, then wandered up here to join you."

Nuic, who had climbed up onto the ledge, shook himself. Colorful droplets sprayed on Elli and Brionna, as well as the jester. But the sprite's own colors remained murky.

"You were asked a question," the sprite declared, "that you haven't yet answered. Just how did you come to the lair of the water dragons?"

"Oh, *that*." He cracked another grin. "I just came through the portal, that's all."

"The portal?" demanded Elli, Brionna, Lleu, and Nuic, all at once.

Surprised by their reaction, Seth took a step backward. He spun his cane deftly in his hand before leaning upon it again. With a look of genuine puzzlement, he explained, "Why, yes. It's just over there, in the next tunnel. Opened up just a few weeks ago, I heard one of the royal longnecks say. A bit soggy, you know, being mostly underwater. But it works. Got me here in no time."

Elli struck her open palm with her fist. "The green light I saw! I *knew* it seemed odd." She spun to face her companions. "If we can just get over there somehow . . ."

She glanced over her shoulder at the pair of guards who had positioned themselves further up the tunnel. They were chanting, their deep voices pulsing with notes that echoed on the rock walls.

"If we can just get over there," she said in a whisper, "we can escape."

Lleu pushed himself to his feet. His lanky frame made him a full head taller than anyone else, and two heads above the hunched jester. "Wait, though. We still don't know where to find the—"

He caught himself, glancing uncertainly at the jester. "The, er, thing we seek."

Elli chewed her lip. "I wish we could find that evil crystal before it's too late." Seeing the priest's face tighten, she shrugged. "It's all right, Lleu. It doesn't matter if he knows what we're after. How could it, if we ourselves don't have a clue where to look?"

Lleu blew a discouraged breath. "Guess you're right. But I'd give anything for just one clue."

The jester stroked his chin. "Too bad I can't help you. I get around a lot in my work, you know. Sometimes I have to leave in, well, something of a hurry, if it's one of those places where the people want to burn, torture, or dismember the first newcomer they find. Which doesn't bring them too many newcomers."

He shook himself, jingling his bells, as if all his jabbering had made him lose his train of thought. "Anyway, I do wish I could help you. Evil crystal, you say? The only one of those I ever saw you wouldn't want to go near anyway! Nor that lout with the pale hands who was guarding it."

"What did you say?" demanded Elli. "*Who* was guarding it?"

Seth blinked at her innocently. "The lout with the pale hands? Bad tomato, rotten to the core." His brow and bald head wrinkled as he tried to remember something. "Name was . . . um, Kul, or Kil, or—"

"Kulwych!" Elli, like the others, caught her breath. This fellow Seth, fool that he was, might have actually happened across the crystal! In that instant, her hopes rekindled.

"Well?" The jester rubbed his hands together and danced another little jig. "What would you like me to do? Juggle some fish, perhaps?"

"No," answered Elli breathlessly. "We need you to tell us where you saw this evil crystal."

"That thing?" He waved in the direction of the dragon guards. "As I said, you wouldn't want to go there."

"Where?"

He smiled meekly. "Shadowroot."

Elli blanched. She looked over at Brionna, who seemed no happier. Then, her voice resolute, she declared, "It makes sense that the sorcerer would go there to hide. Well, if that's where he is, then that's where we must go."

"Wait a second." Lleu studied the jester suspiciously. "There aren't any portals in Shadowroot, at least none that I know about. How did you get there? And how long ago?"

Seth spun his cane nonchalantly. "Oh, just a couple of weeks ago. And I got there by the portal in the upper reaches of Fireroot, the one that overlooks Shadowroot as well. Small matter of a gobsken fortress to avoid, but they haven't the humor to appreciate a good jester anyway."

"Is that so?" asked Lleu, his gaze boring into the jester's head. He turned to Elli. "Something about this doesn't seem right to me."

"What?"

The priest scratched his head. "I don't know, but . . . I'm just not sure if we should listen to anything this jester says."

"Very sensible," commented Seth. "Even *I* wouldn't listen to anything I have to say."

Elli frowned and said to Lleu, "What choice do we really have? He may be wrong, or crazy, or both—but he could also be right." She looked down at Nuic. "What do you think?"

"Hmmmpff," the sprite said, frowning. "I think it's complete lunacy to follow this madman anywhere! Which is why it appeals to you, I should add." He peered at her with his liquid purple eyes. "But the truth is, you're right. We have no choice."

She bent down and picked him up from the ledge. Wet though he was, she pulled him close to her chest. "Let's hope we survive this day."

"I'll just settle for this hour, Elliryanna."

She turned to Lleu and Brionna. "Any ideas how we can get ourselves over to that portal without getting caught?"

The tall priest nodded thoughtfully. "What we need is some sort of distraction." He looked at the silver-winged falcon perched on his shoulder. "Wouldn't you agree, Catha?"

In answer, the bird screeched loudly. Then she leaped into the air and took flight.

21 · Swallowed

CATHA WENT RIGHT TO WORK. SCREECHING wildly, the silver-winged falcon flew down the side tunnel and around the central cavern, diving at waterbirds and surprised dragon guards, causing a considerable stir. The excitement really picked up when she clawed the eye of one dragon, who nearly leaped out of the water and slapped the face of another guard with his great tail. An all-out brawl ensued. Dragons mauled each other with their teeth, smashed ribs and skulls with their tails, knocked huge holes in the cavern walls with their bodies—and sprayed each other with freezing blasts of ice.

Before long, gulls, cranes, cormorants, egrets, kingfishers, flying crabs, and several huge albatrosses joined in the fray, shrieking as they attacked anything that moved. Roars and cries echoed in the tunnels, along with the resounding crunch of icebergs colliding. Soon it was so noisy that no one could possibly hear Elli and her companions, including the jester, swimming to the portal.

Even so, their plan almost failed. Not because of their captors, but because of Shim. It was no easy feat to get him to end his nap and plunge right into the cold seawater. Or to get him to swim over to the place where underwater flames flickered so strangely, throwing bizarre shadows on the tunnel walls. Then came the challenge of getting him—as well as everyone else—to dive down to the shimmering green fire.

Finally, they succeeded. Following Seth, all of them made the dive. Even as Hargol's roars of absolute outrage echoed around his lair, the water rippled with the kicks of Lleu, last to leave the surface. Holding Catha in his arms, he swam out of the dragons' lair—and down to the portal.

A large air pocket, smelling as resinous as a grove of evergreen trees, separated the flames below from the water above. On a ledge of black rock within the pocket, the companions gathered, dripping like freshly caught fish. Elli glanced anxiously up into the water, knowing that a dragon's body could appear at any moment.

"Quick now," declared Brionna, as green firelight danced along her braid. "Bend your thoughts toward the place we want to go. And think of nothing else."

Nuic, riding in Elli's arm, looked over at Shim and turned his most sardonic orange. "For some of us, thinking of nothing is easy. It's thinking of *something* that's hard."

Shim shook his mop of white hair, spraying everyone else with drops. "I knows you is making funs of me," he grumbled. "I just knows it! If I was still bigly, you wouldn't dare treat me so disrespootably. Certainly, wetly, absolutely."

Nuic shifted to steely gray, with flickers of green from the portal. "Body size and brain size are different, you bone-headed fool! If you—"

"Stop," commanded Lleu. "We're wasting time." He checked

the water of the tunnel above their heads. Seeing no sign yet of dragons, he turned to Seth. "All right, jester. Give us a clear picture of this place where we're going. And no rhymes, now."

The jester tensed ever so slightly, though no one else noticed. He didn't like the way the tall priest ordered him around. Not at all. And yet, a jester's lot was to be abused. So he'd just grin and endure it . . . at least for now.

Bobbing his head on his hunched shoulders, he said agreeably, "But of course, kind sir. Imagine the highest portal in Fireroot, so high it's starward of the tallest peak in the realm."

He scanned the anxious faces surrounding him, all tinted by the magical green fire. "No other portal will do, now. Not in Fireroot, nor any other realm. That's the only portal that leads to your crystal."

Elli listened carefully. For her, the need to concentrate clearly on her destination held extra urgency. The last time she had ridden a portal, with Tamwyn, they'd been carried to Mudroot—the very last place she'd wanted to go. The place where gnomes had brutally killed both her parents, taken her prisoner, and kept her in slavery for six long years, before she finally escaped. And even though it was also the place where Tamwyn had saved her life—and she had been moved to save the life of a murderous gnome—Mudroot remained the source of her darkest memories, her fiercest nightmares.

"Remember, now," the jester cautioned. "To Fireroot's highest portal. Nowhere else."

"Snow hare pelts?" asked Shim, his nose scrunched in confusion.

"Fireroot!" shouted Nuic. "Concentrate, you dolt."

At that instant, an enormous leg, covered in shiny blue scales, swept through the air pocket. There was a loud roar from above, and several shouts from the companions, as everyone threw themselves into the flames. The green fire crackled, wavering just a bit more than usual.

And then they were gone—swallowed by the flames.

But not yet safe. Portals, after all, were notoriously dangerous. Some would say they had a mind of their own, occasionally taking people to unexpected places. Serella, the elf queen who was the first to master the art of portalseeking, would have gone even further, having lost many of her people in the paths of green fire. She once declared, "When I ride the portals, death rides with me."

Through the innermost heart of the Great Tree the companions traveled, down radiant rivers of pulsing green light. Resinous aromas washed over them; the breath of Avalon filled them. No longer creatures of body, they flowed like sap and flashed like fire. Small wonder, indeed, that they ever survived.

But survive they did. Moments later, they shot out from another portal, far away from Waterroot. They landed in a twisted heap of arms and legs, cushioned by a soft bed of leaves. All of them were amazed to be alive. And even more amazed, as it happened, to be in . . .

"Mudroot!" snapped Nuic, spitting a mass of leaves and twigs out of his mouth. "How the *harshnazegth* did we get here?"

Lleu, lying underneath the sprite, peered up at him. "I didn't know you could speak dragon."

"I can when I'm furious!" Veins of scarlet raced across Nuic's skin. His very breath seemed tinted with red. Then, as he turned to Elli, his colors softened slightly.

She sat at the edge of the heap, her head sagging between her folded legs. "Not Mudroot," she moaned under her breath. "Not again."

Lleu sat up, which sent the little sprite spinning down into more leaves. "Are you sure that's where we are?" asked the priest. "Seems awfully green here—a jungle, really."

He paused to look at the thick mesh of vines, leaves, moss-barked trees, and huge ferns that surrounded them. Catching his eye, Catha fluttered her wings from her perch on a leafy branch. "If this is Mudroot, where's the mud?"

"Under all the leaves," muttered Elli. She raised her glum face. "We're in the northern part of the realm, the jungles of Africqua."

"She's right," said Brionna, extracting her leg from her long-bow. "I recognize it—all these smells. Catch that hint of guavas? And cinnamon? And vanilla?" She sniffed the air. "It's the only place in the Seven Realms with as many smells as the Forest Fairlyn."

"And it positively stinks!" With a spray of leaves, Nuic finally righted himself. He spat out a shred of bark. Just as he started to speak again, though, Shim rolled over and stretched his twisted arm—swatting Nuic hard in the back. The sprite went tumbling into the leaves once more.

If Nuic had been furious before, he was doubly so now. Scarlet blotches covered his body, pulsing with rage. He was so angry he couldn't speak, only sputter.

But there was one person even more angry. The jester leaped up from the bed of leaves, shaking a wormy clump of dirt from his bald spot. "Mudroot?" he shouted, his face contorted in a most unjesterly expression. *Mudroot?*

Grabbing the cherry wood cane by his feet, he started beating the ground violently. Each blow sent up a small fountain of leaves, bark, and broken twigs. He then slashed a vine in two, which sent a pair of monkeys, who were clinging higher up, into a tizzy of their own. As their angry chattering rose from the branches, the jester exploded in curses as he battered the ground.

"Skull slime! Fried fairies! Troll wipes and bog bottoms!"

The others turned to watch his uncontrolled outburst. Just then, he swung his cane at a thin, bumpy stick that was leaning against the trunk of a tree. The stick, almost as tall as Seth himself, seemed certain to burst into bits from the force of his blow. But a split second before contact, the entire stick twisted sideways. Seth's cane smacked the tree instead, jarring his bones and showering him with nuts, twigs, and loose chips of bark.

Out of the dozen or so bumps on the stick, gangly legs popped into view. A single red eye opened wide near the top end, above a jagged mouth, while a triple forked tongue flitted over the bark of the tree. With an ear-piercing squeal, the stick creature's legs started churning. It shot up the tree trunk and vanished in the greenery.

Caught by surprise, Seth suddenly remembered how he was acting. And how unjesterly he must have appeared. *You fool!* he raged at himself. *Lose control like that again, and you'll ruin everything.*

He tittered nervously, twirling his cane in his hand. "Eh-heh, eh-heh," he chuckled with some effort. "Plenty of good props for a jester here in the jungle."

"So you knew that stick was alive?" asked Elli. She pulled some twigs out of her curls.

"But of course," he replied, taking a deep bow. "Always a crowd pleaser, those stick beasties."

Above his head, Catha whistled doubtfully. Lleu, who was also eyeing the jester skeptically, rose to his feet. He nodded to the falcon. She took off from her branch and drifted down to his shoulder. Brionna stood as well, then gave Shim a hand. Meanwhile, Elli picked up Nuic and brushed the leaves off his skin, which helped his remaining scarlet blotches fade away.

"So," demanded the sprite, "what do we do now?"

Uncertainly, Elli fingered the amulet around her neck. She waved at the portal, whose green flames rose into the air between two gigantic ferns, licking some tangled vines. "We don't go back in there again, that's for sure! We might never get out alive." She turned to Brionna. "Do you know of any other portals—reliable ones, that is—around here?"

The elf maiden tossed her braid over her shoulder. "None. When Granda brought me here, we arrived in southern Mudroot, then walked all the way to this jungle. But that took two weeks, since we wanted to avoid any gnomes."

Elli's jaw clenched at the word. "Always a good idea." She glanced over at Lleu. "Papa once traveled from here to Airroot over the Misty Bridge."

The priest raised his thick eyebrows. "Brave man, your father. The Misty Bridge, from what I've heard, is not for the frail-hearted."

"A whale farted?" asked Shim, shaking his head. "Howly disgusting!"

Lleu paid no attention. "Still, it could be our quickest way out of here."

"And away from the gnomes," added Elli.

"Once we cross the bridge," Lleu cautioned, "we'll still need to travel through the northern part of Airroot to reach the nearest portal, which could take us to upper Fireroot."

Elli nodded. "And from there, we can walk down into Shadowroot." Grim determination filled her face. "To find the corrupted crystal."

"An excellent plan," declared the jester. He bobbed his head eagerly. "Quite excellent."

Lleu peered at Elli. "Are you sure you want to do this, my dear? That route—starting with the Misty Bridge—could be dangerous."

"It's still better than going south into the gnome lands." She ran a hand through her curly hair. "I'll never go anywhere near those beasts again if I can help it."

"Well then," growled Nuic. "Are we just going to stand here jabbering all day? Or what?"

Glancing up at the few stars that she could see through open spaces in the canopy, Elli pointed to the east. "The Misty Bridge is that way. When we get closer, we can climb one of these trees, or a high hill, to locate it exactly."

"Off we go, then," said the jester in a cheery voice. He danced a little jig, then added, "To the Misty Bridge, then on to find your crystal."

And also something else, he said to himself. *Something you don't expect.* His eyes glinted with satisfaction. *Your death.*

The glint brightened. For this disguise as a jester was really one of his best—at least as long as he kept his temper under control. But even with the change of plans caused by that infernal portal, things were now falling into place quite nicely. Better than he'd expected. And he was always someone who expected good results.

For the results depended on him, and him alone. And he didn't get to be Deth Macoll, the most successful assassin in Avalon's history, just by accident. No, he'd gotten there by his consummate skill, his supremely calculating mind, and one thing more: his love of the chase.

And how he loved the chase! The strategy, the patient waiting for just the right moment, and then the kill—and that final instant when he could feel his victim's life bleed away. In that instant of death, he held all the power. Immortal power.

He sighed contentedly. This particular job would be among his most rewarding. How long since he'd had the pleasure of killing not just one person, but several at once? Too long. And to pick up a pair of precious crystals in the bargain—not to mention the one he'd steal from Kulwych, after killing him, too—well, that made this practically a holiday.

For now, though, he would wait. He'd bide his time, looking for the perfect opening to satisfy his sense of drama. He would allow this ragtag bunch of fools to feel hopeful, even successful—and then he'd end his disguise, as well as their lives.

The jester smiled more broadly than he had all day.

22 · Ruins

INTO THE JUNGLE THEY PLUNGED, WITH ELLI and Brionna in the lead. Nuic rode in the crook of Elli's arm, grumbling with every jostle. The jester followed, with Lleu always nearby. Last of all came Shim, trying his best to keep up.

Even when Brionna steered them to an animal trail that ran generally eastward, the trekking was not easy. With every step, they had to push through a thick webbing of fern fronds, draping vines, and branches heavy with leaves, nuts, and ripening fruit. Birds with brilliantly painted tailfeathers, copper and turquoise and emerald green, whistled overhead, causing Catha sometimes to whistle back. Lime green snakes slithered down the trunks of gargantuan palm trees, while heavier snakes speckled with scarlet looped themselves around cedar boughs.

Much as the aromas of ripe papayas, moist breadfruit, sunwarmed almonds, cacao leaves, and vanilla floated through the air, so did butterflies. They glided everywhere, their blue and gold wings flashing as they met the beams of starlight that sliced through the canopy of leaves. Moths also fluttered overhead, or gathered on colorful flowers dripping with nectar. Purple-backed beetles crawled over twisted roots or laid eggs on fern fronds; blue ants marched through the ground leaves, tugging chunks of fleshy fruit or dead crickets twenty times their size; glowing light fliers hummed in the air.

And these were only the creatures that could be seen. High in the branches, monkeys chattered and howled in long, descending scales. Other beings, hidden by the flowering boughs, twittered, barked, piped, and rattled. Even underfoot, Elli sensed the movements of small creatures scurrying or slithering beneath the leaves.

Suddenly she stopped short. Grabbing Brionna by the elbow, she nodded to the left, her face grim. There, adorned with a crown of rust-colored vines, stood a gray, pyramidal stone no bigger than Shim. But one glimpse was all it took to see this was no ordinary stone.

It had eyes. Carved roughly into the top of the pyramid were a pair of deep sockets. An unpolished ruby as big as a fist had been set into each. This gave the statue an eerie look, its huge, bloodshot eyes glaring at anyone who passed.

"Who made it?" asked Elli.

"Someone who didn't want any visitors," Brionna replied.

"Someone in the same mood I'm in right now," muttered Nuic from his seat on Elli's arm.

They kept walking, veering to one side to avoid a mass of thorny grasses as tall as Lleu. Just then Brionna spotted a flat patch of moss at the base of a rock-strewn hill. Curious, she led them over to look more closely. With elvish grace, she bent down to touch the reddish moss, as thick as a sheep's woolen coat, and then turned to the others.

"Just as I thought," she explained. "This moss grows in El

Urien, as well. *Stonebeard*, we call it, because it only grows on rock. By the flatness of this patch, and its rectangular shape, I'd wager it's part of an old . . ." She pushed aside a thick cluster of ferns, revealing several more flat stones that climbed up the hill-side. "Stairway."

"No doubt about it," said Elli, gazing at the mossy steps. Vines had wrapped around some, and bushes had rooted in others and split the stones, but most of the ancient steps looked intact. "Where do they lead, do you think?"

"I think we don't want to find out," suggested Seth. He glanced furtively over his shoulder. "Unless you're in no hurry to find your crystal."

"I *am* in a hurry," Elli replied crisply. "And the best way to save time is to find the Misty Bridge as fast as possible. Whatever was the purpose of these old stairs, they make it easy to climb this hill—and from the top, we should be able to see the bridge."

Without waiting any longer, she sprang up the steps. The others bounded after her—all except Shim, whose body wasn't exactly built for bounding. As they climbed higher, more stones revealed themselves in the jungle growth. A trio of tall pillars, wrapped in vines, stood to one side; a raised platform sat on the other. Next came a fallen tower, and some sort of mound with a slab of white quartz on its side. A pair of scarlet birds with wondrously long, flowing tails took off from the mound as the group approached. Then, as they neared the top of the hill, they saw a ring of col-umns rising out of the trees. Great stone tablets, scrawled with petroglyphs, sat atop the columns. And within the ring sat a foun-dation of immense blocks whose edges had been carved to fit to-gether perfectly. They supported a large pyramidal structure made of translucent quartz. Though part of it had collapsed, leaving a hole in the lower part of the roof, the overall structure was still intact—and its original purpose seemed clear.

"A temple," said Lleu, gazing in awe. "What sort of people built this, here in the middle of Africqua? And how long ago?"

"Who knows?" answered Elli. "But if I go inside the temple and then out that hole in the roof, I shouldn't have much trouble climbing up to the top. It's probably the best view around."

"Are you sure?" asked Nuic, his colors shifting to shadowy gray.

"No . . . but sighting the bridge would help. And besides, when was the last time we were completely sure before we acted?"

Before the sprite could answer, she had started climbing the final steps. Directly ahead, a pair of stone pillars with a crossbeam marked the entryway into the temple. With the others close behind, she stepped inside. Milky white light bathed everything within, turning her hands pale.

Just as the others entered, a guttural grunt sounded above their heads. Suddenly a horde of burly, squat bodies dropped on top of them, knocking them all to the floor. Three-fingered hands grabbed them roughly, while deadly spears aimed at them from every side. Even Brionna's lightning-fast reflexes weren't quick enough to allow her to grab her bow.

"Gnomes," wailed Elli in disbelief. "Why gnomes?"

A grunted command was her only answer. The band of gnomes shoved the companions to their feet, confiscated Brionna's bow and arrows, and marched them across the floor. There must have been at least thirty of them, all scarred, grimy, and hairless but for the ragged tufts on their heads. They herded the companions around a quartz partition, then led them into the structure's central chamber.

The chamber sat directly underneath the point of the pyramid. White light poured down, revealing a stone basin and ax—the equipment of sacrifice—as well as some broken statues, carved bowls, and a long granite table. Next to the table sat an immense throne, carved of gleaming quartz with inlaid amethyst. And on the throne sat the person who was undeniably the gnomes' leader.

The sight of that person made Elli's heart freeze in her chest. Lleu, for his part, stumbled backward in surprise. And then the leader spoke.

"Welcome," said Llynia, still wearing the robe of a Drumadian priestess—and the dark green stain on her chin that Elli had given her at the Baths. "I have been expecting you. Oh yes, ever since my latest vision."

23 · The Moth

DEEP IN THE UNDERGROUND CAVERNS OF Shadowroot, Kulwych paced along a dimly lit corridor, his pale white hands clasped behind his back. Torches flickered on the dank stone walls, illuminating the scars and burned flesh of his mutilated face. The jagged scar that ran from his missing ear down to his chin, the chunk of his nose that was no longer there, and the hollow hole that was once his right eye, all glowed eerily in the torches' flames.

His boots thumped on the stone floor, slowing only to stomp on a tattered gray moth who had landed in front of him. Kulwych chortled to himself as he heard the crunch of its body. It was satisfying to know that, to some creatures at least, he was still the undisputed master.

The permanent scowl on his lipless mouth deepened. Things hadn't been going as he'd planned. No, not at all.

He rounded a bend in the corridor, his one remaining eye trained on the door ahead. Behind that door, Rhita Gawr waited for him. And behind that door, he himself was merely a moth, waiting to be crushed.

In the years since that wretch Merlin had mutilated his face, Kulwych had craved more than anything else the chance to rule the world of Avalon. To rid it of the stench of Merlin, and to re-make it as he chose. He had prayed for help to his lord on high, the great Rhita Gawr, and done everything the spirit warrior had demanded. Why, he had even managed to create a crystal of pure élano in the lake of the White Geyser—despite the meddling of that runt wizard who thought himself the heir of Merlin.

But what, Kulwych wondered, had all this gained him? All those years of suffering alone, of waiting, of planning, and of gath-ering an army of slaves to build his secret dam?

The brow above his lone eye rose hopefully. For there was, even now, a chance. If he could somehow stay clear of Rhita Gawr's wrath—and help him conquer this world—the spirit lord would eventually turn his attention elsewhere. To other worlds: Earth, for example, where that miserable Merlin had gone.

In that event, someone loyal to Rhita Gawr would need to remain in Avalon. To rule it in his name. To destroy any foes who dared resist. And to—

He reached the door. The burly gobsken guard, the replace-ment for the one Deth Macoll had killed, instantly drew back to let him pass. Behind the gobsken's slitlike eyes, Kulwych sensed a touch of fear. This always pleased him.

"Mmmyess, you gobsken trash. You know who is really your master."

He pushed open the door. From the darkness within, bright-ened only by a pulsing bloodred light, came a harsh voice: "And you, my little sorcerer, know who is really yours."

Kulwych gulped. "Y-yes, my lord." He stepped inside, closed the door behind him, and gazed at Rhita Gawr.

"Why do you stare at me like that, Kulwych? Are you sorry now you called for my help?"

"No, my lord. Never! I was just . . ."

"Just what?" hissed the voice.

"Amazed, Master, at how you have grown. You have changed so much since you first arrived in Avalon! No longer are you just a rope of smoke, or a snake that floats upon the air—but a great serpent. Even in the time since I left you this morning, to go check on Harlech's weapons makers, you have grown in size."

"And also, my pet, in power. More than you know."

Rhita Gawr, whose serpentine body had been wrapped tightly around the bloodred crystal of vengélano, uncoiled himself. Streaks of rusty light shimmered over his lengthy form, flashing on the black scales that had only just started to grow. Behind the triangular, snakelike head, a pair of bony nubs had appeared— the first sign of emerging wings. Already he looked less like a serpent . . . and more like a dragon.

As much as Rhita Gawr's shape had changed, however, there was still a trace of himself from weeks before—a hint of the smoke-like being who had resembled a shadow more than anything alive. His eyes. For this serpent's eyes were not merely black. They were absolutely empty. Bottomless beyond any pit or crevasse. Empty of all but nothingness.

Those eyes were the *void*.

As Rhita Gawr pulled himself away from the corrupted crystal, he began to spin slowly. Around and around in the cavern, his barbed tail nearly touching his head, he twirled in a grim but stately dance, to a music that only he could hear. This was the music of power, swelling inside him. Of conquest, growing closer. And of triumph, nearing fulfillment.

As he spun within the dark cavern, black sparks exploded whenever he brushed against the walls. Often his laughter erupted as well, echoing all around. And then Rhita Gawr started to speak. As often as Kulwych had heard that voice, the sound still made his knees wobble and his mouth go dry.

"Now, my little plaything, let me tell you what I have done. I have used the power of this crystal to call an army to my aid."

"Bu-but, my lord, I have already begun to assemble the warriors you asked for."

Still spinning, the monstrous being growled, "Not them, Kulwych! I have called an army of my own—immortal warriors, from the Otherworld."

The sorcerer froze, amazed. "Immortal warriors?"

"Naturally, my pet. Do you think I would rely solely on your motley band of humans and gobsken? And on your limited skills as commander?"

Kulwych's scarred face flushed at this insult, but he kept his slit of a mouth closed.

"They will play a part in my triumph, as will you. But to prevail, I need something stronger. And so I have called to my army of spirits. Yes, and bound them to me through this crystal. Soon they shall enter this world just as I did. They will gather in the stars, growing swiftly stronger. And by the time they are ready to fight, I will have joined them on high. Then I will lead them back down to these wretched realms and finish the work that you have only begun."

Kulwych lowered his head. Like the moth in the cavern, he could feel the approach of the heavy boot that would soon crush whatever remained of his life. And his dreams. "And then," he whispered hoarsely, "I suppose you will discard me."

The near-dragon that was Rhita Gawr finally stopped circling. His empty eyes studied the sorcerer for a moment, glittering subtly from the light of the bloodred crystal. And from satisfaction, as well.

"No, Kulwych, though your haughtiness has tempted me to do just that. As long as you remain loyal to me, and humble in my service, I will do something else with you."

The sorcerer lifted his head slightly. "And that is, Master?"

"I will make you the ruler of Avalon."

Kulwych started, as if a bolt of black lightning had just landed right on him. "Ruler? Mmmyesss?"

"That is right. While I use Avalon to reach other worlds— starting with mortal Earth—you will remain here. And rule it in my stead."

Kulwych could hardly believe what he'd heard. "Truly, Master, I—"

"Spare me your sniveling gratitude! Now tell me the state of your own little army."

The sorcerer snapped to attention. "All goes according to plan, my lord. While Harlech's gobsken are making sturdy weapons, I have sent my ghoulacas all through the realms to contact your allies: humans frustrated by the infantile morality of the Society of the Whole, gobsken, ogres, trolls from the mountains, and changelings where I could find them. I have even won the allegiance of a clan of renegade eaglefolk, ruled by Quenaykha."

He paused, smirking. "And it was surprisingly easy to turn Belamir's Humanity First movement to our advantage. The rank and file may not know it, but they are now entirely at your service."

"So you have infiltrated their leadership?"

Kulwych's lipless mouth turned upward. "Mmmyess, my lord, at the absolute top."

"Good. And these allies know the plan?"

"Only enough to aid you, my lord. They are not all as capable as humans, you know."

The deep, hissing sound from Rhita Gawr's throat made Kulwych stand rigid again. "I have told them all," he said nervously, "to gather in Mudroot, on the Plains of Isenwy. And to make no secret of their movements, so that we can lure as many creatures as possible—creatures still loyal to the Society—into going there, as well, to do battle."

"Very good, my pet. You have done as I asked, without even knowing the details of the trap I have prepared." The triangular head lifted so that it faced Kulwych, eye to eye. "Blind obedience is a quality I cherish, you see."

"Of c-c-course, my lord."

"My ultimate triumph, Kulwych, is but a few weeks away! It gathers, even now, like a violent storm. And when the great horse dies, the storm will come. Ah yes, it will come."

Kulwych's scarred cheek twisted. "I . . . I am sorry, Master, but—"

"You still do not understand?" The bottomless eye moved closer. "Know this above all: No matter how well those wretched humans, elves, and others who still honor Merlin may fight against your army, they will be doomed from the start! You must spread the word among our allies who will converge on the Plains of Isenwy to hold back from war, until they see my sign from the stars."

"Sign?"

"I shall snuff out the central star—the brightest light—in the constellation mortals call Pegasus, the great winged horse. That star, known as the Heart of Pegasus, is more than it appears, much more. And so, when I make it go dark, something marvelous will happen. When the Heart stops beating . . . *the great horse dies.*"

Rhita Gawr paused. "Do not trouble yourself with trying to understand all this, my Kulwych. All you need to know is that, in that very moment, I shall lead my immortal warriors out of the sky! We will descend on our foes—and destroy them completely."

Vigorously, the sorcerer nodded. "I see, I see! A most excellent plan, my lord. The battle will be a truly historic triumph."

"That it will, Kulwych. How tragic you won't be there to witness it."

The sorcerer's knees buckled, and he leaned against the dank stone wall. "Won't be there?"

"No. For I need you to stay here, to guard this crystal. It is far too precious to risk losing, you see. My spirit army is bound to it now. I could take it with me up to the stars, but then it would not be here in the root-realms to assist your troops."

Kulwych's curiosity overcame his bristling disappointment. "And just how will it help my troops?"

"Soon enough, my pet, you shall see."

"But Master . . . must I be the one to stay? And miss your triumphant battle?"

"Yes, Kulwych. For you shall have a battle of your own, I expect. One you will find most rewarding."

The sorcerer's only eye opened wider. "Against whom, my lord?"

A long, crackling laugh echoed in the cavern. "Against your dear friend, Deth Macoll. Just as I have no doubt that he will kill the young priestess and take her crystal of élano, I have no doubt that he will return here—but not to deliver it. He will try to take the vengélano crystal, as well, making himself a power I must contend with. And of course, he will hope to kill you in the process."

Kulwych's white hands curled into fists. "I shall be ready for him."

"Good," answered Rhita Gawr, slashing his tail against the cavern wall in a shower of sparks. "Then I am most pleased."

24 · Food for the Gray Wolf

RETCH. RETCH. AND RETCH AGAIN.

That was all Tamwyn could do when, at last, he awoke. For several minutes, he just lay on his side, curled into a ball. The spasms of coughing and sputtering continued as he expelled as much water as he could from his stomach and lungs. Finally, the convulsions ceased. But the waves of pain that coursed through his body did not.

He took a few gulps of air, coughed again, and breathed some more. Though more than half drowned, he was, at least, alive. But where?

Slowly, head spinning, he propped himself up on one elbow. It took a long moment before his eyes could focus, let alone move as he willed. Then, ignoring the sharp pains in his ribs and all down his neck, he lifted his head just enough to see his surroundings.

He'd landed on another ledge, next to the upward-flowing waterfall. Like the ledge where he'd begun his journey, it was covered with emerald green moss and shallow pools of water—some of which, he suspected, had been vomited out by him. Through the drifting spray of vapors, he could see the twin cascades of wa-ter and light, one spiraling up while the other twirled down. The rising water pounded relentlessly—as did his head.

He closed his eyes, trying to stop his gaze from spinning. Then he recalled that phrase from Krystallus' scroll, something about the view from Merlin's Knothole—that it was *almost as dizzying as the journey*. Well, he couldn't imagine anything more dizzying than the ride he'd just taken. Was it possible that he'd found his way closer to the Knothole?

Weakly, he nodded. Maybe he had—with some help from that crazy hoolah, who had all the brains of a headless troll.

He opened his eyes again. *Wait until I get my hands on him.*

But Henni was nowhere on the ledge. Nowhere at all! Maybe, because he was smaller and lighter than Tamwyn, he'd been car-ried higher by the rising cascade.

Then a second pang struck. He glanced down at his pocket to see how Batty Lad had fared, and discovered that a big piece of his tunic had been ripped away. The cascade had taken a good amount of cloth—as well as his quirky, green-eyed friend.

Batty Lad! Tamwyn shook his sopping wet head. *It's all my fault. I should never have let you come on such a dangerous quest. Poor little fellow . . . I'd only just begun to get to know you. And hadn't even started to figure out what you really were.*

Gone! Both of them. He hung his head for a long moment.

In time, he raised it again. "By the crooked teeth of Babd Catha," he cursed, his voice smothered by the roar of water. "I'd kill Henni all over again, if I could."

Sitting up, he checked himself more closely. He gingerly moved his arms, legs, and neck. Stiff and sore as they were, noth-ing seemed broken. And he did still have his pack, his water flask, and somehow, his staff. As well as whatever parts of his brain hadn't been drowned.

All that aside, though, he was now alone.

Completely alone.

But where? All he knew was that he was somewhere inside the vast expanse of the trunk of the Tree, much higher than the level of that tunnel with the mysterious, brightly painted mural. Besides that, though, he knew nothing. He was more lost than ever! Once again, he wished for some sort of compass that could help him find his location—and his way to the Knothole.

And, after that, the stars. The very stars that Rhita Gawr had darkened—and that would soon bring forth those strange, evil shadows.

With painful slowness, he rose to his feet. He stood there, wobbling unsteadily, until he remembered to pull out his staff. For a while, he just stared at the spiraling waterfall that had brought him here. Then, turning around, he realized that this ledge connected to another tunnel. He'd have to explore it, wherever it might lead.

Aching all over, he started to walk. Like the one he'd trekked through lower down, this tunnel ran horizontally. As he entered, the curtains of moss that clung to the walls soon faded away, revealing the coarse brown wood beneath. Grainy whorls and knots were everywhere, sometimes protruding as rough-hewn crystals that twisted into themselves, sometimes undulating like wooden waves. Tamwyn moved deeper into the tunnel, his footsteps punctuated by the *clack, clack, clack* of his staff.

Suddenly he heard a long, agonized shriek. He'd never heard a voice like that before, but he knew at once it came from a creature at the very edge of death. And it came from farther down the tunnel.

Despite his aching limbs, he hurried on, half-running and half-limping. He ducked just in time to avoid a curling brown stalactite, then turned a corner. The tunnel abruptly widened, opening into a cavern where several passageways intersected. About half as large as the Great Hall of the Heartwood, the cavern overflowed with plant life. Plants of many shapes and colors sprouted from both sides, as well as the ceiling. One variety, with broad, flat leaves, reminded Tamwyn of the bluish green lichen that grew on the bark of Stoneroot's oaks. But here, in the trunk of the Great Tree, the lichen was much bigger, nearly the size of holly bushes.

The shriek came again, reverberating in the cavern. He veered to the left, burst through some shrubbery, and saw a huge brown butterfly being brutally mauled by three gigantic insects. The attackers looked very much like the red-backed termites that Tamwyn had often found chewing on the wood of a fallen branch, but hundreds of times larger. Each of these monsters was at least three times as long as Tamwyn was tall. And given their huge girth, probably ten times as heavy. On top of that, like their smaller cousins, these termites had powerful pincers that could easily rip or crush any wood.

Or any flesh. Right now, two of the termites were tearing at the butterfly's body while one had its jaws closed around a torn wing. Feebly, and without much success, the butterfly was flailing one leg, trying to fight back.

From the corner of his eye, Tamwyn spied another creature, an immense gray wolf with pale green eyes who lurked in the brush. Though fully twice the size of any wolf from the lower realms, the powerful creature moved as gently as a breeze through the bushes. *He's stalking,* Tamwyn realized. *Waiting to eat whatever is left of the termites' prey.*

His brow furrowed. He'd seen, many times in the wild, predators killing their food. But there was something disturbing about the way these giant termites were mauling the butterfly. Somehow he sensed that they weren't killing out of hunger, but out of sheer malice.

And that's wrong. Totally wrong.

Tamwyn leaped over a lichen bush with a wild shout. With his dagger broken, his only weapons were the staff—and sheer ferocity. He used them both to the fullest, clubbing the termites with all his strength, kicking at their enormous eyes, all the while spinning and jumping to avoid their pincers.

He slammed one in the head, just behind its eyes, so hard that it oozed something gray and fell still. Another, who had been ripping into the butterfly's leg, received a jab to the belly that cracked several armored plates. It released the leg and, with a roar of rage, leaped straight at Tamwyn. Just in time, he dodged out of reach—and then saw something that made him freeze.

The termites' prey wasn't a butterfly after all! For the first time, Tamwyn paused long enough to look at the creature he was helping, and realized that it was actually more like a winged man. His skin, dark brown, was shaggy like the bark of a tree. His muscular chest, like his rumpled wings, had been torn by many deep gashes, while both legs were badly mutilated. Silvery brown blood stained most of his body and the simple loincloth he wore around his waist.

Before Tamwyn could jump aside, the giant insect behind him pounced. It knocked him to the ground, and even as he rose again, slashed his back with sword-sharp pincers. Tamwyn shouted in pain and staggered sideways, tripping over the winged man's body. The winged man lifted his head weakly, gazing at him with deep brown eyes. They had no time to speak, but that instant of eye contact had said enough.

Tamwyn rolled to the side, just as a termite's immense body crashed down on the spot. He fought to stand again despite his wounded back. But every motion, like every breath, plunged daggers of pain through his chest.

With a feint, he dodged the savage pincers of one termite, then clobbered the middle of its back with the staff. Red plates splintered as the insect bellowed, arching its back in agony. Tamwyn was about to strike again when the other termite bit the flesh below his hip, tearing a huge gash. Blood spurted and Tamwyn lost his balance, sprawling on the ground.

He'd barely turned over when the termite rose up on its hind parts, preparing to come crashing down on top of him. Since the beast surely weighed more than a horse, this blow would crush his chest. And then, what little remained of him that the termites didn't eat, that prowling wolf surely would.

He spied his staff, just out of reach. And a last, desperate idea struck him. Drawing all the strength he had left, ignoring the pain that coursed through his body, he stretched out his arm farther . . . farther . . .

Got it!

In one swift motion, he swung the staff upright, holding its pointed end high and its gnarled end on the ground. Then, even as the gargantuan beast tipped over, he held it firmly in place. The monster fell forward with an ear-splitting roar of triumph. But its cry turned suddenly to anguish as the staff pierced the base of its neck, its skull, and whatever brain sat within. Black blood gushed in all directions.

Because the termite's writhing death throes had slightly shifted its weight, its body thudded down just to Tamwyn's left, missing him by only a hairsbreadth. He lay next to the impaled beast, panting, his entire body stinging from his wounds. But he was alive.

He rolled over, sat up, and rose shakily to his feet. Bracing one foot against the dead termite, he tugged on his staff until it came free. Remarkably, its magical sheen kept any of the black blood from adhering to it. Ohnyalei, carried long ago by Merlin himself, shone as cleanly as ever.

Just then, Tamwyn heard something move behind him: the one remaining termite. He whirled around, though he was now too weak even to lift the staff. How could he possibly defend himself?

But the beast was fleeing! Tamwyn watched it crawl off through the shrubbery and disappear down one of the passageways. Relieved that he wouldn't have to fight again, he turned to the broken body of the winged man.

The man's deep brown eyes, as richly hued as honey made by brownvelvet bees, tried to focus. And, as had happened so often before, Tamwyn heard the man's thoughts clearly. *You . . . saved me, human son.*

Tamwyn knelt beside him. *Just don't die now, all right?*

The winged man winced. *So many stories . . . yet to tell.*

Tamwyn placed his hand on the worst gash he could find, in the shaggy brown flesh just below the man's collarbone. Suddenly he drew back. This person was hot! Very hot! He'd developed a terrible fever, enough to kill anybody.

Returning his hand to the spot, Tamwyn started willing the

wound to stop bleeding, just as he willed the same for his own torn flesh on his back and hip. But he'd already lost so much blood that the effort made him dizzy. He wobbled unsteadily and barely caught himself from falling over.

Waste not your strength, human son. I am . . . spent.

Not yet! Tamwyn forced his aching back to straighten. *You need help, that's all. Is your home far from here?*

Too far now. All stories must . . . end at last.

Tamwyn wobbled again, his head spinning. He couldn't even hold himself upright! How could he possibly help someone else?

He slumped over, his head smacking the ground by the man's torn wing. He could feel the blood flowing from his wounds, and with it, his remaining strength. Hard as he tried, he could not lift himself up again. Here, he suddenly knew, was the place where he would die.

Though his head swam, he saw some movement at the edge of his vision. The gray wolf! Coming in for the kill.

Tamwyn tried to lift his staff, but even that was impossible. His grip on the shaft relaxed, while a heavy fog seeped into his mind, obscuring his thoughts. Yet he managed to form one last request of the winged man: *At least tell me your name.*

Gwirion. And . . . yours?

But Tamwyn was too weak to reply. Or to see the hungry fire in the gray wolf's eyes as he approached, growling, the hair on his powerful shoulders standing up in a ruff. The wolf's lips drew back, exposing his sharp teeth, just as he started to close his jaws around Tamwyn's neck.

25 · The Golden Wreath

WHEN TAMWYN AWOKE, HE WASN'T SURE he was alive. Or how that could be possible.

But it was.

He twisted his neck, chafed and sore, and looked around at his strange new surroundings. He lay on his back in a small chamber, no bigger than the one-room huts of many shepherds and barley growers he'd known back in Stoneroot. Beneath him was a chipped tile floor, whose original rusty red color barely showed through the layers of black charcoal. The walls and ceiling, made of large panels of tile, were also coated with charcoal. The whole place smelled of smoke—years and years of fires.

He tried to sit up, but his mind spun wildly and he fell back, knocking his head against the floor. It took several minutes for the dizziness and nausea to subside. Finally, he forced himself to roll over, scanning this room that seemed more like a smokehouse than anybody's home.

There was almost no furniture, just an old ironwood table with a pair of matching chairs. A burned bowl and two mugs sat on the table. And a rough-hewn frame on the wall held a tile picture that had long ago been covered with charcoal. Beneath the picture sat a shelf with pots of paint, several splattered brushes, and a small brown box.

But where was the hearth? There wasn't even a space for a cooking fire. Surely whoever built this place didn't just build fires right on the floor? And without fuel?

He saw, stacked in the corner, his pack and staff. *At least they made it here, too,* he thought with relief. *But where is here?*

He had no answer. All he knew was that he'd landed, somehow, in someone's smoky hut. And, from an inner sense that couldn't be explained, he felt sure that he was still deep within the trunk of the Great Tree.

Sadly, he thought about his two companions who hadn't made it this far: Henni and Batty Lad. As quirky (and, in Henni's case, downright dangerous) as they were to be around, he did miss them. Greatly. For although his quest still burned like a fire inside him, without his companions, it was a fire without warmth.

Laboriously, lifting his head as little as possible, he squirmed over to the pack. His hip throbbed in pain, so much that he couldn't bear to move his left leg, let alone put any weight on it. But he managed to slide along, stirring clouds of black ash as he dragged across the floor.

There! He reached the pack. Weakly, he grabbed it. As he pulled it close, it jostled, making the slab of harmóna wood ring like a distant chime. *Elli's harp,* he said to himself, having almost forgotten it was there. And then came a feeling he'd also nearly forgotten: *I wonder where she is right now. And if she's any better off than I am.*

Opening his pack, he grabbed his leathereed flask, unplugged it, and took a drink. As before, every sip of the sweet water from the Great Hall's magical spring soothed his sore limbs. Gave him new strength. And revived his spirits.

Then he noticed something strange about the pack. Tooth marks! Big ones—piercing the top of the leather strap, near where his neck would be if he'd been wearing it. He reached up and touched the scrapes along one side of his neck, just under his ear. Could those scrapes have been from teeth, as well?

Images roiled in his mind: the spectacular mural in the tunnel, the rising water of the cascade, the fight to the death with those monstrous termites. Where was Gwirion? Had he lived, despite that terrible fever? And what had saved Tamwyn from the gray wolf?

He ran his finger over the pack strap, feeling the tooth marks. Could it be? No, no, that was impossible.

His gaze moved again to the tile picture on the wall. Enough streaks of color showed through the charcoal that he could almost make out the image underneath. It seemed vaguely familiar. But what was it?

Grabbing his staff, he angled it toward the picture. Though his arms shook from the effort, he rubbed the tip of the staff over the image inside the frame, knocking off several charred flakes. All at once, he recognized the image—and gasped in surprise.

A flaming man! He looked just like the ones in the mural, but for one detail: This man wore a wreath of golden leaves on his head, much like a crown. His stern mouth and angular jaw gave him a strong look of purpose—but what, Tamwyn wondered, could that purpose have been? Surrounded by orange fire that licked his brawny chest and wings, the man stared down at him with eyes as richly brown as Gwirion's, and just as fierce as Scree's.

But this was no eagleman. This was something entirely different.

Just then, Tamwyn heard voices outside the room. Angry voices. They quickly rose to shouts.

He didn't like the sound of that, not at all. His eyes darted around to look for anything he might use as a weapon. But he had nothing but his staff and a broken dagger—and very little strength.

The door beside the table flew open. It slammed against the burned walls, so hard that a piece of the tile frame fell and splintered on the floor. Tamwyn lunged for one of the knifelike shards just as two men stormed inside. Men with shaggy brown skin, loincloths, and ragged wings, just like Gwirion!

Though they spoke in a tongue that crackled and spat like resinous spruce burning in a fire, Tamwyn understood them easily:

"Kill him, I say! End his story here and now."

"No, no, Ciann. Wait until the high holy day! He's a big beast, this one. He'll make a perfect sacrifice."

"Not perfect, you fool. Only the Golden Wreath is that."

"And when was the last time we had one of those? Dagda only knows! Since before my grandmother told her first tale, at least. I say we keep him until the ceremony, then burn him alive."

"Dead will do! Kill him now, before he gets strong enough to escape. Then—"

Just as the bark-skinned men were about to reach for Tamwyn, he forced himself to sit upright, propping his back against the wall. His head swam and his vision blurred, but he held himself there. Brandishing his piece of broken tile, he roared, "Stay away from me! Away!"

Someone struck him roughly on the shoulder. Tamwyn lashed out, swinging his makeshift blade. One of the men cried out in pain. Then a new voice bellowed, and a scuffle ensued. Something hit Tamwyn's jaw. He slid over sideways, as the tile fell from his hand.

26 · Soulfire

TAMWYN STRUGGLED TO OPEN HIS EYES. THE lids felt heavy, too heavy to move. Yet still he tried.

Even before he opened them, though, he knew he was still in the same room. He could smell the smoke, like the remains of a thousand ancient cooking fires. And he could feel the layers of charcoal on the tiles beneath his hands. But now, at least, he sensed those men were gone.

Who were they? And why did they want to kill him?

At last, his eyes popped open. Just in time to see a bulky, blurry shape bending over him! Coming closer . . .

With all his strength, he tried to sit up. One hand groped blindly for the knifelike shard, while the other pushed desperately against the floor. But his arms quivered and his head burst with pain. More fog obscured his vision. He fell back onto the tiles with a thud.

The shape bent closer.

He tried to lift his head, or one of his hands. But they lay on the charred floor like chunks of lead. He was helpless.

Now the shape was directly above him, staring down at him.

"Don't try to move, human son. You're still too weak. Though somehow you found the strength to fight again just now."

That voice, thought Tamwyn. *I know that voice.* His eyes struggled to focus. "Gwirion!"

"Yes, my friend."

"But you! I thought you were dead. Your wounds . . ."

"My people heal quickly—at least in wounds of the flesh." His brow furrowed. "Even so, it took all the skills of my wife, Tulchinne, to revive me. And also some time: What you would call two whole days have passed since we came here."

"Two days?"

Gwirion rubbed his hairless head. "Yes."

"Those men," said Tamwyn worriedly. "They wanted to—"

"Worry not," declared Gwirion. His eyes, which looked like pools of melted chocolate, watched with compassion, while the corners of his wide mouth turned up in a grateful smile. "We stopped them—Tulchinne, my sister Fraitha, and I. But that was not nearly as difficult as what you did for me."

"But . . . what about that huge gray wolf? Why didn't he just eat us?"

The smile flickered like a wavering candle on Gwirion's face. "He could have, true, and normally would not have hesitated. For here wolves often dine on the termites' leftovers. But wolves are also beasts of rare honor, and deep dignity. When he saw what you did—what courage you showed—he decided to spare us both. So he dragged us here, to my village, just as he'd carry a couple of his own pups. And when Tulchinne found us, he departed."

Tamwyn glanced over at the pack strap, and the tooth marks it bore. "Honor lives in surprising places."

"Indeed it does," Gwirion replied, looking not at the pack strap, but at Tamwyn himself. He bent lower and placed the palm of his hand on the young man's brow.

Suddenly Tamwyn shook his head. "Your hand—so hot! You have that fever again."

Gwirion drew back his hand. His wide mouth twisted in such a way that he seemed to be amused and sorrowful at the same time. "Fever? No, this is my normal temperature, though it is much cooler than it should be."

"Cooler? I don't understand."

Gwirion scratched the shaggy, barklike skin of his brow. "You see, human son, our fires have long burned low."

"Fires?"

"The fires of my people, the Ayanowyn."

That word again! Tamwyn remembered how it had popped into his head, from some magical insight, at the painted mural. He started to speak, but before he could, Gwirion held up both his brown hands.

"Be silent, my friend. It is time, I can tell, for a story. One of the few remaining skills of my people."

He whistled to himself thoughtfully, as if deciding where to begin—a series of low, wandering notes. At last, he shifted his loincloth and sat down on the floor, legs folded. He was so close that Tamwyn could feel the heat emanating from his skin. Yet all that warmth didn't seem to trouble Gwirion in the least. Rather, it was the tale of his own people that made him scowl as he spoke. Despite the glory of his words, there was none at all in his face.

"Many thousands of flames ago, even as the first streams of élano stirred inside the trunk of the Great Tree—what we call the

Middle Realm—our people arrived in this world. Led by Ogallad the Worthy, we flew down to these lands, our bodies burning every bit as bright as our destiny."

Tamwyn stirred. "Flew *down*? Your people came from the branches?"

"No, human son. We came from the stars."

Tamwyn sucked in his breath. *From the stars.* "And when you say your people were burning . . ."

"I mean we burned with fire that springs from the soul— *llalowyn* in our language, the hottest fire known to mortal beings. And when we passed into Avalon, Dagda himself greeted us. He told us that we would be masters of the Middle Realm for many generations, and that our people would inspire many wondrous stories which would long outlive us—whether in the songs of bards or in the murals of painters. *For stories*, he said, *are as immortal as the gods.* Dagda then crowned Ogallad with a Golden Wreath to signify our glorious future."

Suddenly Tamwyn understood. Gwirion's people were the same ones he'd seen pictured! Fire angels—though somehow their fires had been extinguished. So they *were* real, after all.

He indicated the charred image on the wall. "Is that him? Your first leader?"

Gwirion looked both pained and proud. "That is Ogallad, his soulfire burning bright." He peered at Tamwyn. "And now, I expect, you want to know what happened to our flames."

The young man nodded.

"In the days of *Lumaria col Lir*—the Age of Great Light—my people flourished. We built magnificent cities of colorful tile, made with the heat of our own flames, in the caverns of Avalon's trunk. We ventured far from the Middle Realm, both starward and rootward, though mostly down into the root-realms. Why, it was my people who brought the first light ever to shine in Shadowroot."

Despite the pain, Tamwyn lifted his head. "Not the Lost City of Light?"

"Indeed." A distant fire kindled in Gwirion's eyes. "We gave light to the land, placing torches by the thousands on the streets and in the buildings. And we also gave light to the hearts of the people there, by sharing all the stories we knew, and teaching them to do the same. We even built them a great library just to hold all their books and maps."

He paused, savoring the image of that city. "Dianarra, we named it. City of Fallen Stars, for it seemed that we had brought the light from high above to the darkest depths below."

He looked past Tamwyn to the scorched wall, and somewhere beyond. "Years later, as you must know, the dark elves doused those lights. Then the City's name proved apt, for it had truly Fallen. But by then my people had fallen as well. Into darkness and decline, our greatest stories all but forgotten."

"What happened?"

Somberly, he ruffled his ragged wings, then whistled a few forlorn notes. "Our greatness turned to greed. We believed, sometimes correctly but ever more intolerantly, that our ways of living were superior to others. We imposed our customs, and our will, on peoples throughout the Middle Realm. If they dared resist, we burned their homes, their crops . . . and sometimes even their children. For we told ourselves that only we knew *the right*; only we understood *the good*."

He sighed. "At the same time, we started thinking of the Great Tree as our land, our possession, to exploit and use however we liked. We grew wasteful, destructive, shortsighted. We burned forests to clear land for grazing our captive beasts, even if it clogged the air and sullied our streams. Then we moved on to other forests and did the same, over and over again. Always, mind you, in the name of what was *right* and *good*. Why, we even destroyed the trees that held our precious Golden Wreath, symbol of our highest destiny! In time, the Ayanowyn had turned much of the Middle Realm into a wasteland."

His voice lost the spark and crackle of flames and began to hiss, like embers doused with water. "The greatest wasteland of all, though, was inside ourselves."

He thumped his chest. "And so, in time, our soulfires burned low, then went out completely. Now we do not flame, but merely smolder. We give no light. Why, even our wings have shriveled, so we can no longer fly!"

Sadly, he shook his head. "Today my people create no new stories through our wise choices and heroic deeds. We only repeat the tales of old glories, those we can still remember, even though we know such times will never come again. Unless . . ."

"Unless what?" Tamwyn pushed himself up onto his elbow, then slowly sat up. He faced Gwirion, peering into his deep brown eyes. "You must still have hope."

The winged man shrugged. "Hope is a spark that blows on the wind. If it does not soon find kindling to burn, it goes out forever."

"But you said *unless.*"

It was a long moment before Gwirion responded. "There is a prophecy, the final vision of our people's last seer. Her name was Mananaun, and she died just recently, a mere eighty flames ago. She prophesied that one day, the Ayanowyn will somehow regain the wisdom of our hearts and the power of our wings. On that day, we will fly out of the darkness we have made for ourselves . . . and back into the light."

That painting! Tamwyn recalled the striking image of Gwirion's people soaring into a brighter sky.

"Not only that," continued Gwirion, "our soulfire will rekindle, and burn as bright as before. Then we will, at last, return to the stars from whence we came so long ago—and be met once again by Dagda himself. And in that meeting, he will give us a great gift."

"What?"

Gwirion's eyes gleamed. "Our people's true name. And so would begin another great age for our people—as storied, perhaps, as Lumaria col Lir."

He shook himself, as if waking from a dream. "But none of this will ever happen! We have fallen too far. Our name will always be Ayanowyn, which itself is much too grand for what we have become. It means, in our tongue—"

"Fire angels," finished Tamwyn.

Gwirion stared at him in surprise. "You have unusual talents, my friend. Very unusual. And something more. I feel that, in some mysterious way, you attract *goodness* to yourself."

"Ha! If only you knew the truth."

"I feel sure of this, quite sure. Why else did that wolf do what he did?"

"Maybe he just wasn't hungry."

"Not likely. No, you remind me of a story about Angus Oge—an explorer, and a man of unusual kindness, who lived in the early days of my people. It is said that once he trekked across a remote part of the Middle Realm, a place so lifeless that he could find no food to eat. All he had was muddy water, for tens of flames on end. He grew steadily weaker. With his last remaining strength, he used his soulfire to boil some water in his ironwood pot, hoping to find at least a sprig of herbs to make some tea. But he found nothing. He knew now that he would die. Then, at the very final moment before his story ended, a wild hare bounded over—and jumped right into his pot."

Tamwyn frowned. "Usually, Gwirion, it's *me* who jumps into the boiling pot."

His friend laughed, a sound like vibrant fire crackling.

"It's true." Tamwyn's expression darkened. "Back in the root-realms, we, too, have a prophecy. It says that one person, the child of the Dark Prophecy, will someday cause the end of Avalon. The ruin of this world." After a long pause, he said, "And that person is me."

Gwirion studied him, then declared, "I do not believe this."

"But it's true."

"No, I think not. Prophecies can be hard to interpret. Or simply wrong. Our destinies can take as many shapes as a flame, you know! For we may be given our colors and brushes by the gods, but we paint our stories ourselves."

He glanced over at Tamwyn's staff that, even in this smoky room, still gave off a hint of hemlock. "You are like your staff, really. Plain to look at, perhaps, but with something very powerful inside. Yes, I can feel it! You have your own soulfire, though it cannot be seen. And I suspect that, one day, it will burn bright indeed."

Tamwyn looked down at his tattered tunic and leggings, so torn and bloodied. "That's hard to believe."

Suddenly Gwirion started. "By the fires of Ogallad! We have been through so much, but I don't even know your name."

"Tamwyn. It means—"

"Dark Flame. I know."

"You, too, have unusual talents."

Gwirion smiled. "Not really. Your name is from the flamelon people, is it not?"

Tamwyn nodded. "My mother was a flamelon."

Gwirion reached over with a muscular arm, scarred from their battle in the tunnel. He clamped his warm hand on Tamwyn's shoulder. "Then we are cousins, you and I. For in days long past, my people and yours intermarried. That is how, I have heard, the flamelons gained the ability to hurl fire from their hands."

"That skill didn't pass on to me, I'm afraid." Tamwyn raised his hands and turned them slowly before his face. "I can't make any magical fire. Only illusions."

"Perhaps one day you will," Gwirion replied. "After all, magical fire must first be kindled in the soul."

Tamwyn gazed at this bark-skinned man who seemed, at once, so sad and so assured. Despite Tamwyn's doubts, there was something in Gwirion's words that gave him a touch of hope.

At that moment, the winged man leaned forward. "What work do you do among your people?"

"Whatever work I can find, mostly. My favorite job is being a wilderness guide."

"Ah, so you are an explorer like Angus Oge?"

"No, not really. But my father . . ." Abruptly, he caught himself. "Gwirion. Have any other humans ever come through this realm?"

Thoughtfully, he rubbed the shaggy skin of his neck. "Once, and only once."

Tamwyn's face lit up. "Tell me!"

"It was many flames ago. In human years, I would say, almost twenty. A man came through this village—the last survivor, he said, of his group. The rest had perished in a terrible attack by the termites, in this case scores of them. The only reason he survived, he said, was his torch."

Tamwyn started. He would have leaped to his feet, if he'd had the strength. "That was Krystallus," he declared. "My father."

Gwirion's brown eyes peered at him. "Yes, I see the resemblance now. Though his hair was gray and yours is black, there is a kinship in your faces. And in your soulfires. For he was very brave, and very proud. He was injured, but would not take our help. And he was on his way, he said, to the stars! I told him that was terribly dangerous, even foolhardy, though in my heart I envied his boldness."

Tamwyn's heart swelled at this news. "Then you will feel the same toward me. For my quest, too, is to find the way to the stars. And to rekindle those that have been darkened."

Gwirion whistled in astonishment. "Your kinship to your father goes far deeper than your faces."

"Do you know," the young man asked anxiously, "which way he went?"

"Yes, and I will show you. Once you are well enough to walk, that is."

Tamwyn tried to push himself to his feet, but the hip that the termite had bitten exploded with pain. Groaning, he fell back on the charred tile floor. A cloud of soot rose up from the spot and settled on his torn leggings.

Weakly, he shook his head. "I wish I could go now."

"Yes, my friend, I know. But you will be ready soon." His eyes narrowed. "You *must* be ready soon."

Tamwyn cocked his head, inquiring.

"In just thirteen flames—less than a week by your way of counting time—is our high holy day, what we call Wynerria, or Fires of Faith. It marks the day when Ogallad first arrived in this realm."

He paused, a wistful look on his face. "In ancient times, when the glory of my people was as great as our numbers, Wynerria was the grandest celebration of the year. Bonfires burned in every cavern, in giant ironwood hearths so the Great Tree would not be harmed. Stories were told, paintings were crafted, and music was shared by all. At the height of festivities, a Golden Wreath—still plentiful in our forests—was cast into the flames as an emblem of Dagda's ever-bright splendor."

"And does this celebration still happen?"

"Only in a burned-out ember of itself, I fear. Today, our numbers have declined, so much that only this miserable little village is left. Instead of the great celebration we once had, all that remains are meaningless rituals. And since the last Golden Wreath disappeared, some villagers—let by that fool, Ciann, who attacked you—have taken to burning living creatures as a sacrifice to Dagda. So the whole meaning of the day has been utterly lost. The Dagda I believe in wants life, not death, to honor him! We have gone from fire angels . . . to fallen angels."

Tamwyn swallowed, but he could no longer taste the sweetness of his magical water. The smell of charcoal in this hut seemed to grow stronger. "So they wanted to use me as the sacrifice."

Glumly, Gwirion nodded. "That is why you must leave as soon as you are well enough to walk. Before the holy day, in any case. The nearer to that day we get, the more dangerous for you. If Ciann and his allies are in a frenzy for sacrifice, I probably won't be able to hold them off again—not even with the help of my wife and sister."

He glanced at the door. "They should be returning very soon, by the way, with the supplies that we need."

"Good. I look forward to meeting them when I'm not fighting for my life."

Tamwyn's gaze moved slowly around the blackened walls of the room, coming to rest on the picture of Ogallad aflame. For some time he examined the Golden Wreath that Ogallad wore upon his head. At last, he said, "Mistletoe. It looks like mistletoe."

Seeing Gwirion's puzzled expression, he explained, "A plant that grows in my homeland. I've seen it often in the wilderness. People sometimes call it *the golden bough*. And our bards will tell you that, back in the days of Avalon's birth, those golden leaves were believed to hold some sort of special power. Though what that power might have been has long been forgotten."

His friend smiled sadly. "It is always a kind of death when a story is forgotten. But I am glad to know that those leaves still grow somewhere."

Tamwyn tapped the warm skin of the man's forearm. "So tell me, Gwirion. What kind of work do you do? Are you, too, an explorer?"

"No, human son. I am an artist—a storypainter, as we say. Mostly I do not paint new murals, but just restore the old ones. They are everywhere in the Middle Realm, in tunnels carved by water, gnawed by termites, or opened by the flows of élano."

"I saw one," Tamwyn recalled, his voice full of wonder. "In a tunnel lower down, near the cascades. It was so full of life, and colors."

"And stories." Gwirion waved at his shelf of paint pots and

brushes. "I was out looking for some leaves of the *fomorra* plant, which I need for all my blues and purples, when those giant termites attacked me." He turned back to Tamwyn. "And if you hadn't appeared, that would have been the end of my story."

"Gwirion, do your people have any stories about the stars? About what they really are? Why they burn . . . or sometimes go dark?"

"No," he said solemnly. "Though I have often wished we did. I think those tales—those times—are just too far away. They have passed out of our minds, I fear, because we can no longer understand them. And how can we tell stories if we have not the words? How can we paint them if we have forgotten the colors?"

Gwirion's gaze moved to the charred picture on the wall. "Stories are a people's memories, you see. They can be disturbing, encouraging, and sometimes . . . inspiring. They hold all our losses, gains, sufferings, glories, and longings. But before we can have the story, we must have the meaning."

"I understand," agreed Tamwyn. "Stories are like a mirror we hold up to ourselves."

"That's right. But they are more than just the mirror, and the image we see in it. They are also whatever invisible truth lies behind."

Tamwyn squeezed Gwirion's arm. "I am glad we met, you and I."

The bark-skinned man grinned. "In gladder times, I would have considered it a sign of forgiveness from Dagda." Then, as quick as a torch blown out by the wind, the grin disappeared. "But the sign we really need is a Golden Wreath."

He looked glumly at his companion. "There is one more part of Mananaun's prophecy, something I didn't tell you before. She said that we will know our time of rebirth has truly arrived when a Golden Wreath suddenly appears."

"Just like that?"

"Yes. It will appear, she said, not in the lands around our village, as in days of old—but magically, on the door of one person's home. And that person will be the new leader of our fallen people, the one to lead us back into the firelight. In other words—the next Ogallad."

Tamwyn glanced up at the picture. "It could happen, I suppose."

"No, my friend. As much as I wish that were so, my people have fallen too far."

"But it's possible."

"No, it is not." Gwirion's wide mouth turned down. "By the Thousand Flames, it is not."

27 • Gwirion's Gift

OVER THE NEXT SEVERAL DAYS, GWIRION DID whatever he could to help Tamwyn heal. For time was disappearing faster than a candle's dying flame.

Aided by his wife, Tulchinne, and his sister, Fraitha, the bark-skinned man worked hard to bind wounds and stem infections. All this was made more difficult by how deeply the termite's pincers had penetrated Tamwyn's hip, and how badly the muscles and skin had been torn. But after plenty of bandages, repeated cleansings, and many hearty meals of *lauva*—a creamy, charred grain spiced with something like nutmeg that Tulchinne served in an ironwood bowl—Tamwyn's strength began to return.

"I do love this stuff," he mumbled, his mouth full of lauva, from his resting place on the floor. This was the third bowl he had downed that morning. "It's the best porridge I've ever tasted."

"But of course, Tamwyn," answered Fraitha. She was seated at the table, repairing a hole in her shawl with some sturdy red threads of a vine called *hurlyen*. "It was made by my sister-in-law, famous for her cooking throughout the Middle Realm."

Tulchinne looked up from where she was kneeling, near

Gwirion's shelf of paint pots, grinding grain with her mortar and pestle. "Don't be absurd! If I'm famous for my cooking, it's just in this little hut. And only then because you hate to cook, and Gwirion doesn't know a jar of spice from a den of mice."

Gwirion, who was whistling softly as he mixed some dark green paint at the table, didn't respond.

Fraitha, however, burst out laughing. The sound reminded Tamwyn of resins popping in a fire. Then she turned her head—which was, like those of all her people, completely hairless—toward their human guest. "You do seem stronger, Tamwyn."

"Hungrier, anyway," he replied as he shoveled some more lauva into his mouth.

"That's a start," commented Tulchinne. She paused in her work long enough to draw her own shawl higher on her shoulders. As the traditional garb of Ayanowyn women, the heavy shawls helped to retain their body heat. This one covered Tulchinne's back as well as her crumpled wings.

Gwirion abruptly stopped whistling. "You'll need to do better than that, Tamwyn." His voice, like his expression, was grim. In that moment he looked almost as stern as the tile picture of Ogallad on the wall behind him. "We're running out of time."

Tamwyn set down his food. His own face turned grim, for he knew that he was also losing valuable time on his quest. *My ultimate triumph*, the vision of Rhita Gawr had boasted, *is but a few weeks away*. However many more days he'd need before he was well enough to walk again, it was too many!

"I'll try standing on my own today," he announced to them all. "Really, I think I'm strong enough."

"Good," replied Gwirion. "Then tomorrow, if you're able, you can begin walking around."

"Outside?" asked Tamwyn, motioning toward the door of the hut.

"No, my friend." Gwirion's scowl deepened. "Why risk enraging Ciann and his followers any more than they already are?"

Reluctantly, Tamwyn nodded. Even now, he could hear the sounds of people chanting and drums pounding beyond the door. As the high holy day approached, the village was growing increasingly restless.

"I must try again to talk with Ciann," declared Gwirion with resolve. "To convince him that his whole way of thinking is wrong. And that you are not just some beast to be sacrificed, but a friend to be helped on your way."

"Good luck trying," said Tulchinne skeptically. "That fellow has about as much brains as an empty bowl! And you, my good husband, haven't much more if you really think your plan will work."

Gwirion squinted at her and said testily, "So, my good wife, do you have a better one?"

"No," she snapped. "But at least I know enough to understand we need one."

At the table, Gwirion's expression softened. "You're right, you know." With a teasing edge, he added, "As always."

Tulchinne grinned, even as she continued to grind some more grain. "You hear that, Tamwyn? That simple truth is why we've been able to stay married as long as we have."

"And how long is that?" asked Tamwyn.

"Thirty-eight years," she replied. Then, with a glance at her husband, she added, "Though at times it feels more like fifty."

"Or five hundred," grumbled Gwirion. Then, to Tamwyn's surprise, he beamed at Tulchinne. And even more surprisingly, she smiled back.

Seeing the two of them spar so good-naturedly made Tamwyn think about his own relationship with Elli. Could they, someday, learn to get along that well?

"Gwirion," he asked impulsively, "how do you two really make it work? Thirty-eight years is a long time."

The winged man replied, but in a voice that could have been serious—or then again, could have been joking. "It's easy, really. I like to whistle, and she likes to cook. So we each provide some form of enjoyment for the other."

Tamwyn nodded, thinking that this could indeed be a valuable notion.

Then Tulchinne shook her head. "It's not that simple, though. What he didn't tell you is that I have always loved the music of whistling, but whenever I try to do it . . ." She winced. "Small birds drop dead at our doorstep."

Gwirion laughed. "And for my part, I dearly love to smell things cooking, and certainly like to fill myself with food. But hard as I try, I just can't cook."

Tamwyn chuckled at the irony of this. "So you fill each other's gaps, like two pieces of dovetailed woodwork." Then, with a bemused look, he asked, "Why can't you cook?"

"Too stupid," teased Tulchinne before her husband could answer.

"That," agreed Gwirion, "plus something else. Something I did as a child. You see," he confessed, "I tried to eat some burning coals, to make my soulfire burn brighter. What a thing to do! I permanently scarred my tongue and throat. And while the experience left me wiser, I suppose, it also ruined my sense of taste."

His deep brown eyes studied Tamwyn. "So in the end, there

is really not much I can tell you about relationships. Except that staying together, grand as it can be, isn't always easy."

With a scowl, the young man replied, "That much I already know."

For the rest of that day, Tamwyn practiced standing without support, pushing himself as hard as he could. Finally, he succeeded. Though he managed to stand only a few minutes, it was, as Tulchinne had said, a start. And after that, he improved swiftly. By the end of the following day, he was limping clumsily around the charred floor of the hut.

"Just wait until Gwirion sees you walking," said Tulchinne, sounding both anxious and relieved. She added a sprinkle of crushed ginger to the salad she was preparing at the table. "He'll be back soon from that folly of trying to make Ciann understand. And ready at last to make some other plans."

Tamwyn leaned against the wall, resting, "I'm ready, too."

"None too soon," said Fraitha, putting down the amber flute she had been playing. "The high holy day is tomorrow."

Just then, Gwirion strode in. He shut the door behind him with a resounding slam. "Curse them," he grumbled. Then, turning to Tulchinne, he lamented, "You were right, yet again. The rituals begin at dawn."

"Including," Tamwyn asked gravely, "the sacrifice?"

"Yes. And Ciann even told me, in that sneering way of his, that he'd stop by here tomorrow before dawn. *To fetch something valuable*, as he put it."

"That moron!" exclaimed Fraitha.

"Soon to be a murderer," added Tulchinne, "if we don't find some way to stop him."

Gwirion rubbed the shaggy skin of his brow. "Here we are, on the very night before Wynerria, living in fear of our own people! Why can't they understand that sacrifices just confirm our unworthiness in the eyes of Dagda? Instead of new stories to tell, we offer only anger and ignorance."

"Gwirion," said Tamwyn, "I can walk on my own now! Right after you left, I started." To prove his point, he stepped awkwardly over to the other side of the hut.

The rich brown eyes widened. "Then you must leave tonight! Just before dawn, when the élanolight out there is dimmest."

"No," Tamwyn objected. With a grimace, he bent his stiff left leg. "They will be expecting that. Instead, I will leave now—while most of them are eating supper. Catch them unprepared, maybe."

Gwirion scrutinized him. "It just might work. But are you sure you can walk well enough?"

"No. But it's worth a try."

"Then I'm coming with you. To show you the way to escape from the cavern that holds our village. And, if necessary, to fight off Ciann."

"All right," Tamwyn agreed. "But I wish you—"

"Wait," commanded Tulchinne, rising from her seat at the ironwood table. "This is foolish! There are probably guards outside, even now. You'll both be caught."

"There's no other way," answered Gwirion.

"But there is!" she insisted. Stepping over to a hook on the wall, she grabbed the shawl, one of her spares, that was hanging there. Woven of heavy vine threads, it rustled as it moved. She carried the shawl over to Tamwyn and threw it over his shoulders.

"Here," she declared. "Wear this. Now, hunch down a bit, so

you're not so tall. And when you go outside, pull it up over your head so that none of your hair will show. In the dark out there, those ruffians will think you are Fraitha or myself! Avalon knows, they've seen us going in and out of here often enough."

"It won't work," objected Gwirion.

"But it will!" Tulchinne faced him squarely. "At least it might. And that is better than your plan, which is as sure to fail as a bard without a tongue."

Gwirion ruffled his wings and looked over at Tamwyn. "It is up to you, my friend."

He nodded. "I'll go with Tulchinne's plan." Turning back to her, he raised an eyebrow. "You know, maybe you really *are* always right."

She didn't smile. "We shall see, if you actually manage to escape."

"Indeed." Gwirion walked over to join them. He put his hand on Tamwyn's shoulder. "Are you sure? At least, if I come with you, I could hold them off while you get away."

Tamwyn's long black hair brushed against his shoulders as he shook his head. "No, this way is better. With my leg like this, I couldn't outrun anybody who chased me. My best hope for escape is to be disguised. And alone."

Gwirion sighed. "All right, then. But if you meet any trouble, you must shout your loudest. I will sprint to your side."

"As will I," declared Tulchinne.

"And I," added Fraitha.

"I know you will. Now, where do I need to go?"

"To the place we call *Amon Holm*, which means, in your tongue, *Secret Stairway*."

Tamwyn groaned. "I won't be very good on stairs."

"Never mind that," continued Gwirion, a strange gleam in his eye. "It is the only passage in or out of our village that isn't patrolled. Here is what you must do to find it: Go out this door and turn left. Cross through the village, to the hill that rises steeply all the way up to the cavern wall. Climb it. But be careful of the thorn bushes, which are everywhere—and savagely barbed. Right at the very top, where you think you cannot go higher, there is a black stalagmite. Push against it and you will find the Stairway."

"Where does it lead?"

Gwirion's eyes lifted toward the smoke-blackened ceiling. "Up, up, and up. You must take it as high as you can go, to a place we call *Nuada Ildana*, or Window to the Stars. That is an actual opening in the trunk—where the stars, not élano, are the source of light." He paused, searching for a better way to describe it. "In your world, you might call it a great knothole."

Tamwyn caught his breath. Merlin's Knothole! So this Stairway was the steeply rising pathway he'd seen in the wall painting!

"It is a remarkable place," Gwirion went on, "the highest point in the Middle Realm. Mind you, it is a long climb up to the Knothole—whether you go by the Stairway, or some other way such as the Spiral Cascades. After all, you are climbing through the very trunk of the Great Tree! But once you arrive there, you can leave the inside of the trunk and stand out on the surface, for in that place the Tree bulges outward in a great burl that holds the valley of the Knothole. And Tamwyn . . . from Nuada Ildana you can actually see the branches! Possibly even climb to them. And beyond—to the stars."

He drew a deep breath. "One more thing you should know. This was also the route chosen by your father."

Even as he finished speaking, someone passing by the hut

shouted a string of angry epithets. Tamwyn couldn't catch the words, but the feeling behind them was unmistakable.

Gwirion's strong hand, warm as a fire coal, squeezed his shoulder. "Before you go, I have a gift for you."

"You have given me enough already."

"No, not nearly."

Rustling his wings, he strode over to his shelf of paint pots and picked up the small brown box that rested there. Opening it, he moved aside some glittering crystals of wood—red cedar, black ebony, silver-green willow, and others—to retrieve a vial, no bigger than the quartz bell on Tamwyn's hip. Carved of ironwood, the vial looked unbreakable.

Gwirion held it to his ear and gave it a shake. "Still there," he declared. Then, stepping back across the room, he put the vial into Tamwyn's hand.

"Take care of this," he whispered. "It holds a single drop of a precious liquid, what we call *Dagda's dew*. My father's father, one of the last of our people who could still fly, brought this back from a journey up into the branches."

He glanced at his wife and sister, who nodded in turn, then looked at Tamwyn. "It is said that a single drop of Dagda's dew, placed on your forehead, will give you a rare sort of sight."

Tamwyn squeezed the vial in his palm. "What sort?"

"Long vision—over vast distances." Gwirion gave him a hopeful look. "It only lasts a while, if its powers have not faded. But it might be useful to you on your way to the stars."

Their gazes locked. It seemed that a line of clear light stretched between them, reaching across the smoky air of the room, and the far greater gap between two very different peoples. Finally, Tamwyn spoke.

"Thank you, Gwirion."

"My friend, you are welcome. May your story be long and glorious! Now . . . just try to survive tonight."

"And you, tomorrow."

Tamwyn limped over to his pack and pushed the vial down inside. He heard the crinkle of his father's scroll, which only hardened his determination. Then, grasping the tooth-marked strap, he put it on. It took a moment, and some help from Tulchinne, to cover both his head and the pack with the shawl, but finally he was ready. He grabbed his staff and hobbled over to the door.

With a final look back at his friends, he slipped out into the night.

28 · Death Is Near

WEARING THE HEAVY SHAWL, TAMWYN stepped out Gwirion's door. His night vision improved after just a few steps—enough that he could clearly see two men standing opposite the door, on the other side of a dirt pathway. Grumpily, they eyed him, their shaggy-skinned faces scowling. Then, to his relief, they shrugged and went back to eating sticks of dried meat. He drew up the shawl, making sure that his head and long hair were completely covered. And then he moved off as quickly as he could, not daring to look back.

Although the village lay in shadow, he could make out the shapes of other tile huts, as well as some larger structures that could have been stables, taverns, and traders' posts. More dirt pathways ran in jagged lines between the buildings. And scattered throughout the settlement, enormous stalagmites towered like cylindrical trees, rising twenty or thirty times his own height.

He glanced up at the cavern's ceiling, so far away that it seemed like a rough-hewn sky. But this sky had no stars. Like the giant stalagmites, it glowed with the faintly green luminescence of élano.

He thought back to what Gwirion had said about this

élanolight—that it dimmed at night and brightened again at dawn. *Just like the stars*, he mused. Did the Great Tree and its mysterious flows of élano cause that to happen, or was it somehow connected to the stars themselves?

Yet as he limped along one of the pathways, Tamwyn knew that the dim light alone couldn't explain how well he was seeing. *No doubt about it*, he thought, pausing to avoid stepping on a cricket, *my night vision is stronger than before*.

He wondered why. Was it his powers, continuing to expand? Or just something about this cavern?

He nodded to himself, for he knew in his heart that this was yet another aspect of his growing powers. He still knew so little about them, yet he feared them less than he once did. Ever since they'd helped to save Scree, those strange, undefined forces down inside himself had felt less like enemies and more like . . . well, unfamiliar allies. Would he ever truly learn to master them?

He halted, hunching over with the shawl drawn tight, as a group of people bustled by, their arms loaded with putrid-smelling dung, as well as some scraggly bushes that had been pulled out by the roots. Fuel, no doubt, for the morning's bonfire.

Tamwyn remained hunched and motionless, trying his best to look like a villager, as the group passed. They didn't seem to notice him—until, at the last, an old man slowed down and stared at him. His gray eyes widened suspiciously. After a few seconds, he continued on his way. But there was a look on his face that left Tamwyn feeling uneasy.

I've got to get to that Stairway. And fast.

He shuffled along, trying not to limp too visibly. Another group of five or six people passed him, chanting vigorously. One of them pounded on a hide drum as he marched. Tamwyn heard one particular chant over and over:

> *Death is near,*
> *So is flight.*
> *Flames appear!*
> *End this night.*

Turning a corner by some sort of pottery works, where stacks of bowls and tiles rested by outdoor kilns, Tamwyn found himself facing a steep hill. Rough, granular dirt covered it, along with twisted bushes with thousands of murderous thorns. In the dim glow of élano, the thorny hill looked haunted as well as dangerous.

It's not many places that make me wish I wore boots, he thought, rubbing one of his callused feet into the dirt. *But that hill is one of them. Even a deer would have trouble avoiding all those thorns.*

His thoughts leaped, as swiftly as a stag, to the thrill of running like a deer. Now, *there* was a kind of magic that hadn't been troublesome to master! Maybe because running freely had always been so natural to him, he hadn't resisted the power to shift into a deer. Or confused that power with too much thinking. In any case, if his hip hadn't been hurt so badly, he could try to summon the magic of a deer right now, and bound up this—

A shout from behind halted his thoughts. "There!" someone cried. "On the hill."

"Don't let him get away," a hoarse voice bellowed. "Could be the outsider we're going to sacrifice!"

"Run!"

Tamwyn bolted onto the hillside. He remembered well what

Gwirion had said: The entrance to the Stairway was all the way at the top. Could he make it before they caught him?

He scrambled up the slope, climbing awkwardly but steadily, despite the thorns that tore at his leggings. All of a sudden his left leg buckled beneath him. He sprawled on the ground, rolling in the dirt like a loose pebble. When at last he stopped, his mind kept on spinning.

Fiery hot tongs of pain squeezed his sore hip, burning muscle and bone. But there wasn't time to tend to that now. He wiped the dirt out of his eyes and fought to get up again, using his staff as an extra leg. Despite the pain and the remnant dizziness, he kept climbing.

Three dark figures reached the base of the hill below him. One of them pointed. Shouts rang out.

Tamwyn hopped over the snaking branch of a thorn bush. His feet slid on the loose dirt, making every step a hurdle. Even without his injury, and in daylight, this slope would have been difficult to surmount.

He could hear, behind him, his pursuers' angry shouts. Getting closer! They were gaining fast.

Sweat streamed down his brow, stinging his eyes. Ahead, an especially large cluster of murderous-looking thornbushes blocked his path: There must have been seven or eight of them intertwined. Jabbing his staff into the ground, he swerved to climb around them.

Just as he crossed uphill of the cluster, he stepped on a slab of packed dirt. With a sudden grinding sound, it broke loose. He slammed to the ground, hitting his knee as well as his head. Dirt sprayed into the air as he slid backward—right into the cluster of thorns.

Finally, his body stopped. He lay on his back, panting, staring up into a deadly jungle. Jagged points dug into his skin, raked his arms, and tore his clothes. One monstrous, barbed thorn, as big as a dagger blade, was directly above his face, aimed right at his eye.

It took all his strength of will not to cry out, for that would tell his pursuers exactly where he was. Bad enough that he was stabbed, bruised, and pinned so tight that he could barely move. Or even breathe.

Just then he heard the winged men struggling up the slope. They'd reached the cluster of bushes! Judging by their wheezing and cursing, they weren't very pleased with their situation—or their prey. Tamwyn held his breath and watched them from the corner of his eye.

"By the bard Helvin's ghost, where did he go?"

"Fell down a pit, mayhaps."

"No, he was just here, I tell you! I saw him clear as—"

"Night. Mayhaps he really was a ghost."

"Look! Would a ghost wear this?"

To Tamwyn's horror, one of the winged men picked up his shawl. It must have come off when he'd fallen, just before he slid backward into the bushes! The fellow held it up, scanning the slope for any sign of its wearer. His companions did the same, their ragged wings opening and closing as they searched. One of them, Tamwyn felt sure, looked straight at him for several endless seconds.

Finally, the man cast the shawl aside. "Bah! If he did tumble down a pit, that would be the last of his story. Just what he deserves, I say."

"Right. Call it an early sacrifice."

"Are you sure you really saw him? Could have been that ale."

"I saw him, all right! But some more ale would taste good right now."

"Plenty good."

With that, the trio turned to go. They trampled down the hillside, their harsh voices fading into the night.

Tamwyn sighed in relief. He had escaped! Now all he had to do was wriggle out of this maze of thorns without slicing himself to bits. Which wouldn't be easy.

Slowly, carefully, he turned onto his right side. He started to squirm—when suddenly he glimpsed something astonishing. He froze. And then he blinked, making sure that he wasn't just imagining it.

But no, it was there! Wrapped around a branch deep inside the maze of thorns. Impossible to see, except from this angle.

Mistletoe. The small, shiny leaves shone like burnished gold even in such dim light.

Twisting his body, Tamwyn stretched out one arm as far as he could. There! He wrapped his fingers around the golden bough and gently pulled it free from the thorns. Then, oblivious to the additional pokes and scrapes on his arm, shoulder, and neck, he drew it to himself. And wriggled out of the cluster of bushes.

He sat there, streaked with blood, but glad beyond words. Light from the cavern's ceiling filtered down, faintly illuminating his body—and the prize he held in his hands. For a long moment he studied the leaves in admiration, curling them around his forearm. At last, he nodded.

For he knew exactly what he was going to do with this radiant bough.

•   •   •

It took more than two hours for Tamwyn to make his way back down the hillside, his head and pack covered with the shawl. Much of that time he'd spent huddled, motionless, in dark corners of the village, avoiding the roaming bands of chanters. As well as the drunkards. And he must have tripped half a dozen times, owing to his injured hip. Even now, it throbbed painfully.

Yet that did not concern him. For he stood, at last, at his destination—just outside the door to Gwirion's humble home.

He waited until there were no passersby, and no people lurking in the shadows. Then, as quietly as the breaking light of dawn, he stepped over to the door. Gently, he removed a sprig of dried herbs that was hanging from a hook. In its place on the door, he hung the circular wreath that he had made from the mistletoe.

A Golden Wreath. Just as Mananaun had prophesied, these villagers—all that remained of a once-magnificent people known as fire angels—would now have a new leader.

A new beginning.

And perhaps, a new destiny.

Good luck, my friend, he thought as he stepped back from the door. *May you someday burn as bright as the stars.*

Tamwyn limped back into the shadows. Without another look back, he started once again on his trek.

29 · The New Age to Come

LYNIA STUDIED THE PRISONERS ARRAYED before her. And the many spear-wielding gnomes who stood around them, filling the central chamber of the ancient temple. Her face, pale in the milky light shining through the ceiling of translucent quartz, showed the hint of a grin. With the composure of someone who could command the present, and also discern the future, she ran her fingers through her straight blonde hair.

Still savoring the reactions of Elli and Lleu, her former colleagues at the Society of the Whole, she was in no hurry to speak. After all, she was Llynia the Seer, as Hanwan Belamir had dubbed her. And this wretched group before her—who were they, really? Nothing but gnomes in human guise, closer to mosquitoes than to herself. Her grin broadened ever so slightly: Mosquitoes deserved to be swatted.

Calmly, she adjusted the band holding a deep red ruby that sat upon her brow. Then, with an air of thoughtfulness, she rubbed her green-stained chin. At last she spoke.

"You don't look well, my young apprentice. No, not well at all."

"How can I be well if I'm your captive? Let us go this instant!"

Llynia leaned forward on the throne, her own glare locked with Elli's, staring so intensely that she didn't even notice the amulet of leaves around the younger woman's neck. Then, forcing her voice to sound calm, she said, "It is not for you to give orders, young apprentice."

"I am not your apprentice!" Elli took a step forward, stopping only at the points of spears that pushed against her chest. "You are a disgrace to the Society."

"Possibly so," Llynia replied, leaning back in her throne. She fingered the clasp, shaped like an oak tree, on the collar of her robe. "But to be disgraced by an obsolete sect is actually a form of honor." She sighed ruefully. "You, however—*you* are a disgrace of the worst sort. A disgrace to your own kind! To humanity, the creatures made in the true image of Dagda and Lorilanda."

"Who taught you that, Llynia?" demanded Lleu, his hands on the hips of his Drumadian robe. "Your new mentor, Belamir?"

Even in the milky light, her face darkened. The green patch on her chin looked more than ever like a beard. "Why yes, Hanwan has taught me much. Including," she spat, "the worthlessness of those such as you, who cling blindly to the old ways."

"And what are the *new* ways?" he shot back. "Are they anything more than the comforting certainty of your own arrogance? And the unending tug of your own greed?"

Her fingers gripped the arms of the throne, squeezing tightly. "Humans are the greatest of mortal creatures! Some, though, refuse to accept that fact. For with the blessing of our many gifts comes a responsibility—to *care* for our world, and help its lesser creatures."

Nuic, whose scarlet color didn't seem the least bit dimmed by the temple, coughed as if he was choking. He squirmed in Elli's arms, turning the Galator toward his back where it wouldn't be seen. Then, his voice as sharp as the gnomes' spears, he declared: "You mean to *devour* our world, and enslave other creatures."

"I mean nothing of the kind!" Llynia's outburst echoed within the quartz walls. "Don't you understand that we have the wisdom and power to remake the world?"

Lleu's dark eyebrows drew together. "Like you remade the compound?"

She looked, for the first time, uncertain. "What do you mean?"

"It's all been destroyed! And with it, the life of Coerria."

Llynia seemed to wince. "I know nothing of this." Suddenly her expression hardened. "You are lying! Trying to trick me into straying from the path. If such a thing really were to happen, I'd have seen it in a vision. And besides," she added coldly, "Coerria's time is past, even as the old order is past."

"But—"

"But nothing! This is the time of Humanity First. The rise of an age when humans will, at last, leave their mark everywhere in Avalon."

Lleu frowned. "Can't you see, Llynia, that it sometimes takes far greater wisdom to leave no mark at all? That it gives us far greater power, in the end, to honor all forms of life as much as our own?"

"You are mad not to understand! Animals, birds, fish in the seas—they are our children, to be led. Our underlings, to be commanded. And sometimes our foes, to be destroyed. But *never*, despite all those misguided teachings of Elen and Rhia, our equals."

Again Elli spoke up. Her voice remained quiet, barely more than a whisper. But her words seemed to swell, filling the whole temple. "Can we glow like the light flyer? Tell me. Sing like the meadowlark? Tell me. Or leap like the antelope? And tell me this, as well: Can we listen to the language of trees, as can the elves? Swim for days in the darkest depths of the sea, as do the mer people? Or fly higher than the clouds, like the eaglefolk?"

Ignoring Llynia's prolonged, contemptuous yawn, Elli continued, her voice still quiet, yet no less ringing. Where the words came from, she had no idea. She only knew that they came.

"Those creatures I named—and all the others—they're not just our equals. They are our sisters and brothers, our fellow journeyers, borne by the same uncertain winds of choice and chance. They share our mortal longings, our triumphs and tragedies. They deserve, no less than we do, to live and breathe and grow before they die."

As she spoke, Nuic continued to glare at the woman on the throne. But his colors melted into blues and greens. And the maryth's tiny hand reached out to touch the back of Elli's wrist.

"How lovely," said Llynia, patting her open mouth. "You speak, perhaps, of the past. Yet I, with the gift of visions, speak of the future."

"And just what future do you see?" demanded Lleu, pushing a spearhead away from his face.

The priestess relaxed into her throne. "At Hanwan's request, I came here two weeks ago, to offer the gnomes a chance to survive in the new age to come. To serve, while we reshape Avalon, as our helpers."

"As your mercenaries," grumbled Nuic.

"Helpers," repeated Llynia. "Of course, gnomes being gnomes, I had to offer them payment."

"Spoils of war," corrected Nuic. "So here you are, bartering with the very same creatures you once said you detested."

"All for a higher cause." Her face twisted into a sly smile. "Unlike you, though, I will soon be leaving this forgettable land. I would have gone yesterday, in fact, the alliance having been forged. Then came my vision of your imminent arrival in this ruined temple of some lost religion—whose fate, I should add, was rather like the one that will soon befall the Society of the Whole."

"And everyone else, too!" Elli stepped forward, her voice quaking with passion. "I know you hate me, Llynia. But you've got to listen. *Rhita Gawr is here in Avalon.* It's true! He's planning to conquer Avalon—and other worlds, too. Soon! In just—"

"Wait," commanded the priestess, taken aback. "Rhita Gawr? Here?"

"Yes."

Llynia leaned forward, looking more skeptical by the second. "Where did you ever hear such a thing?"

"A vision. Almost two weeks ago, on top of Hallia's Peak. It came to—"

"A vision?" scoffed Llynia, her face reddening. "Came to *you*?"

"It's true," insisted Elli. "And not just me. Others saw it, too! Even . . . the Lady."

The mere mention of the Lady of the Lake, whose rejection still smarted, made Llynia's face flush even more. "How dare you try to tell me about visions? Me—a true seer! How dare you try to tell me *anything*, you impudent whelp?"

"Llynia," pleaded Elli. "You must listen."

"I must do nothing!" she snarled. "Our conversation is *finished*, apprentice."

Elli glared at her, eyes aflame.

Llynia raised her hand and made a harsh, guttural sound that called all the gnomes to attention. Then, speaking slowly in the Common Tongue, she told them to take the prisoners to the underground chamber. And to keep the prisoners alive, at least as long as they caused no trouble. Although they seemed disappointed at the second part of the command, the gnomes grunted their approval. Outside the temple, monkeys chattered raucously in the jungle—but their voices seemed melodic compared to the gnomes'.

Throughout all this, the jester gnashed his teeth, considering his options. He could, of course, kill the girl, the irksome priest, and probably a few gnomes, in short order. What would that gain him, though? Even for a killer as accomplished as himself, there were simply too many of these three-fingered toads for him to get away alive. And with the crystals.

Curse that flawed portal! he thought. Everything had been going so well until then. Why, he'd even guessed correctly that the Lady had sent them to the highlord of the water dragons, to learn the whereabouts of Kulwych's crystal. Which would, before he was through, belong not to Kulwych, but to himself.

His fingers tapped against the shaft of his cane—a slow, menacing rhythm. Control. He had to regain control. That was what he loved most about this business, after all, right down to the ultimate control of another person's life. Or death. Nothing was more exhilarating than that!

For now, though, he'd have to wait. To bide his time. And to wait for the moment of weakness, of vulnerability, that always came. And then . . . he would strike.

At that moment, a sharp spearpoint poked him hard in the back. He whirled around to see a particularly scarred gnome, urging him to start walking. The other prisoners had already begun to move out of the chamber. Narrowing his eyes, Deth Macoll said to himself, *I'll go, you toad. But I'll see you again before we're through. That's a promise.*

Elli, who was at the front of the group, suddenly stopped. Despite the snarls and grunts of the gnomes around her, and their angry shoves, she held her ground and turned back to Llynia. The priestess was watching from her throne, satisfaction written all over her pallid face.

"Wait," demanded Elli. "What was that you said about a new age to come? What exactly did you mean?"

Llynia growled some sort of command, and the gnomes' shoving ceased. "I suppose," she said in a leisurely tone, "it would do no harm for you to know about it. For unlike your so-called vision, this truly *is* coming. And soon."

She made a mocking frown. "So sorry to tell you, though, since you will feel no end of torment. You see, there will soon be a terrible battle, a battle that will determine the fate of Avalon. And I fear that many of your dear friends will have to die."

Elli, Lleu, and Brionna all gasped. Catha whistled uncertainly, while Nuic went completely black. Only Shim, who hadn't heard a word of what she'd said, and the jester, preoccupied with his thoughts, showed no reaction.

Llynia continued, fingering her clasp. "Two opposing armies will soon start to gather, on the Plains of Isenwy south of here.

One of them," she said disdainfully, "is a ragtag assembly of creatures—well, come to think of it, creatures like *you*. Led by elves from El Urien, no doubt, since they have always had the audacity to consider themselves equal to humans."

She paused to savor Brionna's glare, then went on. "The elves, I am sure, have picked up a few recruits among humans—reactionary villagers, faith-blinded priests, and the like. My guess is that a few old allies from the War of Storms will join them, as well, such as eaglefolk, dwarves, and perhaps one or two others."

She couldn't suppress a satisfied chortle. "The other group—not really an army but a peacekeeping force—will have even more humans, those open to the teachings of Hanwan Belamir. And joining them will be many other peace-loving creatures."

"Such as gnomes and gobsken, no doubt," said Nuic acidly.

"Perhaps," Llynia replied, with a wave of her hand. "But they are welcome only because they can help the higher cause."

"Which is?" asked Lleu.

"Peace. Harmony. Freedom. All of which can only be attained, and preserved over time, if humanity takes charge."

Elli snorted. "And for that to happen you need a war? A massacre, maybe? Llynia, just listen to yourself! You were once a priestess, for Avalon's sake!"

"Yes," she replied grimly. "For Avalon's sake." She leaned forward on the throne, peering straight at Elli. "And that is why, despite the likes of you—whose every breath mocks the special role of humanity—I have insisted to Hanwan that before the great battle begins, mercy must prevail. All the defenders of the old order will be given a chance to surrender. To lay down their weapons and walk hand in hand with humanity into a bright new future."

Brionna bristled. "Or die."

Llynia sighed with genuine regret. "If necessary. Hanwan and I hope dearly that it will not come to that." She scratched the dark patch on her chin, pondering. "But if that is what it takes to remake our world, then so be it."

The prisoners traded glances—part outrage, part grief, part helplessness. Just as Llynia started to speak again, Nuic's caustic voice cut her off.

"Congratulations, Lady Greenbeard. In no time at all, you've become a tyrant of gnomes, an ally of gobsken, and—though you refuse to see it—a servant of Rhita Gawr. That takes rare talent."

Even in the milky light of the temple, her cheeks turned as red as a ripe apple. Before she could respond, though, Elli asked a question.

"Where is your maryth, Fairlyn? She always loved you, protected you with her own branches, and filled your days with wonderful smells. So where is she now?"

For the first time since they had arrived here, Llynia's gaze faltered. The change was nearly imperceptible, but Elli noticed. She guessed that Llynia had been wounded, not just by her words, but by some deeper loss.

"She left you, didn't she?" Elli raised her voice, driving her point home. "She just couldn't take what you've become."

Llynia's wrathful glare returned. "Gnomes," she barked. "Take them away. Right now!"

30 · Hidden Blood

THUD.

The heavy bar that blocked the entrance to the underground chamber slammed down. Seconds before, Elli had turned away from the door—just as the last three-fingered hands had pushed Shim through. The little fellow had stumbled and fallen against one of the granite walls. Right now, he was rubbing his sore shoulder, muttering to himself. Brionna, who looked equally glum, sat beside him, leaning against the wall.

A dungeon, Elli thought as she gazed around the cold, dank room. It felt like the inside of someone's grave. *Maybe whoever built this place used it to keep people about to be sacrificed. Or people, like me, who just couldn't stay out of trouble.*

She slapped her thigh as she paced across the room, still holding Nuic. How foolish she'd been to have veered from her quest! She'd only managed to make everything worse.

And yet now, at least, she knew some valuable information about the coming battle—thanks to that sorry excuse for a priestess. But what good was information if she and her friends were just going to rot here in this dungeon?

Indeed, as she could see, there could be no escape from this place. It had no other entrance and no apparent weaknesses, just four stone walls and a stone floor, with no cracks in any of the slabs. A small air vent, set with granite bars, opened in the ceiling, which allowed a single shaft of light to drift down from the temple above. A little more light came from the circular window that had been bored through the door. Just outside, two savage-looking gnomes sat on a stone bench, drinking something that smelled like rancid beer.

Elli grumbled aloud, "How could Llynia not listen to me? Why can't she see that she's just being used by White Hands and Rhita Gawr?"

"Arrogance," answered Lleu, who was leaning against a wall, arms folded across his chest. "That age-old human trait."

Elli just nodded, feeling heavier than just Nuic's weight could explain. With a groan, she flopped down beside Brionna. Her head tilted back, resting against the stone wall—her pillow, she knew, at least for a while.

Maybe a very, very long while.

"Hmmmpff. Don't expect me to say anything helpful or encouraging," grumbled Nuic from her lap. "It's just not my nature."

Despite her dark mood, Elli chuckled. "I like your nature the way it is, old friend."

"That's good, Elliryanna, since you haven't any choice."

Brionna lifted her braid, then threw it over her shoulder. It smacked against the wall, loud enough that one of the gnomes shambled over and put his face to the circular window. He peered inside, growling, then went back to drinking with his cohort.

"Come join our party," Lleu called merrily after him. "We've got lots of good food."

Catha screeched as she paced across his shoulder, clearly scold-ing him for making light of their situation.

But Lleu persisted. He turned to the jester, who was seated apart from the others, in the far corner of the room. "Well now, master Seth. How about showing us some entertainment? We're truly a captive audience, you know!"

The fellow didn't seem to appreciate Lleu's joke. Instead, he shot the priest a look that could have curdled milk.

"I wish Scree were here," muttered the elf maiden. "He's al-ways so good in a fight."

"That's because you give him so much practice," observed Nuic dryly.

Brionna didn't laugh.

Elli reached over and put a hand on her knee. "I miss some-one, too. Remember what you told me about candle wax? Well, right then I didn't understand, or want to admit it. But now, well, I do."

Brionna nodded somberly. "It's not just Scree I miss, whatever sort of friend he might have been. Mostly, I wish I still had . . ." She straightened her back, rubbing the scar from the slave mas-ter's whip into the wall. "Some family."

Elli sighed, then said, "You know, in all those years the gnomes made me their slave, working in their smoky tunnels, there was one thing I wanted even more than my freedom."

The elf turned toward her. "What?"

"My family." She nodded, making her abundant curls bounce. "To see them again, just for a day—that's what I wished for most of all."

She paused, drumming her fingers on her flask of water from the Secret Spring. "Which makes it even more absurd that I wasted some of this water to heal that filthy gnome who attacked Tamwyn and me. What stupidity!"

"Maybe," said Brionna, "or maybe not. Granda had a favorite rhyme that he picked up somewhere in his travels:

> *"See the creatures great and small,*
> *Made so diff'rent, each from all:*
> *Amble, slither, fly, or swim—*
> *Yet still in each, so deep within,*
> *Runs the hidden blood of kin."*

"Kin?" repeated Elli doubtfully. "Not the gnomes."

"Hard to see, maybe, but it's true. After all, isn't that what you said to Llynia? *They're our fellow journeyers, our sisters and brothers.*"

Elli said nothing.

The elf nudged her teasingly. "Look here, even Shim and I are related." She leaned over and asked into his ear, "Aren't we, dear uncle?"

But the old fellow just looked at her blankly. "Don't tries to be funnily, Rowanna. I knows I you don't really means it."

He squeezed his fists tightly. "If only I was still a bigly lad! Then I'd just stand up and lift off this whole ceililing."

Across the room, Lleu leaned his direction. "How *did* you get small again, Shim?" he asked, practically shouting in order to be heard.

The little giant rubbed his wrinkled cheeks. "I don't knows! It justly happened, leaving me forever shrunkelled."

"Maybe not forever," said Brionna into his ear.

"For many years, at leastly!" He scrunched his bulbous nose

at her. "If only I did understand, then mabily I could reversify things. But I don't, so of coursedly I can't."

"When did you first notice?" shouted the priest.

Shim's white head nodded. "Oh, that much I knows exactly! It was back in the War of Storms, in the Yearly of Avalon 498."

"The year," Brionna recalled, "of the Battle of the Withered Spring. That was the last time," she added with a glance at Elli, "the Drumadians' compound was ever attacked."

"Yes, Rowanna. That's rightly." Shim cocked his head, remembering. "It was a fightly battle, much too bloodsy for me. But I still fought, because without us giants, those flamelonly types would have surely winned. And in that battle, our giantly leader was Jubolda."

He opened his arms wide. "Bigly as a hillside she was, justly like her daughters." He chortled. "In factually, I *saved* one of her daughters, I did. By being so clumsily! When they had her all tied up in knotly ropes, I came running over to help. But I tripped and fell with a crashly big bang. Lucksily, though, I fell right on tops of the flamelons."

He clapped his hands for emphasis. "That was the end for them! A smooshily end."

Brionna nodded. "Very smooshily."

"But when did you start getting small?" shouted Lleu.

"Rightly after that."

"Are you sure?" demanded the elf maiden. "Did anything else happen to you?"

Shim shrugged his small shoulders. "Wellsy now, justly one thing." He blushed. "But it's surely not important."

"We'll decide that," Lleu bellowed. "Tell us."

His blush deepened. "Well, allsy right. Jubolda's daughter was named Bonlog Mountain-Mouth." He paused, glancing around the room. "For a goodly reason, too. And after I saved her, she tried to thanks me with a kiss!" He shivered from head to toe. "All too slobberly, let me tell you."

Trying to stifle her laughter, Brionna asked, "So what happened?"

"I runs away. And fast, lassie! As fast as I could, up into the mountains. The lastly thing I remember was hearing Bonlog's rumbumbily voice behind me, shouting some nastily things. She was, methinks, a little upset."

"Sounds that way," muttered Nuic, from his seat in Elli's lap.

"To keep away from her slobberly self," Shim went on, "I hides in the mountains for a longly time." A frown came over his face. "That's when the shrunkelling started. And got worsely and worsely."

"Hmmmpff." The sprite waved a tiny hand. "That's because she cursed you, idiot."

"Whatly?"

"Cursed you!" he roared. "Set a spell on you for humiliating her."

Shim's pink eyes widened. It was as if he'd just witnessed, for the very first time, the wondrous flash of golden light at starset. "A curse," he muttered. "You mabily be right! Now I justly needs to undo it."

Nuic shook his head. "I knew Jubolda's daughters. And you were right to run! But they had giantess sorcery thick in their blood. A curse from one of them can't ever be undone, except perhaps by Merlin himself. And I doubt even he would succeed."

While Shim may not have caught all Nuic's words, he didn't

miss the meaning. He scowled, and his head drooped. "So I is stuckly, then. Shrunkelled forever."

Brionna wrapped her arm around his shoulders, yet he didn't seem to notice.

A renewed sense of gloom settled over the companions. Elli sighed bitterly, watching Nuic's color swiftly darken. Lleu turned to the shadows, as Catha fluttered her wings restlessly. Brionna, like the jester in the corner, just stared at the granite floor.

"We're lost," said Elli despairingly. "Our quest is over. I've failed the Lady, and now Avalon is doomed. And we're stuck here in this dungeon until we die."

No one replied. Her words seemed to hover in the dank room like some thick, noxious fume. Slowly, it seeped into their skin, their lungs, and their minds, poisoning them by degrees.

An hour or more passed. None of them so much as stirred. The light from the air vent dimmed to nearly nothing, as nightfall came to the jungles outside the temple.

Without warning, there was a heavy grating sound just outside the entrance. Then a thud—and the heavy bar that blocked the door fell to the floor. A three-fingered hand reached inside, shoving the door open with a savage grunt.

"Merlin's beard," exclaimed Lleu. "They've come to kill us!"

Brionna leaped to her feet with elvish speed. Elli stood as well, cradling Nuic, and Lleu stepped over to them. The jester, too, rose swiftly and silently, brandishing his cane.

The gnome, however, did something unexpected. Something that made the companions freeze in place. Instead of rushing inside, he merely stood in the doorway and threw some objects into the darkened room. They clattered on the stone floor by Brionna's feet.

"My longbow," she said, awestruck. "And my arrows."

The gnome watched her as, in one swift motion, she grabbed them up and slung the quiver over her shoulder. Then he turned to Elli, his dark, bulging eyes peering deep into hers. Even before he raised his hand to touch the three jagged scars in the middle of his chest, she recognized him.

Her throat tightened. Yet she didn't need to speak. The look they exchanged said enough.

The gnome grunted urgently, then waved for them to follow. Stealthily, he led them past the other guard at the door, now slumped on the stone bench in a drunken stupor. Back up the stairs they crept, past more sleeping captors. The jester, who came last, took the opportunity to make sure that one of them—the guard who had rudely poked him in the back—would not wake up in the morning.

Down a narrow corridor they stole, avoiding the temple's central chamber. Ever so quietly, the gnome slid through a hole in the wall, where a palm tree had fallen against one of the slabs of quartz. He waited outside, until the last of them had passed through and the whole group stood beneath the trees in back of the temple. Then, with a final glance at Elli, he grunted and slipped off into the jungle, his squat form disappearing into the dark mesh of vines.

For a few heartbeats, the companions watched him disappear. Elli then looked skyward and found some stars shining through gaps in the trees. She paused for an instant, remembering the night with Tamwyn on the Stargazing Stone, but there wasn't time to think about that now. She pointed to the east, then plunged into the forest, following an animal trail that wound its way through the moist ferns and fruit-heavy branches.

All through the night they trekked. Monkeys chattered overhead, while a few nocturnal birds whistled eerily. Often, in thicker growth, it was only Brionna's superb vision that enabled them to keep moving. Even that failed once, when they found themselves in the midst of a dark and trackless swamp. Then they turned for help to Catha, who flew ahead and picked out a route from the air. Mostly, however, they kept moving. And mostly in silence—although Shim couldn't seem to stop falling over toppled trees, cracking sticks underfoot, and scaring unseen creatures into angry growls or hisses.

As dawn arrived, and the stars overhead began to brighten, the companions finally left the jungle behind. Wearily, they scaled a steep hill sprinkled with stubby brown grass. At the top, they all plopped down to rest. They were exhausted, and still hungry, despite the tangy fruits they'd eaten during the night. But they were free.

Scanning the rows upon rows of undulating brown hills that faded into the distant clouds, Elli smiled in satisfaction. "The Mud Hills. And over there," she said with a wave at the horizon, "is the Misty Bridge."

Brionna, too, gazed at the vista, but her own expression was far more glum. "And our route to the corrupted crystal."

Something about her voice made Elli turn toward her. "What's troubling you, Brionna?"

"Nothing," her friend replied crisply.

But Elli's instincts told her otherwise. "Something's on your mind. Now, what is it?"

Brionna's deep green eyes gazed at her. "Well, if you must know, I've been thinking about what Llynia told us. About the battle, and the elves from my homeland." She drew a slow, unsteady breath. "It made me feel . . . well, that for the first time on this journey, I'd like to be in two places at once."

She shrugged, running her hand along her bow that lay beside her on the grass. "But I can't. So I'd best just put all that out of my mind, right? Come on now, let's get moving! We're wasting time here." She stood up, ready to leave.

Elli, too, rose to her feet, but only to face the elf who seemed so sturdy and yet so slender. "You really feel that torn?"

Somberly, Brionna nodded.

"And what would you do if you went to join the elves?"

"Tell them what I've learned. And, if need be, fight beside them."

Elli frowned. "Must you? Wouldn't it be better to convince them to stop, to stay in Woodroot? The elves, after all, are such peaceful folk."

"Not now, we aren't. Not when such a threat to our world, our way of life, has arisen. Listen, did Merlin just rest when Rhita Gawr's blight started spreading through El Urien? And did Rhiannon sit idly by when the War of Storms erupted? They were people of peace, as am I. But with what we know now, we must act. Do whatever we can to save our world."

"I understand," said Elli, her voice hushed.

"So do I," declared Lleu. He stood, straightening his lanky form. Turning to the rolling hills to the east, he confessed, "You see, I've been feeling the same way myself."

The falcon on his shoulder clacked her beak in surprise, but he continued speaking to Elli. "All night long, as we walked, I've been wondering if I could just get to Belamir. Bring him back to his senses, if I can! Show him the horror of where all this is leading. Convince him to call it all off, while he still can."

Elli cocked her head doubtfully. "You really think that's likely?"

"I don't know until I try. But it *is* possible. After all, he's not really wicked, just misguided."

"Hmmmpff," said Nuic with a snort. "Wickedly misguided, if you ask me."

"Perhaps so. But if there's any chance to reach him—" He caught himself, glanced at Brionna, then faced Elli again. "What am I saying, though? I belong here with you. All of us do."

"That's right," agreed the elf maiden, twisting her long braid around her forearm. "So let's get going."

Slowly, Elli shook her head. "I don't think so. You both have been the truest companions anyone could ask for, but if there are other things calling to you, then maybe you should listen to them."

The elf maiden regarded her lovingly, her eyes shining in the dawn light. "You'd really allow us to go?"

"No," she replied, forcing a smile. "But I'd *command* you to go."

Lines of worry scored Brionna's brow. "What about the crystal? The quest?"

"I can manage just fine," declared Elli. "After all, I'll still have Nuic." Indicating the little giant now dozing on the grass, she added with a smirk, "Just do me this favor, though? If you do go, take Shim with *you*."

Brionna gave a nod, then asked simply, "You're sure?"

"I'm sure. This is right for you." She turned to Lleu. "And also for you."

The priest studied her doubtfully. "Perhaps so. But half of me—my wiser half, probably—wants to come with you to Shadowroot and destroy that crystal."

No, thought the jester from his seat on the grass just a bit apart from the others. *Not your wiser half. For if you stayed with her much longer, you'd die shortly. In a terrible accident.*

A barely visible grin stole across his sallow face. *Things are going my way again, how lovely.* He would miss dearly the chance to dispatch that foolish priest, but the girl—and the crystals—would be his before long.

As if, in his intuitive ear, he'd sensed the jester's true intentions, Lleu leaned closer to Elli. "My biggest worry for you," he whispered, "isn't so much what you'll have to face in Shadowroot. I know, somehow, that you can find that sorcerer and destroy his crystal. Even if you must outwit Rhita Gawr himself to do it. No, my biggest worry is that fellow over there. Something about him troubles me, though I'm not quite sure what."

Elli merely waved his concern aside. "You worry too much. Just like Papa always did."

His thick, dark eyebrows drew together. "And like your father, I have something very important to worry about."

Feeling the warmth of his words, she almost grinned. "I'll be fine, Lleu. Really. And besides, I still need the jester, remember? He's the only one who knows how to find the corrupted crystal."

That's right, thought Deth Macoll, who had overheard everything. His bells jingled as he bobbed his head. *How lucky for you.*

"Then it's decided," declared Brionna. "Let's travel together, Lleu, as far as we can. Both of us can head first for Isenwy." Catching a worried look from Elli, she added, "Keeping alert for any more gnomes, of course. If no elves have arrived there yet, we can take the Isenwy portal to Woodroot. Granda did that many times, so it's bound to work."

"Hmmmpff," sneered Nuic, shifting his weight on the grass. "*No* portal is bound to work. See you in Airroot."

Brionna didn't seem to hear. She was gazing thoughtfully at Elli. "Hear me, now. I know only a little about Shadowroot."

"You nearly died there, you once told me."

Brionna's face tightened. "Yes. That horrible, unending darkness almost—but that's a disease only found in elves. And truly, I would face that darkness again a dozen times over to help you! I would, if only I didn't have to fight for the survival of my people."

"I know, Brionna."

"What you need to know, though, is this. Granda told me that even though Shadowroot has always been on the dark side of the Tree, long ago there was some light there, as well. Not much, perhaps, but still some. And remember? There was even a city there—founded by winged people from the stars, they say—called the Lost City of Light. Before the dark elves destroyed it, museos sang, gardens blossomed, bards performed, and bonfires burned endlessly. There was even a portal that brought people from all over Avalon."

"Then all that ended."

"It did end. But all? We can't be sure." Her green eyes probed Elli's. "There are great dangers in Shadowroot. And terrible creatures—not just dark elves, but death dreamers and others who have not even been named. But there may also yet be, in some hidden corners of the realm, a sliver or two of light."

Elli's hand wrapped around hers. "You've taught me something, you know."

Brionna shook her head. "It's just a bit of history I learned from Granda."

"Not that," said Elli with a twinkle. "I'm thinking of something else."

"What?"

"You've taught me what it's like to have a sister."

Together, they shared a look that was itself a smile.

Part

III

31 · Final Battle

SCREE CLIMBED THE RIDGE OF FIRE-blackened rocks. He moved stealthily, keeping to the shadows. For after three arduous days of trekking through the hills of the Volcano Lands—over charred vales, sheer cliffs, and scorched streambeds—he was finally nearing the nests of the Bram Kaie clan.

Now only this last ridge separated him from the clan's leader, Quenaykha. From the brutal warrior who had murdered Arc-kaya. And from what he knew would be his own final battle.

He clacked his jaw, beaklike, as he moved, thinking of the village healer who had been so generous to him. Was it because Arc-kaya had lost her own son, and Scree his own mother, that they had bonded so readily? Whatever the reason, he'd felt a growing connection with her—until it was abruptly severed.

A plume of sulfurous smoke blew past, making his eyes water. He stopped, leaning against a charred boulder, blinking to clear his vision. He could still see Arc-kaya's face bending over him in the first days after his fever broke, her fluffy gray hair shining in the starlight. And he could still feel the weight of her lifeless body in his arms as he carried her to the burial mound. He glanced down at his anklet of gray hair, now blackened by the ash of Fireroot's volcanic peaks. *Soar high, run free . . .*

A flame vent erupted by his feet. With an eagleman's reflexes, he leaped aside—though slower than usual because of his wounded thigh. Orange flames licked his leg, singeing some of his hairs that could become feathers at will.

Upward he climbed, as his thoughts turned unexpectedly to that golden-eyed eagleboy he had met in Arc-kaya's village. Something about that boy, whose pride and ferocity couldn't hide how much he had lost in the attack, reminded Scree of his younger self.

His sharp eyes spied, in the shadow of a rock covered with char-lichen, a lone blossom. Firebloom—the only flower that grew on these ridges, and yet another reminder of his younger self. For on the day he'd met Queen, he'd given her a blossom just like that one. Skilled actor that she was, she'd seemed enthralled by it, stroking those orange petals that fluttered like tiny feathers—just as she'd seemed enthralled by him.

"What a broken yolk I had for a head!" he muttered angrily. "To think that I ever believed her for a second."

He scraped his sharply pointed toenails, so close to talons, against the sooty pebbles. Sure, he'd been fully grown physically when all that had happened, having reached adulthood at age five or six like all eaglefolk. But inside, he'd been just a fledgling. Queen, he was certain, had known that right from the start—but it hadn't kept her from taking ruthless advantage of his naivete and, yes, his need for affection.

At last, his thoughts settled back to where they had remained for most of the past several days: how to stop the murder and thievery of the Bram Kaie clan. That was the best—probably the only—way now he could help Tamwyn, Elli, and Brionna. As well as Avalon.

The answer was clear. His only hope of success was to challenge the clan's leader, and to prevail in a fight to the death. One of eaglefolk's most basic traditions had always been that the policies of a leader, in this case Queen, would last until he or she died. And then only the person who had won the fight for succession could set new policies for the clan.

Trouble was, what if the Bram Kaie, who valued so few traditions, no longer honored that one? Or even if they did, what if Scree somehow succeeded in removing Queen from power—and then was himself killed, before he could even begin to change the clan's ways? What if he was killed by that brutal young warrior, who would have no trouble at all continuing Queen's treachery?

He shook his head, even as he neared the crest of the ridge. He couldn't answer those questions. All he could do was try his best to stop Queen, as well as that warrior, from doing any more harm.

Scree topped the ridge. Immediately, he crouched behind a boulder, scanning the clan's village. Or, more accurately, fortress. For the nests of the Bram Kaie had changed greatly since he'd seen them last, being more numerous, more sturdy—and far more wealthy.

Tall copper torches, bejeweled statues of soaring eagles, and silken flags decorated broad avenues paved with planks of black obsidian. Every nest—and there were now more than twenty of them—was fortified with iron bars; spiraling stairways of oak, elm, and mahogany allowed eaglefolk to enter and depart without climbing on the nests themselves. The spoils of raiding and plundering lay everywhere: Scree recognized a rocking chair carved in the elaborate style of the Mellwyn clan, a chest of shiny kitchen utensils that could only have come from the metalworkers of southern Olanabram, and a winged kite that he'd seen once being flown by several eaglechildren near the River of Fire.

The whole village gleamed of new wealth—and also with the reddish glow of the clouds that always hung over the Volcano Lands. It looked as if the entire settlement had taken on the hue of molten lava. Or, perhaps, dried blood.

Sentries, armed with bows and arrows as well as spears, patrolled the streets. All wore red leg bands, and grim expressions on their faces. They were gathering at one spot in particular, around a torch that stood just outside the village. A large crowd of eaglefolk had formed there, as sentries paced to and fro. What, Scree wondered, was going on?

As he watched, trying to peer through the mass of eaglefolk milling about, a dusty brown snake slithered by him—and right over his foot. But Scree neither moved nor made any sound. If he was to have even a chance to succeed, he'd need to stay completely unnoticed until he suddenly struck, transforming into eagle form and attacking Queen before any of those sentries could loose their arrows.

The crowd grew steadily more restless. Some people shouted angrily, and a few youths started shoving each other roughly. People were clearly upset about something. By the minute, the eaglefolk grew more unruly, and the guards more anxious.

What's this all about?

Then Scree got his answer—as well as his opportunity. His whole body tensed as he saw an eaglewoman stride purposefully out from behind a nest, approaching the crowd. Tall and muscular, she wore dozens of golden rings in her flowing auburn hair.

Queen. Scree immediately recognized her determined gait,

her shapely form, and above all, her penetrating yellow eyes. He recognized, too, the way she held her head, and even the way she breathed. Suddenly, without warning, the memory of her breathing—so very close, chest to chest—flashed through his mind. It made him shudder.

Focus, Scree! No time now for such nonsense.

He studied her face. That had certainly changed, looking much more haggard than he remembered, a mask of unending worry. Her lips, once so full, so soft—now were pinched as tight as a closed beak.

As she approached the crowd, the eaglefolk parted, though some needed a push from a sentry to stand aside. At last Scree could see, from his vantage point behind the boulder, why so many people had gathered there: Sprawled on the ground beneath the torch lay the blood-smeared corpse of an eaglewoman. The same one that Scree had seen being flown back to the village moments before, by a band of warriors.

Scree clenched his jaw. The woman, whoever she was, had been brutally battered, her wings broken, the talons severed from her legs. By the black tips still visible on her wingfeathers, he could tell that she had belonged to the clan. Yet, from what was left of her, she seemed too old and frail to fight—a most unlikely warrior.

Who had done this? he wondered. It was one thing to be killed, another to be mauled so viciously. Had she been attacked in revenge for one of the clan's raids?

Queen bent over the corpse for a moment, inspecting it, even as several bystanders grumbled angrily. Then, with all the authority of the clan's leader, she straightened and raised her hand for silence.

"Kree-ella betrayed us all," she declared. Waving at the crowd, she shouted, "Every last one of us! Traitor that she was, she slipped away last night to warn another clan of our attack. And if she had succeeded, it could have cost the Bram Kaie many lives, and many valuables. That is why I commanded that she be captured and killed."

And tortured, thought Scree grimly.

As another wrathful murmur rose from the crowd, he suddenly realized something that made him catch his breath. All this anger wasn't directed at the dead eaglewoman, but at Queen herself! Heads shook, faces scowled, and people pointed accusing fingers at their leader.

But Queen hardly seemed to notice. Utterly unmoved, she showed not even a trace of fear or remorse. Strong, hard, and unforgiving, she stood before her people. Then, raising her hand again, she continued speaking.

"Kree-ella was the mother of some of you, I know. And the teacher of many more, who learned the skills of flight under her care. But she deserved to be killed! As does anyone who betrays our clan."

She swung around and pointed at a pair of warriors. "Guards! Light this torch, then hang her body there for all to see."

As one warrior struck a flame and ignited the torch, the other thrust Kree-ella's body upward, roughly impaling it on the torch's decorative copper spikes. Meanwhile, the crowd's angry murmurs swelled louder than ever. Fists clenched; feet scraped against the blackened ground. Yet for all the discontent, no one dared to challenge Queen directly.

"Just look around you," the leader intoned. "Everything our clan has gained in these years, all the riches you see, are here because I, Quenaykha, taught you about loyalty. To your clan, your cause, and your ruler."

A few heads bowed, though the angry chatter did not go away. "This woman," she said with a final wave at the dangling corpse, "brought this punishment on herself, by her own disloyalty. And so she shall hang here, under this torch that will blaze day and night, as an example to all."

She gazed at the crowd, her face rigid. Finally, she started to turn away, when a tall young man stepped out of the crowd. Bare chested, in the custom of eaglemen in their human form, he looked lean but strong. He bowed to Queen—then abruptly whirled on her, drawing a dagger from his leggings.

Queen clearly hadn't expected the attack. She spun to the side, but the young man's dagger plunged straight at her chest. Just when the blade was about to penetrate her flesh—

Ffffffttt. An arrow pierced his neck. He gasped as blood spurted from his severed artery. Twisting, he collapsed and fell dead at Queen's feet.

As the crowd fell silent, another young man stepped boldly forward. Still holding the heavy wooden bow that he had just used, he faced Queen, his expression as grim as her own. Like the attacker, he was around seven years old, but fully grown as an eagleman, the equivalent of a human in his twenties. And he was powerfully built: Although shorter than the other young man, he was much broader in the shoulders and more thickly muscled. His mouth seemed twisted into a permanent, haughty sneer.

Scree knew him at once. *The brutal warrior.*

Crouching lower behind the boulder, Scree debated what to do next, his fingers drumming on the anklet of Arc-kaya's hair. Should he attack both of them at once? Or wait for a chance to catch Queen alone? But what if that chance never came? He kneaded the sore muscles of his thigh. Already he felt stiffer than he should, to succeed at swooping down from this ridge in a surprise attack.

Better wait and watch a little longer, he decided at last, shifting his weight impatiently. *But not much longer*. He turned his attention back to the scene below.

"Thank you, good Maulkee," declared Queen. "You have shown once again your loyalty to your ruler."

His broad back straightened. To the astonishment of many in the crowd, as well as Scree, he answered her in a rough voice: "Not to my ruler, but to my clan."

Queen stiffened. The light from the torch that burned above them was no brighter than her savage yellow eyes. "So," she growled, "do you dare to challenge me?"

"I do," he declared. "Not in the cowardly way of an assassin," he said with a kick at the body of the man he'd just killed, "but in the long-standing tradition of our people. Talon-to-talon combat."

So, Scree thought to himself, *the tradition has survived*.

"To the death," she snarled.

He dropped his bow and tore off his quiver, facing her squarely. "To the death."

Queen's eyes blazed. "I expected that someday I would face a challenge from you, Maulkee. But not so soon! How convenient for you that the people are so angered by Kree-ella's death. They'll be less likely to see this as the raw treachery that it is."

"The way *you* gained power," he spat back at her. Then, his sneer broadening, he added, "You taught me long ago to surprise my prey, didn't you? Just like a good mother."

Scree pushed back from the boulder, astonished. His mother? He would actually kill *his own mother*?

Below Scree's hiding place, the crowd buzzed with anticipation. Eaglefolk called to others, still in their nests, that a battle for the clan's leadership was about to begin. People hurried down stairways and dashed through the obsidian streets, eager to witness the fight.

A swirling spiral of dust lifted off the ridge, sped through the village, then died. Above, rusty red clouds rolled across the sky, seeming to darken steadily.

Queen, meanwhile, put her hands on her hips and scowled at her challenger. "You may be my son, but you were never any smarter than a cliff hare."

"Is that so?" he said, starting to circle her.

"At least," she taunted, "you won't live long enough to do much damage. Today, in fact, will be your last."

"We'll see," he retorted.

All at once, they leaped upward, instantly transforming into winged warriors. The villagers fell back, leaving plenty of room for the battle. Talons slashed the air, and the shrieking cry of eaglefolk—half human, half eagle—echoed across the volcanic ridge.

Several people's height above the ground, they flew straight into each other, swiping wildly with their talons. As their powerful wings collided, several black-tipped feathers tore loose and drifted slowly downward.

Queen suddenly flipped over in midair. Her talons raked Maulkee's ribs, drawing first blood. But in that same instant he rolled aside, spinning through the air, and bashed her jaw with the bony edge of his wing. She screeched and fell back to the ground, sending up a cloud of soot and ash.

With a cry of vengeance, he followed. Swiftly, he plunged out of the sky and landed right on top of her. Pinning her with his weight, he raised a deadly talon to swipe at her throat—when she unexpectedly arched her back and rolled, throwing him off. He slid across the rocks, barely missing a pit of bubbling, steaming lava. Instead, he slammed into the post of the flaming torch. The dangling corpse broke loose and fell on top of his chest.

In the split second the warrior needed to hurl the corpse aside, Queen pounced. She slashed his face, trying to cut his throat. But he caught her leg with his powerful wing and jerked down with such force that her limb snapped. She hobbled backward, wincing in pain, trying desperately to stand on her one unbroken leg.

Maulkee made short work of her. Throwing her to the ground, he brutally stomped on her wings, breaking them under his weight. With a savage slash, he cut her neck, severing muscles and tendons so that her head drooped helplessly. Then, with a mighty kick in the chest, he sent her hurtling outside the awestruck ring of villagers.

Queen lay in a heap of bloodied feathers on the ground. Unable to move, bleeding profusely, she couldn't even lift her head in defiance. Maulkee kicked some ashes into her eyes, then walked away, leaving her to die in slow agony.

"So much for the reign of Quenaykha," he sneered as he strode away.

Scree watched, his heart pounding. He waited as Maulkee, followed by most of the villagers, moved off, quickly disappearing into the maze of nests. Of those who didn't follow, nobody—not a single one of her former subjects—went to tend to the fallen ruler. Cautiously, Scree stepped out of the shadow of the boulder and clambered down the ridge, avoiding flame vents, pits of molten lava, and fire plants along the way. A moment later, he was kneeling over Queen's broken body.

Now that he saw her like this, dying before his eyes, his old rage and hurt seemed less overwhelming. In fact, despite himself, he felt a stirring of something close to sadness. He gently turned her head, looked into her stricken face, and said simply: "Hello, Queen."

For a long moment, she tried to focus. Then, in a flash, her bloodshot eyes widened in astonishment. In a hoarse voice, she whispered, "You?"

"Yes, me. I came back."

"To kill me, no doubt." She tried to swallow, but ended up coughing. "Well, that worthless upstart saved you the trouble."

"So he did," said Scree grimly. "Now I just have him left to kill."

She looked at him with an unreadable expression. At last, she asked in her rough whisper, "You still have the staff?"

His old anger suddenly surged. "That's all you ever really wanted, isn't it? No, I don't have it anymore! If you really must know, I gave it away. To its rightful keeper."

Her face tightened; its harshness returned. "Then you are even stupider than I thought."

"And you must have thought me pretty stupid to think I'd fall for . . ." He turned away, his hooked nose angled upward.

A touch of softness came back to her gaze. "Scree," she said weakly. "There's something I must tell you. Something important."

Surprised by her tone, he turned back to her. "What is it?"

"You need to know this. Your—"

"Look there!" someone over by the nests shouted. "A stranger."

"Get him!"

Scree leaped to his feet. But before he could even begin to transform into his eagle shape, two sentries had drawn their bows, nocked with deadly arrows aimed straight at his chest. "Move and you die," one of them barked.

Scree could only glare at them.

Two more sentries came running over. With a nod from one of the bowmen, they shoved Scree toward the village. One of them held the point of a spear at his back.

"Let's take him to Maulkee."

"That'll be fun to watch."

Scree glanced back at the bloody heap that was Queen. Their eyes met for barely an instant, then the sentries started marching their prisoner into the village.

32 • Precious to Have, Painful to Lose

SURROUNDED BY FOUR WELL-MUSCLED sentries armed with arrows and spears, Scree was marched past the still-flaming torch—and toward the fortified nests of the Bram Kaie clan. Overhead, the bloodstained sky of Fireroot cast a reddish light on the village, and on the prisoner.

Scree's sharp toenails scraped against the pumice and ash that covered the ground. What a troll-brained dolt he was! Instead of remaining in hiding, waiting to pounce on the clan's new leader, he had gone over to speak with Queen. Such a foolish, stupid, sentimental thing to do! Now he'd lost the best chance he'd ever have to take control of this clan, and to change their treacherous ways forever.

At that instant, Maulkee himself came striding toward them, his feet slapping the obsidian street and then the bare ground by the torch. As he approached, his sneering face looked Scree up and down. "Well, well," he declared. "A spy!"

He stepped closer to Scree, glowering at him. "Where did you come from, spy?"

"From Iye Kalakya," came the reply. "The last village you plundered."

Maulkee spat on his prisoner's face, then watched as the spittle dripped slowly down the stern jaw. "Not very bright, are you? And tell me now, why did you come?"

"To kill you," answered Scree through clenched teeth, his whole body quaking with rage.

Maulkee started to turn away, then suddenly spun around and punched Scree hard in the abdomen. As the prisoner groaned and doubled over, the four sentries grinned at each other. Their new leader knew how to handle this sort of rubbish, all right.

A few other eaglefolk drifted over, hoping to see some more excitement. Meanwhile, Scree straightened up again. He stood as tall as ever, just as if he'd never been punched. And looked Maulkee squarely in the eye.

In that instant, an odd feeling struck him. Beyond that hateful sneer, beyond the violence in that gaze, there was something in Maulkee's face that looked strangely . . . familiar. That he'd seen somewhere before—even before the slaying of Arc-kaya. Yet he knew that wasn't possible.

Scree just brushed the feeling aside. No doubt he was just picking up on the young warrior's resemblance to his mother—the same woman whom the warrior had just mutilated and left to die.

"Well then," Maulkee said haughtily, "I've wasted enough of my time on you." He shot a glance at the helpless form that was all that remained of Quenaykha. "And her."

As he turned to leave, he flicked his hand casually at Scree. "Kill him," he ordered the sentries. "I don't care how, just do it. Then hang what's left of him to that torch, as a warning to any other spies."

Maulkee started to stride back toward the nests.

"Wait," commanded Scree. His voice rang out with such authority that even the new leader of the Bram Kaie clan could not ignore it.

He whirled around and faced Scree again. Impatiently, he snapped, "You waste my time. Why?"

Scree's eyes narrowed. "Because I *challenge* you, Maulkee. Here and now."

Astounded, the young eagleman exclaimed, "You *what?*"

"I challenge you! Talon-to-talon combat to the death."

"Challenge me? For leadership?" Maulkee scoffed, pacing on the ash-covered ground. "You're crazy as well as stupid! You're not even a member of this clan."

"What's the matter?" demanded Scree, his voice as cutting as any talon. "Afraid you will lose? Afraid your time as ruler will be the shortest in eaglefolk history?"

Maulkee hissed with anger. The sentries, however, traded intrigued glances. This wasn't at all what they'd expected. No prisoner had ever done something so audacious! But their glances also carried a question: If Maulkee was too timid to accept the prisoner's challenge for leadership, was he really fit to be their leader?

Unwilling to back down in front of his warriors, Maulkee growled, "All right, then. Release him!"

"Look," shouted one of the villagers. "Another challenge."

"Come quickly," another cried.

Soon dozens of eaglefolk dashed to the scene. Men, women, and children gathered, giving a wide berth to the two warriors about to battle. Several more eaglefolk scaled the side of the nearest nest, while others stood atop stairways, to gain a better view from above. A pair of youths quickly climbed the nearest bejeweled statue of an eagle, perching on the outstretched wings. People milled everywhere, though they were still careful to avoid the flame vents and pits of bubbling lava that dotted the base of the ridge—as well as the corpse of Kree-ella and the motionless form of their fallen ruler, Quenaykha. The entire village, from its gilded nests to its fire-blackened surroundings, buzzed with anticipation.

The two adversaries started to circle. Their wrathful gazes locked, while their muscular arms lifted as if they were already wings. Then, at an unseen signal, both Scree and Maulkee leaped into the air. A blood-freezing screech reverberated across the volcanic slopes.

They crashed together, hardly a man's height off the ground. Flapping their mighty wings, they tumbled through the air, slashing wildly with their talons. Over and over they rolled, a blurred mass of feathers, talons, and powerful legs.

The bony edge of Scree's wing caught his adversary in the side of his head. Maulkee lashed out with his talons, ripping the feathered skin of Scree's shoulder. Yet neither showed any desire to retreat. They fought on in midair, pummeling and slicing each other brutally, their bodies whirling over the ground.

Noticing a bloody gash in Scree's ribs, Maulkee leaped at it and bit fiercely, tearing off a huge chunk of flesh. Before Scree could pull away, his winged adversary ripped the spot again and again with his talons.

Suddenly Scree feinted one way, then rolled, hoping to get behind Maulkee. The ploy worked: Before the warrior could turn around, Scree slammed a wing into the back of his head. Too dazed to keep flying, Maulkee fell to the ground. In an explosion of black ash, he smashed into a large flame vent, so hard the vent's charred cone snapped off.

Roaring with fury, Scree pounced, as blood streamed from his side. But he landed with such force that his leg, still weak from the shard that Tamwyn had removed, buckled underneath him. He stumbled, barely avoiding a bubbling pit of molten lava.

Just as he regained his balance, and spun around to face Maulkee, the broken vent erupted in a blast of fire. Orange flames belched forth, with a cloud of sulfurous smoke, right into Scree's face. Fire singed his eyes, blinding him. Even as he blinked helplessly, trying to see, Maulkee's powerful wing slammed into his head, sending him sprawling.

Scree hit the ground next to the bubbling pit. Lying there, he realized that his sight was starting to return, though not fast enough. He could see only blurry shadows—one in particular, which towered over him.

"So, you like the taste of fire, do you?" Maulkee laughed haughtily. "Maybe after I kill you, I'll roast you for supper, just like a cliff hare."

Scree sat up, blinking madly to clear his vision. But he still couldn't see! In another few seconds, he'd be dead. Same as Arckaya! Only worse—because she'd never had any chance to defeat this bloodthirsty brute. Scree, by contrast, had been given a chance, but had bungled it badly.

Instinct, not sight, told him that Maulkee was just about to jump on top of him and slit his throat. And so Scree did something both desperate and bold. Even though he could hardly see the lava pit, he shoved his wings as hard as he could into the ground and flipped his entire body into the air. He spun over the steaming pit, barely missing its edge when he crashed on the other side.

Maulkee, meanwhile, had started to pounce. When Scree flipped, the surprised young warrior stumbled, flapping his great wings to regain his balance. Only at the last instant before he fell into the lava, he caught himself.

Just then, Scree's broad wing bashed him from behind. Even as he realized that his adversary had tricked him by flying back across the pit, Maulkee screeched in terror. His wings flapped desperately, unable this time to keep himself from plunging into the cauldron of molten rock.

Maulkee's final scream echoed among the nests, ending with a loud gurgle of lava. A sulfurous wind blew across the volcanic ridge, carrying the smell of melted flesh across the village. The people of the Bram Kaie clan, meanwhile, stood as still as their nests, surprised that they had lost their leader yet again.

Painfully, Scree landed beside the lava pit. He stared down into it for a long moment, his vision now nearly restored. After a glance at his anklet, he raised his yellow-rimmed eyes to the sky above. Loud and long, he screeched in triumph.

His feathers melted away as he transformed again into his human form. Grimy sweat glistened on his broad, muscular back, and blood oozed from the deep gash in his side, but he stood with all the glory of a victor. He turned and, limping slightly, walked back to the huddled form of Queen.

Kneeling beside her, he turned her head so she could see him. Through glazed eyes, she studied him, then smiled bitterly. "So now you are the leader of my clan."

"Only long enough to bring your clan back into the world of other eaglefolk."

"Bah," she spat, coughing weakly. "Then you will reduce them . . ." She coughed again. "To a life of hardship and poverty."

"And *you* reduced them to a life of crime and dishonor."

"Fool!" she rasped, licking her dry lips. "At least you should know . . . what you're giving up. A sorcerer, named Kulwych, offered me and my people wealth, great wealth, to ally with him." She released a painful moan. "Even now he gathers his army—on the Plains of Isenwy. An army that will conquer Avalon! And if the clan fights alongside him, he promised us riches beyond our dreams."

Scree rolled his shoulder as if ruffling his wings. "I know Kulwych. And his evil swordsman. And I'd never fight alongside him! Never."

Her yellow eyes narrowed. "You sound like my weakest subjects. Too squeamish . . . to fight."

"That, Queen, I am not."

"Then you're just . . . a salamander-headed fool."

He grinned imperceptibly. "Now, that's probably true."

She started to respond, but fell into a violent fit of coughing. When, at last, the coughs subsided, her face was ashen. Scree looked down at her flowing auburn hair, now streaked with her own blood, and felt again the sting of sadness.

"Is that," he asked gently, "the important thing you were going to say? Before Maulkee's guards captured me?"

"No, Scree." Her voice, barely a whisper, quavered like the wind on the ridge. "I wanted you to know . . . that Maulkee . . . was your son."

If half the volcano that rose above the village had broken off and fallen on top of Scree, it would not have hit him any harder than this news. For a long moment, he couldn't even breathe. At last, he asked in disbelief, "My son?"

She looked at him, trying to keep her eyes open. "Yes, Scree. *Our* son."

He shook his head, remembering in a flash the words he'd said to Arc-kaya: *Your son was your family. Nothing is more precious to have, or more painful to lose.*

"Scree," she whispered weakly.

He peered down at her, all his torment and confusion on his face. "Yes?"

"I want you to know . . ." Her voice faded as her eyes closed. But she rallied, enough to open them again and say one more phrase: "I always regretted . . ."

She never finished. Quenaykha, ruthless leader of the Bram Kaie clan, lay dead. To Scree, however, she was something else: the mother of his only child.

The son he had just killed.

He hung his head, feeling a swirl of conflicting emotions, but most of all, sorrow.

33 · The Secret Stairway

FOR TAMWYN, SLIPPING BACK THROUGH Gwirion's village without being seen was not his toughest challenge that night. Nor was climbing back up the hill, avoiding thornbushes and treacherous pits, or ignoring the throbbing pain of his wounds.

No, his toughest challenge, after he'd found the stalagmite that marked the entrance to the Secret Stairway, was simply containing his own excitement. Enough so he could pay close attention. For the very first rule of being a traveler in the wilderness, as he knew well, was *awareness is everything.*

But really, how could he not feel like celebrating? He may not have found the special compass that he'd wished for, to guide him through the upper reaches of Avalon—but he did have, at least, a general idea of his position inside the trunk of the Great Tree. And even better, he knew where he was going: up the Stairway, which had looked like a silvery ribbon in that wall painting he'd seen in the tunnel. And which would, Gwirion promised, take him to the place called Window to the Stars.

Merlin's Knothole. A place where he could actually see the

branches, as well as beyond. And where he could, perhaps, find his way to the stars.

In time, I hope, to relight them! His eyes narrowed in determination. *And to stop those shapes, those shadows, from entering Avalon.*

As he placed his hand on the black stalagmite that Gwirion had described, he felt a surge of another kind of excitement, as well—an excitement that rose from deep inside himself, like élano within the Great Tree. *This is my father's route.*

All he needed to do now was push the stalagmite aside and enter the Stairway. And then, as Gwirion had told him, climb it as high as he could go.

He winced slightly, feeling the persistent ache in his wounded hip—not to mention his back, his knee, his arm, and so many other places. It wasn't going to be easy to mount stairs! Let alone stairs that had to rise hundreds of leagues. Thousands, perhaps. For this stairway stretched all the way up to the Knothole, which sat just below the Tree's branches.

To give himself extra strength, he pulled out his leathereed flask. Eagerly, he took a swallow of the sweet water, and then another, feeling its power move through his whole body. Power that would help sustain him during the long climb ahead.

As he stowed the flask, he suddenly felt an ache, deeper than any muscles, for the friends no longer with him. How he missed them all! He thought of Gwirion, who by now must have discovered the gift that Tamwyn had left on his door—a gift that would change his life, and maybe that of his whole people. He thought of Henni and Batty Lad, lost in the Spiral Cascades. And he thought of Scree, who should be well enough now to be up and moving around—as well as skull-cracking angry at Tamwyn for leaving on this quest without him.

Finally, he thought of Elli. She could make him madder than anyone else in Avalon. Even her perpetually grumpy little sprite was a dream to be around sometimes, compared to her. And yet . . . she made him feel, at other times, as if he could fly without wings. Or sit by her side for hours and never need to say a word. Or feel that, clumsy and foolish as he was, he might just do anything he tried.

He closed the pack, feeling its leather strap that had been torn by the teeth of a wolf. *As soon as I can fix my dagger,* he vowed, *I'm going back to work on that slab of harmóna wood. Even if she never sees it, I want to make her what I promised.*

Then, after sliding his staff into its sheath so that he could push with both hands, he leaned against the stalagmite. With a groaning scrape, it slid sideways, revealing a thin, mossy stairway in a tunnel that plunged straight down into the hillside.

Down? Tamwyn wondered. *This must connect, somewhere below, to the Stairway itself,* he reasoned. *And then I'll start going up. And up.*

Leaning forward, he peered into the tunnel, hoping that the dim élanolight, together with his night vision, would tell him more. But he couldn't see anything. Just steep, mossy stairs leading down into darkness.

He could, however, hear something. Water! Rushing like a river. *Now, that's odd. Well, maybe the stairs pass by a river. I'll find out soon enough.*

All his excitement swelled anew. He would, indeed, find out! He placed his foot on the top step, not bothering to look closely . . . in which case he might have noticed that a big piece of the step had broken off.

Tamwyn put his weight on the foot—and open air. With a

sudden lurch forward, he fell straight into the tunnel, plunging down the chute, bashing over the steps as he slid on the wet moss. Even without hearing the stalagmite snap closed above him, he knew he was trapped: Now he'd only stop when he reached the very bottom. And that promised to hurt, even more than this tumble. Falling so fast, he couldn't even brace himself for the crash that he knew would soon come.

But it didn't. Instead—

Splaaasssh!

He landed with a shower of spray in the river he had heard moments before. Water sloshed over him, drenching his body completely, pouring in tiny rivulets across his face as he came up for air, spluttering. This was no ordinary river, however, as he soon realized. It was slightly warm, surprisingly smooth—and flowing straight up.

Up! This river was, indeed, rising speedily higher inside the trunk of the Great Tree. Like the Spiral Cascades that had carried Tamwyn upward for some distance, this waterway lifted vertically—and, it seemed to him, endlessly. Higher and higher it bore him now, like a waterfall in reverse.

Yet unlike the gargantuan waterfall of the Spiral Cascades, this river didn't batter and pummel him into unconsciousness. Nor did its waters rise as light descended, with strains of music swirling along the way. Instead, this waterway simply flowed and flowed, lifting him as easily as an updraft of wind lifts a single leaf.

So this is the Stairway! In a flash, it all made sense. This was why the wall painting had used that watery silver color to show the route. And this was why Gwirion hadn't seemed concerned at all about Tamwyn's injuries when telling him to climb as high as possible.

Like a droplet of water himself, Tamwyn rode the rising current. The only sound he heard was the endless ripple and slosh of the water surrounding him; the only smell was the rich, nectar-sweet aroma of wet wood and moist air. Because of the élano in the water, the river glowed milky white, with occasional sparks of green—a ribbon of light as well as liquid deep inside the Tree.

Steadily higher he was carried, through leagues upon leagues of vertical distance. Every so often he would spy a tributary river flowing into his own, or a stream that would split off and plunge deep into the heartwood. Over and over he glimpsed ledges and side tunnels that just begged to be explored. What other, un-known realms was he riding through? What other, strange peoples was he near? He knew only that the answers were beyond any-thing he could imagine.

As he rode upward, he began to notice two things about the river. First, it seemed to be growing gradually smaller, narrowing as it worked its way higher in the trunk. And second, its warm waters seemed to be soothing his wounds. He could bend his legs easily now, even bring his knees up to his chest. His scrapes and bruises had vanished; his strength had returned. And neither his hip nor his back throbbed with pain anymore, for the first time in many days.

But how? Perhaps it was the water's warmth itself, or the gen-tle massage of the ripples on his body. Or perhaps, like the healing water that Elli carried in her water gourd, the élano in this river could restore wounded flesh and bone through its own powerful magic.

Ever higher he flowed, for hour after hour—possibly day after day. Tamwyn had no way to tell. Wholly sustained by the élano-rich water, he felt neither hunger nor thirst, nor any need for sleep. He just rode the rising cascade.

Upward, upward, the river carried him. Distance was without measure; time was without meaning. The only certainties were the water and the Tree.

Finally, the river narrowed so much that he sensed he was moving more slowly. Fairly soon, its force wouldn't be strong enough to lift him any higher. Slower and slower he progressed, until he'd nearly stopped. Though part of him hated to leave this wondrous waterway, he knew the time had come, and he started to look for a way out.

Just ahead, he spied a narrow ledge, thick with luxurious green moss. It connected, he could see, to some sort of tunnel that ran into the trunk. Rolling over, he reached out his hand.

Barely grasping the ledge, he hauled himself onto the moss. Water poured off him as if he were a scrap of bark that had floated for ages on end. He lay there on his back for several minutes, listening to the splash and gurgle of the river that had carried him so very high, so very far.

At last, heaving himself onto his hands and knees, he looked more closely at the tunnel ahead. Its ceiling was quite low, so he'd have to crawl. But it did, at least, seem to be horizontal, running perpendicular to the river. He glanced behind for one more view of the waterway. And then, feeling physically better than he had in some time—since leaving Hallia's Peak—he crawled into the tunnel.

Low as it was, the passageway posed no obstacles. Whether it had been carved by an ancient stream, bored by termites, or hollowed by the workings of élano, he couldn't tell. The wood around him glowed dimly, allowing him to observe the subtle changes in texture, color, and grain. Every so often he spotted miniature crystals of purple, pink, black, gold, and white that had sprouted on the walls. And in the cracks of wood he found velvety moss, flakes of lichen, and once, a row of the smallest toadstools he'd ever seen, marching up the wall like a tiny trekking party.

More than anything, as he crawled farther away from the river, he noticed the silence. Broken only by his own breathing, the occasional knock of his staff against the tunnel wall, and the distant whisper of water, the silence seemed to swell as if it were truly a different kind of sound. He sensed, as he had sometimes in the quiet of mountain evenings, the simple beauty and sheer weight of silence. It was not an absence, but a presence; not a denial, but an invitation. An invitation to listen at last to himself, to belong wholly to the world.

In time, he noticed a change in the air. It was drier, as well as cooler. And it smelled of something—something vaguely familiar.

Outside, he realized all of a sudden. *It smells like outside the Tree.*

He kept crawling, picking up his speed. After a while, he noticed another change. Farther ahead, the tunnel looked different somehow. Brighter, and whiter.

Light! By the Thousand Groves, there's light ahead!

Tamwyn smiled. For he could tell that this light didn't come from élano. No, he felt certain. This light came from the stars.

34 · Fierce Wind

TAMWYN, CRAWLING AS FAST AS HE COULD toward the light, finally neared the tunnel's end. The hard wood under his hands, knees, and toes softened into moist brown soil, while tiny green sprigs grew here and there. He slid under a spiderweb, luminous with dew, that stretched across the top of the tunnel, and found himself facing a round hole rimmed with thick green grass. A golden cricket on the grass, startled by his approach, chirped and hopped away.

Before poking his head out the hole, he paused, savoring the memory of the stillness and beauty that he'd just passed through. And he also needed a moment to blink his eyes—for the light coming through this hole was brighter than any he'd seen in days. At last, heart pounding, he slowly pushed his head outside.

Even before he'd fully emerged, he froze. For as astounding as it was to smell wet grass again, to feel chill air blow against his cheek, and to hear the whoosh of distant wind, what truly struck him was the sight. He felt exactly as if he'd just crawled through a window.

A window to the stars.

Pulling himself, together with his pack and staff, all the way out of the hole, he just lay on his back on the grass, gazing in astonishment at the sky. The stars above him didn't merely sparkle, as they had so often during his years of camping in Stoneroot. Rather, these stars flamed like celestial torches—brighter than he'd ever seen, nearer than he'd ever expected to find. He felt, if only his arms were just a little longer, that he could reach up and feel the very warmth of their fires.

Suddenly, he noticed something odd. Long streaks of shadow rose out of one horizon and ran across the sky, like rivers of darkness, swallowing hundreds of stars. Were these the same shadows he'd seen in the vision? Was he already too late?

His heart raced. Then, peering at the darkened streaks, he realized that they didn't fill him with the same sort of bone-deep dread he'd felt before. Nor did they really seem to have swallowed any stars. Rather, they were *blocking* the stars. These shadows were actually solid shapes that ran between him and everything beyond.

Branches! I'm seeing branches! He shook his head in awe, following the shadows' curling contours. *So this really is Merlin's Knothole,* he said to himself, only half believing it was true. *The place where branches can be seen. The place my father came, years ago, on his own journey to the stars.*

He sat up, scanning the terrain around him. He was in a valley, deep and round, full of lush green grasses that grew thickest down on its floor. And just as he'd seen in the wall painting down inside the trunk, the Knothole bulged out, burl-like, from the side of the Great Tree—holding this valley like an enormous, cupped hand.

The entire bowl wasn't very large, reminding him of the small glacial valleys in Stoneroot's high peaks. Yet unlike that realm far below, this land showed no trace at all of winter. Could Merlin's Knothole, he wondered, have seasons unlike anywhere else? Or no season but spring?

His gaze moved to the rim. Unlike the verdant valley floor, almost nothing grew on the encircling brown hills. Where he now sat, he was about halfway up the slope; both the rim and the valley's bottom looked only a short walk away. Yet he could also see far greater distances from here: Beyond the rim closest to the trunk of the Tree, rough ridges climbed steadily toward the branches . . . and eventually, the stars.

Sitting there in the grass, he again raised his eyes starward. He began to pick out a few of his favorite constellations—surprisingly difficult because of the unusual brightness of every point of light—when he saw the vacant hole that had once held the Wizard's Staff. All the terror and uncertainty of that night atop Hallia's Peak came rushing back to him. Could he still get up there in time? Could he figure out what those infinitely dark shapes, which he'd seen pouring through the hole, really were? And could he find some way to stop them, for the sake of Avalon?

Abruptly, a fresh breeze rustled the grasses around him, and he caught a rich new smell on the air. It wafted toward him from the verdant fields at the bottom of the valley. He knew that smell from somewhere. Yes, from back in the villages of Stoneroot.

Gardens! He shook his head in disbelief. Gardens, way up here? Yet there could be no doubt about that smell: freshly turned soil, ripening leaves, fruit on branch and vine.

Peering more closely at the valley floor, he could now make out, near a deep ravine, the parallel lines of furrowed plots. There was a small but thick forest nearby, as well as a group of leafy trees planted in straight rows—an orchard. And not far away, a pile of oddly shaped items that just might be baskets and garden tools.

Someone lives down there, he thought in amazement. Climbing to his feet and pulling out his staff from its sheath, he added, *Just who, I'm going to find out.*

He hesitated, leaning on his staff. It seemed quite odd that, except for the gardens, he could see no other signs of people. No houses, pathways, or smoke trails from cooking fires. Yet someone, he felt sure, was down there. And had been down there for quite some time—long enough to have planted that orchard. And also long enough, perhaps, to have met his father.

He swallowed. Or to actually *be* . . .

Just then a small lizard, with a scaly green back and darting orange eyes, crawled out of the grass by the tip of the staff. Surprised, the creature halted, staring up at this strange visitor, before placing its front legs on the staff and lifting itself higher for a closer look. The orange eyes studied Tamwyn closely.

The young man returned the gaze, then asked in the silent language that had always helped him talk with other creatures, *Good lizard, would you tell me who made those gardens?*

It blinked at him, and Tamwyn sensed it was about to reply. Suddenly, a keening cry echoed overhead. The lizard instantly scurried off into the grasses.

Tamwyn looked up at the bird who had scared off his conversation partner. It was larger than a hawk, more like the great blue herons he'd seen diving for fish from the cliffs on Stoneroot's marshy coast. But no heron could do what this bird did next.

Its broad wings tilted, so that its feathers faced an especially bright cluster of stars, which Tamwyn recognized as his old favorite, the constellation Pegasus. All at once, the bird's wings and tailfeathers flashed like dazzling prisms. Arcs of rainbow colors burst forth, painting a wispy cloud nearby with rays of lavender, green, yellow, and scarlet that shimmered with misty brilliance.

Tamwyn's eyes widened in wonder. Those wings were almost as radiant as a starset! Never, in all his wanderings, had he seen a bird so magnificent. Nor had he heard of anything like this in the songs of bards. Either this bird was unique to Merlin's Knothole, or it could be found only in the upper reaches of the Great Tree.

Prism bird, he said to himself. *That's what I'll call you.*

The great bird keened again. This time Tamwyn heard not the cry of a predator, but the song of an exultant flier, whose every wingbeat flashed joyful colors across the sky. As he watched, it veered again, painting yet another cloud as it passed.

Turning back to the valley floor, and its mysterious gardens, he started to stride down the slope. Thick grasses, cool underfoot, swished against his leggings. As he swung left to walk around a little knoll, he noticed a dense grove of scraggly trees, quite unlike the leafy ones down lower in the orchard. Just then, the fluttering breeze suddenly strengthened.

Mightily! The wind tore across the Knothole, whipping up clouds of dirt from the surrounding hills and flattening the grasses on the upper slopes. It nearly hurled Tamwyn off his feet. Only with the help of his staff did he keep from being blown over, and even then it wasn't easy. As the air screamed around him, he made for the shelter of the scraggly trees, which were bending in unison under the weight of the wind.

He dived into the grove, rolling to a stop against the smooth trunk of one of the largest trees. After blinking the dirt from his eyes, he examined its shape—quite unlike any tree he'd seen before. Its big, burly roots plunged into the soil of the field, keeping the tree from blowing away. But the rest of it seemed thin and warped, like an old piece of driftwood that had finally floated ashore after years at sea. If standing straight up, it would have been about twice his height, a knobby, weather-beaten specimen. In fact, this tree, like all the others in the grove, had no bark, just wood polished smooth by the wind. And no leaves, either— merely thick tufts of grass that sprouted here and there on trunks and limbs.

For an instant, he sensed something else about these trees. Something odd that his inner magic perceived, akin to an emotion. Fright? But could such an emotion be coming from the trees? Before he could learn any more, the feeling quickly vanished, blown away by the next howling gust.

He noticed just then that these twisted, leafless trees had interlocked their branches. Of course! How better to survive these brutal winds up here above the valley floor? That was also why, no doubt, they grew blades of grass instead of larger leaves that could easily be ripped away.

At last, the wind subsided. The tree trunks lifted, as the long grasses surrounding the grove raised their grain-clustered tops. Tamwyn, too, sat up higher. He breathed a sigh of relief that such winds didn't blow down in the root-realms—except, perhaps, in Airroot. Up here, though, on the trunk of Avalon just below its branches, the wind seemed a fact of life, as ordinary as starset.

Just as he was about to get up again, the tree that he was leaning against shook violently. Tamwyn slid off, then realized that the ground beneath him was quaking just as much. He tried to rise, or even to crawl, but the wild tremors knocked him flat on his face. Dirt sprayed all over him. There was a loud popping sound as the trees' burly roots pulled out of the ground. He curled into a ball, expecting one or more trees to fall on top of him.

Nothing fell. The quaking ceased.

Tamwyn shook the dirt out of his hair, sat up—and suddenly understood. He could only gasp in astonishment.

All that shaking hadn't come from the ground, but from the trees themselves! They were standing around him, their roots splayed on the grassy turf, their branches no longer intertwined. The trees—or whatever they really were—had gathered around him in a circle, leaning their faces closer to scrutinize him.

For they did indeed have faces, midway up their scraggly, many-limbed bodies. Each face had a ragged slit for a mouth, a double knob that might have been a nose, and most striking of all, a single, vertical eye, as tall and narrow as a twig. The ring of tall eyes examined Tamwyn, never blinking.

Suddenly he felt a powerful rush of fear. Whether it came from himself or from these bizarre creatures, he couldn't quite tell. But instinct made him jump to his feet, leap over the roots in his way, and escape as fast as he could down the grassy slope.

The creatures pursued him, their roots slapping against the ground and their grassy limbs swishing through the air like a wintry wind. As fast as Tamwyn ran, he could hear them thumping down the slope behind him, gaining every second. Anxiously, he turned his head to see how close they really were.

Without warning, he tripped on a tussock of grass. Pitching forward, he cried out as he fell, rolling downhill. Finally he came to a stop. Spitting the grass from his mouth, he started to regain his feet—when one of the creatures' knobby limbs slammed hard against his back.

The force of the blow knocked him flat on his face. Worse yet,

the creature began to thrust all its weight onto the limb, pushing down on his back. No matter how much he wriggled, Tamwyn couldn't escape. Nor even breathe. And the limb grew swiftly
heavier. In another few seconds, the weight would surely crush his
ribs—or break his back.

"Heeeevashhh! Heeeevashhh!"

As the sharp, hissing sound rent the air, the creature suddenly
froze, and ceased crushing Tamwyn. To his astonishment, it lifted
its limb slightly—not enough that he could extract himself, but
just enough that he could breathe again.

"Oiyanishhhla. Shhheralass, oiyanishhhla!"

Slowly—and, Tamwyn sensed, reluctantly—the creature raised
its limb another notch. He pulled himself free, spinning away on
the grass. Panting, he knelt on the slope, eager to see who, or
what, had stopped the creature from killing him.

A tall, broad-chested figure in a hooded cloak strode toward
him. With a sharp wave of his hand, the figure cried out again,
louder than before. This time, the knobby creature and its companions actually backed away. With a hiss of disappointment, they
turned and slowly shuffled off toward higher ground, their root-
legs thumping on the turf.

Tamwyn watched them for a few seconds to be sure they were
really leaving, then faced the cloaked figure again. At that instant,
the figure pulled back his hood.

A man! All the way up here in Merlin's Knothole!

Tamwyn bit his lip. Carefully, he scrutinized the face of this
stranger, whose long gray hair and coal-black eyes, gleaming in
the starlight, made Tamwyn think, for an instant, that this just
might be the person he'd longed his whole life to find.

Yet he knew, in the very next instant, it was not. As much às

Tamwyn wanted to believe that he had finally found his father, he felt sure, by some inner sight that had nothing to do with the eyes, that this was someone else. But who? And how did he come to be in this place?

The burly man furrowed his brow, as if he were asking himself the very same questions. At last, in a voice that seemed to echo in his barrel chest, he said simply, "Yer a long way from home, lad."

Tamwyn reached for his staff and rose to his feet. With a nod, he answered, "So are you, I'll wager."

"Then ye'd lose, lad. This valley be me rightful home. Has been now fer . . ." He paused, counting. "Seventeen years. An' in all that time, yer me first guest."

Tamwyn stiffened. Seventeen years. The time of his father's expedition! This man might have been part of the team Krystallus had assembled—in which case he'd surely know what had happened to that team. As well as its leader.

Yet as much as he hungered to find out, Tamwyn sensed that the time wasn't yet right to ask. He'd hold back, at least for the moment.

"Long enough," the man went on, with a shake of his gray locks, "to learn the tongue o' them drumalin's."

"For which I'm very grateful!" Tamwyn smiled, then asked, "Drumalings? Is that what you call those creatures?"

"Aye. That be not their name fer theirselves, which rolls on an' on like a damn waterfall, somethin' like *hershnaganshalasha-nooshkalash*. But that be what I took to callin' them—after the Old Fincayran word fer tree, ye know."

"Druma."

"Right, lad." He stroked his curly gray beard for a moment,

then extended his immense hand. "Me name be Ethaun. An' yers?"

"Tamwyn." He cleared his throat, then asked the question that burned inside him: "Did you, by chance, come to this place with—"

"Ye must be hungry," Ethaun declared, cutting him off. "Come on, I was jest fixin' me own breakfast when I heard yer shout. So now ye can join me fer some eats."

Without waiting for a reply, he turned and started down the grassy slope, angling toward the ravine at the bottom. With a sigh, Tamwyn followed along behind.

35 · A Name from the Past

ETHAUN, WHO SEEMED AS BURLY AS A BEAR, led Tamwyn down the slope into the thicker grasses of the valley floor. To the young man's surprise, his guide veered away from the gardens and orchard, and toward the deep ravine. *Where is he taking me?* Tamwyn wondered.

Just as they neared the edge of the ravine, which dropped five or six times Tamwyn's height into the fertile ground, he saw a staircase wrought of something that resembled ironwood. The steep stairs led down to a simple earthen hut, its roof made of mossy wooden shingles with a sturdy stone chimney at one end. Outside the hut's doorway sat a substantial pile of firewood, a chopping block, and dozens of assorted garden tools—hoes, saws, rakes, pruning shears, and the like—many of which looked broken or only half-built.

Of course, thought Tamwyn as he climbed down the stairway. *He lives down here to stay out of the wind! Or maybe*, he added grimly, *out of the reach of those drumalings.*

Following Ethaun's broad form, he stepped into the hut and set down his pack and staff. As he closed the door behind him, a stone bell that hung on the back of the door jangled. Tamwyn smiled, knowing that his host, like himself, must have spent some time in Stoneroot, the land of bells. As if in response, the small quartz bell on Tamwyn's hip sounded a note of its own.

With only one window, the hut was quite dark, in addition to reeking of smoke. But as Tamwyn's eyes adjusted, he realized that some of the darkness was, in fact, smoke. A thick, dark cloud hovered near the ceiling above the hearth.

Ethaun bent over the hearth coals and blew a long, steady breath. The coals immediately burst into flames, filling the hut with more light—as well as more smoke. He tossed a good-size slab of wood onto the fire, sending up a fountain of sparks.

Then Ethaun stepped over to a sturdy wooden table, which held a large carving knife, a blackened pipe—and the largest melon Tamwyn had ever seen, fully as big as a troll's head. The barrel-chested man started to pick up the knife, then stopped and turned back to Tamwyn.

"Tickle me toenails," he declared, breaking into a wide, gaptoothed grin. "I'm fergettin' me manners! Not used to visitors, ye know." He motioned to a stool by the wall. "Jest slide that over here, lad, so we both can sit at the table."

As he stepped across the earthen floor to the stool, Tamwyn gazed around Ethaun's dwelling. It seemed very crowded—and very human. Under the table sat a straw basket full of pipes, most of them carved from hardwood burls, along with a sack of pipeweed that looked like dried leaves of lemon balm. Over by one wall sat a straw pallet with a ragged cloth blanket. And stuffed partially under the pallet's edge was a torn copy of a book he recognized: *Cyclo Avalon*, the famous Drumadian text by Lleu of the One Ear.

Against the opposite wall, many smaller tools hung on hooks.

There were hammers of several sizes and shapes, knives, tongs, thin-bladed saws, a set of chisels—and many implements that Tamwyn couldn't recognize, including some sort of glass globe in a leather strap. All the tools showed considerable craftsmanship, whether they had been made from wrought iron, polished hardwood, or chipped stone.

In the far corner of the hut sat a set of triangular shelves, drooping from the weight of the chunks of iron ore, slabs of obsidian, and coils of heavy rope that they supported. Nearby rested several large bags, overflowing with colorful seeds. And in baskets by the shelves sat more enormous fruits and vegetables, all jumbled together. These included a bunch of fist-sized grapes, a single carrot as long as Tamwyn's arm, a leaf of lettuce that could have covered his entire back, a batch of giant scallions, and a turnip that looked about as heavy as one of the iron chunks.

Tamwyn's gaze moved back to the hearth. Shaped as a semi-circle, and built from blocks of granite, the hearth and its chimney took up most of one wall. Beside it rested a flat, oblong hunk of rock that looked very much like an anvil.

All at once, Tamwyn realized this place wasn't just a home. It was also a smithy! He nodded to himself as he spotted the heavy, charred apron hanging from a hook over by the tools.

"Well, lad, are ye comin' to breakfast er not?" called Ethaun from his seat—a pair of unopened seed bags by the table. "Bite me boots, this melon be tasty."

Tamwyn grabbed the stool and slid it over to the table. Seeing the hefty slice that his host had set aside for him, he took a big bite of the melon's juicy white center. For some time after that, the only sounds within the hut were chomping teeth and dribbling juices.

Although Tamwyn ached to ask about his father, he could

sense that Ethaun would need to be in the proper mood. So, bid-ing his time, he asked instead about the strange creatures who had nearly killed him.

"Meant no harm to ye, them drumalin's," declared Ethaun as he cut himself another slice of melon.

"No harm?" asked Tamwyn, incredulous. "That beast nearly broke my back!"

"Not knowin'ly," the gray-bearded man insisted. "It was jest overly scared, ye see. Truth be told, them drumalin's be scared o' everythin'. Even their own bitty little green mustaches! Not to mention that wild wind up there on the slopes, which scares them even though they can anchor theirselves with rootyfeet."

"I still say," countered Tamwyn, pausing to swallow, "they're dangerous."

"Maybe so, lad. But they're also spectac'ler gardeners." He waved his big hand at the baskets of fruits and vegetables. "'Course, they never grow anythin' but salads an' fruit. But count me curls, they do that well! An' all year round, too, since it never gets so cold here as to frost er snow. Why, they even grow me all the firewood I need fer me smithin'."

He paused, his eyes suddenly bright, and leaned toward Tam-wyn. "Ye don't have any dried strips o' meat in yer pack there, do ye?"

"No. Sorry about that."

"Not so sorry as me! Seventeen years without a single lick o' meat, think o' that."

Tamwyn nodded, deciding that maybe the time had finally come. "So tell me," he said as casually as he could, "whatever brought you to this remote place?"

Ethaun slowly wiped his mouth with the back of his hand, then spoke as if he hadn't heard the question. "Soon after I arrived, it strikes me these gardeners do pretty well with their bony stick-fingers, but what if they had a few real garden tools? So I makes them a trade. They gets some tools, an' I gets all the food I can ever eat."

"But tell me, Ethaun. When you came here, did you—"

"Here, lad. Have a carrot."

Tamwyn peered straight at him. "Just tell me this. Did you come here with a man named Krystallus?"

At the mention of that name, Ethaun suddenly looked troubled. He set down his melon rind. "Now that be a name from the past," he said finally, his voice as low as a thrumming grouse. "But aye, I did travel with him, leastways fer a while."

"A while?"

Picking up his pipe, Ethaun chewed on its stem for a moment. Then, in one deft motion, he took a pinch of pipeweed and pushed it into the bowl with his little finger. From his tunic pocket he grabbed a pair of iron stones, much like the ones Tamwyn himself carried, and lit a spark. After a few thoughtful puffs, he finally spoke again.

"That be a long tale, lad. Are ye sure ye'd like to hear it right now?"

Tamwyn's face looked just as hard as the stones of the hearth. "I'm sure."

He took another puff. "Well, I s'pose it'd do me good to tell somebody. Been a dragon's age, it has, since it all happened."

36 · The Dagger's Blade

ETHAUN LEANED BACK ON THE SEED BAGS that formed his chair, gazing across the wooden table at Tamwyn. "Ye see, I always wanted to be an explorer. To go places, aye! Places so amazin' that I couldn't even imagine them. Even though I'd seen naught but the inside o' me old master's smithy in Stoneroot, that was me dream."

He sucked on his smoke-blackened pipe. "An' so I ran away, I did, after hearin' that the greatest explorer o' them all, Krystallus hisself, was roundin' up brave folks to join him on his biggest journey ever. A journey people said might go all the way to the stars."

Tamwyn's gaze bored into him. "Yes?"

"Well, I was so very young, Krystallus didn't want me along. Said it was jest too damn dangerous. But I tried me best to convince him he'd need a good smith, as I'd worked the hammer an' tongs since boyhood. Still he said no. But I pestered him an' pestered him, bein' the sort o' lad who jest wouldn't give up."

He chewed on his pipe for a moment, eyeing Tamwyn. "A lot like ye, methinks."

Grinning, Tamwyn nodded. "And what happened?"

"Well, finally, he changed his mind. Said I could come an' be a second smith, as well as pot washer, seam stitcher, an' all-round helper. Told me that, with the twelve folks he already had in his group, I'd make it a lucky thirteen."

Ethaun turned toward his wall cluttered with tools, his face wistful. "Well, I was happier than a pig in paradise! An' fer the first few weeks, it was a great adventure, fer certain. I saw jest about everthin' I'd ever hoped fer—portals, painted tunnels, upside down waterfalls, ye name it."

Suddenly he scowled. "Then one day, jest when we was settin' up camp in a cavern, them termites came out o' nowhere! Hulkin', fearsome beasts, with slashers like giant broadswords, an' hungry fer blood. I seen them first, but I . . ."

After his voice faded, the hut was silent, as if the earthen walls themselves were waiting for him to continue. The cloud of smoke, hovering above the hearth, seemed to darken. And it was Tamwyn who spoke next, for his intuition told him what had happened. Quietly, he asked, "You didn't stay to fight, like the others, did you?"

"Jest ran off an' hid! Tremblin' like a worthless leaf in the wind." Ethaun bit so hard on his pipe the stem snapped, spilling pipeweed onto the floor. He spat out the end that had been in his mouth. "Not exactly like an explorer, eh?"

Tamwyn pinched his lips together. "That's nothing compared to some of the fool things I've done."

The man just grunted and stroked his curly beard. "I've wished a hundred times, if I've wished once, to live them moments again. To do right fer me mates. An' 'specially fer Krystallus, a better man than any who ever walked the paths o' Avalon."

Tamwyn's eyes shone, though he said nothing.

Ethaun heaved a sigh. "None o' them survived, not a single bloody one."

"All of them died?"

"That be right, lad. All o' them." Bitterly, he added, "Except fer lucky number thirteen."

"But," protested Tamwyn. "I heard Krystallus *did* survive. And that he came up here to the Knothole, just as I did."

Ethaun shook his hairy head. "Not that I know about, lad. An' that means, I'm afeared, it never happened."

"How can you be certain?" Tamwyn banged his fist on the table. "You can't be!"

The big man got up and fetched another pipe and a different sack of pipeweed, which smelled like crushed needles of cedar. Biting the pipe stem, he filled the bowl, lit the weed, and took a first puff. Then, moving slowly, he returned to the table and sat down on the seed bags.

"It be like this, ye see. When I comes out o' hidin', I went back to the battle scene. An' counted the bodies, mangled though they was. Twelve, all together. Nobody survived, I tell ye. Nobody."

Seeing the disbelief in Tamwyn's expression, he went on. "Anyways, I came up here straightaway after that. Rode the bloomin' waterfall, I did, far as I could. Used me tarp to ride higher—like a big sail that was lifted by the water. Then I jest followed tunnels fer days an' days, growin' weak from hunger. I was sure that I was goin' to die—an' that I deserved to die. Somehow, though, I jest happened to find a tunnel that took me here, to this very valley."

He chewed vigorously on the pipe for a moment, then puffed a few times. "If any other man was ever here, don't ye think I'd know about it? An' in all these years, I've seen nobody else wearin' two legs. Until ye came along."

"Are you sure?"

"Aye."

Tamwyn squinted at him. "I *still* think he came here, just as Gwirion said. And even if he was badly injured, the élano in the water should have healed him, as it did me." Turning away, he added under his breath, "I just can't believe he's dead."

For some time, neither spoke. Finally, Ethaun blew a ring of smoke toward his hearth, and said, "I'm sorry, lad. Ye must o' been pretty young when Krystallus left the root-realms. But . . . did ye know him?"

Hoarsely, Tamwyn whispered, "I would have liked to."

"Well, well. Now I understan'!" boomed Ethaun. He leaned back on the seed bags, his strong hands clasping one of his knees. "Makes perfect sense, it does."

Tamwyn looked over at him. Could he have guessed the truth?

Ethaun gave a knowing nod. "Yer a young explorer, too, aren't ye? Jest like I was."

Tamwyn just stared at him blankly. All the hopes, all the longings, he'd allowed himself to feel—now crushed. He still wasn't willing to let them go completely . . . but he didn't really believe them anymore. He felt strangely empty inside. He still had the friends he'd left behind on Hallia's Peak, of course, as well as his quest. But if he'd lost any hope of ever finding his father, then he'd also lost part of himself.

"Well now, lad," said the smith. "Seein' as yer an explorer, an' likely have a long ways more to go, do ye have anythin' that be needin' fixin'? I'm still fairly good with the hammer an' tongs."

Absently, Tamwyn shook his head. "All I have is an old dagger that I broke on a living stone. But it's so old and rusted you probably can't fix it."

Ethaun leaned forward, crashing his burly forearms down on the table. "I'll be the judge o' that, lad. Where be it? In yer pack? I'll jest fetch it fer a look."

Suddenly afraid that Ethaun would open the pack and find the scroll from Krystallus—which he didn't want to talk about right now—Tamwyn got up himself. He walked across the earthen floor to his pack, reached inside, and pulled out the dagger's broken handle and blade. Glumly, he dropped them on the blacksmith's lap.

Even as Tamwyn shuffled over to the window, to see the swelling light of dawn slowly brighten the ravine, Ethaun took an oily rag from the table and started to polish the rusty blade. A few seconds later, the burly fellow whistled. Tamwyn spun back around to see him gazing at the blade with something close to awe.

"What?" asked the young man skeptically. "It's just an old thing I plowed up in a farmer's field. He called it *a gift from the land*, but that's just a fancy way of saying it's an old, beat-up dagger nobody wanted."

Ethaun didn't respond. All his concentration was on the broken blade. He polished it some more, shifted his bulk so that more starlight from the window struck the metal, then mumbled some archaic-sounding words.

Finally, he lowered the blade and peered at Tamwyn. "No, lad. Yer wrong. This here be somethin' special."

"How?" Tamwyn walked back to have a look, almost tripping over a half-made garden rake that lay on the floor. "I tell you, it's just—"

As if for the first time, he saw the subtle marks engraved on the side of the blade. What he'd thought were merely random scratches were really some kind of script! Like an ancient stream, the script meandered down the length of the blade. How in Avalon's name could he have carried this with him for so long without ever realizing what those marks were?

He scoffed at himself. *Because you never looked closely enough, you dolt!*

Ethaun's big finger jabbed at the script. "This be Old Fincayran, bet me top teeth. See here? How them letters curl back on theirselves? I seen some writin' jest like this, ages ago, on me old master's most prized possession, a real ancient shield. He'd never let me touch it, aye, but I sure looked at it plenty. An' a bard who came through our village showed me how to read its meanin'."

Tamwyn bent down on one knee to look more closely. "Can you read this?"

"Some parts, leastways." Brow furrowed, he puffed some on his pipe. "It says somethin' like, *Hallow be this blade when held by Merlin's heir.*"

Tamwyn's heart leaped over its next beat. Merlin's heir? Could that really be the dagger's destiny? And could he really be its rightful owner?

He glanced over his shoulder at his staff by the door. It could have been just a trick of the dawn light coming through the window, but for an instant, the seven symbols carved in the wooden shaft seemed to glow eerily. Then the staff returned to normal.

"Can't figure what that could mean," grumbled Ethaun. He set the blade back down on his lap and picked up the rusted handle. Examining it, he scratched the side of his beard. "One thin' be sure, though. This dagger was made long ago, an' by elvish folk."

"Elves? How can you tell?"

He pointed to the sweeping designs, barely visible, that ran along the handle's edges. "Only elvish metalworkers from Old Fincayra did that." He turned it over, then ran his cracked and blackened fingernail along the underside, revealing some more script. "Whoa! Will ye look at that?"

"What does it say?"

"Not real sure," he muttered, scraping away some more layers of dirt and rust. "I can't see none o' the first part, but it ends with some sort o' name. Startin' with an *R*, then an *h*, *i*, *t*—"

"Rhita Gawr!"

"Yer right, lad." Ethaun's pipe wriggled in his mouth as he chewed thoughtfully. "But Rhita Gawr be a wicked spirit! Why should the elvish folk be makin' mortal weapons with a spirit's name?"

"Because long ago," declared Tamwyn in a flash of insight, "before Rhita Gawr became a spirit, he was a mortal man. A warlord."

He ran his finger along the handle's edge. "I've heard songs about those days, Ethaun. Terrible things happened. Rhita Gawr rose to power by massacring families, burning villages, and poisoning crops—to stamp out anyone who opposed him. And he came down harder on the elves than anyone, because only they had the skill to make magical weapons."

The blacksmith looked at him doubtfully. "Magic blades? Never seen one o' them in all me years! Ye've been hearin' too many fanciful tales from bards, lad."

"Maybe so. But this one could really have some sort of magic."

"Even if it does," said Ethaun, shaking his head, "that still don't explain why the blade's got Gawr's name writ on it."

"Because the elves could have made this weapon to fight him, don't you see? Maybe in their own time—or maybe, if they could read the future, in some future time."

"Which could be why it says that bit about the heir o' Merlin?"

Tamwyn said nothing.

Ethaun tapped on the metal, which rang clear and cold, like a faraway bell. "Leastways, it still be a treasure. Even without any magic, a real beauty." He turned to Tamwyn. "I'll fix it fer ye, right now."

While Tamwyn watched, the man strapped on his apron and built up the fire, squeezing his bellows to make it burn hot. He set out a tall bucket of cold water, as well as several rags made from leathereed. Wielding his tools with the same ease and confidence as an expert swordsman wielding his blade, Ethaun alternately heated, hammered, twisted, and tempered the dagger. Clangs, squeals, and hisses reverberated around the hut.

At last, the smith wiped his brow with the sleeve of his tunic, and pulled the reforged dagger out of the fire for the last time. Holding it with the tongs, he turned it around, inspecting it from every angle. With a grunt of approval, he set it down on the anvil to cool.

He stretched his huge arms wide. "Well, tickle me toes, that be a good day's work!" With a glance at Tamwyn, he said, "Might jest take a wee nap, do ye mind? As it happened, I was out an' about fairly early this mornin'."

The young man grinned. "I know."

As he watched Ethaun drop his bulk onto the straw pallet, an idea rose in Tamwyn's mind. Walking over to his pack, he pulled out the slab of harmóna wood. For a long while he sat beside the hearth, feeling the wood and studying its orange-streaked grain, while Ethaun snored contentedly.

At last, when the dagger had cooled enough to hold, Tamwyn took it and began to carve Elli's harp. Gradually, the slab's triangular shape began to change. Almost, the outlines of a soundbox could be seen; almost, the space for strings, imagined. Curling chips of wood sprinkled the stone hearth, humming ever so delicately as they grew warm from the nearby coals.

Ethaun, in time, woke up. Sitting up on the pallet, he stretched his arms, scratched his beard, and then noticed Tamwyn. Rising, he strode over.

"Well, now," he exclaimed, "toast me turnips! If ye should ever stop explorin', lad, ye could pass fer a woodcarver."

"No," said Tamwyn with a shake of his black locks. "But on this carving, the wood is helping. And maybe the blade, as well."

The big fellow raised an eyebrow. "Ye know," he said in a rough whisper, "the legends from Old Fincayra are mighty strange at times. But one o' the strangest says that a young wizard only came into power when he carved his first musical instrument."

Tamwyn stopped carving and gave him a wink. Imitating the smith's tone of voice from before, he said, "Magic instruments? Never seen one o' them in all me years! Ye've been hearin' too many fanciful tales, lad."

Ethaun burst out laughing, his lungs heaving with all the force of his bellows. Finally, he stopped, though his eyes kept smiling. Quite gently for such a powerful man, he placed his hand on Tamwyn's shoulder.

"Ye know, lad, I'm glad ye came here to me part o' the world. Real glad." He peered at the young man thoughtfully, and then a strange expression came over his face. "So . . . I'm goin' to tell ye somethin' I swore never to reveal."

Tamwyn ceased working on the harp. He looked up at his bearded host, unsure what to expect.

After a long pause, Ethaun said softly, "Krystallus *did* come here."

Tamwyn jolted. "But you said—"

"I know, I know. Fergive me. But ye see, he made me promise never to tell."

"Why?" asked Tamwyn, still stunned.

"Well, lad," said Ethaun slowly, as if the words themselves hurt his tongue. "What he said was he didn't want no people from the root-realms comin' up here, searchin' fer his famous torch, hopin' to claim it fer theirselves."

In a flash, Tamwyn remembered what Nuic had said about that torch, and the only way Krystallus would ever set it down. He opened his mouth to speak, but no words came.

"But methinks his real reason was different. Methinks he jest didn't want no people tryin' to carry back his body."

All the blood drained from Tamwyn's face. "His . . . body?"

"Aye, lad. Ye see, he arrived here shortly after me, lived with me fer jest a while, and then—died."

Died. The word dropped on Tamwyn with the weight of an anvil.

"He was hurt bad, real bad—but not in his body. His wounds from them bloody termites had all healed somehow. No, he died from . . ."

"What?"

Ethaun's gaze moved to the hearth. Orange and gray coals still crackled, as waves of warmth made the air above them tremble. "It could pain ye greatly to hear, lad."

"Tell me," croaked Tamwyn.

Ethaun cleared his throat. "He died, pure an' simple, from grief."

Tamwyn's head felt heavier than iron ore, but he managed a nod. "Did he tell you . . . why?"

"Aye, lad. Said he'd lost everythin' he ever really cared about. His friends, his hopes, an' worst o' all, the two people he loved most—his wife an' son. An' then he told me that he'd lost some-thin' else, too. Somethin' that had finally left him fer good."

"His will to live," whispered Tamwyn.

"Yer right, lad."

Tamwyn studied the smith. "Did he say anything else?"

Ethaun drew a deep breath. "Aye. He said he fergave me fer runnin' off like I did. An' fer not fightin' by his side, as well. Told me that he'd been afeared hisself, many times, more than he could even count. An' then he said . . ."

"Yes?"

"That me true heart . . . was the heart o' an explorer."

Tamwyn gazed at him steadily through misted eyes. "And so you buried him up here, as close as he ever got to the stars."

"Aye. With me bare han's, I dug his grave."

He squeezed Tamwyn's shoulder just slightly. "An' lad," he whispered, "I'll take ye to see the grave." He nodded slowly. "Fer ye see, I've finally realized that yer his son."

37 · The View from the Grave

WIND WHISTLED AS TAMWYN AND ETHAUN trekked through the fields of tall grasses, climbing up to the rim of Merlin's Knothole. Their long locks, as well as Ethaun's beard, streamed out behind them. Though the wind this afternoon only came in gusts, with long moments of tranquility in between, whenever the gusts came the men had to lean over drastically just to keep standing.

Grasses waved all around them, a rippling sea of green, as they worked their way higher. The daytime sky was brighter than Tamwyn had ever seen, so bright that every tree, rock, or blade of grass was flooded with light, and every shadow crisp and dark. The smells of garden vegetables and freshly turned soil gradually lessened as the two men trekked farther above the valley floor.

Meanwhile, clusters of drumalings stood silently watching with narrow, vertical eyes, their knobby limbs gleaming in the starlight. Every so often, some of them would pull their burly roots out of the ground with loud popping noises, spraying dirt, and follow the two humans up the slope. *Scared o' everythin'*, Ethaun had

362

described them—and although Tamwyn didn't try to talk with them, he could feel their currents of fear and doubt.

Both of them were gasping for breath by the time they reached the upper edge of the grasses, above the place where Tamwyn had emerged from the tunnel. They didn't take time to rest, however. Just a brief pause to look back at the fertile gardens below was all they gave themselves. Then they started to climb one of the brown hills that ringed the Knothole.

Soon the last tufts of grass gave way to crusty brown soil and scattered stones. Every few paces, a new gust of wind tore across the rim, whipping their faces with clouds of dirt. Already Tamwyn had grit in his mouth, ears, and eyes.

Of course, he thought as he hiked up the hillside. *Nothing grows up here on the rim because of the wind!* He chuckled to himself, thinking that for any seed to stay in place long enough to root, it would have to weigh as much as Ethaun.

Glancing over at the burly blacksmith who was huffing by his side, he added, *And that's a lot.*

Just as they neared the top of the rim, a powerful gust roared across the hills. The air howled furiously. Both of them crouched down as dirt swirled around them, stinging any exposed skin, even the backs of their hands. Finally, the wind blew itself out. As they rose again, Ethaun pointed to a small but deep cleft higher on the hill.

"See that notch, me lad? That be the place." He worked his tongue and spat out some grit. "Protected from the wind it be, leastways mostly. An' yet up here, close to the stars. That be why I picked it fer the grave."

Tamwyn merely nodded. This wasn't how he had hoped to find his father.

Up the last stretch of hillside they trudged. As the gravesite came fully into view, Tamwyn paused to look at it. Leaning on his staff, with wind tousling his hair, he could see a low mound of soil within the notch. The site was unmarked and unadorned, except for a single wooden pole. The torch!

At that instant, a keening cry echoed above their heads. Tamwyn looked up to see another prism bird. As it spun skyward, its wings spread wide and its feathers flashed, sending streams of color across the sky. One cloud, directly behind the top of the torch, caught the wash of brilliance, exploding with light for a brief, shining moment.

"Well, I'll be a talkin' turnip," said Ethaun in awe. "There be no bird er beast more beautiful than that, anywhere in Avalon."

Tamwyn nodded and started walking toward the gravesite again, thinking about what he'd just seen. It looked just as if the torch itself had burst into colorful flames. An omen, perhaps? Or just another false hope?

The real torch, he could see clearly as they approached, was dark. Dead and dark.

As he entered the notch, just behind Ethaun, the wind abruptly ceased. Tamwyn strode over to the mound of hardpacked soil. Awkwardly, he set down his staff and knelt beside it. He lowered his head, staring into the ground, wishing he could see right through the layers of soil—the layers between life and death—to look upon the man named Krystallus Eopia.

His father.

He saw nothing, though. Nothing but dirt.

Slowly, he lifted his head. Ethaun, too, was kneeling by the grave. He looked up at the same time and their gazes met.

"Ye know," his growling voice rumbled, "we're jest the opposite, ye an' me."

"How so?"

He gave his beard a thoughtful tug. "Well, fer me, knowin' Krystallus, even fer a little while, was the best part o' me life. From the very first moment he let me join the group, he always looked out fer me. Even shared his breakfast biscuits with me, he did! An' while I never said so to him, I always wished . . . he was really me father. Though o' course, he wasn't."

Tamwyn nodded grimly. "So you knew him, but he wasn't your father. And for me—just the opposite."

The smith's dark eyes glittered. "Rot me roots, a bad deal fer both o' us! But Tamwyn . . ."

"Yes?"

"At least he really *was* yer father."

Tamwyn turned back to the grave. Under his breath, he said, "I'd rather have known him."

At last, his eyes lifted again. He studied the torch. Its pole was made of simple, unpolished wood—no more remarkable than his own staff had seemed before he'd uttered the magical phrase that made its runes appear. And the top of the torch was merely a charred, oily rag, wrapped tightly and secured with twine.

Even so, he sensed some power within it. Magical power, that rubbed against his own like a pair of iron stones. But would that rubbing, he wondered, produce a spark that could burst into flame?

"Tell me about this torch," he said to Ethaun.

The man shrugged. "It burned, an' not jest now an' then but all the time. Day an' night. That be all I knows. Fer as long as

Krystallus lived, it flamed away. Then, the very instant he died, it went dark. Jest like that."

"But how did it burn? Do you know?"

"No, lad. Nobody knows. Not even Krystallus, methinks." He scratched his hairy chin. "Only one person knows, I suspect, an' that be Merlin hisself."

"Merlin?"

"Aye. Krystallus said that Merlin gave him the torch, an' made it flame, way long ago. So the wizard must have knowed. But he be long gone."

"Maybe he left a clue," suggested Tamwyn. He got up and circled the dark torch, inspecting it closely. Yet he saw nothing even remotely helpful. It seemed no more unusual than the straw that Ethaun had used for the pallet in his hut.

Still, he did feel something, from down deep in its core. Something magical. If only he knew how to reach it!

At that moment, Ethaun rose. Standing beside Tamwyn, he seemed like a huge, pitted boulder, as much part of the hillside as the notch itself. "It be time," he growled, "fer me to go. Got some smithin' to do fer them rootyfeeted friends o' mine."

Tamwyn nodded. "Thanks. For everything."

"Yer welcome, lad." He reached his burly arms around Tamwyn and gave him a powerful, bone-cracking hug. "I'm thankful, too, ye came here."

Releasing his hold, Ethaun fumbled in the pockets of his tunic. "There be a little gift I want to give ye now, to help ye on yer journey."

"No, really. You don't need to."

"'Course I don't need to! But I truly want to." He pulled

something from the folds of a cloth: a glass globe held inside a leather strap. "Here, lad. Take it."

Tamwyn hesitated. "I saw that on your wall. What is it?"

"It be somethin' that Krystallus hisself gave to me, afore he died. Told me to take care o' it fer him." He cleared his throat. "An' that I have."

"Ethaun, are you sure?"

"Listen, lad. Do ye think I've got any use fer it, havin' made this valley me home? No, yer the only one who'll be needin' a compass."

A compass. Tamwyn held his breath as he took the globe from the smith's weathered hand. Here was the very thing he had longed for!

Carefully, he examined it. Inside the globe, held by hair-thin wires, were a pair of silver arrows. One, like every compass in Avalon, rotated horizontally and always pointed westward—toward El Urien, for travelers in the root-realms. But there was also another arrow, which had been set to rotate on a vertical axis, and always pointed starward! So no matter how lost a traveler might be, or how far beneath the surface, he or she could always find the direction of the roots below and the stars above.

Eager to see if it really worked, Tamwyn carried the compass outside the notch that sheltered the gravesite. Though the wind suddenly whipped his face and tore at his tunic, he held tight to the globe as he carried it over to the farthest tip of the rim where he could stand.

Ahead of him, rising steeply higher, he could see the rugged ridges of Avalon's upper trunk, lifting into the misty horizon. And beyond that, starkly etched against the bright afternoon sky, were the shadowed shapes of the branches—even easier to see than they had been before. They reached up into the sky, flowing like uncharted rivers, until they disappeared at last into the brightness above.

As the wind howled all around him, he peered into the globe. Sure enough, the starward arrow was pointing straight at the place where the branches faded into open sky—the realm of the stars.

Smiling with satisfaction, Tamwyn headed back, leaning to keep his balance against the wind. When he reentered the notch, and the wind abruptly stopped, he faced the broad-shouldered smith.

"What a marvelous gift," he said gratefully.

"Jest might prove useful," said Ethaun with a wink. "Fer a real Avalon explorer."

"Right," Tamwyn replied. "And now here's another gift. For another explorer." He slipped off his pack. Even as he stuffed the compass inside, he pulled out the lock of gray hair that had been tied around his father's scroll. Placing it in Ethaun's hand, he said, "You know where this came from."

The big man blinked in surprise. "That I do, lad."

"You should have it."

"But . . ." the smith protested, trying to give it back, "yer his son."

"And so, in a way, are you. So keep it. Please."

Ethaun dragged a sooty hand across one of his eyes. Then he squeezed the lock tight, nodded farewell, and turned to go. He shambled off down the slope, looking very much like a bear going back to his den.

Tamwyn watched him go, then turned back to the grave. His gaze roamed across the mound, and to the soft dirt surrounding it. He could see his own knee's print from where he had knelt, as well as his footprints and the marks of Ethaun's boots. Then, to his utter astonishment, he saw something else: a footprint left by neither of them.

The footprint of a hoolah.

Tamwyn bent to look more closely. There could be no mistake. The outline was just as clear as could be. And the imprint was no more than a couple of days old.

Henni! Could he still be alive? And wandering here in the upper reaches of Avalon? With Batty Lad, too, perhaps? No, the chances of that were just too remote. He shouldn't raise his hopes. And yet . . .

He scanned the area around the notch. There were no paths, no signs of anyone else. Ogres' uncles, if that hoolah was really here, where had he gone?

He lifted his gaze higher, toward the branches and stars. If Henni had somehow survived, and had found his way up to the Knothole, it was at least remotely possible that he'd also found some way to climb up there, into the branches. And yet, if that were true, how could Tamwyn ever hope to catch sight of him? Those distances were simply far too vast to find anything as small as a hoolah.

An idea suddenly struck him. The vial of Dagda's dew! What had Gwirion told him it could do? *A single drop, placed on your forehead, gives a rare kind of sight—long vision over vast distances.*

"Just what I need," declared Tamwyn.

He grabbed the ironwood vial out of his pack, unplugged it, and poured a single drop of glistening liquid onto his fingertip. Holding his breath in anticipation, he touched the drop to the middle of his forehead. Then, realizing that there was still a bit of Dagda's dew left in the vial—perhaps one more drop—he quickly plugged it again and replaced it in his pack.

He stood, spear straight, looking up at the shadowy branch that seemed nearest. Waiting. Just waiting.

Nothing happened. Could the liquid have lost its magic? Or had he done something wrong?

All at once, everything in his vision shivered and blurred, as if he'd stepped into a waterfall. Images streamed before him, all stretched out of proportion. Light and colors streaked, clotted, burst apart, and streaked again.

Suddenly his vision returned. He was staring right into the face of a bizarre winged creature, as ferocious as any dragon, with spiraling tusks, jagged blue teeth, and hundreds of faceted eyes. Flying straight at him!

Tamwyn ducked, throwing his forearm across his face for protection. Then suddenly he realized the truth. That creature was hundreds of leagues away! Somewhere on one of Avalon's branches, a monster with huge tusks and leathery wings soared. But not here.

He stood straight again, planting his feet in the soil of the gravesite, and trained his gaze skyward, toward the branch far above. Wherever that ferocious creature had gone, he couldn't see it now. Instead, he saw a new landscape, one that looked like a great forest. Except that this forest bent and flowed like an ocean. Gigantic waves flowed through the wooded hills and valleys, lifting the trees skyward, plunging them into deep hollows, and lifting them all over again. *What kind of place is that, where the land flaps like a windblown cape and never stays firm under your feet?*

He shook his head in amazement, which shifted his vision. Now he was looking at a ring of purple waterfalls. They didn't flow upward, like the Spiral Cascades, although their spray did. But the spray didn't rise into clouds, as it would have in the root-realms. Instead, it gathered into great, sparkling spheres of lavender-colored mist. Part water, part air, and part light, these spheres twirled in the sky, before exploding into countless rain-drops that then fell on the hills above the falls.

Tamwyn gasped with surprise. In the last instant before they burst apart, the misty spheres hardened into something as smooth as glass. And in that fleeting instant, varied images appeared on the glassy surface: brightly colored butterflies with eight wings apiece; a wide, red-fruited tree that seemed to be sprouting right out of a cloud; and an enormous, black dragon, whose hateful glare gave Tamwyn a shiver.

No! his inner voice exclaimed. For now he glimpsed in one of those crystalline spheres a face that he recognized. His own face! He was shouting something, pleading, something about the stars—

Then it was gone. The whole image exploded into lavender rain.

Without thinking, he turned away. Suddenly he found himself staring, close up, at a group of stars. The constellation Pegasus! There were the stars that marked the horse's head, wings, hooves, and tail, so blazingly bright that he was forced to squint just to look at them. And there—the central star that burned brighter than all the rest, the one called the Heart of Pegasus.

Tamwyn peered at this star—and suddenly blinked in astonish-ment. The Heart of Pegasus seemed to be beating! He opened his eyes just a sliver more, as wide as he could stand, to look more closely. And yes, that star was indeed pulsing like the heart of a great steed. *Why, I wonder, would it do that?*

A lizard scurried, just then, across his foot. Tamwyn flinched in surprise. In doing so, he lost sight of the pulsing star. He started to look for it again, but found himself gazing instead at a different constellation.

A darkened constellation.

The black hole that had once been the Wizard's Staff.

He stared hard at the spot where those seven stars had once burned so bright, hoping to find some clue about what had really happened to them. And what all this had to do with Rhita Gawr.

Something strange caught his attention. Peering closely, he could detect vague circles of light up there. Yes . . . seven of them. And the circles—each no more than a thin, glowing thread—sat in precisely the same places as the lost stars! Could they be the stars themselves, but in another form? Or covered up somehow?

Though his whole body shook with excitement, Tamwyn fought to keep himself steady. He had to know more! To understand what this meant! The stars, or some parts of them, were still there. And if they were still there . . . they could, perhaps, be lit again.

He swallowed. Could only Merlin himself do such a thing?

Startled, he noticed something else. Dark, formless shapes seemed to be crossing in front of the rings of light. Just like the shapes in the vision atop Hallia's Peak! Always moving outward, they flowed like ominous clouds, reeking of evil. Whatever they were, they seemed to be emerging from *within* the circles.

What in Avalon's name are those shapes? He was still no closer to answering that question than he'd been on the night of the vision. And now his time—Avalon's time—was almost gone.

He sucked in his breath. *I wish Elli were here right now! To-gether, we could figure this out.*

Indeed, he wished she were here for many reasons. To help him understand those dark shapes, yes—but also to show her the harp he was making. And simply to look upon her face, her hazel green eyes.

He froze. Maybe there *was* a way.

It would require all the strength of his enhanced vision. And all the new power growing inside himself—power that was partly from magic, and partly from something else.

Tamwyn sat down in the dirt, leaning his back against the torch that his father had carried all the way to this place. In case its powers just might augment his own, he grasped hold of the staff. And then he did something remarkable.

He closed his eyes. For this kind of seeing, he knew in his heart, had nothing to do with normal sight.

"Elli," he said, then fell silent.

38 · Distant Music

ELLI GULPED. AND WRAPPED HER FINGERS even more tightly around the two thin, silvery ropes, one that stretched along her left side and one along her right. A third rope ran under her feet—all that stood between her and a free fall into endless oblivion.

From the corner of her eye, she glanced downward. Swirling clouds of mist—with no shape, no boundaries, and absolutely no bottom—churned beneath her, as far as she could see. Supported by nothing except these three long ropes of tightly spun clouds, which had been strung centuries before across the airy chasm between Mudroot and Airroot, she couldn't take another step. She couldn't even move, except to shudder.

The Misty Bridge! How could I have been so foolhardy to try this?

As she shuddered again, the sprite Nuic wriggled anxiously on her shoulder. His color deepening into a dark azure blue, he said calmly, "It may surprise you to hear this, my dear, but you might actually get to the other side quicker if you start walking again."

Elli didn't answer. She just continued to squeeze the ropes of glistening cloudthread, her body frozen in place.

"Come now, Elliryanna," coaxed Nuic. "That idiot jester is probably all the way over to the other side by now."

"I can't," she said shakily. "Just . . . can't."

"Hmmmpff, is that so? Halfway across the bridge, and now you decide to quit? Just how do you plan to explain your change of heart to Rhia? Tamwyn? And Coerria?"

The mention of those names made her scowl. *He's right, you dolt! If you don't start moving again, you've just abandoned everything.*

But how could she move when these three ropes, swaying under her weight, seemed no more substantial than strands of spider's thread?

Spider's thread. The words reminded her of Coerria's magnificent garb, the spider's silk gown that had been worn by every High Priestess since Elen. She glanced down at the scrap of the dress, brought to her by the Sapphire Unicorn, that hung right now from her belt. *Those threads may not look very strong,* she told herself, *but they've lasted for a thousand years.*

Slowly, she drew a breath. Her fingers slid up and down the ropes on either side, feeling the silken strands. *Perhaps these, too, are stronger than they seem.*

"Well, Elliryanna?" came the sprite's voice in her ear. "Are you going to start walking again or not?"

"All right, all right, you crusty old goat." She started to move ever so cautiously, sliding one foot along the bridge. "I was just enjoying the view, you know."

"Hmmmpff. Which is why you're still quaking like a leaf in a hurricane."

"That isn't me," she declared, taking another small step on the rope. "It's this blasted bridge, wobbling all over the place."

She took another step, then another, running her hands along the cloudthread railings. With each movement, the whole bridge bounced, sending waves of vibrations up and down the ropes. Mist swirled in bottomless depths below, but she tried with all her will to resist looking down again. And to keep on walking.

After two dozen more steps, she glanced back over her shoulder—hardly more comforting than looking down. She was still somewhere in the middle of the bridge, unable to see the great pillars of hardened mud that anchored the ropes behind her, and equally unable to see whatever lay ahead. All she saw in both directions were the three spindly ropes disappearing into swirls of mist.

"Who made this bridge, anyway?" she asked, trying to think about something besides falling to her death.

Without warning—her foot slipped sideways off the bottom rope. She gasped, teetering, and seized the railings with all her strength. A few seconds later, her foot was back where it should have been. But her heart continued to gallop.

Nuic, clinging tightly to her shoulder, sounded slightly breathless as he answered her question. "Sylphs built it. No surprise there, since they simply love to float around, busying themselves with inane projects." With a hint of pride, he added, "This bridge, one of their more practical ideas, was organized by my old friend Le-fen-flaith."

Thin lines of silver seeped into his azure blue skin. "When it was all done, in the Year of Avalon 702, Rhiannon and I were the first to cross it. Le-fen-flaith himself guided us, and then took us across Y Swylarna, all the way to the sacred birthplace of the sylphs."

Elli continued edging forward, moving toe by toe across the chasm. "And your friend also named it?"

"He did," scoffed Nuic. "But great architect that he was,

naming things was not exactly his strength. Called it Trishila o Mageloo, which means something syrupy like *the air sighs sweetly.*" His color shifted to barf brown. "Thankfully, in time, travelers came to call it the Misty Bridge."

Elli grinned, knowing full well that Nuic was doing his best to distract her, hoping to keep her mind off the danger of slipping again and plunging into nothingness. "I *like* the idea of air sighing sweetly. Could make a good song."

"Hmmmpff. Watch out, or I might sing it to you."

"Fine. Just warn me first, so I can—" She caught herself, glimpsing something more solid than the mist ahead. "The other side! We're almost there."

"About time," Nuic grumbled, his color settling back to silvery blue.

In just a few more steps, they would reach the Airroot side of the bridge. Even as she moved closer, Elli studied how the structure was anchored. Instead of mud pillars to hold the ropes, twin columns of what looked like frozen clouds rose out of a platform made of the same material. A layer of curling mist rose off the platform, making it resemble a flat-bottomed cloud.

"That's cloudcake," Nuic explained, anticipating Elli's question. "The closest thing to stone in Y Swylarna, found only near the Air Falls of Silmannon. And yes, it's hard enough to stand on, as you can tell from that fool who's waiting there now."

The jester stepped toward them through the chest-high swirls of mist. When he reached the edge of the platform, he made the mistake of leaning on his cane, which immediately sank halfway down into the cloudcake due to its narrow point. He nearly fell over, then waved his arms wildly to regain his balance. Finally, with a loud grunt, he pulled his cane free.

"Look there," Elli said, feeling almost giddy with relief to be nearly off the bridge. "He's even clumsier than Tamwyn."

"Tamwyn's more likeable, though. In a, hmmmpff, repulsive sort of way."

Elli glanced at her bracelet, braided from the yellow stems of astral flowers, but said nothing. She knew that Nuic understood she'd been thinking often about Tamwyn. Just not *how* often.

With one final step, she left the bridge. It took a moment for her still-swaying body to realize that she was, at last, standing on something more solid—and steady—than cloudthread rope. And another moment to realize that she'd actually crossed over the Misty Bridge. She felt a gentle tap against her ear: a congratulatory pat from Nuic.

She turned around slowly, scanning this new landscape. Or, more accurately, cloudscape. Clouds of distinctive shapes and sizes hovered or drifted nearby: some flat and smooth as ax blades, others high and lumpy as spruce trees; some nearly as solid as fortified castles, others more wispy than dandelion seeds. Although several clouds moved freely, vaporous bridges, ladders, and walkways connected many of them. A large group, stacked on top of each other like floating platforms, were connected by intricate webs of silver cloudthread—the work, it appeared, of a clan of giant spiders.

Her gaze then turned to the cloud that supported them now. Beyond the platform, it looked fairly dense—maybe even thick enough to walk on. The narrow cloud tilted gradually upward, so that it resembled a long, rising ridge.

"What the trolls' teeth is that?" She pointed to a huge cloud in the distance, shaped like a mass of rolling hills. Rising off its misty slopes were thousands of hazy pinnacles, sharply pointed at the top. More like pillars of light than anything solid, they covered the cloud completely.

"The great Forest Afloat," answered Nuic, an unusual tone of admiration in his voice. "It's full of eonia-lalo trees, whose bark is almost invisible, even when you're standing among them. The whole forest moves freely around the realm. So it's impossible to guess, on any given day, just where it will appear next."

"Just like me," chuckled Seth, who had stepped to Elli's side. "Jesters are always on the move, you know—often to escape our adoring crowds, especially the ones wielding axes and knives. I come and go just like the clouds."

"More like the plague," grumbled Nuic.

Seth's grin broadened, and he slapped his side. Bells up and down the arms of his jerkin jingled playfully. His thoughts, however, were anything but playful, for he had definitely made up his mind that killing this annoying little sprite would be part of his pleasure. He'd do it first, too, so the girl could watch. The only question was whether he should stab Nuic with the hidden blade, bludgeon him to death with the cane—or simply throw the little beast over the edge.

Throw him over, Seth decided. *The shrieks will be lovely. And of course*, he thought smugly, *there is another question—when to do it.*

His flinty gray eyes narrowed. *I grow weary of this charade. And eager to possess my crystals! Besides, this setting is quite perfect. So dramatic, so remote. I shall do it soon. Very soon.*

"Look there!" cried Elli, pointing to a group of nine or ten thin, vaporous forms, nearly transparent, that were sailing across the sky. Moving rapidly, they were carried by some peculiar wind of their own, which didn't seem to touch any of the larger clouds nearby. "They look more like a flock of birds than a bunch of clouds, don't they?"

"Hmmmpff. That's because they *are* more like a flock of birds, you fool. Those are sylphs—flying off to the Harplands, by the looks of it."

Elli watched the vaporous forms, hardly more substantial than the air itself. After a moment, she reached up and touched a tiny foot of the maryth on her shoulder. "Did you say Harplands?"

"That's right. Listen."

To the sound of your breathing, said the jester to himself. *While it lasts—which won't be long, my sweet.*

Elli, meanwhile, was listening to the airy sounds of Y Swylarna. Beyond the steady swish of distant winds, she thought she could hear a deeper, whooshing sound—perhaps the Air Falls that Nuic had mentioned. But hard as she tried, she couldn't hear anything that sounded at all like harps.

"Sorry, Nuic. Maybe your Harplands are just too far away."

The sprite's color turned an impatient orange. "Or maybe humans' ears are made of wood, just like their brains. Perhaps if we walk up to a higher point on this cloud ridge, you can hear better. And see better, too—so I can point out our route."

Good idea, thought Seth, bobbing his head. *The higher you are, the farther you'll fall.*

Elli, with Nuic on her shoulder, stepped off the cloudcake platform and started to walk up the long, gradual rise—although walking didn't really describe it. *Bouncing* suited it better, for with every step, her body sank deeper and rose higher than she'd ever experienced before. Each stride was almost as much vertical as horizontal. Elli felt as if she were stepping over an enormous, immensely soft pillow. But this misty pillow made every step easier, since the cloud kept springing back firmly underfoot.

Once Elli became used to the new, bouncy rhythm of her gait, she quite liked the feeling. After a glance back at the jester, she concluded that he, too, was enjoying their pillow-walk, even though his face seemed more a mask of his emotions than a true expression of them. No doubt, she guessed, that was the way with all jesters: They were always performing.

As they climbed the long, gradual slope, Elli scanned some more of the surrounding airscape. Vapors, tinted light green or lavender, twisted and curled everywhere, wrapping themselves around denser clouds like radiant ribbons—or around each other, like transparent snakes. In the gaps between clouds, brilliant pools of sky opened, impossibly blue. Like melted sapphires shot through with light, the pools glittered invitingly.

All the while, as she took springy steps higher, gentle breezes tickled her chin and tousled her hair. So light was the wind, she almost wished that she could leap up and float along with it, borne through the ocean of air.

Then, to her left, she saw something surprising: an entire cloud dotted with thousands of tiny blue points. Like a celestial field of blueberries, the cloud sparkled with this misty crop. Elli licked her lips, remembering the feast of berries they'd eaten just after landing in Waterroot. Did fruits grow in this realm, as well?

She was just about to ask Nuic, when overhead she heard a swelling cacophony. Birds! Hundreds and hundreds of birds, several flocks combined, flew out of a cloud. There were black cormorants, cranes with long necks, pointy-beaked sandpipers, hawks, jays, terns, kitiwakes with silver wings, and even a few pure white owls. Squawking and piping, hooting and whistling, the birds' noisy chatter drowned out every other sound, even the rush of faraway winds.

Only after they had flown a good distance, disappearing into a dark bank of clouds, did their calls finally fade away. Elli shook her head and commented, "Loudest birds I ever heard."

Nuic tugged on one of her curls and declared, "Then you've never been to the Isles of Birds, many leagues east of here. Where that group is heading, I'll wager. Why, there are so many birds nesting there, all year round, that the noise is almost deafening."

"So there must be thousands."

"Try millions, Elliryanna! So many birds that when all of them rise into the sky, they block out the light and it seems like nighttime until they land again."

As Elli tried to imagine such a sight, Nuic suddenly pointed to a steep rise ahead, lifting like a summit at the northernmost edge of the cloud. "There," he declared. "That spot will do. From the top, we can see how far we have to go."

And how far you have to fall, thought the man striding behind them, a jesterly grin on his face.

With quick, bouncy steps, they mounted the rise. At the top, a wide vista opened to the north. There were scores of thin, intertwining clouds that had woven themselves into a great tapestry of mist; a range of massive clouds, even taller than the high peaks of Olanabram; dozens of luminous rainbows, all rising side by side; and on the horizon, a stormy maelstrom that crackled constantly with lightning. But what captured Elli's attention more than any of these sights was a misty valley in the distance where tall, graceful spirals of vapor twirled and spun in an airy, ongoing dance.

"The Dancing Grounds of the Mist Maidens," said Nuic, following her gaze. "Among the strangest sights—and strangest creatures—of this realm. Just imagine what it would be like if you—"

"Wait," Elli said, cutting him off. "I think I can hear the harps!"

She closed her eyes, listening not just with her ears but with all of herself, opening every pore of her skin to the world of sound. She heard the beating of her heart, the breathing of her lungs, and the swish and whistle of distant winds. But now, beyond all that, she also heard something else—a tender, lilting music that seemed the perfect accompaniment to the Mist Maidens' dance.

Harps. They sang with long, sweeping notes that held the lightness of air and the sweetness of starlight, rippling with overtones. The music of the harps' strings swelled louder, receded, then lifted anew and hung there, warbling, before finally fading away—only to rise again.

Elli opened her eyes again, though the vaporous creatures' spiraling dance now seemed only possible because of the harps' music. "It's like . . . well, like the air *itself* is singing."

"It is," replied Nuic, sitting close to her ear. "Those are aeolian harps, you see. Scores and scores of them, resting on the slopes of those mountainous clouds over there. The sylphs themselves crafted them, and tuned them over several centuries. For strings they used only the finest strands of vaporthread, stretched between clouds so tightly that even the slightest brush of wind will vibrate them. And so it does, making the finest music—outside of museos, of course—anywhere in the Seven Realms."

She sighed, remembering the lilting harp music that her father had played for her so often, years ago. And the harp that he had given her before he died—which Tamwyn had accidentally crushed on the first day they'd met. Yet even without the instrument, she could still hear its music, still feel its enchantment.

Nuic gently tapped her cheek. "And mind you, all this music is more than just entertaining. It's also useful. People around here predict changes in the weather based on what they hear in the Harplands. Not too accurately, mind you, but at least it's better than an ogre's bunion."

Elli listened for another moment, then said, "It's more than just sound, isn't it? It's also feeling. Layers and layers of feeling."

Nuic paused, himself listening, before he spoke again. "Some sylphs who have studied the harps say those strings respond to more than just wind. They can also pick up the emotions of people nearby—anger, love, fear, and the like. Hmmmpff, I don't believe it myself, but they claim it's possible to sense, sometimes, changes in the overall balance of things. Approaching danger, for example."

Even as he spoke, the music swelled the slightest bit louder.

Elli gasped. She took a big step backward on the cloudy knoll, startling Nuic so much that he nearly fell off her shoulder. Seth, meanwhile, remained still, watching calmly.

"There," Elli shouted, pointing at an enormous, dark shape that was rising on the horizon. "Look there!"

The huge shape lifted higher, poking through the surrounding clouds. A head! It turned toward them, even as it opened powerful jaws with hundreds of gleaming teeth. The jewels in its gargantuan crown flashed, yet not so brightly as its wrathful green eyes. Two ears straightened, dangling gigantic earrings of pearls and kelp.

"Hargol!" she cried. "He's here."

"Hold on, Elliryanna," declared Nuic. "Do you think a water dragon, who can swim but not fly, could get very far in Airroot?"

"Then . . ." she said, staring at the gigantic head. "What is it?"

"The Veils of Illusion," he replied coolly. "Clouds with a disturbing magic of their own. They can take the form of whatever fears may be riding the wind."

Elli shook her head, scattering some wisps of mist that had settled on her curls. "Let's avoid that place, shall we?"

"That we can do," declared the sprite. "But to follow your plan—going to that portal in upper Airroot, and then on to Shadowroot for the corrupted crystal—we'll have to pass through some *other* dangerous places. Very dangerous."

Seth, who was standing right behind them, smirked wickedly.

In the distance, the music from the Harplands grew suddenly louder. And also slightly discordant, as if some of the vaporthread strings had suddenly broken.

Slowly, Seth straightened his hunched shoulders. His little bells sounded, even as the distant harps jangled out of harmony. "As for myself," he declared, "I rather prefer *this* dangerous place."

Struck by his newly malevolent tone, Elli spun around to face him. "What do you mean?"

"This." The jester clicked the hidden button on his cane. Instantly, a gleaming dagger blade extended from its tip. Quicker than Elli's eyes could follow, he swung up the cane so that the blade's tip aimed straight at her chest.

Instinctively, she took a hasty step backward. And she might have taken another, if she hadn't found herself standing on the very edge of the cloud—with a sheer drop into bottomless vapors right behind her.

Nuic, whose skin color had shifted to a mix of crimson and black, grumbled, "Trouble, like clouds, comes in many forms."

"Couldn't have said it better myself," clucked their assailant. He jabbed the blade toward her chest again. "You see, I'll be taking those little trinkets of yours—both of them."

"Not unless you kill us first," spat Elli, her hands curling into fists.

His sallow face grinned crookedly. "If you insist, my little gumdrop." His dagger blade pricked the amulet around her neck, pulling apart the leaves so that he could see the luminous crystal beneath them. "Oh yes indeed, how very nice."

Elli shook her head, heedless of the blade. The crystal flashed brilliantly, shooting out rays of white, green, and blue light. Very slowly, he lowered the blade, dragging it down her robe until it rested just above her heart. He held that position, clearly enjoying the feeling of being in complete control.

"You see," he said with a smirk, "my real name isn't Seth. No, no. My *real* name is Deth. Deth Macoll."

"How appropriate," grumbled Nuic. "But it doesn't suit you as well as some other names. Fraud, Coward, and Madman, for instance."

Deth Macoll's face reddened. "Is that so, you little loudmouth?" In a flash, he raised the blade to point right between Nuic's purple eyes. "So glad you reminded me that I'd like to kill you first. Now, any more insults before you get skewered?"

"The best insults are true," shot back the sprite. "You *are* a fraud. As well as a coward! I'll wager you're just scared to death of Kulwych. You would never have dared to take us to his hiding place, anyway. Why, you probably don't even know where it really is!"

The assassin's face turned nearly as crimson as Nuic, while the wind harps swelled to a dissonant chorus. Shaking with rage, he snarled, "You think so? Well, he's somewhere even deeper than a dark elf's grave." He raised an eyebrow. "But if you think I'm going to tell you any more than that, you're wrong."

"Hmmmpff. So you *don't* know."

"I do! But the only thing worth knowing is that very soon his crystal will be joining the ones worn by you and the girl. Right inside my pocket!"

At that instant, three things happened at once. Deth Macoll thrust his murderous blade at the sprite. Elli swiftly sidestepped and grabbed the assailant's wrist. But before she could start to fight for the blade, Nuic leaped at her head, grasping her abundant curls.

She wrenched backward as the force of his leap threw her off the edge of the cloud. Both Elli and Nuic fell downward into the endless well of mist. And they weren't alone. Pulled by Elli's grip, Deth Macoll pitched forward and tumbled over the edge, swinging his cane wildly.

All three of them plummeted down into the swirling vapors.

39 · What Wind That Blows

SO LOUD WAS THE *WHOOSHHHHH* OF AIR ALL around, Elli couldn't hear her own scream. Down, down, down she fell, tearing through gauzy shreds of mist, plunging into utter emptiness. Nothing could stop her fall—and nothing could save her quest.

Yet even as she spun downward, she reached behind her head to grab Nuic. He didn't let go easily, tearing out whatever curls he held in his tiny hands, but finally she clutched him to her chest. Their eyes met. And for Elli, this was their very last chance to read each other's gaze.

Strange, she thought as she peered into his liquid purple eyes, *he doesn't look at all afraid—*

A trail of silver threads suddenly burst out of the crease in Nuic's back. Instantly, the threads popped into a wide parachute, giving the sprite a sharp tug. Elli barely held on to him. Then, abruptly, the whoosh of air quieted. They were floating like a huge, windblown seed through the vaporous air.

Again their eyes met. And she suddenly could imagine his crusty rebuke: *Stump-headed fool! How could you forget about my parachute? We mountain dwellers don't just walk everywhere, you know.*

Just then a broad, wedge-shaped cloud, dense enough to stand on, came into view. Nuic twisted hard to the left, trying to shift the parachute. They veered sharply sideways.

Trails of mist from the side of the cloud flowed over them, making it difficult to see. Even so, Elli spied the darker, denser edge of its core, and reached for it. Keeping Nuic tightly in one arm, she stretched with all her will. Her fingers nearly pulled out of their sockets as she tried to grasp hold.

Too late! They slid downward, bouncing off the underside of the cloud. The parachute caught on something and twisted with a wrenching jolt, spinning them in midair. They plunged downward again.

Whooshhhhh! A savage gust tore into them, sheering them sideways. The blast of wind was so strong that Elli lurched and turned upside down, almost losing her grip on Nuic.

But that twist was just enough to untangle the parachute. The silver threads popped again, slowing their fall. They sailed through the air, making gentle turns, as if they were dancing an aerial ballet.

"There!" cried Elli, pointing to a rumpled cloud to the right. Though it wasn't very big, and didn't seem to be attached to anything else, at least it looked dense enough to provide a safe landing—if only they could reach it.

Nuic twisted hard. They veered right, as Elli reached out her hand, stretching as far as she possibly could.

Closer they came, and closer. Misty fingers reached out to them, drawing them near. Elli spied a firm edge and reached, reached farther . . . and touched it! As her hand wrapped around the edge, she pulled with all her strength. They thudded down onto the surface, rolled through the rising vapors, and finally came to a stop.

Elli lay her head back on the cloud, her brown curls scattered around her head like an unruly halo, and sighed in relief. This cloud was softer, wetter, and even more springy, than the ridge cloud they had walked upon. Yet it was, at least, somewhat solid. Enough to hold them for a while.

Nuic wriggled free and sat down in the spongy vapors beside her. With a sharp squeeze of his shoulders, he released the parachute—all except for one strand that had twisted around his leg. He untangled himself, flicked the strand away, and watched as the parachute blew free again, drifting over the edge of the cloud and out of sight.

"Well, Elliryanna, looks like we made it." His color warmed to rich pink. "And it looks like our friendly jester didn't." His rosy hues deepened. "I quite enjoyed seeing him plunge down into the mist, writhing uncontrollably and squealing like a baby boar."

Elli rolled over on the cloud and propped herself on her elbow. Her arm sank into the soft, slightly moist surface. She scrutinized him closely, as if she were reading some hidden script beneath his skin.

"You knew he was a fraud all along, didn't you?"

The sprite winked at her. "Very good! I knew you'd catch on eventually."

"But how did you know?"

"It was easy, really. No one as mean-faced as him could really make it as a jester."

She blew away a floating wisp of mist that had settled on her nose. "Then why did you wait so long?"

"Hmmmpff. Isn't that obvious? Because we needed to know where that fiend Kulwych is hiding! And now, my dear, we do."

"No, we don't. He refused to tell you, remember?"

"Hmmmpff. So he thought! He said, if you recall, that Kulwych is *somewhere even deeper than a dark elf's grave.*"

Elli shrugged. "And?"

"And that tells us he's down deep underground—which, in Shadowroot, means one of the dark elves' abandoned mines. Wherever the deepest mine may be, I'll wager that's where we'll find Kulwych."

Slowly, a grin spread over her face. "You really are a sly one, Nuic."

"You've only now figured that out?"

"But wait," she protested. "How are we supposed to find this old mine?"

"How should I know?" he grumbled. "I'm no explorer! You'll just have to find a map or something."

Elli just stared at him. "A map? Of Shadowroot? It would be easier to find a friendly dark elf somewhere and ask him for directions."

"Hmmmpff." Nuic folded his arms. "Do that, then. But whatever you do, be quick about it!"

She merely frowned. "The deepest mine in the darkest realm," she muttered, her voice joyless. "That's the kind of place people visit only in their worst nightmares. Not on purpose."

The sprite grabbed some shreds of mist and then drummed his moist fingers on his belly, just above the Galator. "That's true, I'm afraid. Finding it will be hard enough, especially with so little time. But something tells me that *entering* it will be even harder. And who knows what we'll meet down inside?"

"A jester, perhaps."

Lightning-quick, Elli sat up to see who had spoken. Just like Nuic beside her, she scowled to see a gray shape striding toward them through the mist rising off the cloud. She leaped to her feet, ready to fight to the death.

"Or even a bard," said the misty figure, stepping through the vapors.

To Elli's astonishment, not to mention relief, it was not Deth Macoll. For no master of disguise, unless he was also a changeling, could have made such a dramatic change. This fellow wore a bushy beard that stuck out on both sides, a lopsided old hat, and an extremely silly grin. And even without the hat, he stood at least a head taller than the assassin.

Even so, Elli looked at this stranger with suspicion, her fists raised. She glanced down at Nuic, standing in the vapors by her feet. Strikingly, his colors showed no concern whatsoever. His skin swirled with warm yellows and greens. She looked back at the man—and suddenly recognized him.

"You're the bard on the hillside! The one who led us to Brionna. And who Tamwyn said he'd met before." She almost winced, hearing herself say his name . . . for now she missed him more than she would have believed possible.

The man twirled one tip of his sideways-growing beard and bowed slightly. "Olewyn the bard, at your service."

"Nuic the sprite at yours," came the voice by Elli's feet. "Or, as my friends call me—"

"Nuic the grump," she finished. "And my name is Elliryanna Lailoken, or just Elli."

"Hmmmpff. Just *rude*, if you ask me."

The bard's silly grin widened. "Pleased to meet you, Nuic the

Grump and Elli the Rude. You never can predict who or what you'll encounter on a passing cloud. Pure chance, you know."

He shook himself jauntily and plopped down on the cloud, legs crossed beneath him. Then he stretched out his arms and wiggled his fingers. "Ah," he sighed dreamily. "How nice to rest."

Following his lead, both Elli and Nuic sat back down. As she wriggled a bit deeper into the soft mass of vapors, Elli examined the bard. She couldn't decide whether he was really very old or very young, rather less than he appeared or rather more. With this fellow, it was extremely hard to tell. Just as it was hard to tell whether something other than what he called *pure chance* had brought him here.

"A song, anyone?" offered Olewyn merrily.

"Hmmmpff," muttered Nuic. "I'd prefer a meal."

"Ah, we can provide that, too." The bard nodded, as if agreeing with himself, then reached into the folds of his baggy cloak. He pulled out a dark and grainy slab that could have passed for the bark of an oak. "Here, try some of my homemade bread."

With an arduous effort, he managed to tear the slab into rough halves. Then, still huffing from the strain, he handed a piece to each of them. Elli, who was trying not to live up to her reputation as rude, reluctantly took one. She tried a cautious nibble.

At first, as she'd expected, it tasted just like wood. After a few chews, however, it softened up remarkably, then suddenly dissolved into a tangy, minty liquid. Almost as soon as she swallowed, she felt renewed strength surging through her limbs. She took another bite, larger this time. And then another.

As the taste of fresh mint tingled on her tongue, she asked, "What is this called?"

"Ambrosia bread," Olewyn replied. "You like it?"

"Oh yefff, vewy mufff." She swallowed. "Really, I do."

"Good," declared the bard. "It's my tastiest recipe. Matter of fact, it's my *only* recipe. In any case, while you and Grump the Nuic keep eating, I shall give you a song. With the help of my dearest friend, of course."

Elli, chuckling and chewing at the same time, watched as he reached up and grabbed the brim of his lopsided hat. With dramatic flair, he lifted off the hat and revealed a small creature who was sitting atop his head. Blue-skinned with flecks of gold, shaped like a teardrop, the creature was unmistakable.

"Your museo," she said, delighted to see—and, even more, to hear—this magical creature again. She knew just how rare museos were in Avalon: not so rare as a Sapphire Unicorn, perhaps, but still almost never seen. Certainly not as close as this.

The bard twirled one side of his beard, thinking. Then, with a knowing look, he pulled a small lute out of his cloak. He plucked it once and announced, "This ballad, though brief, is one of our favorites. Written, they say, by Rhiannon herself, when she was High Priestess."

Elli and Nuic exchanged a glance, which bespoke their love for both Rhia and Coerria. Without thinking, Elli reached up to her amulet, feeling the crystal hidden beneath its leaves.

Just then, the museo began to hum—a rolling, layered hum that filled Elli with such a rush of emotions she felt almost giddy. She swayed, light-headed, glad that she was sitting down. As the museo's deep, vibrating hum rolled through her, she slid farther down into the vaporous cushion of the cloud.

The humming swelled louder, while distant strains of wind harps rose to join it. And at last, the bard himself began to sing:

Sway, broad boughs of Avalon,
Shielding from the storm—
Bend so far, yet never break:
Ev'ry day newborn,
Mystery's true form.

Rise, tall trunk of Middle Realm,
Stretching ever high—
Reach for misty, branching trails:
Stairway to the sky,
Stars are flaming nigh.

Sink, great roots of Seven Realms,
Plunging under sleep—
Hold the farthest, lowest lands:
Celebrate or weep,
Wonders ever deep.

The museo kept humming for a moment longer, a low, rolling note that vibrated the very marrow of Elli's bones. She felt as if a wave of sound and feeling had just washed over her, leaving her sadder, wiser, and richer than before. And she longed to plunge deeper into that wave, to ride its currents, to feel its swell, over and over again.

When at last the museo ceased, no one stirred or spoke for quite some time. Other than the faraway music of the Harplands and the gentle breath of the wind across the cloud, there was no sound. Yet for Elli, the memory of the museo's hum and bard's song was more than enough to lift her heart.

It was the bard who first spoke again. "And so, good travelers, where will you voyage next?"

Elli started to answer, then caught herself. Having learned her lesson, she wasn't sure it was wise to reveal to anyone—even a friendly bard—where they were going. That was why she looked so surprised when Nuic raised his voice.

"To Shadowroot," the sprite declared. "By whatever route we can. And as fast as we can! We have work to do there—important work, that could mean the life or death of Avalon."

The bard raised his thick eyebrows.

Sensing his doubt, Nuic growled, "Can't you understand what I'm saying? All the wonders of this world, all the places where you roam, all the people you care about—will be lost if we don't succeed."

The sprite blew a frustrated breath as his colors darkened. "And where are we now? Stuck on this cloud, drifting through Airroot! And even if, by some miracle, we ride it all the way to a portal, we're still a good way from our goal, since no portal can take us into Shadowroot. So however you look at it, we have a long ride—and a longer trek—ahead of us."

Glumly, Elli added, "And almost no time."

Olewyn's brow, already lined, wrinkled some more. "There is, you know, a faster way."

"What?" demanded both of them at once.

He leaned forward as a shred of mist wrapped around his beard. In a whisper, he said, "You could ride the wind."

"What?" exclaimed Elli. "You don't expect us to believe that, do you?"

"That's up to you," said the bard. "It's not easy, mind you, and it requires the greatest concentration you can muster—even more than riding through a portal. Not to mention a fair bit of courage."

Suddenly, his face contorted. "How foolish of me! The only people who can ride the wind are those who carry a magical object of great power. That is why, I am told, Merlin could do it in days long past. Not by his own magic, but by that of his staff, Ohnyalei. So unless you have something of that nature, I'm afraid this idea won't help you."

Elli and Nuic shared a glance—uncertain but intrigued. After all, they did possess two of the most powerful magical objects in Avalon.

"How exactly does it work?" asked Nuic. "If it really does work, that is."

"Well," began the bard with a wave at the air beyond the cloud, "it's quite simple, really. You stand at the edge of a cloud, hold tight to your source of magic, and think hard about where you want the wind to carry you. And then . . ."

His expression turned somewhat sheepish. "Then you jump."

Elli's eyes opened to their widest. "You can't be serious."

"Well now, how do you suppose I ever got to this cloud in the first place?"

She frowned skeptically. "Where's your magical object, then?"

He rolled his eyes upward. Perfectly on cue, the teardrop-shaped creature on his head took a bow, making its translucent robe shimmer in the misty starlight.

"Your museo?"

"Of course. For a bard, there can be no greater magic."

She shook her head. "I still don't believe you."

He regarded her thoughtfully. "You look quite tired, my dear. Perhaps you'd feel differently after some rest."

"Of course I'm tired," she retorted. "But I don't see how some rest will change the fact you think we should jump off a cloud!"

The bard answered by strumming a chord on his lute.

Before Elli could say another word, the museo began to hum again. This time, its magical music wrapped around her like a blanket, warming her deeply. She tried to protest, but instead she could only yawn.

As the vibrating voice swelled louder, all the gathered exhaustion of the journey welled up inside her. Even if she'd wanted to resist, she didn't have the strength. Her eyelids drooped heavily. Before she knew it, she was settling down into a welcoming bed that seemed every bit as soft as a cloud.

So quickly did she fall asleep that she barely even heard the bard begin his ballad:

> *Fair Avalon, the Tree of Life*
> *That ev'ry creature knows—*
> *A world part Heaven and part Earth*
> *And part what wind that blows.*

40 · The Thousand Groves

ELLI DREAMED, NOT SURPRISINGLY, THAT SHE was floating on a cloud. She sat up to view her surroundings, turning her head slowly as she took in the vista. Mist swirled and vapors billowed overhead, the air was moist against her cheeks, and a fluttering breeze tousled her curls. All around, wispy clouds drifted through the hazy air, glowing as they passed through slanted beams of starlight.

Yet this was clearly a different cloud than the one where she'd been lulled to sleep by magical music. For this cloud held no bard, no museo, and no Nuic. She was utterly alone.

Then she heard footsteps.

Padding softly across the moist, squishy surface of the cloud, someone drew nearer. And nearer. She spun around to face the source of the sound, but saw nothing beyond the veils of rising mist.

She leaped to her feet, which slapped on the surface. Still she could see no one else on the cloud. Yet the footsteps only grew louder.

Suddenly she noticed rays of green light, striping her forearms and the front of her robe. They were coming from her crystal of élano! Astounded, she reached her fingers toward the amulet that hung around her neck. As she gently parted the oak, ash, and hawthorn leaves, more rays, blindingly bright, shot forth. Unlike the crystal's normal color—white with hints of green and blue—this time it was entirely green.

Just then she saw a matching green in the mist just in front of her. It looked like—could it be? *Tamwyn's staff*, glowing green along its full length.

Then a hand materialized out of the vapors, grabbing hold of the staff. An arm followed, a sturdy shoulder, some loose black hair . . .

Tamwyn! He stood there on the cloud, facing her. His coal black eyes glittered.

"Hello, Elli."

It took a few seconds for her to speak. "Tamwyn?"

The corner of his mouth lifted slightly. "It's me."

She shook her curls, thicker than a tangle of newly sprouted ferns. "Is this . . . a dream?"

"Mmm, well—yes and no. We're somewhere that's not quite real, but not quite a dream, either. It's a place *in between*. And I've come to you by magic. My own magic."

She raised a skeptical eyebrow.

He nodded, swishing his locks against his shoulders. "I'm not afraid of it anymore, Elli! That's what scared me so much, back at the Stargazing Stone. Why, I thought it might . . ."

"Might what?"

"Hurt you." His tone softened. "And that was the last thing I wanted."

She studied him for a moment. "My guess is that you were

scared of more than just your magic, Tamwyn. But this does help explain why you acted like such—"

"A dolt," he finished.

"An idiot, I was going to say." She nodded for emphasis. "And, you know, being an idiot is your specialty! Really, I wouldn't recognize you if you weren't like that some of the time."

"Much of the time," he said, suddenly wondering whether he had made a big mistake in coming here. "If you're going to berate me," he said resignedly, "I guess that's what I deserve."

She cocked her head. "I'm not going to berate you, Tamwyn." Her voice dropped to a bare whisper. "But I am going to say . . . I've missed you."

"You have?" He swallowed. "Well, you know, I—well . . ."

"What?"

He gathered himself. "I've missed you, too."

She burst out laughing, and around her shoulders, thin shreds of mist shimmered and spun.

He took her hand. "Elli, I've seen some terrible things. And some wonderful things, too."

"So have I."

"Where are you now?"

"In Airroot, about to . . ." She caught herself before telling him the outlandish idea the bard had proposed. "About to go to Shadowroot. Then down a deep mine—to destroy Kulwych's crystal."

He grimaced. "Which is also Rhita Gawr's crystal."

Worry filled her face. "Tamwyn, they've corrupted it somehow. Made it evil. Rhia gave me this," she added, pointing at her amulet, "so at least I might have a chance."

He blew a long breath, scattering the rising strands of mist from the cloud. "A deep mine in Shadowroot. Just the sort of place White Hands and his master would hide themselves—until they're finally ready to attack." He shook his head. "How will you find them, though? How will you know where to go in that perpetual darkness?"

Her gaze fell. "I don't know. What we really need, as Nuic says, is a map. But that's impossible."

Tamwyn squeezed her hand. "Wait, now. I just remembered something! You see, I have a new friend, who healed my wounds after a battle."

She stiffened, recalling the scene in the Galator. "Who is she?"

"He," Tamwyn corrected, not noticing that she relaxed again. "His name is Gwirion. A really good man—and a born leader. Just the right person to save his people, I think."

Her hazel eyes sparkled. "Like you."

He blushed, shaking his head. "No, not like me." Then, remembering what he'd wanted to say, he explained, "Gwirion told me something about the Lost City of Light—Dianarra, they called it long ago. He said there was a great library there, a place to hold books, and also maps."

She caught her breath. "So if I can find that old library—"

"You could, maybe, find your way to the evil crystal."

"You know, Tamwyn, you're smarter than you think."

He scoffed, releasing her hand to wave a knot of mist away from his nose. "If I were really smart, I'd know what those dark shapes are by now."

"The ones we saw in the vision? Flowing out of the vanished constellation?"

"Not just out of the constellation, Elli. Out of the *stars*. Somehow they're coming out of the stars themselves."

Bewildered, she peered at him. "I don't understand."

"Listen," he explained. "Right now, I'm almost up to the branches. And I've seen the stars—closer than ever before." Anxious lines spread around his eyes like dark webs. "And Elli . . . I've discovered something. The seven stars of the Wizard's Staff *are not completely dark.*"

"They're not? But—we can't see them anymore."

"Not from the root-realms, true. But they're still there, I'm sure of it. They're just *blocked* somehow. Like some sort of doors have shut over them."

Her expression turned still more dubious. "Doors?"

"I don't know . . ." He shook himself, exasperated, sending the wisps of mist floating nearby into whorls and spins. "That's just what it looked like, that's all. Then I saw those shapes, darker than smoke, moving out of the thin rings of light where the stars used to be."

She clucked at him. "If your doorways are closed, how can anything move out of them?"

All of a sudden, he slammed his fist hard into his palm. "That's it, Elli!"

"That's what?" she asked, her face a mask of puzzlement.

"The key to the stars!" He was so excited now, his whole body shook. "They really *are* doors. Don't you see? But instead of being closed now, they're opened!"

She stared at him, more puzzled than ever.

He took her hand again. "Listen. The stars *themselves* are doorways. Doorways of fire! Made of the brightest fire of all—pure light, almost. And they burn that strongly so they will always remain closed. Impassable. Unless, that is . . . one of the gods wanted to open them."

"Like Rhita Gawr?"

"That's right."

"But where," she pressed, "do those doorways lead?"

"To other realms. Other worlds." He halted, realizing just what he was saying. "Other trees."

Elli's eyes widened. "The stars! So all the lights we see above us are really *paths to other worlds*—mortal Earth, the Otherworld of the gods, and more. So many more. Why, there are hundreds, no, *thousands*, of worlds out there."

"The Thousand Groves! So that's what it means." He looked at her in wonder. "All these years I've wondered about the stars, what they really are—I've also wondered about that phrase."

"Rhia said you'd understand its meaning someday, remember? When we were with her there in New Arbassa."

"I remember," he said dryly. "That was the time you almost murdered me."

"Really?" She shrugged innocently. "There have been so many times like that, I don't recall."

He grinned, releasing her hand. "But now," he continued, excited again, "we really *do* understand! That's why Avalon is so important, Elli. This *is* the world in between. The world whose tree connects to all the other worlds, all the other trees, in the Thousand Groves."

Slowly, she wrapped one of her curls around her finger. "Which is why Rhita Gawr wants to control Avalon. For if he can just do that, he can control all the rest of the worlds, as well."

"Exactly. We are the bridge, the world in between—just as Lost Fincayra was in the days of Merlin."

"But Tamwyn," she asked, "if the stars are really doorways— doorways of fire, as you said—just *why* are they aflame? Why aren't they simply left open, and unobstructed?"

He inhaled slowly. "Because, I think, Dagda and Lorilanda want one primary thing for each world—that it should be allowed to find its own way. Just as they want that for each creature, which is why we have free will. And if each world remains separate from the others, then it can create its own destiny."

Grimly, Elli pondered his words. "So Rhita Gawr violated that principle by opening those doorways in the Wizard's Staff. But why? Where do those doorways lead?"

"To the Otherworld of immortal spirits." Tamwyn ground his teeth. "I'm sure of it! That's a world so immense, with so many layers, it could have seven doorways. Normally, they are closed, dividing the spirit realm from ours. But no longer. That's how Rhita Gawr came here, to Avalon. And those dark shapes—"

"Must be his warriors!" exclaimed Elli. "Terrible warriors, who will fight for Rhita Gawr whenever he calls them. Hordes of them, too—which is why he opened all the doors, not just one."

They looked at each other, amid the rising vapors, hardly able to believe their own words. Finally, Tamwyn sighed and said, "Deathless warriors from the spirit world! No mortal army could ever defeat them. No wonder Rhita Gawr, in that vision, spoke of his *ultimate triumph*."

Just as glumly, Elli commented, "They must be starting to mass up there, just waiting for his command."

"Which will come *when the great horse dies*." Tamwyn ran a hand through his hair. "Trouble is, we haven't any clue what that means."

"We *do* know it's going to happen soon," she reminded him. "Rhita Gawr said, that night on Hallia's Peak, that there were just a few weeks left. And that was two weeks ago. So we have—at most—one week left."

"One week," muttered Tamwyn, waving away some vapors in front of his face. "And then that horse will die. Along with the rest of us."

He scowled in frustration. "But what horse is that? The same one my father wrote about—or a different one? And besides, the only horse I've seen on this quest isn't really a horse at all."

Curious, Elli moved a bit closer. "What do you mean?"

"Oh, nothing," he grumbled. "Just Pegasus. You know, the constellation. I was just looking at its central star, the one called the Heart of Pegasus . . . and Elli, it actually seemed to be *beating*. Why, I don't know."

"Beating?"

"Yes. Like a real h—" He caught himself. "Elli! If that star goes out—and the heart stops beating—then . . ."

"The great horse will die," they both said at once.

But the excitement of their revelation swiftly faded, overwhelmed by the scale of their challenge. Discouraged, Elli asked, "How can we ever stop all this from happening?"

"You, by finding your way to White Hands and that evil crystal. It must be important to Rhita Gawr's plans somehow, or they wouldn't have gone through so much trouble to make it. And then—you must destroy it. Whatever it takes."

Resolutely, she nodded.

Tamwyn's eyes narrowed. "And me, by climbing all the rest of the way to the stars. By getting to the Wizard's Staff, before Rhita Gawr commands his warriors to attack. And by finding some way to relight those stars—close those doors—before it's too late."

Despite the moisture in the air, his throat felt suddenly dry. "It won't be easy for either of us," he said hoarsely.

Her hazel eyes watched him for some time before she asked, "What about your search for your father?"

"I found him," he whispered. "His grave, at least."

Her gaze fell. "I'm . . . so sorry, Tamwyn."

He drew a deep breath and looked at her tenderly. "That's not all I've found, Elli." Then, with care, he stripped off his pack. "I have something for you."

He pulled out the half-carved harp. The harmóna wood, streaked with orange, seemed to glow in the misty light. Delicate shreds of vapor curled around its contours, seeming to caress the wood.

At the sight of the harp, she gasped. "Really?"

"A bit late," he said bashfully, "and it's not done yet. But if we actually . . . well, make it through all this, I'll give it to you."

"That's right," she agreed. "You'll give it to me yourself."

A moment of quiet passed, then she added, "And I have something for *you*."

She stepped forward. Gracefully, she leaned into him, just enough that their lips touched, feeling warm in the coolness of the mist. And though the kiss itself didn't last very long, something about it promised to linger long after.

As they pulled apart, Tamwyn replaced the wood in his pack and slung the strap over his shoulder. Holding his staff, he gazed at Elli one last time. Then, without a word, he turned and melted away into the swirling vapors.

Epilogue · The Specter

"COME ON, YOU LAZY LOUT, WAKE UP!"

Nuic's voice pierced the magical blanket that still wrapped Elli, though not enough to wake her. The sprite, now a very impatient red, shook her again.

Suddenly she started, and lifted her head from the soft, vaporous pillow of the cloud. "Tamwyn?" she asked, half expecting to see him.

"No," groused Nuic. "Just ugly old me. Now wake up, will you?"

"All right," she moaned, shaking the drowsiness from her head. Moisture from the cloud, which had completely soaked her curls, splattered Nuic in a spray of droplets.

"Don't try to humor me with a shower, Elliryanna. It's high time you got up. And time we decided what to do."

All at once, she remembered. The bard. The museo. And that wild idea of riding the wind.

"Where is the bard?" she asked, blinking her still-sleepy eyes.

"Gone," declared Nuic. "No doubt he leaped off the cloud while we were fast asleep. He could be in another realm by now."

She peered at him. "Do you really think it works?" Craning her neck, she watched some shreds of mist, hardly firmer than air itself, sailing past the edge of their cloud.

"I don't know," said the sprite, studying her with his liquid purple eyes. "But it just might. And it would be a lot faster than just riding on this fluffy boat, hoping we might land somewhere eventually. Meanwhile, you can be sure that our enemies aren't just sitting around! Rhita Gawr is doing everything he can to prepare himself, his allies—and that crystal—to conquer Avalon."

She wrapped one of her dangling curls around her finger, much as shreds of mist were doing. "You actually think we could ride the wind all the way to Shadowroot?"

Nuic's skin showed veins of green, the same color as the Galator around his middle. "I don't know, Elliryanna. But I do think we should try. We have so little time. And the power of our two crystals can't be fathomed."

She frowned at him. "Nuic, you're supposed to be the saner one of us. But you're sounding as foolish as *me*, for Avalon's sake! Or that silly-bearded old bard."

Her lips pursed thoughtfully. "Who is he, do you think? Just what he says, or something more?"

"Hmmmpff. I don't know, but I can tell you one thing."

"What?"

"He seems to get around a lot. Woodroot one day, Airroot the next. Almost as if—"

"He rode on the wind," Elli finished.

She gazed at him intently for a long moment, as thin trails of mist flowed past them. "All right," she declared at last, her voice firmly resolved. "It's time for us to leap off a cloud."

"And to see," Nuic added gravely, "just *what wind that blows.*"

• • •

Slowly, Scree lifted his head.

As a sulfurous wind gusted over the charred volcanic ridge, dusting him with ash, he glanced down at the auburn-haired woman who lay dead in his arms. The fallen leader of the Bram Kaie clan. The mother of his son.

"The son I myself killed," Scree grumbled, tasting something far more bitter than the volcanic ash on his tongue.

His gaze roamed from Queen's lifeless face to the deep gash in his side, and then to his own bloodstained feet. He couldn't tell whether that blood had come from himself, from Queen, or from the young warrior he had killed. All he knew was that it would never truly wash away.

He scowled. That young warrior had been brutal, arrogant, and ruthless. As well as a murderer—of innocent people such as Arc-kaya. But he was also, in this cruel gust of fate's wind, Scree's own son.

Hearing some movement, he turned. Villagers were congregating—leaving their nests, climbing down from stairways and statues where they'd witnessed the battle. More were coming, as well, hurrying down the obsidian-paved streets, tugging their friends and carrying their babies.

Despite all the gleaming wealth of their village, to Scree these people looked almost as confused and bereft as he himself felt. Yet their wounds from this day, unlike his, could be healed.

For although they had lost their leadership—and, more important, their way as a people—they could, perhaps, find that again.

The eaglefolk moved closer, surrounding him in a large circle of bodies, pressing as close as they dared. Children with anxious faces, women and men with fear in their eyes, frail elders, and battle-hardened sentries—all peered at Scree. Their faces, every one, seemed to ask the same question: *Will you now lead us?*

Scree blinked his yellow-rimmed eyes. Today's tragedy was only the latest one he'd known: His mother had been killed by cruel men; his adopted mother hadn't lived much longer; his father he'd never even known. Arc-kaya, who had been so kind to him, he had lost in just a few beats of a wing. Brionna he had treated so oafishly that he'd probably driven her away for good. And Tamwyn, his only true family, was by now probably dead, or lost among the stars.

And these people still want me to lead? he asked himself. *Me— who only brings sorrow wherever I go?*

As if by magic, the anxious faces in the crowd suddenly seemed joined by those other faces—belonging to the people he had once loved, and who had loved him. There was Tamwyn. Brionna. And Arc-kaya. As well as that ancient wizard who had, so long ago, trusted Scree to protect his precious staff.

All those faces, old and new, looked at him with expectant eyes. Hopeful eyes. Wanting him to bring something more than sorrow to his life, his people, and his world.

Still, Scree debated what to do. Leave these wretched eaglefolk right now, and never return? Or stay here and try to lead them?

If he left, he would still have his grief—though he'd also have his freedom, something he'd always prized. But if he stayed, he would do his best to remake this clan, as well as their destiny. He would join the great battle for Avalon, soon to happen on the Plains of Isenwy. And even if he perished in that fight—he would at least know that he had, for once, soared as high as he possibly could.

Drawing a deep breath, he set down Queen's body and rose, grinding pumice and black ash under his feet. Ignoring his wounds, some visible and some not, he stood tall and grim, the rust-red light from the sky reflected on his face. At last, he spoke to the hushed crowd.

"I am Scree," he declared. His voice echoed across the fire-blackened ridge. "And I am your new leader."

• • •

Tamwyn opened his eyes again. Above his head, a prism bird's wingfeathers flashed in the starlight, painting the clouds with brilliant streaks of color.

But the greater brilliance, and the deeper glow, was in the image that still lingered in his head. The image of Elli, her hazel eyes looking into his own, with the shared hope that they might somehow survive the days to come. And stand together—not in a magical dream, but in real life.

He took a deep breath. Pushing off from the hardpacked soil, he rose to his feet. Once again, he peered at the simple mound of his father's grave. And at the darkened torch that marked it.

An idea seized him. He pulled his newly reforged dagger out of its sheath and sliced a strip of leather off the flap of his pack. Then, with the tip of his blade, he carved these words into the leather:

Here lies the body
of
my father,
Krystallus Eopia,
though his spirit
shall ever roam
the highest reaches
of
The Great Tree
of
Avalon.

Placing the leather on top of the grave, he anchored it with a hefty stone and stepped back to view what he'd done. After a few seconds, he nodded to himself, then turned his gaze back to the torch.

In a flash, he knew what else he must do. What his father would want him to do.

Tamwyn stepped forward and grasped the torch's wooden pole. With a sharp tug, he pulled it out of the ground. And then, using his twine, he tied the torch to the strap of his pack so that the pole rested securely against his back.

To be sure, the torch was dark—as dark as his own future. But this much he knew: He would carry this torch, burning or not, just as his father before him had carried it. He would try to find the way to rekindle its flame—and, if possible, other flames, as well.

For he would carry this torch all the way to the stars.

• • •

Deep in the darkest reaches of Shadowroot, a specter rose out of the blackness of eternal night. Darker even than the blighted land itself, the lightless sky, or the mine shaft from whence it came, the specter lifted into the air and flew skyward.

Had any eyes been able to see its emergence, they would have instantly shut tight. Out of terror—the deep, primal terror that shrieks soundlessly in mortals' worst nightmares. For this specter had taken the shape of a gruesome dragon, utterly dark, with eyes that held nothing but the void.

The shape of Rhita Gawr.

The warrior spirit, now fully re-formed in a dragon's guise, beat his enormous, leathery wings. His eyes, blacker than the night, gleamed. Everything was going well, very well indeed.

Even that child's magician, Kulwych, has done his part, the dragon gloated silently. *And soon*, he thought, with such appetite that rivers of saliva rolled out from his jaws and down his scaly neck, *this miserable little world shall be mine.*

The wings beat powerfully, carrying him ever higher. *And with it, all the other worlds. Every last one of them!*

Laughter, as empty as the void itself, crackled from the dragon's throat. Shadowed clouds nearby exploded with black lightning and blasts of thunder. He drooled some more, for he could already taste his long-awaited conquest. Just as he would taste it all through this flight, all the way to the stars.

A Brief History of Avalon

S ONE WORLD DIES, ANOTHER IS BORN. IT IS a time both dark and bright, a moment of miracles.

In the mist-shrouded land of Fincayra, an isle long forgotten is suddenly found, a small band of children defeats an army of death, and a people disgraced win their wings at last. And in the greatest miracle of all, a young wizard called Merlin earns his true name: Olo Eopia, great man of many worlds, many times. And yet . . . even as Fincayra is saved, it is lost—passing forever into the Otherworld of Spirits.

But in that very moment, a new world appears. Born of a seed that beats like a heart, a seed won by Merlin on his journey through a magical mirror, this new world is a tree: the Great Tree. It stands as a bridge between Earth and Heaven, between mortal and immortal, between shifting seas and eternal mist.

Its landscape is immense, full of wonders and surprises. Its populace is as far-flung as the stars on high. Its essence is part hope, part tragedy, part mystery.

Its name is Avalon.

—the celebrated opening lines of the bard Willenia's history of Avalon, widely known as "Born of a Seed That Beats Like a Heart"

Year 0:
Merlin plants the seed that beats like a heart. A tree is born: the Great Tree of Avalon.

THE AGE OF FLOWERING

Year 1:
Creatures of all kinds migrate to the new world, or appear mysteriously, perhaps from the sacred mud of Malóch. The first age of Avalon, the Age of Flowering, begins.

Year 1:
Elen of the Sapphire Eyes and her daughter Rhiannon found a new faith, the Society of the Whole, and become its first priestesses. The Society is dedicated to promoting harmony among all living creatures, and to protecting the Great Tree that supports and sustains all life. The new faith focuses on seven sacred Elements—what Elen called "the seven sacred parts that together make the Whole." They are: Earth, Air, Fire, Water, Life, LightDark, and Mystery.

Year 2:
The great spirit Dagda, god of wisdom, visits both Elen and Rhia in a dream. He reveals that there are seven separate roots of Avalon, each with its own distinct landscapes and populations—and that their new faith will eventually reach into all of them. With Dagda's help, Elen, Rhia, and their original followers (plus several giants, led by Merlin's old friend, Shim) make a journey to Lost Fincayra, to the great circle of stones that was site of the famous Dance of the Giants. Together, they transport the sacred stones all the way back to Avalon. The circle is rebuilt deep in the realm of

Stoneroot, and becomes the Great Temple in the center of a new compound that is dedicated to the Society of the Whole.

Year 18:

The Drumadians—as the Society of the Whole is commonly called, in honor of Lost Fincayra's Druma Wood—ordain their first group of priestesses and priests. They include Lleu of the One Ear; Cwen, last of the treelings; and (to the surprise of many) Babd Catha, the Ogre's Bane.

Year 27:

Merlin returns to Avalon—to explore its mysteries, and more important, to wed the deer woman Hallia. They are married under shining stars in the high peaks of upper Olanabram. This region is the only place in the seven root-realms where the lower part of Avalon's trunk can actually be seen, rising into the ever-swirling mist. (The trunk can also be seen from the Swaying Sea, but this strange place is normally not considered part of the Great Tree's roots.) Here, atop the highest mountain in the Seven Realms, which Merlin names Hallia's Peak, they exchange their vows of loyalty and love. The wedding, announced by canyon eagles soaring on high, includes more varied kinds of creatures than have assembled anywhere since the Great Council of Fincayra after the Dance of Giants long ago. By the grace of Dagda, they are joined by three spirit-beings, as well: the brave hawk, Trouble, who sits on Merlin's shoulder; the wise bard, Cairpré, who stands by Elen's side throughout the entire ceremony; and the deer man, Eremon, who is the devoted brother of Hallia. Even the dwarf ruler, Urnalda, attends—along with the great white spider known as the Grand Elusa; the jester, Bumbelwy; the giant, Shim; the scrubamuck-loving creature, Ballymag; and the dragon queen, Gwynnia; plus several of her fire-breathing children. The ceremonies are conducted by Elen and Rhia, founders of the Society of the Whole, the priest Lleu of the One Ear, and the priestess Cwen of the treelings. (Babd Catha is also invited, but chooses to battle ogres instead.) According to legend, the great spirits Dagda and Lorilanda also come, and give the newlyweds their everlasting blessings.

Year 27:

Krystallus Eopia, son of Merlin and Hallia, is born. Celebrations last for years—especially among the fun-loving hoolahs and sprites. Although the newborn is almost crushed when the giant Shim tries to kiss him, Krystallus survives and grows into a healthy child. While he is nonmagical, since wizards' powers often skip generations, his wizard's blood assures him a long life. Even as an infant, he shows an unusual penchant for exploring. Like his mother, he loves to run, though he cannot move with the speed and grace of a deer.

Year 33:

The mysterious Rugged Path, connecting the realms of Stoneroot and Woodroot, is discovered by a young lad named Fergus. Legend tells that Fergus found the path when he followed a strange white doe—who might really have been the spirit Lorilanda, goddess of birth, flowering, and renewal. The legend also says that the path runs only in one direction, though which direction—and why—remains unclear. Since very few travelers have ever reported finding the path, and since those reports seem unreliable, most people doubt that the path even exists.

Year 37:

Elen dies. She is grateful for her mortal years and yet deeply glad that she can at last rejoin her love, the bard Cairpré, in the land of the spirits. The great spirit Dagda himself, in the form of an enormous stag, comes personally to Avalon to guide her to the Otherworld. Rhia assumes Elen's responsibilities as High Priestess of the Society of the Whole.

Year 51:

Travel within the Seven Realms, through the use of enchanted portals, is discovered by the wood elf Serella. She becomes the first queen of the wood elves, and over time she learns much about this dangerous art. In her words, "Portalseeking is a difficult way to travel, yet an easy way to die." She leads several expeditions to Waterroot which culminate in the founding of Caer Serella, the original colony of water elves. However, her first expedition to Shadowroot ends in complete disaster—and her own death.

Year 130:

A terrible blight appears in the upper reaches of Woodroot, killing everything it touches. Rhia, believing this to be the work of the evil spirit Rhita Gawr, seeks help from Merlin.

Year 131:

As the blight spreads, destroying trees and other living creatures in Woodroot's forests, Merlin takes Rhia and her trusted companion, the priest Lleu of the One Ear, on a remarkable journey. Traveling through portals known only to Merlin, they voyage deep inside the Great Tree. There they find a great subterranean lake that holds magical white water. After the lake's water rises to the surface at the White Geyser of Crystallia, in upper Waterroot, it separates into the seven colors of the spectrum (at Prism Gorge) and flows to many places, giving both water and color to everything it meets. Merlin reveals to Rhia and Lleu that this white water gains its magic from its high concentration of *élano*, the most powerful—and most elusive—magical substance in all of Avalon. Produced as sap deep within the Great Tree's roots, élano combines all seven sacred Elements, and is, in Merlin's words, "the true life-giving force of this world." At the great subterranean lake, Merlin gathers a small crystal of élano with the help of his staff—whose name, Ohnyalei, means *spirit of grace* in the Fincayran Old Tongue. Then he, Rhia, and Lleu return to Woodroot and place the crystal at the origin of the blight. Thanks to the power of élano, the blight recedes and finally disappears. Woodroot's forests are healed.

Year 132:

Rhia, as High Priestess, introduces her followers to élano, the essential life-giving sap of the Great Tree. Soon thereafter, Lleu of the One Ear publishes his masterwork, *Cyclo Avalon*. This book sets down everything that Lleu has learned about the seven sacred Elements, the portals within the Tree, and the lore of élano. It becomes the primary text for Drumadians throughout Avalon.

Year 192:

After a final journey to her ancestral home, the site of the legendary Carpet Caerlochlann, Hallia dies. So profound is Merlin's grief that he climbs high into the jagged mountains of Stoneroot and does not speak with anyone, even his sister Rhia, for many months.

Year 193:

Merlin finally descends from the mountains—but only to depart from Avalon. He must leave, he tells his dearest friends, to devote himself entirely to a new challenge in another world: educating a young man named Arthur in the land of Britannia, part of mortal Earth. He hints, without revealing any details, that the fates of Earth and Avalon are somehow entwined.

Year 237:

Krystallus, now an accomplished explorer, founds the Eopia College of Mapmakers in Waterroot. As its emblem, he chooses the star within a circle, ancient symbol for the magic of Leaping between places and times.

THE AGE OF STORMS

Year 284:

Without any warning, the stars of one of Avalon's most prominent constellations, the Wizard's Staff, go dark. One by one, the seven stars in the constellation—symbolizing the legendary Seven Songs of Merlin, by which both the wizard and his staff came into their true powers—disappear. The process takes only three weeks. Star watchers agree that this portends something ominous for Avalon. The Age of Storms has begun.

Year 284:

War breaks out between dwarves and dragons in the realm of Fireroot, sparked by disputes over the underground caverns of Flaming Jewels. Although these two peoples have cooperated for centuries in harvesting as well as preserving the jewels, their unity finally crumbles. The skilled dwarves regard the jewels as sacred, and want to harvest them only deliberately over long periods of time. By contrast, the dragons (and their allies, the flamelons) want to take immediate advantage of all the wealth and power that the jewels could provide. The fighting escalates, sweeping up other peoples—even some clans of normally peaceful faeries. Alliances form, pitting dwarves, most elves and humans, giants, and eaglefolk against the dragons, flamelons, dark elves, avaricious humans, and gobsken. Meanwhile, marauding ogres and trolls take advantage of the chaos. In the widening conflict, only the sylphs, mudmakers, and some museos remain neutral . . . while the hoolahs simply enjoy all the excitement.

Year 300:

The war worsens, spreading across the Seven Realms of Avalon. Drumadian Elders debate the true nature of the War of Storms: Is it limited exclusively to Avalon? Or is it really just a skirmish in the greater ongoing battle of the spirits—the clash between the brutal Rhita Gawr, whose goal is to control all the worlds, and the allies Lorilanda and Dagda, who want free peoples to choose for themselves? To most of Avalon's citizens, however, such a question is irrelevant. For them, the War of Storms is simply a time of struggle, hardship, and grief.

Year 413:

Rhia, who has grown deeply disillusioned with the brutality of Avalon's warring peoples—and also with the growing rigidity of the Society of the Whole—resigns as High Priestess. She departs for some remote part of Avalon, and is never heard from again. Some believe that she traveled to mortal Earth to rejoin Merlin; others believe that she merely wandered alone until, at last, she died.

Year 421:
Halaad, child of the mudmakers, is gravely wounded by a band of gnomes. Seeking safety, she crawls to the edge of a bubbling spring. Miraculously, her wounds heal. The Secret Spring of Halaad becomes famous in story and song—but its location remains hidden to all but the elusive mudmakers.

Year 472:
Bendegeit, highlord of the water dragons, presses for peace. On the eve of the first treaty, however, some dragons revolt. In the terrible battle that follows, Bendegeit is killed. The war rages on with renewed ferocity.

Year 498:
In early spring, when the first blossoms have appeared on the trees, an army of flamelons and dragons attacks Stoneroot. In the Battle of the Withered Spring, many villages are destroyed, countless lives are lost, and even the Great Temple of the Drumadians is scorched with flames. Only with the help of the mountain giants, led by Jubolda and her three daughters, are the invaders finally defeated. In the heat of the battle, Jubolda's eldest daughter, Bonlog Mountain-Mouth, is saved when her attackers are crushed by Shim, the old friend of Merlin. But when she tries to thank him with a kiss, he shrieks and flees into the highlands. Bonlog Mountain-Mouth tries to punish Shim for this humiliation, but cannot find him. Shim remains in hiding for many years.

Year 545:

The Lady of the Lake, a mysterious enchantress, first appears in the deepest forests of Woodroot. She issues a call for peace, spread throughout the Seven Realms by the small winged creatures called light flyers, but her words are not heeded.

Year 693:

The great wizard Merlin finally returns from Britannia. He leads the Battle of Fires Unending, which destroys the last alliance of dark elves and fire dragons. The flamelons reluctantly surrender. Gobsken, sensing defeat, scatter to the far reaches of the Seven Realms. Peace is restored at last.

THE AGE OF RIPENING

Year 693:

The great Treaty of the Swaying Sea, crafted by the Lady of the Lake, is signed by representatives of all known peoples except gnomes, ogres, trolls, gobsken, changelings, and death dreamers. The Age of Storms is over; the Age of Ripening begins.

Year 694:

Merlin again vanishes, but not before he announces that he expects never to return to Avalon. He declares solemnly that unless some new wizard appears—which is highly unlikely—the varied peoples of Avalon must look to themselves to find justice and peace. As a final, parting gesture, he travels to the stars with the aid of a great dragon named Basilgarrad—and then magically rekindles the seven stars of the Wizard's Staff, the constellation whose destruction presaged the terrible Age of Storms.

Year 694:

Soon after Merlin departs, the Lady of the Lake makes a chilling prediction, which comes to be known as the Dark Prophecy: A time will come when all the stars of Avalon will grow steadily darker, until there is a total stellar eclipse that lasts a whole year. And in that year, a child will be born who will bring about the very end of Avalon, the one and only world shared by all creatures alike—human and non-human, mortal and immortal. Only Merlin's true heir, the Lady of the Lake adds, might save Avalon. But she says no more about who the wizard's heir might be, or how he or she could defeat the child of the Dark Prophecy. And so throughout the realms, people wonder: *Who will be the child of the Dark Prophecy? And who will be the true heir of Merlin?*

Year 702:

Le-fen-flaith, greatest architect of the sylphs of Airroot, completes his most ambitious (and useful) project to date: building a bridge, from ropes of spun cloudthread, spanning the misty gap between Airroot and Mudroot. He names it *Trishila o Mageloo* which means *the air sighs sweetly* in the sylphs' native language. But in time, most travelers come to call it the Misty Bridge. The first people to cross it, other than sylphs, are the Lady of the Lake and her friend Nuic, a pinnacle sprite.

Year 717:

Krystallus, exceptionally long-lived due to his wizard's ancestry, and already the first person to have explored many parts of Avalon's roots, becomes the first ever to reach the Great Hall of the Heartwood. In the Great Hall he finds a single portal that could lead to all Seven Realms—but no way to go higher in the Tree. He vows to return one day, and to find some way to travel upward, perhaps even all the way to the stars.

Year 842:

In the remote realm of Woodroot, the old teacher Hanwan Belamir gains renown for his bold new ideas about agriculture and craftsmanship, which lead to more productive farms as well as more comfort and leisure for villagers. Some even begin to call him Olo Belamir—the first person to be hailed in that way since the birth of Avalon, when Merlin was proclaimed Olo Eopia. While the man himself humbly scoffs at such praise, his Academy of Prosperity thrives.

Year 900:

Belamir's teachings continue to spread. Although wood elves and others resent his theories about humanity's "special role" in Avalon, more and more humans support him. As Belamir's following grows, his fame reaches into other realms.

Year 985:

As the Dark Prophecy predicted, a creeping eclipse slowly covers the stars of Avalon. So begins the much-feared Year of Darkness. Every realm (except the flamelon stronghold of Fireroot) declares a ban against having any new children during this time, out of fear that one of them could be the child of the Dark Prophecy. Some peoples, such as dwarves and water dragons, take the further step of killing any offspring born this year. Throughout the Seven Realms, Drumadian followers seek to find the dreaded child—as well as the true heir of Merlin.

Year 985:

Despite the pervasive darkness, Krystallus continues his explorations. He voyages to the realm of the flamelons, even though outsiders—especially those with human blood—have never been welcome there. Soon after he arrives, his party is attacked, and the survivors are captured. Somehow Krystallus escapes, with the help of an unidentified friend. (Some believe it is Halona, princess of the flamelons, who helps him; others point to signs that his ally is an eaglewoman.) Ignoring the danger of the Dark Prophecy, Krystallus and his rescuer are wed and conceive a child. Just after giving birth, however, the mother and newborn son disappear.

Year 987:

Beset with grief over the loss of his wife and child, Krystallus sets out on another journey, his most ambitious quest ever: to find a route upward into the very trunk and limbs of the Great Tree. Some believe, however, that his true goal is something even more perilous—to solve at last the great mystery of Avalon's stars. Or is he really fleeing from his grief? Whatever his goal, he does not succeed, for somewhere on this quest, he perishes. His long life, and many explorations, finally come to an end.

Year 1002:

Seventeen years have now passed since the Year of Darkness. Troubles are mounting across the Seven Realms: fights between humans and other kinds of creatures; severe drought—and a strange graying of colors—in the upper reaches of Stoneroot, Waterroot, and Woodroot; attacks by nearly invisible killer birds called ghoulacas; and a vague sense of growing evil. Many people believe that all this proves that the dreaded child of the Dark Prophecy is alive and coming into power. They pray openly for the true heir of Merlin—or the long-departed wizard himself—to appear at last and save Avalon.

Year 1002:

Late in the year, as the drought worsens, the stars of a major constellation—the Wizard's Staff—begin to go out. This has happened only once before, other than in the Year of Darkness: at the start of the Age of Storms in the Year of Avalon 284. No one knows why this is happening, or how to stop it. But most people fear that the vanishing of the Wizard's Staff can mean only one thing: the final ruin of Avalon.

Turn the page for a sneak peek at the next
installment of the Merlin saga:

BOOK 11

THE ETERNAL FLAME

Prologue:
The Unmaking Knife

Kulwych's chortle, while no louder than the thin stream of water trickling down the cavern wall, was unmistakably mirthful. He rubbed his pale white hands together. In the throbbing light of the crystal beside him—the only light in this cavern far beneath the surface of Shadowroot—his scarred face glowed with anticipation.

"Soon," he whispered to himself. "Mmmyesss, very soon."

Spying a small beetle crawling across the dank stone wall, he reached up and snatched it. Slowly, he crushed its body between his thumb and forefinger, savoring each and every crack of its shell and gush of its organs.

"This is how I will deal with you, Deth Macoll." He whispered the words with relish, imagining his long-awaited chance to kill the assassin. For he knew that Deth Macoll would soon return, seeking payment for the pure élano that he'd been sent to steal.

The sorcerer wiped the remains of the beetle on his cloak. Then, inspecting the smooth flesh of his fingers, he nodded confidently. "And that is how, mmmyesss, I will deal with anyone who dares to challenge me—the new ruler of Avalon."

The crystal, resting on the stone pedestal by his side, pulsed with reddish light. Rays shimmered in the jagged scar that cleaved his face; within his hollow eye socket, scabs and swollen veins glistened. And once again, he cackled with mirth.

He knew that his master, the spirit warlord Rhita Gawr, had promised him such power, and had even used that phrase, *the ruler of Avalon.* In less than one week's time, Rhita Gawr, now in the form of an immense dragon, would extinguish the pulsing star called the Heart of Pegasus—a star that was really much more than it appeared. And then, in a great moment of triumph, Rhita Gawr would lead an army of deathless warriors down from the sky. They would destroy the ragtag alliance of mortal creatures—elves, eaglefolk, giants, and any foolish humans still loyal to the Society of the Whole—who were now gathering on the Plains of Isenwy. Unless, of course, Kulwych's own army had already crushed the mortals by then.

Having secured Avalon, the precious world between all worlds, Rhita Gawr would then turn to his next conquest: mortal Earth. That would leave Kulwych alone to dominate Avalon. To rid it forever of the foul stench of Merlin. And to remake it however he chose.

His lone eye studied the crystal on the pedestal. Small as it was, this crystal of corrupted élano—vengélano, as Rhita Gawr had named it—held unfathomable power. It could destroy any flesh, poison any water, crumble any stone. More important, it could guide the spirit warriors of Rhita Gawr, for the warlord had called to them through the crystal, even as he had bound them to its power.

"And now," whispered the sorcerer, "you shall do one thing more."

Reaching into the pocket of his cloak, he pulled out a savage-looking claw, the parting gift of Rhita Gawr before he'd flown off to the stars. Black and shiny as the dragon's own scales, it was, in fact, only the tip of a claw, though it was still as big as Kulwych's whole hand. Its curled tip narrowed to a point sharper than a dagger; its base showed the gouges of teeth, since Rhita Gawr had bitten it off his own foreleg.

Deftly, Kulwych tied a leather cord around the claw, making a simple necklace. He fixed the knot with a sturdy spell of binding. Then, recalling the words that his master had taught him, he concentrated all his will on the corrupted crystal, lifted the claw, and began to chant:

> *Vengélano, power dark,*
> *Fill this vessel with thy spark.*
> *Let it wield Unmaking Knife:*
> *Slashing, piercing, sowing strife.*
> *Carving out the heart of life!*

A faint crackling sound started to come from the claw, as if something smoldered deep inside. Louder the sound grew, and louder, swelling steadily until it echoed throughout the cavern. Abruptly, all the noise ceased—just as a small red spark appeared on the claw's surface. It spread swiftly, like molten lava, replacing the black sheen with a dull red glow.

"Excellent," gloated the sorcerer. He examined the glowing claw, twirling it in the throbbing light. "Here is a weapon fit for a great warrior. Mmmyesss, and a great ruler."

Part

I

1 · To Ride the Wind

JUMP? THOUGHT ELLI, INCREDULOUS AT HER own folly. *Am I really about to jump off a cloud?*

A sharp gust of wind suddenly rocked her forward, making her swing her arms wildly just to keep her balance. Her feet—submerged in the moist, spongy cloud where she and Nuic had rested—dug in more firmly. For a breathless moment, she teetered there on the edge, before finally managing to stand still again. Yet her heart kept pounding.

For she had glimpsed what lay below her: a bottomless swirl of mist, vapors, and nothingness. She was, indeed, about to leap off a cloud. And there were only shreds of mist to break the unending plunge.

"Well, Elliryanna?" snapped the pinnacle sprite at her feet, his liquid purple eyes squinting with doubt. "Are you ever going to do it? Or are you just going to wait here until we both sprout wings?"

"I'll do it, Nuic." With difficulty, she swallowed. "Just not yet."

"Hmmmpff," he replied. Slowly, his skin color darkened to leaden gray. "Maybe I should try to plant an herb garden while we wait."

Elli didn't answer. She merely gazed out at the misty realm of Y Swylarna, commonly called Airroot, that seemed to stretch forever before them. One hand clasped her belt, touching the silken strip torn from High Priestess Coerria's gown. The strip fluttered in the breeze, along with the hem of Elli's simple Drumadian robe and her thick brown curls.

Although made of mist, the airscape before her held as many shapes and colors as any realm of land. Green, gold, and lavender ribbons of vapor wrapped around the denser clouds. In the distance, scores of spiraling forms rose higher, twirling endlessly: the Dancing Ground of the Mist Maidens. Beyond these airy figures, an enormous flock of birds—joined by a few vaporous sylphs—flew toward a brilliant blue patch of sky that glowed like a starlit sapphire.

And as she watched, she listened. To the steady swish of winds all around; to the deep whooshing of the Air Falls of Silmannon; to the eerie, sucking sound of a distant maelstrom; and to the long, rippling notes of aeolian harps—music that always reminded her of Tamwyn. Thinking of their brief meeting in her dream, and their even briefer kiss, she blew a long sigh.

But the sound she heard more clearly than any other was the fearful pounding within her chest. *Jump? Into that?* she thought, shaking her head.

Suddenly she remembered the shrill scream of Deth Macoll, when the assassin had fallen off a cloud much like this one—and plummeted to his death. Instinctively, her feet crept back from the edge. She had only moved a tiny bit, but Nuic had noticed. Though he said nothing, his skin darkened to the color of a storm cloud.

Just then the wind slackened. Now, instead of the ceaseless

rush of air, she felt just a gentle tickle on her brow, almost a caress. In that instant, she recalled the old bard who had appeared so unexpectedly—and his soulful song about *what wind that blows*. Those eyes of his, so old and yet so young, had made her want to trust him, although his notion of leaping off a cloud and riding the wind had seemed utterly preposterous.

And still seemed that way.

The breeze tickled her chin. To her surprise, she heard in her mind the bard's very words, almost as if he were whispering into her ear.

It's quite simple, really. You just stand at the edge of a cloud, hold tight to your magic crystal, and think hard about where you want the wind to carry you.

Quite simple! Elli shook her head. It really was preposterous.

And yet . . . the old bard's words had reached her somehow. They had even convinced crusty old Nuic. On top of all that, there didn't seem to be any other explanation for how the bard himself got around, moving so quickly from one realm to another.

She twisted one of her curls, wondering. Even though her common sense—and all her better judgment—told her that this whole idea was idiotic, it just might work. After all, the crystals that she and Nuic wore held enormous power. In the opinion of Rhia, the Lady of the Lake, they possessed more magic than anything else in Avalon—save perhaps Merlin's staff, the legendary Ohnyalei.

Or perhaps, she thought with a shudder, the crystal of élano that was now in the hands of that murderer Kulwych, who served Rhita Gawr. For that crystal, unlike the pure one that she carried, had been turned into a terrible weapon. Who could say whether the person who wielded it could ever be stopped?

Yet that, she knew, was her task. To find Kulwych, who was hiding somewhere down in the deepest mine of the darkest realm. And to use whatever powers she and her crystal could muster to prevent him from destroying Avalon.

But she had too little time to do all this! Less than a week, if she had figured correctly. Just as Tamwyn had far too little time to find his way to the stars and stop Rhita Gawr.

In the distance, the music of the harps' vaporthread strings swelled louder. Their tones seemed more clear now, as well as more urgent. As Elli listened, the strings rose to a high, warbling pitch that sounded like a desperate plea.

A memory of Tamwyn flashed across her mind: He was showing her the partly carved harp that he'd been working on, hoping to give it to Elli if they actually made it through all this alive. More than ever, she felt sure that destroying Kulwych's crystal would also help Tamwyn succeed. After all, the corrupted crystal was the tool of Kulwych, who was himself the tool of Rhita Gawr. Somehow, in a way she couldn't begin to guess, succeeding in her quest could possibly help Tamwyn succeed in his.

She drew a deep breath and stepped closer to the edge. Grimly, she glanced down at Nuic, who nodded impatiently. And then—

She jumped.

For an instant she hovered in the air, just long enough to see Nuic also leap off the cloud. Then she began to fall! Tumbling, twirling head over feet, she plunged downward faster and faster. Air whooshed past, flapping her gown and yanking her hair. Tears streamed from her eyes. Panic suddenly flooded her mind, obscuring all her thoughts.

Except one. A voice broke through, a voice she recognized as the bard's. *Think hard,* he had said. *Think hard about where you want the wind to carry you.*

Calling on every bit of will she possessed, she fought back her panic and concentrated on Shadowroot, that realm of eternal night. No one but dark elves and death dreamers—and now the sorcerer she sought—chose to live there; very few had even dared to explore its terrain since the fighting that had closed its only portal and destroyed the City of Light. Darkness was the soul of this realm, hiding its mysteries forever.

Still falling! For an instant Elli's concentration shattered, and the air tore at her as she plummeted down, down, down. Without thinking, she grasped the amulet of leaves that held her crystal. With all her remaining strength, she bent her thoughts again toward Shadowroot, and the task she wanted so badly to accomplish.

With a sharp jolt, her falling ceased. The wind seemed to stop, to vanish completely. Then she felt herself lifting, floating like a feather in an updraft.

All at once, she realized the truth. The wind hadn't vanished. It was simply supporting her, bearing her body in its invisible arms. Though she could feel it no longer, it was all around her, carrying her with ease.

She was riding the wind.

Not far above her, Nuic floated. His own tiny hand clutched the green jewel of the Galator, while his color had changed to a contented shade of blue. Turning toward Elli, he gave a wry grin. She could almost hear his gruff voice saying, *Took you long enough, Elliryanna.*

The wind swelled beneath them like a rolling wave. Swiftly it bore them, through airy avenues between clouds, and through shimmering veils of mist that burst into circular rainbows as soon as they approached. They rode over clouds and under them, rising upward at times and swooping downward at others, always moving steadily northward.

Over the Harplands they flew, listening to notes that now seemed as lilting as a child's laughter. To the east, Elli could see the massive, curling cloud that Nuic called Windwhistle Point. And on the horizon, a splash of violet and scarlet made her wonder whether she had glimpsed the famous Cloud Gardens of the faeries.

Slowly, the shreds of mist around them began to thin. The air grew clearer, as well as drier. Elli caught a faint whiff of sulfur, like eggs gone terribly bad. The wind carried them over a huge, lumbering cloud—and all of a sudden she saw volcanoes below.

Fireroot! Now, as far as she could see, marched the ridges of Rahnawyn's fire-blackened peaks. Their cliffs glowed with streaks of orange lava, while their summits swirled with clouds of red and gray ash. Noxious fumes poured out of flame vents, billowing as they rose skyward. All across this scorched landscape, fires flickered on the cliffs and heavy smoke poured out of deep crevasses.

Onward the wind carried them, through red-tinted clouds that dusted them with ash. At one point, as they passed above a desolate, charred ridge, Elli spied a crater surrounded by crooked spires of rock. Could that be, she wondered, the place that Scree had once described? The crater that had been his childhood home, and also Tamwyn's? She cringed, thinking of Tamwyn, who so loved the forests of El Urien, living in this place without any greenery at all. And she cringed again, recalling her own years without any trees or vines or flowers—the years she'd spent as a slave to those gnomes who had killed her parents and then kept her captive underground.

She coughed, trying to rid her throat of its bitter taste, even as a sulfurous cloud made her eyes water. She turned away from Nuic, not sure why she didn't want him to see.

Then, beyond the crater's rim, she caught sight of the molten River of Fire, and beyond that, several enormous towers. Conical in shape, they resembled perfectly formed volcanoes, crowned with turrets that arched skyward like erupting lava. Made of polished red stone, the towers gleamed in the light of the huge, intense fires that roared beneath them. Were they the forges of the flamelons, the warlike people who made such elaborate weaponry and building materials? Or were they, perhaps, the famous flamelon palaces—buildings that held, if the bards' tales were true, many marvelous inventions found nowhere else in Avalon?

All at once, the sky started to darken. Starlight faded from the sky, while the air grew swiftly colder. Below, the landscape disappeared, and even the bright fires of Rahnawyn soon flickered and vanished. Elli turned her head toward Nuic, but she could no longer see him. She called out, but heard no reply.

Into the deepening darkness she sailed, borne by the unbroken wind. Unable to see any landmarks below, nor even any clouds, Elli felt increasingly disoriented. Was she still moving at all? Was Nuic still with her?

A vague feeling of terror swelled inside her chest. If she was, indeed, entering Shadowroot, how would she ever find her way? How would she even survive?

Suddenly the wind sputtered. A fierce blast of air jolted her sideways; another slapped her face so hard that she tumbled backward through the blackness. Just then she heard air whoosh-ing wildly around her, and she realized that she was falling. Falling fast! Before she could scream, or even squeeze her crystal more tightly, she hit the ground with a brutal thud.

She lay there, motionless, in the darkness—the darkness of eternal night.